SAMAK THE AYYAR

SAMAK THE AYYAR

A TALE OF ANCIENT PERSIA

TRANSLATED BY

FREYDOON RASSOULI

ADAPTED BY

JORDAN MECHNER

Columbia University Press *New York*

COLUMBIA
UNIVERSITY
PRESS

Columbia University Press gratefully acknowledges the generous support for this book provided by a Publisher's Circle member.

Columbia University Press
Publishers Since 1893
New York   Chichester, West Sussex
cup.columbia.edu

Library of Congress Cataloging-in-Publication Data
Names: Rassouli, translator. | Mechner, Jordan, adapter.
Title: Samak the Ayyar : a tale of ancient Persia / translated by Freydoon Rassouli; adapted by Jordan Mechner.
Other titles: Samak-i 'Ayyār. English.
Description: New York : Columbia University Press, 2021.
Identifiers: LCCN 2020050392 (print) | LCCN 2020050393 (ebook) | ISBN 9780231198783 (hardback) | ISBN 9780231198790 (trade paperback) | ISBN 9780231552813 (ebook)
Subjects: LCSH: Tales—Iran.
Classification: LCC PK6450.9.A1 S2613 2021 (print) | LCC PK6450.9.A1 (ebook) | DDC 891/.5531–dc23
LC record available at https://lccn.loc.gov/2020050392
LC ebook record available at https://lccn.loc.gov/2020050393

Cover design: Julia Kushnirsky
Cover image: Freydoon Rassouli

CONTENTS

INTRODUCTION

Jordan Mechner

THE day I met Rassouli, he shared a childhood memory of afternoons spent with his uncle in a teahouse in Isfahan, a historic city in central Iran, listening spellbound to adventure tales spun by a storyteller in the ancient Persian oral tradition that had produced the *Thousand and One Nights*. The stories that had most enthralled him as a boy, he told me, featured as their main hero an *ayyar* named Samak—a member of a class of warriors in Persia with deep roots going back thousands of years.

I grew up in New York in the 1970s; my exposure to Persian lore had been second- or third-hand, through illustrated children's editions of the *Nights*, Hollywood derivatives like the 1940 Technicolor *Thief of Baghdad* (starring Conrad Veidt as a scheming vizier named Jaffar), *Mad* magazine, and *Ali Baba Bunny*. (Fourth-hand might be more like it.) The power of those ancient tales and archetypes nonetheless came through vividly enough to inspire me to create, in my twenties, a video game called *Prince of Persia*.

Over the next two decades, researching and writing *Prince of Persia* sequels, reboots, and adaptations for increasingly high-resolution platforms (from the 280 x 192 pixel Apple II computer screen to a 4K Disney live-action movie starring Ben Kingsley as a scheming vizier named Nizam), I'd gained an amateur's familiarity with the thousand-year-old source material, especially the *Nights* and Ferdowsi's *Shahnameh*. But in all my reading, I'd never heard of ayyars. Rassouli made them sound like a kind of Persian Robin Hood or ronin. I was fascinated.

Rassouli explained that although ayyars came from a lower social class, their code of brotherhood was noble, including loyalty, honor, self-sacrifice, and never turning away the hand that reaches out for help. Samak is not just a brute-force warrior but a trickster who foresees dangers and problems before anyone else and prevents them through decisive and surprising action. He embodies a heroic ethic that has resonated in stories for every generation, and one that the world needs now as much as ever.

Rassouli pulled a volume from his shelf and opened to a page at random. As he began to read, translating on the fly from archaic Persian into English, chills ran down my spine. Here was an adventure set in ancient Persia involving a beautiful princess, a treacherous vizier, kings, armies, witches, and an agile hero who scaled walls and snuck into palaces. More than just an entertaining tale, it offered vivid glimpses of the everyday life of the era, with details I hadn't been able to find anywhere else. It was the source material *Prince of Persia* had always wanted but never had.

The friend who introduced me to Rassouli had described him as an Iranian-born painter and writer, passionate about Persian history and culture, who had translated the poetry of Rumi, Hafiz, Attar, Omar Khayyam, and others. I'd come to him hoping to enrich and deepen my understanding of *Prince of Persia*'s world and mythology as I worked with a team of designers and artists preparing to pitch a new take on the franchise.

I told Rassouli that I absolutely had to get my hands on an English edition of *Samak-e Ayyar*. He explained that there wasn't one; the original work was unknown outside of Iran and even to most Iranians. It was a small miracle that it had survived in written form at all. The Mongol invasions of the thirteenth century had burned Persia's libraries and destroyed a vast swath of its literature. The tales of Samak, as part of Persia's oral tradition, were believed lost until the 1960s, when a scholar visiting the Bodleian Library in Oxford, England, made an unexpected discovery. An old Persian manuscript that had been preserved for its color illustrations—the oldest in the museum's collection—was in fact *Samak-e Ayyar*, transcribed in the twelfth century from a still older manuscript by one or more unknown scribes, recording the narration of a master storyteller from Shiraz.

Dr. Parviz Natel Khanlari, Iranian poet and professor of language and literature, reconstituted the archaic Persian text from disparate source materials (including a missing volume that turned up later in a sixteenth-century Turkish translation in the British Museum). Thus *Samak-e Ayyar* was published for the first time in a limited edition in Tehran in 1969. It promptly went out of print.

It seemed—and still seems—incredible to me that popular modern-language editions of *Samak* haven't been published around the world, as have the better-known (but not more deserving) tales of Aladdin, Sinbad, Ali Baba, and the *Thousand and One Nights*. By the time Rassouli and I said goodbye at the end of our first evening together, we had pledged to fill that gap. It felt like destiny had entrusted us with a mission. Rassouli had never played a video game, much less expected to join a team that was creating one; I had never expected to adapt a twelve-hundred-page archaic Persian manuscript. But thanks to Samak the trickster and the unlikely chain of events that led me to Rassouli's studio, it was obvious that this was what we needed to do.

How Rassouli collected all six out-of-print volumes of *Samak-e Ayyar* is an adventure tale in itself. He enlisted his brother to take a road trip from Isfahan to an antiquarian bookstore in

Nishapur, and then a plane flight from Tehran to Dubai to mail the books to Los Angeles (package shipments from Iran to the United States having been suspended due to the political situation at the time).

Ironically, the video game project that had brought us together ended up being cancelled in preproduction. (That's a tale to be told another time. The workings of the game industry can be as arcane as those of Abbasid kings and viziers.) By then, Rassouli was deep into translating the Persian manuscript with no intention of stopping. When an ayyar accepts a mission, you can be sure he will complete it, even if the promised reward is withdrawn or circumstances take an unfavorable turn. Video game or no, Samak had inspired our commitment and loyalty, as he does for Sorkhvard, Ruzafzun, Atashak, and other characters in the book.

ABOUT THE TRANSLATION

Our priority was to create an entertaining, readable, yet faithful and complete modern-language version of *Samak-e Ayyar* to make this great work accessible for the first time to a global audience.

In general, we tried to use plain language and avoid unfamiliar terms. The word *ayyar* is an exception: the concept is so central to the story that we had to keep it. We dare to hope that *ayyar* may one day enter the popular lexicon, like *samurai* and *ronin*, terms that were also once unknown in the West.

For other Persian words with no direct Western equivalent, we wrote around them. Rather than try to define *javanmardi*, for example, we sought to translate its essence using phrases like brotherhood, honor, loyalty, altruism, and noble conduct, all of which the term connotes.

Because I read no Persian, Rassouli's first step was to render a raw literal English translation of Khanlari's work. Eliminating materials extraneous to the story flow—poems inserted later, requests for prayers for the scribes at the beginnings and ends of dictation sessions, ritually repeated rhymes that Persian storytellers used (and still do) while waiting for the audience to gather and to collect money at the ends of their performances—he divided the story roughly into chapters, which he handed on to me.

As *Samak* unspooled before my eyes, I became addicted, eagerly awaiting Rassouli's weekly emails to find out what happened next. The deft interweaving of a large, diverse cast of characters, with parallel action in multiple locations, alternating visceral combat and epic battle scenes with humor and intimate moments, was like an HBO series. Its world felt both archaic and startlingly modern. Female ayyars are brave, deadly, and vulnerable; princes and warriors drink wine in army tents on the eve of battle; nobles and commoners struggle to reconcile their hearts with duty to leaders who unleash a devastating, avoidable civil war. The triangle of friendship, loyalty, sexual attraction, envy, and gender-role frustration that binds Samak, Sorkhvard, and Ruzafzun, to take one example, felt like it could have been written yesterday rather than in the ninth century.

That said, creating a unified narrative from Khanlari's assemblage posed a challenge. *Samak-e Ayyar* was never a literary work by an author like Ferdowsi's *Shahnameh* but a folk tale transcribed from a storyteller's live performances. (The storyteller himself may have been illiterate.) Even if the task weren't complicated by gaps, missing pages, inconsistencies among recopied sections from different historical periods, and changes in narrator, the narrative itself is sometimes self-contradictory. A traveler makes a journey in one day that is described elsewhere as taking a month. A person on foot arrives before a rider on horseback. A character established as being in a particular place disappears from the action for a stretch, as if the storyteller had forgotten he was there. Two characters meet for the first time, unaware that they already shared an escapade several chapters earlier. The pacing is uneven: the death of a minor character is described in detail, while one central to the story is dispatched abruptly with no fanfare.

Such discrepancies are understandable in a complex story recited by a storyteller accustomed to improvising and adapting his memorized material to suit the occasion. We can assume he was never given the opportunity to go back and edit the transcription as a whole. It would be beyond remarkable if the manuscript's thousand-odd pages fit together perfectly.

In a printed book, where the reader can flip back and compare one passage with another fifty pages earlier, inconsistencies are more distracting than in a story heard aloud. An unedited manuscript makes for a bumpy read. As much as Rassouli and I wanted to be faithful to the original, it became clear that a strict literal translation would be a book few readers would have the patience to finish. Some dramatic license was required.

For example, considering the vizier Mehran's importance in part I, the way Samak deals with him and Surkhkafar in chapters 33–37 of part II seemed too desultory, dependent on coincidence and illogical behavior. I tweaked the original action beats to achieve the same end result in a way that felt more plausible to me and consistent with the setup, characters, and world established by the storyteller. Elsewhere, I took smaller liberties of adding dialogue, description, or action to flesh out moments that wanted it, or I streamlined narration that felt tedious or repetitive. Such changes can become a slippery slope. I hope the reader will find ours judicious and in keeping with both the spirit and the detail of the original.

Given *Samak's* large cast of characters and diverse world map, our approach to names deserves a note. We retained Persian names of most places and characters, occasionally translating them (Stone Alley, Twelve Canyons) or parts of them (Falaki Fortress, Dabur the Demon Slayer). Our guiding intention was to make it as painless as possible for readers to understand the action.

In the story, the prince of Persia journeys from his father's capital city, Halab, across a desert to a remote—but still Persian—mountainous region where the kings of rival city-states Chin and Machin vie for power, drawing tribal leaders from surrounding territories into their ever-expanding war. Rassouli and I interpreted names like Halab, Chin, and Machin (which means "beyond Chin") as evocative of a timeless storyteller's realm rather than literal history or geography. We felt that to seek modern English equivalents, encouraging the reader to identify them with cities or nations whose coordinates can be found today on Google Maps, would be misleading.

The tale of Samak was already old when it was written down in the twelfth (or ninth?) century. Many character names evoke Persian archetypes and myths that date from pre-Islamic times. *Mahpari* means "moon fairy"; *Khorshid Shah* means "sun king." These too we left untranslated.

The one indisputably identifiable place is the ancient land in which *Samak*'s storytellers and audience lived—Persia, whose culture and proud allure have endured for thousands of years, from long before this tale was put to paper until our present day.

Here is the first of five volumes of *Samak the Ayyar*, translated and adapted by Rassouli and me. We hope you enjoy it . . . and that these pages open a window into an enchanted world of princes and ayyars, intrigue, romance, and adventure, shaped by the collective genius of generations of Persian storytellers.

PART I

SECTION 1

The Princess of Chin

1

THE SUN PRINCE

THROUGH the centuries, storytellers have passed down the tale of a king who once ruled Persia from his capital city of Halab. His name was Marzban Shah. He was a just and generous ruler, beloved by his subjects and all of his servants. He had everything he needed to live a blessed and joyful life—except a son to inherit his kingdom. The king prayed day and night with all his heart to God to grant him a child, but his prayers had not been answered. The lack of a son grieved him deeply.

Marzban Shah had a vizier named Haman who had served him devotedly for many years. One day, he summoned Haman and said: "O wise and kind vizier! You know that I have wealth, many treasures, and devoted subjects. Yet all of this means nothing to me without a son to take my place when I am gone. I want you to explore the astrological predictions and tell me if I will ever be blessed with an heir."

The vizier replied: "Your wish is my command." He left the court, went to his palace, and took a seven-sided, four-level astrolabe in hand. Holding it toward the sun, he looked through all 360 degrees of the universe until he saw a newborn in the third house. Haman hurried back to Marzban Shah and said, to the king's delight: "O my king, it is your destiny to have a most powerful and blessed son." He added: "The stars say that he will be born to a princess from a foreign land who has already married and had a child."

Perplexed, Marzban Shah told Haman to find out which king's daughter matched this description so that he might seek her out. The vizier made inquiries and returned with the news: "The king of Iraq has a daughter named Golnahr who recently gave birth to a son. Her husband was killed, and she is now mourning his death."

On the king's orders, Haman opened the doors to the royal treasury and picked out one hundred bags containing a thousand golden nuggets, a crown covered with precious jewels, and one hundred gold-embroidered robes. The vizier sent these gifts along with fifty slaves to Somaregh, the king of Iraq, to request the princess's hand in marriage.

Somaregh received Marzban Shah's envoy with splendor. The emissary was escorted into the palace, seated on a gold chair near the king, and served wine and delicious food. He then took out the letter from Marzban Shah, kissed it, and placed it on the step of the king's throne. The letter said:

"In the name of the Creator of the World, this letter is from Marzban Shah, king of Persia, to Somaregh, supreme ruler of the land of Iraq. We have been informed that the great king has a daughter whom we wish to marry. We trust that Your Majesty will not turn away our hand so that the child of this marriage may inherit our crowns and unite our two kingdoms. As for the princess's son, we will adopt and raise him as our own."

Somaregh was pleased by Marzban Shah's message and the impressive array of treasures. He ordered the judges, dignitaries, and governors of his kingdom to gather to witness the engagement of his daughter Golnahr to the king of Persia.

The next day, the princess started her journey to Halab, accompanied by one hundred beautiful bond maidens, one hundred servants, and one hundred horses. She carried a jeweled crown and a precious ring as gifts for Marzban Shah.

When the king heard the news that Princess Golnahr was on her way, he ordered the streets of Halab decorated with mirrors and flowers. Minstrels sang and played joyful music on every corner in anticipation of their future queen's arrival.

Golnahr's caravan was met outside the city by forty carriages adorned with flowers, two hundred servants dressed in white, and one hundred beautiful maidens in colorful dresses. They placed the princess on a litter of roses and carried her to the city gates, where Haman and a welcoming committee greeted her with open arms. Crowds lined the streets as Golnahr was carried on her litter through the city to the king's palace. The next evening, the dignitaries of the kingdom gathered for a splendid feast at the royal palace to celebrate the marriage of Golnahr and Marzban Shah.

Soon after the wedding, Queen Golnahr became pregnant and gave birth to a son of extraordinary beauty. When the king saw his son's face shining like the sun, which had risen and broken the horizon at the very moment he was born, he decided to name him Khorshid Shah: the sun king.

All across Persia, the people celebrated the prince's arrival. The doors to the royal kitchens were opened to the king's subjects for an entire month, and the people thrived under Marzban Shah's just and benevolent rule. At Queen Golnahr's request, her son Farokhruz was brought from Iraq to join his mother. The king received Farokhruz with kindness and noticed the two-year-old boy's striking resemblance to his own newborn son.

The two princes grew up together as best friends and received a royal education and training starting at age four. By the time and thin, her mouth like a newly opened rose. A blush bloomed on her cheeks. Her belly was as white as flour, her breasts like two pomegranates on a silver plate. She wore a pale silk robe that showed every contour of her perfect body. Her soft skin shone like the silver moon. A necklace of pearls peeked out from under the thin scarf that covered her long, lustrous black hair and slender neck. Lightly, like an angel in a breeze, she rose and looked at the prince.

When the girl's eyes met Khorshid Shah's, his heart began to beat as fast as a hummingbird's wings. He was speechless and could see nothing but her loveliness. He felt a strange sensation that he had never experienced before. He wondered what this beautiful girl was doing in the middle of this barren desert.

"Who are you?" the girl asked. "Where did you come from? Why do you look so puzzled?"

Khorshid Shah tried a few times to speak and finally whispered: "O lovely one! What are *you*, such a great beauty, doing in this desert? Are you an angel from heaven, or is this a dream, and are you a fairy? In all my life I have never seen anyone as beautiful as you."

The princess (for she was indeed a princess) seemed as confused as he. She had awakened to find a young man in her room, standing as straight and tall as a cypress tree. His face shone like the sun, shaded by the beginnings of a youthful beard. He was so handsome that he might have been painted by the greatest artists of the world. She asked: "How did you get here?"

It occurred to Khorshid Shah that such a girl must surely have guards who would burst in and attack him at any moment. But he felt that seeing her had given him the strength to defeat an army of a thousand warriors.

Khorshid Shah's mind was racing when he noticed a golden bowl filled with water next to the cushions. Realizing that he was extremely thirsty, he asked if he could have some water. The princess picked up a golden goblet, filled it, and handed it to Khorshid Shah. No sooner had the prince drunk the water than dizziness overcame him. He fell to the ground unconscious.

Meanwhile, back at the camp, the hunting party was waiting for the prince to return and becoming anxious in his absence. The two generals asked Farokhruz to remain at camp while they rode out to look for Khorshid Shah. For several days they climbed every hill and crossed every meadow. At last they spotted the prince's horse in the distance.

As the generals approached the horse, they saw the prince lying unconscious on the ground. The men lifted his head, poured water into his mouth, and attended to him until he opened his eyes.

The prince sat up and looked around for the pavilion and the girl. There was no sign of either one. With tears in his eyes he told the generals what had happened to him: "I've met a girl who has captured my heart. But I don't know anything about her, not even her name. How can I find her again?"

At first the generals had difficulty believing the prince's story. Then the prince noticed a strange new ring on his finger. He showed it to the generals: "She must have put it on my finger while I slept!" This was proof that he hadn't just imagined the episode.

All three mounted their horses and rode back through the meadows until they reached the hunting camp. The prince, eager to find out the secret of the ring, insisted that they head straight back to the city. The hunting party rushed to gather their belongings and they all rode back to town after Khorshid Shah.

2

THE MYSTERY OF THE RING

In the past, whenever the prince returned from a hunt, he went first to his father. This time he did not go to the king but went straight to his own palace. When Marzban Shah saw the hunting party return without his son, he became worried and asked about him. The generals told him that Khorshid Shah was not feeling well. This answer did not satisfy Marzban Shah. He demanded the truth, whereupon the generals told him the whole story of what had happened to the prince.

The king went at once to his son's palace, followed by his vizier Haman. The prince was lying in bed, running a high fever. The king sat at his son's bedside and placed his hand on his forehead. Khorshid Shah opened his eyes, sat up, and thanked his father for having come to see him. He said nothing about his encounter with the mysterious girl in the desert.

The king told his son: "O light of my eyes, why don't you open your heart to me? Tell me what is troubling you, and I will find a remedy for your pain."

The prince realized that his father already knew the story. He said: "O great father, we rode and hunted for six days in the mountains and deserts. On the seventh day, my brother and I went hunting together in a meadow, where I saw a magnificent zebra. I told my brother to let me catch the animal by myself, and I followed the zebra to a barren desert. There I found a pavilion and inside it the most beautiful girl I've ever seen. I fell in love with her. She slipped this ring onto my finger while I slept."

The king looked at the ring but could not read the writing on it, nor did he recognize the images. He gave it to his vizier to examine.

Haman, despite his wisdom, was unable to decipher the cryptic symbols on the seal of the ring. He called on all the learned experts of the kingdom, but not one could identify the symbols.

The vizier said: "O great king! Perhaps we should place the ring in the bazaar and announce throughout the kingdom that anyone who can read it will receive one thousand golden dinars from the royal treasury." The king agreed, and they tied the ring on a cord in the middle of the main bazaar and assigned a guard to watch over it.

The bazaar was a place where merchants and tradesmen came from many different lands. Word spread, and many well-known people came to see the ring, but none could read what was written on it.

Four months passed. The prince's condition grew worse as he pined for the mysterious girl. He lost the strength even to rise from his bed, and his voice grew weak. The greatest physicians and healers of the kingdom tried to cure him, but there was no use. The only remedy for a lover is the beloved.

News of the prince's illness spread through the country. His mother, Queen Golnahr, spent long hours weeping at his bedside. The king began to fear for his son's life and asked the vizier to consult Khorshid Shah's astrological charts. Haman called in expert astrologists who wrote down their findings to share with the king.

Haman returned and said: "O great king, the prince is suffering from the love he has developed for this girl from a foreign land. The predictions indicate that he will leave his home and family and travel far away. It is his destiny to rule for forty years over a vast territory including seven countries and achieve what no ruler has achieved before." Hearing this, Marzban Shah dearly hoped that these predictions would come true.

One day, an old man in threadbare clothes walking with a cane passed through the bazaar and saw the crowd gathered around the ring. He asked them why they were so interested in it. He was told of the reward of one thousand dinars from the king's royal treasury that awaited whoever could solve its mystery.

The old man examined the ring, then looked up and stated: "I know who this ring belongs to." Hearing this, the people took the old man straight to the royal palace, where he was brought before the king.

Haman the vizier suggested that it might be best if the man shared his secrets in the presence of the prince. The queen and Farokhruz joined them, and they all went to Khorshid Shah's bedroom. The king said: "Sit up, my son, to hear what this man has to say, for it seems that he knows something about the ring and its owner!"

Upon the king's command, the old man revealed: "O wonderful prince! This ring belongs to Princess Mahpari, the daughter of Faghfur Shah, the king of Chin. It is her name that the script on the seal spells out in an enigmatic way."

Eagerly the prince asked: "Is she married?"

The old man replied: "She is not. She is dominated by her nurse, an extremely clever witch named Shervaneh. This witch has set three challenges that must be met by anyone who seeks the princess's hand in marriage. Her witchcraft is so powerful that even the king, with all his army and servants and subjects, does not dare oppose her. Twenty princes have sought to marry the princess. Not one has performed these tasks successfully."

"What tasks?" asked the prince. The old man explained that the first challenge was to tame a wild horse; the second, to wrestle a giant Abyssinian warrior and pin him to the ground; and the third, to find a talking cypress tree.

Hearing these words, Marzban Shah went into deep thought. Finally, he said to the prince: "My son, if this problem could be resolved with gold and jewels, I would do it. If I could solve it by sending an army to conquer Chin, I would do it. But this situation is beyond my reach."

The old man bowed down and said: "O great king! Your son's quest to marry the princess Mahpari can end only in disaster." To the prince he said: "Your present suffering is the result of Shervaneh's witchcraft. She has used the princess to entrap you in her snare, like many other important and vulnerable princes before you. I am sure that the zebra you followed was none other than her."

During this conversation, Haman watched the old man with growing suspicion. The king ordered his guards to open the treasury doors and give the stranger one thousand golden dinars along with a gold-embroidered robe. The old man accepted his reward and left.

Once he was gone, Haman shared his feelings with the king and the prince. "Something about that old man seemed not right. I wonder if he might have been Shervaneh herself, disguised by witchcraft." He urged the prince to forget Mahpari.

Khorshid Shah resisted at first, but he finally followed the vizier's advice and began to work on his own mind and meditate. After a few days, his health improved and soon he was able to put on his royal robes and resume his regular duties. Within a month he was back to his old self.

One morning, the prince waited until everyone but the king had left the royal court. He approached his father's throne and asked permission to travel to Chin to seek the hand of Princess Mahpari in marriage. He explained that although he acted as though he had recovered, his soul was still suffering greatly with love.

The king reminded his son of the old man's warning and the vizier's suspicions: "O my son, if you travel to Chin, I fear we may never see you alive again. Your mother and I could not bear to lose you. Please forget this impossible love."

The prince cried out: "O father! Have mercy on your son. You don't know the pain I am in. First it was passion that made me ill. Now this passion has turned to love, and my soul is filled with sadness. It's destroying my balance. I've lost all perspective. If I cannot go after the princess, I will die of grief. Please let me go!" He entreated his father: "I know I can win Mahpari and take her as my wife. With her at my side, I could be a great king. Without her, I won't be fit for the crown." But still the king refused to let his son leave.

The prince's sorrow increased day by day, to the point that it made life difficult for the king and queen. One day, Haman the vizier kissed the ground in front of the king and said to him: "O greatness! Patience is not the remedy for lovers. Perhaps it would be wise to allow the prince to make this journey despite our misgivings. Remember, we have heard from the astrologers that this will end in a happy result and the prince will realize his heart's desire."

The king finally gave in and agreed to let the prince travel to Chin to seek the princess's hand in marriage.

3

THE WITCH NURSE

As soon as the king's decision was announced, everyone began to prepare what was needed for the prince's long journey. The doors to the treasury were opened and gold, silver, and jewels were gathered as offerings for his future bride.

Marzban Shah called his two greatest generals and ordered them to accompany the prince on his mission to win the princess. He told them: "My son is young and inexperienced in the ways of the world. I count on you to watch over him, advise him, and protect him." The generals bowed down and assured the king that they would do this.

The day of departure arrived. The sound of drums echoed through the capital. All the army generals and dignitaries came to bid the prince goodbye and wish him well. The king and queen had tears in their eyes as they said farewell to their son.

Farokhruz stepped forward and said: "O mother, if it breaks your heart to be separated from Khorshid Shah, imagine how I feel! He is my brother and dearest companion. If it is his destiny to rule, it is my destiny to protect him. My life away from him would make no sense. I beg you, order me to go with him and be his shield." Seeing her hesitate, he added fiercely: "If you don't let me go, I'll run away or kill myself."

The queen reluctantly gave her consent. Khorshid Shah and Farokhruz mounted their horses. They set forth, the two generals riding at their sides, followed by one thousand soldiers.

The journey was long and difficult. For many days they traveled across rugged mountains, open meadows, and dry lands. Stage to stage, caravansary to caravansary, and post to post they continued, until they reached the edge of a barren plateau. All they could see ahead of them was parched earth, with neither water, nor food, nor resting place in sight. On the recommendation of their guides and scouts, the army gathered enough supplies to last them forty days and set out into the desert.

The wasteland was a fearsome place of phantoms, giants, and monsters. Before they were halfway across, one general said to the other: "Why are we following the orders of a child? We could instead take this wealth and army and be masters of our own fate."

The two generals decided to get rid of Khorshid Shah and his brother. They called in the prince's personal chef and offered him a large reward of gold and silver coins to poison the two brothers' meals.

The chef thought to himself: "If I do this, the two generals will surely kill me as well, out of worry that I might reveal their horrible deed." He went to Khorshid Shah and told him of the generals' proposal. The prince thanked the chef and offered him an even greater reward for poisoning the generals' meal instead of his. So it was that the two warlords died that night instead of the two princes.

The army continued across the desert, journeying through cold, frozen places until they reached the walls of Chin. There they set up camp and awaited permission to enter the city.

When Faghfur Shah, the king of Chin, heard the news of their arrival, he ordered his vizier, Mehran, to discover the identities of these people camped outside the city wall. Mehran sent a group of scouts, who quickly returned, saying: "The prince of Persia, son of Marzban Shah, has come with his brother and an army to ask for the hand of Princess Mahpari in marriage."

Hearing this news, Faghfur Shah became anxious. He lamented to Mehran: "I wish I had no daughter! So many kings and princes who wanted to marry her have been lost thanks to the witchcraft of that nurse of hers. Now Marzban Shah's son will meet the same fate, and I will have him for an enemy."

Mehran told the king: "You are not to blame. Everyone knows that the problem is Shervaneh and her witchcraft. We have no choice but to allow the prince of Persia to enter." Faghfur Shah agreed and sent Mehran to greet Khorshid Shah and welcome him into the city.

When the two princes heard that Faghfur Shah's messenger was on his way, Farokhruz told Khorshid Shah: "My brother, I am afraid that you will lose your life in this mission. Listen to my idea: You and I look much alike. We're the same height. Our hair and voices are the same. Even our own servants sometimes mistake us for one another when they can't tell us apart by our clothes. Let me go to the king dressed as you, and you become Farokhruz. No one will know we've changed places. If they arrest me, you will still be free and can deliver me from their trap."

Khorshid Shah replied: "My dear brother, we are here on my account. If there is danger, I must face it, not you." But Farokhruz insisted and eventually convinced the prince that his way was best. The two brothers exchanged garments. Farokhruz put on Khorshid Shah's crown and seated himself on the throne, while the real prince stood beside him and ordered that Mehran, the vizier of Chin, be shown into their tent.

Mehran entered the royal pavilion and welcomed Farokhruz, believing him to be the prince of Persia. Shortly thereafter, the city gates were opened, and the two brothers with their entourage entered the city and headed directly to Faghfur Shah's palace.

The kingdom of Chin was well organized and clean. On every corner one could hear the sounds of music and laughter. Faghfur Shah's palace compound was set within a large garden overlooking the entire city. In front of the main entrance gate, which was made of many different metals, all reflecting heaven, one hundred servants lined up to welcome the visitors. Guards wearing golden helmets came forward and helped Farokhruz dismount. Chamberlains drew aside golden curtains and announced the arrival of the prince of Persia.

Farokhruz and Khorshid Shah entered the royal court, a vast hall of white marble inlaid with turquoise. In its center was a pond filled with exotic gold and silver fish. Beyond it, on a throne made of ivory, teak, ebony, and sandalwood, sat Faghfur Shah on four cushions, wearing his crown. Two lines of servants stood at attention in silken robes and hats adorned with silver and pearls.

Faghfur Shah welcomed Farokhruz with open arms and had him seated on a golden throne beside his own. Servants brought food and wine. After they had eaten and drunk their fill, their hands were washed in rose water. Minstrels entered and played music, dancers danced, and their wine goblets were filled again and again.

Faghfur Shah asked Farokhruz what had brought him to Chin. Farokhruz responded: "O great king! I have come all the way from Halab to ask you for your daughter's hand in marriage, to unite our royal families and our two lands."

Uneasily Faghfur Shah responded: "O great prince! There is no one in the world who would not want to have you as his son-in-law. But I beg you to withdraw your proposal, for I am worried that it will not be to your benefit. The decision about my daughter's marriage is in the hands of her nurse, Shervaneh, who is a very controlling witch. Twenty princes have come before you seeking to marry my daughter, and all of them have fallen into Shervaneh's trap. I am afraid that you will lose your life in this endeavor."

Farokhruz thanked the king for his warning but said that he was determined to go ahead with his proposal. He requested permission to see the Princess Mahpari.

Faghfur Shah sent for his daughter to come to the throne room. Shervaneh, who never left the princess's side, made her up and dressed her to be even more beautiful than usual. As the princess entered the royal court, Shervaneh followed closely behind her. Faghfur Shah ordered everyone to leave the hall except for Mehran the vizier, Farokhruz, and Khorshid Shah, who stood next to his brother.

When Mahpari entered, Khorshid Shah's heart began to pound at the sight of the princess's amazing beauty. His knees trembled and he was on the verge of fainting when he heard Shervaneh asking: "Who is the one requesting the princess's hand in marriage?"

Farokhruz responded: "I am."

The nurse asked Farokhruz: "Are you aware of the conditions for this marriage?" Farokhruz confirmed that he was willing and ready to tame the wild horse, wrestle with the powerful warrior, and find the talking cypress tree.

Early the next morning, Faghfur Shah and his dignitaries took their seats in the arena. His queen sat beside him, his daughter at his other side. Beside the princess sat her witch nurse, Shervaneh.

Khorshid Shah strode into the arena, wearing his own armor. Since the two brothers looked so alike, no one noticed the change, not even Shervaneh.

On Shervaneh's orders, the stable gates opened. An enormous horse almost the size of an elephant charged across the arena straight at the prince. Khorshid Shah threw his lasso around the horse's neck, but with one powerful surge the horse broke free and attacked him.

Khorshid Shah made a fist and punched the horse in the jaw with all his might. The horse's head dipped down. Khorshid Shah grabbed both the horse's ears and swiftly jumped on its back. The giant horse bucked and reared but could not move his head nor break the prince's grip. At last the horse gave up and became tame in Khorshid Shah's hands.

Now it was time for the prince to show off the riding skills he had learned in Halab. He demonstrated some spectacular and unusual moves that made the crowd cheer in admiration.

The next day, the arena was prepared again, and everyone took their places. This time, the prince had to wrestle a huge Abyssinian warrior, a man built like a mountain and wearing only a leopard skin. The two fighters grappled and their struggle began.

The fight went on until Khorshid Shah, in one quick move, placed his hands between the warrior's legs and lifted him above his head. He spun him around several times and slammed the huge wrestler down onto the ground so hard the crowd heard his back break. The people rose to their feet, shouting in joy and hailing the prince. He bowed to them and strode out of the arena, leaving his defeated opponent flat on the ground.

On the third day, Farokhruz again entered the palace pretending to be Khorshid Shah, while his brother walked behind him. The king, princess, and witch nurse awaited them. Shervaneh, angry that her first two challenges had failed, addressed Farokhruz: "Tell me where the talking cypress tree can be found!"

Farokhruz replied: "May I have three days to find the answer?"

The witch shrieked: "No! You have no time!" With that, she flew toward Farokhruz, grabbed him by the shoulders and lifted him high into the air. Before the astonished eyes of Khorshid Shah and the entire court, the witch flew out the palace gates with Farokhruz.

4

A MINSTREL MAIDEN

KHORSHID Shah was devastated. His brother Farokhruz, who had taken his place to protect him, had been kidnapped. The prince rode furiously from Faghfur Shah's palace back to his own pavilion on the outskirts of the city.

For several days Khorshid Shah sat in solitude, with his thoughts in a tumult and one question rising above all: How can a man fight witchcraft and sorcery? This was a challenge for which his training had not prepared him.

On the third day the prince rose, mounted his horse, and rode into the city bazaar. All day long he visited various shops, searching for any clue that might help him rescue his brother from the hands of the witch nurse.

Late in the afternoon, passing through the cloth dealers' bazaar, Khorshid Shah noticed a powerful-looking man riding on horseback, surrounded by an entourage of warriors. "Who is that?" he asked a vendor.

He was told that the rider was Shaghal, head of the *ayyars*, a group that wielded great power in the city. Although the ayyars had no official standing, all citizens knew that they could turn to them for protection in case of injustice.

Khorshid Shah watched the group of ayyars with interest. Walking in front of Shaghal was a well-built young man about the prince's own age, clad in felt. This was Shaghal's adopted son, named Samak. It occurred to the prince that perhaps these ayyars could help him find and rescue his brother.

The next day, Khorshid Shah gathered his entourage and told them to disperse inside the city, concealing their weapons. He then took a bag full of gold coins, mounted his horse, and set out alone on a quest to find Shaghal.

Khorshid Shah soon arrived at the ayyar headquarters. Seeing the door guarded by two muscular men, he said: "Tell your master that someone associated with the prince of Persia wants to see him."

Shaghal, who was aware of the recent events at Faghfur Shah's court, told the guards to let the stranger in. Like everyone else, Shaghal believed that Khorshid Shah, the prince of Persia, had been kidnapped by the witch.

As the prince entered, he saw Shaghal sitting and talking with several ayyars, including his apprentice Samak. Before them was a tray of fruit and a jug of wine, and in each man's hand a goblet. The ayyars raised their goblets and drank to the safety of the people.

Shaghal welcomed the prince with open arms. He expressed respect for the king of Persia and sadness that his son had been kidnapped.

After accepting some fruit and wine, Khorshid Shah asked Shaghal: "Tell me, what are the principles of the ayyars?"

Shaghal replied: "There is no limit to being an ayyar, but there are seventy-two principles that every ayyar knows. I will tell you the two most important: To keep secrets, and to help those in need."

Hearing this, Khorshid Shah said: "Now that I know ayyars are bound to keep secrets, I will reveal to you that I am Khorshid Shah, son of Marzban Shah, king of Persia. The one who was kidnapped by the witch is my brother Farokhruz, who took my place and put himself in danger to protect me."

Shaghal absorbed this information. Then he said: "Farokhruz risked his life for the good of his kingdom. This shows courage and nobility that is in keeping with our brotherhood's code. Therefore, we ayyars will dedicate our services to free him." He raised his goblet of wine to salute Farokhruz. The other ayyars did the same. Then Shaghal accepted the bag of gold coins the prince offered him as a royal gift.

The prince asked Shaghal if he could visit the princess Mahpari and find out from her where his brother was being held. Shaghal replied: "This would not be easy. The witch nurse guards the princess so well that even a bird does not dare fly above her palace."

Samak, who had been listening quietly, turned to Shaghal and said: "O master! One of Mahpari's handmaidens is like a mother to me. Her name is Ruhafza. We can go to her and ask if she can get Khorshid Shah into the princess's palace." The prince and Shaghal accepted Samak's offer. They spent the rest of that day and a good part of the night eating, drinking, and enjoying each other's company until they all fell asleep.

At dawn, Khorshid Shah, Shaghal, and Samak went to Ruhafza's home before she left for the princess's palace. Samak kissed Ruhafza's hand and said: "I need to ask a great favor of you, who are closer to me than my own mother. I hope you will not turn me down."

Ruhafza replied: "Samak, you know I would do anything for you."

Samak asked: "Dear mother, you know some of the principles of the ayyars because you have seen me practice them. Can you recall them?"

Ruhafza replied: "One that stands out for me is that you never push away the hand that stretches toward you for help. Another is that you never reveal someone's secret to others."

Samak said: "I am glad you remember these principles, because I have a secret to tell you." He then revealed that the stranger with him was none other than the prince of Persia, who had come to Chin to marry Mahpari. Ruhafza asked: "How can this be? Prince Khorshid Shah was kidnapped by the witch Shervaneh."

"No, my dear mother," said Samak. "The one the witch kidnapped was Farokhruz, the prince's brother. Now Khorshid Shah wants to enter the royal compound to find out where his brother is being kept so that he may free him."

Ruhafza said: "My son, this will be difficult. You know that witch has total control over who enters and leaves the palace."

Samak responded: "This is why only you can help us."

Ruhafza thought for a minute, then said: "Let the prince stay here with me until I can find some way to take him into the royal compound."

Shaghal and Samak left the house. Ruhafza asked Khorshid Shah many questions. When she discovered that the prince was able to sing and play musical instruments, she knew how she would get him in to see Mahpari.

• • •

A few days later came Nowruz, the first day of spring and the Persian New Year. Ruhafza decorated the prince's hands and feet with henna and made him up to look like a beautiful young girl. She combed his hair and placed a gold silk turban on his head. Inside the turban she hid a small container filled with sleeping powder. Finally, she wrapped a lasso around the prince's chest under his clothing. Then she took him with her to the palace to join the New Year celebration.

The Nowruz garden was filled with early spring flowers. Amidst the colorful blossoms sat Princess Mahpari on her throne, shining like the sun. Everyone who entered the garden went first to Mahpari, kissed her hand, and offered her a Nowruz gift. In return, the princess gave each visitor a bag of gold coins.

At the peak of the ceremony, while musicians, dancers, and magicians all performed their arts, Ruhafza entered the garden with Khorshid Shah and escorted him to Mahpari's throne. She kissed her hand, saying: "My princess, I have brought you this girl as a special Nowruz present. She is a minstrel who will devote her talents to entertain you privately at night. I hope you will be pleased with her."

Mahpari thanked her handmaiden and gave her a bag of gold coins. Khorshid Shah was mesmerized by the princess's beauty. He kissed her hand and sat down beside Ruhafza on the opposite side of the princess from the witch nurse, Shervaneh.

As the day came to an end and night settled over the garden, the visitors departed one by one. The last to leave was Ruhafza, leaving Khorshid Shah alone with the princess and Shervaneh in Mahpari's private chambers.

Now that everyone had gone, the prince picked up a lute and began to play a love song, singing in a high falsetto. Mahpari and Shervaneh were enraptured by the sweetness of his voice and the beauty of the melody. Khorshid Shah took advantage of their distraction to pour sleeping powder in their wine goblets when they weren't looking.

Princess Mahpari, in ecstasy, raised her goblet in honor of the wonderful minstrel maiden. The witch did likewise. Before long, the goblets were empty and both women were unconscious on the tiled floor.

Khorshid Shah slung the witch Shervaneh over his shoulder and headed for the garden's outer wall. The night was dark, and many guards were still half drunk from the day's celebration. Khorshid Shah hid from them as he made his way through the garden to the outer wall of the palace compound. Setting his unconscious captive on the ground, he threw the lasso high and fastened its noose onto a battlement atop the wall. He then tied the witch to the other end of the lasso and climbed the rope himself. At the top of the wall, his feet braced firmly against the battlement, he pulled Shervaneh up and then lowered her down the other side. Once they were outside the wall, he headed for the ayyar headquarters.

Samak and Shaghal, who had been waiting anxiously for news of the prince, rejoiced to see him arrive carrying the witch over his shoulder. "Leave her to us," they told Khorshid Shah. They fastened Shervaneh's hands and feet to a wall with heavy chains.

Khorshid Shah said goodbye to the ayyars and headed back to the royal palace. He used the lasso to climb the wall into the garden the same way he had left. Still in minstrel maiden's garb, he found a safe spot to rest under a tree with his lute. He hoped that the ayyars would soon find out from the witch where she had imprisoned Farokhruz and send him word through Ruhafza.

Meanwhile, Shaghal and Samak waited until Shervaneh regained consciousness. The moment she opened her eyes and found herself chained, she understood what had happened to her.

"Where have you hidden Khorshid Shah?" Shaghal asked.

Shervaneh replied scornfully: "I will never tell you!"

Shaghal and Samak began beating Shervaneh, demanding that she reveal the prince's whereabouts. But she refused to speak a word.

Back at the palace, evening fell, and Khorshid Shah still had no word from Ruhafza. He returned to Mahpari's private chamber. The princess welcomed the minstrel maiden who had played so splendidly for her the night before. At her request, Khorshid Shah resumed playing, singing the most beautiful love songs he knew. When Mahpari's attention was distracted, he again seized the opportunity to pour sleeping powder into her wine goblet.

5

THE WITCH'S DUNGEON

SOON after Princess Mahpari drank the wine, she fell into a deep sleep. Khorshid Shah left her chamber and began to explore the royal compound, searching for Farokhruz.

In the darkness of the garden he discovered a hidden passageway. As he entered, a huge guard wielding a fearsome sword stepped out and blocked his path, shouting: "Who the devil let you in here? No one may enter, not even the king himself. Get out of here before I chop you into pieces!"

Hearing this, Khorshid Shah felt certain he was in the right place. In a sweet, girlish voice, he said: "Forgive me! I am a new maiden in the court and I don't know the way around here yet. I was singing to the princess. Now that she has gone to sleep, I am looking for a place to spend the night. Can you help me?"

The guard took a keen look at Khorshid Shah. In the dim light of a burning torch in the passageway, he saw a beautiful and willing maiden. His eyes gleamed and he said: "O lovely girl! I overheard your voice last night and dearly wished to see you up close. Can it be that my wish has come true? Would you sing for me?"

Khorshid Shah replied: "It would be my pleasure to sing for a strong man like you! But I am afraid if I sing here in this passageway, it might awaken others. Is there some private place we can go to be together?"

The guard's heart leapt. "Follow me," he said. He led Khorshid Shah through the passageway and down a flight of stairs into a hidden room. It was dark except for one dim torch. The guard poured a cup of wine for Khorshid Shah, one for himself, and the two began drinking.

Khorshid Shah played his lute, singing enticingly in a soft voice, until the guard was overcome with lust. The prince seized the moment to pour sleeping powder into the guard's wine.

Soon the guard's head dipped and he slumped unconscious. Immediately Khorshid Shah took the burning torch from the wall and began searching for a way out that might lead him to his brother. Before long, he found a massive locked door.

Khorshid Shah returned to the sleeping guard, took the key chain from his neck, and used the keys to open the multiple locks on the door. Pushing it open, he found himself in an empty room. In its center was a large heavy millstone. Using all his strength, Khorshid Shah pushed the millstone aside, revealing a deep hole in the floor and gaping darkness below.

Beside the hole lay a rope ladder that Khorshid Shah lowered into the darkness. Holding his torch in one hand, he descended about fifty steps until he reached the bottom.

In the dim light of the dungeon, twenty prisoners turned toward him. They sat in groups with their hands and feet chained together, each group around a single lit candle. All were young men who had come to Chin in hopes of marrying Princess Mahpari.

Khorshid Shah searched the prisoners' faces until he recognized Farokhruz among them. Approaching him, he removed his maiden's disguise. Farokhruz cried out with joy. Khorshid Shah held his brother in his arms and they wept in relief. Farokhruz asked: "How on earth did you get in here?"

Khorshid Shah responded: "I'll explain later." He then unlocked his brother's chains.

Addressing the other prisoners, Khorshid Shah said: "If we all leave together now, the palace guards will catch us. Be patient one more night. Tomorrow I will return with help and free you all."

Khorshid Shah and Farokhruz climbed the rope ladder out of the dungeon. Khorshid Shah pushed the millstone back into place, relocked the door, and replaced the key chain around the sleeping guard's neck.

Exiting the passageway into the garden, the two men stole through the darkness of the compound until they reached the outer wall. Khorshid Shah threw the lasso as he had done the night before, and he and his brother climbed over the wall.

Once on the other side, Khorshid Shah said to his brother: "The ones who helped us are the ayyars Shaghal and Samak and the princess's handmaiden Ruhafza. Go to the ayyar headquarters, tell them everything, and make plans to return tomorrow night and free the others." He showed Farokhruz the path. The two brothers embraced farewell. Khorshid Shah then climbed back over the wall and returned to Mahpari's chamber.

He found the princess still sleeping soundly as he had left her. Now that his brother was free and Shervaneh imprisoned, all Khorshid Shah's attention went to his beloved, for whom he had endured so much trouble. The dream he had cherished since their first encounter in the desert was about to come true. He was alone with Mahpari. His heart began to beat so hard it echoed through the room.

Khorshid Shah moved close to the sleeping princess. He yearned to take her in his arms and kiss her. But he controlled his desire, picked up his lute, and continued playing. All night long, he sang soft love songs to Mahpari. With the first rays of morning, the princess stirred and awoke, pleased to see the minstrel maiden still singing faithfully for her.

Meanwhile, Farokhruz arrived at the ayyar headquarters just after dawn. Shaghal and Samak held him in their arms and thanked God for his safety. Farokhruz told them everything that had happened to him, beginning with his capture and ending with Khorshid Shah's promise to free the other prisoners.

Shaghal sent Samak to Ruhafza with a message for Khorshid Shah: "Tell the prince we will meet him at midnight outside the palace wall."

Early that evening, Khorshid Shah returned to Mahpari's chamber for the third night, still in maiden's dress. The princess was happy to see the minstrel maiden again, and happy that the witch nurse had not returned. "She must have gone to celebrate Nowruz with her own friends and relatives," the princess told the prince. "Now that we are alone and she is not here to spoil our fun, sing me a happy song!"

Khorshid Shah sang and played. The princess danced joyfully around the columns of the chamber with the freedom and lively energy of youth.

The prince was spellbound by Mahpari's grace and beauty as she danced. He could not take his eyes off her, and he wished the night would never end. But he remembered the promise he had made to the imprisoned suitors. At the right moment, he again poured powder into Mahpari's wine goblet, and soon the princess was asleep.

Khorshid Shah took his lute and returned to the dungeon passageway. The guard, unaware that Farokhruz had been released, was excited to see the minstrel maiden again. Apologizing for having fallen asleep the night before, he promised that tonight he would stay awake long enough to be good company. He took

Khorshid Shah back to the private room and began drinking while the prince played and sang for him.

Khorshid Shah once again used sleeping powder to put the guard to sleep. He left the dungeon, climbed the compound's outer wall, and found Shaghal and Samak waiting on the other side with a group of their men. It was just after midnight. The prince removed his maiden disguise. He, Shaghal, and Samak used their lassos to scale the palace wall while the rest of the ayyars remained outside below.

Khorshid Shah guided Samak and Shaghal through the gardens into the dungeon passageway. Samak took a look at the unconscious guard and said: "This evil man has been helping the witch for a long time and deserves to die." He pulled a dagger from inside his coat and cut off the guard's head. Khorshid Shah took the guard's key chain and the torch and headed for the dungeon, followed by Samak and Shaghal.

The twenty imprisoned young men were excited to see them. Samak, Shaghal, and Khorshid Shah removed the chains from the prisoners' necks, hands, and feet, and helped them climb the rope ladder one by one.

Once all the suitors were in the garden, Samak gathered them together and announced: "This is Khorshid Shah, the prince of Persia. He risked his life to capture the witch nurse and free you. He has come to Chin to marry Princess Mahpari. You must all promise to respect his wish."

All the suitors gave their promise. Samak then told the prince: "It will be difficult to take everyone over the wall. These men have been in chains a long time and some are too weak to climb."

Khorshid Shah agreed: "We must go out through the main gate." He led the way through the palace grounds in the darkness.

When the king's soldiers guarding the gate saw the prisoners approaching, they drew their swords and attacked. A fierce combat began in the predawn light. The ayyars waiting outside the palace wall heard the noise and ran to join the battle. Soon all the guards were slain. Khorshid Shah and his group headed for the ayyar headquarters, arriving just before sunrise.

When Mahpari woke up and wondered what had become of the minstrel maiden, she sent one of her handmaidens to look for her. The girl entered the secret passageway, saw the dead guard, and screamed. She ran back to Mahpari and told her what she had seen.

Soon the whole palace knew that Shervaneh's prisoners had escaped, a number of guards had been killed, and the witch nurse was nowhere to be found.

Faghfur Shah called for his vizier. Mehran said: "I suspect the hand of the ayyars. Let us summon Shaghal and Samak."

When Shaghal and Samak entered, Faghfur Shah greeted them and said: "Strange things have been happening in the palace compound. Is it possible that the ayyars might have had something to do with the disappearance of my daughter's nurse, the escape of those prisoners, and the killing of my royal guards?"

Samak, seeing his master hesitate, spoke up quickly: "Your Majesty, we cannot lie to you. Khorshid Shah came to us for help to free his brother Farokhruz from the witch nurse's snare, and we did not refuse him."

"Bring them to me!" ordered Faghfur Shah.

Samak went straight from the royal court to the ayyar headquarters, where Khorshid Shah and Farokhruz were resting from their ordeal while the ayyars and prisoners celebrated their freedom. No one was paying any attention to Shervaneh.

Samak immediately saw that Shervaneh had been using her powers to weaken the iron chain binding her hands and feet, and that she was on the point of breaking loose. He could imagine the harm she would cause if she were free in the ayyar headquarters.

He walked up to her and said: "O wicked witch! It seems to me you are taking great pains trying to release yourself from these shackles. I will save you the trouble and set you free forever!" With those words, Samak drew his dagger and cut off Shervaneh's head. He then put her head into a leather bag.

To Khorshid Shah and Farokhruz he said: "Come with me." The two princes followed Samak to Faghfur Shah's palace.

Samak strode into the royal court, opened the leather bag and shook out its contents. The entire court gasped as the witch's bloody head rolled across the floor and came to a stop in front of Faghfur Shah's throne.

Everyone looked to the king for his reaction.

Faghfur Shah, who had long been concerned and unhappy about Shervaneh's influence over his daughter, looked pleased. He asked: "Have you also brought me the prince and his brother?"

At a gesture from Samak, Khorshid Shah entered the throne room, preceded by Farokhruz. Everyone was mesmerized by the prince's beauty, elegance, and charm. Faghfur Shah welcomed him and invited him to sit on his right side on a special silken seat.

When the tale of the past few days' events reached Princess Mahpari, she became curious to see Khorshid Shah for herself. Entering the royal court, her eyes went first to Farokhruz, who had previously been presented to her as the prince of Persia, and only then to the young man sitting on her father's right.

Seeing the prince, Mahpari's heart leapt. She recognized him not only as the maiden minstrel whose singing and playing had enchanted her, but as the stranger she had fallen in love with in a dream. In that dream, more than a year ago, she had embraced him in a distant desert tent and slipped her ring onto his finger as a token of her love. Awakening to find herself in her own chambers with only her witch nurse for company, she had wept with bitterness at night for months thereafter wishing that the dream were real. Now here he was, seated at her father's side. Instantly Mahpari was consumed with love and wanted nothing in life but to become Khorshid Shah's queen.

Friendly discussions went on among everyone present at the court, following which Faghfur Shah announced that his daughter would be married to the prince of Persia in ten days.

6

THE VIZIER'S SON

FAGHFUR Shah's vizier Mehran had a son named Qabiz who was his pride and joy. Qabiz was a great warrior, so skilled in the use of every kind of weapon that there was not a man in all of Chin who dared to face him in combat.

Qabiz was in love with Mahpari, but his father had warned him not to reveal his feelings out of fear that his son would be caught in Shervaneh's snare.

The day Qabiz heard the witch nurse was dead, he saw his opportunity. When Mehran returned from court, Qabiz knelt before him with tears in his eyes and spoke of his great love for Mahpari. "O father, you have served the king faithfully for many years. Would you now let a foreigner marry into the royal family instead of your own son? I beg you to use your influence to prevent this marriage."

Moved by his son's words, Mehran promised: "My son, I will do what I can."

The next day, Mehran found a moment to be alone with the king. He warned him: "Your Majesty, I am troubled by this promise you have made to Khorshid Shah. The other suitors whom the witch captured are royal princes and sons of noblemen from many countries. I worry that being passed over for this marriage among the one thousand others in the king's stables. Its jewel-encrusted saddle sparkled in the sunlight. Farokhruz rode at his brother's side, followed in orderly procession by Samak, Shaghal, a group of ayyars, and then the foreign princes and noblemen who had been released from the witch's dungeon.

The group of riders stopped in the center of the arena. Horns were blown and drums were beaten. The crowd became quiet.

Mehran the vizier stood up and read the king's decree. He then declared: "Let the suitors for the hand of Princess Mahpari step forth and introduce themselves."

A royal prince rode out from among the suitors and shouted: "O great king, nobles, and citizens! We, who were imprisoned by the wicked witch, owe our freedom to the prince of Persia. We have promised him not to contest his claim. We therefore yield."

Before anyone could react, Mehran called out accusingly: "Khorshid Shah! Can it be that you have made these brave men promise not to fight you? Is it your wish to avoid combat in this manner?"

Khorshid Shah did not want to show weakness in front of Mahpari and the public. He replied: "If you insist, let those who wish to marry the princess fight until only one champion remains. I will then fight that champion myself."

Mehran consulted briefly with the king and announced: "This suggestion is acceptable to His Majesty. Let the combat begin!"

Khorshid Shah and the ayyars moved to one side of the arena, and the other suitors faced each other to fight. The crowd roared as twenty princes and noblemen, mounted on fine horses, all with different armor, backgrounds, and fighting styles, threw themselves into battle.

Watching from the edge of the arena was Mehran's son, Qabiz, quietly studying the warriors' techniques and awaiting an opportune moment to enter the field himself.

Cheers went up each time a fighter was downed and his body carried from the field. As the combat continued, the contenders were eliminated until only one remained—Bahman, the prince of Oman, a mighty warrior.

The crowd roared. Raising his fist in triumph, Bahman turned his horse toward the prince. "Khorshid Shah!" he shouted. "Come and face me!"

Khorshid Shah was ready. As he rode out into the arena to face the champion, Mehran's voice rang out: "True heroes do not attack those who are worn out from combat!"

The prince hesitated. Mehran then shouted: "If anyone else here wishes to marry the princess, let him enter the arena and challenge Khorshid Shah!"

Even before the vizier had finished his invitation, a group of prepared soldiers rode into the arena, attacking Khorshid Shah from all sides. A bloody combat ensued. Khorshid Shah fought heroically, eliminating his attackers one by one, until he was left alone. Tired and bleeding from many wounds, Khorshid Shah turned again to face Bahman.

The crowd roared with excitement. Having seen both princes fight with skill and courage, their loyalty was equally divided between the two champions.

The two warriors charged toward each other, shooting arrows from horseback until they came within range. They fought with mace, sword, and dagger until Bahman's horse slipped and fell, tumbling him onto the ground. Khorshid Shah likewise dismounted as Bahman scrambled to his feet to face him. The two princes fought hand-to-hand, weapons and shields clashing, until Bahman was disarmed.

Khorshid Shah threw down his own weapon. He stepped in close, seized his opponent by the waist, lifted him above his head, and threw him flat onto the ground. A cheer went up from the crowd. Mahpari smiled with joy.

Now Qabiz, who had been standing by and watching the combat since the beginning, saw his opportunity. He spurred his horse and rode into the arena toward Khorshid Shah. The prince, exhausted and wounded, turned to see Qabiz riding toward him.

Samak jumped from his seat and sprinted into the arena. Qabiz was almost upon the prince when Samak ran in between them. "Now you attack a wounded warrior?" he shouted. Qabiz's horse reared. Samak grabbed the reins, saying: "The words of your father the vizier should have been meant for you!" And he pulled Qabiz down from his horse in one clever move.

Snarling, Qabiz drew his sword and faced Samak on foot. The two men circled, fighting hand-to-hand. Suddenly Samak side-stepped and plunged his dagger into Qabiz's heart so deeply that the tip came out his back. Samak withdrew the blade and Qabiz fell to the ground, dead.

The crowd surged to their feet with a roar. The most famous warrior of Chin had been killed before their eyes. As people poured from the stands into the arena, Samak and other ayyars circled around Khorshid Shah to protect him.

Fearing a riot, the king ordered the royal guards to clear the arena. Guards rode in and began pushing the crowd back. Amid the chaos, the king announced: "Let it be known that the marriage of Mahpari to Khorshid Shah will take place as planned!"

The vanquished suitors left Chin to journey back to their homes—the survivors to recover from their wounds, the dead to be buried. The body of Qabiz was taken to the vizier's palace to be prepared for burial in the city's main cemetery.

Qabiz's death at the hand of Samak was an unbearable blow to Mehran the vizier. Not only had he lost his beloved son, but Chin had lost its greatest hero. In grief and anguish, Mehran began to plot his vengeance against Samak and Khorshid Shah.

7

A FATAL BANQUET

With the princess's wedding only five days away, Mehran sought some way to delay it. He sent for Shirafcan, a seasoned warrior who had supervised his son's training. The vizier knew that Shirafcan was also mourning Qabiz's death.

When Shirafcan arrived at the vizier's palace, Mehran embraced him like a brother and said: "Now that Qabiz is no longer with us, you are the greatest warrior of Chin. It is you who should marry Princess Mahpari and succeed Faghfur Shah as the next ruler of our kingdom, not the foreigner Khorshid Shah."

Shirafcan's eyes gleamed. His own wife had died years ago. Like Qabiz, he harbored a secret love for Mahpari. Eagerly, he said: "O great vizier, how can I help make this happen?"

Mehran replied: "Our first step must be to prevent this marriage to Khorshid Shah. I suggest that we kidnap the princess and hide her in a safe place." Shirafcan agreed with this plan.

The vizier said: "I will send to you a man named Shabkhiz, a dedicated slave who is skilled at digging underground tunnels. He will follow your every order. As for the rest, I have confidence in your skill and judgment."

Shirafcan assured him: "You can count on me."

tied her up, and pulled her into the tunnel he was digging under the wall. Mahpari was completely immobilized. Shabkhiz left her there in the tunnel and hurried to inform Shirafcan so that they could return and carry the princess away.

Unfortunately for Shabkhiz, his path led him right past Samak, who was searching the darkness nearby for Mahpari. Shabkhiz ducked his head and hurried along the path, but Samak's sharp eyes spotted him in the dark. Samak grabbed Shabkhiz by the neck, demanding: "You bastard, what have you done with the princess? Tell me or I'll send you straight to hell!"

Shabkhiz whimpered: "What princess? I'm innocent! I swear I don't know what you're talking about!"

Samak said: "I'll show you what I'm talking about!" He tied a rope around Shabkhiz's neck and dragged him like a mule to the ayyar headquarters.

Meanwhile, Shirafcan, who had been waiting for Shabkhiz to return from digging the tunnel, became concerned. He decided to go by the royal palace and check on the slave's progress.

As Shirafcan searched the darkness along the outside of the palace wall, he heard a moan. He followed the sound and discovered the entrance to the tunnel, which Shabkhiz had concealed. Shirafcan crawled into the tunnel on hands and knees. There he found Mahpari tied up.

Quickly he dragged her out, lifted her over his shoulder, and carried her to the vizier's palace. Mehran ordered his servants to put the princess in a bedroom where she would be comfortable, to attend to her injuries, and to make sure that she could not escape.

Shirafcan explained how he had found the princess in the tunnel, and that Shabkhiz was nowhere to be found.

"You did well," said Mehran. "Now go home and leave the rest to me."

• • •

Shortly before dawn, one of Mahpari's maidens came to check on the princess and saw the guard lying dead outside her door. She screamed and called for help. Soon the whole palace knew that the princess was missing.

Hearing the news, Faghfur Shah thought to himself: "This sounds like the work of the ayyars." He sent a messenger to summon Shaghal.

Meanwhile, Samak and Shaghal had interrogated Shabkhiz, who had confessed everything. They hurried to the palace and found the tunnel Shabkhiz had dug, but there was no sign of Mahpari. Samak concluded that she had to be in the custody of the vizier Mehran.

By then the sky was light. Samak and Shaghal saw the king's messenger approaching. "The king wishes to see you," said the messenger. Samak replied: "That suits us, for we also want to see the king."

The messenger brought the two ayyars to the women's quarters, where Faghfur Shah was waiting. The king said angrily: "Tell me, in all my life, when have I ever done anything unpleasant to you? I have left you alone and never interfered with your activities in the city. Why have you turned against me and kidnapped my only daughter? You speak of fairness, but your actions are those of thieves. Return her at once before the whole world learns of this outrage!"

Samak bowed to Faghfur Shah and said: "Your Majesty, I assure you your daughter is not with us. This is what happened: Last night, I broke into her chamber and took her willingly for her own protection, because I feared the vizier Mehran would act against her. I was right. While I was taking her down the wall of the palace, a servant of Mehran cut the rope and stole her away. She is now in the hands of your vizier."

Faghfur Shah shouted: "Mehran! What does my vizier want with my daughter? What did I do to deserve this torment?" He then dismissed Samak and Shaghal, declaring: "I will get to the bottom of this." Faghfur Shah sent a messenger to bring Mehran immediately.

When the vizier arrived at the court, Faghfur Shah said: "I trusted you as my vizier. I thought you were here to help me rule the country peacefully. Now you dare to kidnap my daughter behind my back! Do you deny it? Speak up before I have your head cut off!"

Mehran bowed and said: "Your Majesty! My only thought was to protect your daughter. One of my slaves saw her being kidnapped by Samak the ayyar. The villain had tied her with a rope and was lowering her down the palace wall. My slave cut her loose and brought her to my palace for her safety. Had he not acted quickly, your daughter would now be in the hands of the ayyars, and God knows what they would have done to her!"

Seeing that he had the king's attention, Mehran continued: "Those ayyars murdered my son. They have slain your guards, good men who were loyal to you. Now they break into your palace in the night and steal your daughter, and you blame me? If my slave had not been there at the right moment, she could have been lost to us forever. I think I have done Your Majesty a great service."

Mehran saw that the king was listening and pressed his advantage. "Your Highness, the ayyars are destroying our nation. The way things are going, soon it will be they, not you, who rule the kingdom. History will say that Faghfur Shah was defeated by only sixty ayyars. I urge you to get rid of them and put an end to all these troubles." Mehran continued: "Your Majesty asks what I have done with your daughter? My answer is I have saved her from a gang of lowly rogues. I will return her today to her chambers, safe and sound. If you still believe I did you wrong, I will kill myself right here in front of you."

Faghfur Shah went into deep thought. Mehran's words made sense to him. He said: "I have often thought that the ayyars have become too powerful. But how can we get rid of them? The people trust them. Their network extends throughout the kingdom. Do you have a suggestion?"

Mehran asked the king: "Can we speak alone?" Faghfur Shah gestured for everyone to leave the hall.

When the two men were alone, Mehran said: "I have an idea for how we can eliminate the ayyars." The king leaned forward, listening.

Mehran continued: "We will hold a feast on the night before your daughter's wedding. Let us invite the ayyars along with Khorshid Shah and his brother. It will be natural to require the guests to leave their weapons at the entrance so that no one is armed at the royal table. We will offer them delicious food and wine, with musicians and dancers to lull them into a relaxed state. Once they are drunk and their bellies are full, I will give the signal, and guards hidden behind the drapes and curtains will fall upon the ayyars and kill every one of them. Then our land will be free of them, and Your Majesty will have peace of mind."

Faghfur Shah thought for a minute and said: "Make the arrangements as you have described."

The vizier returned home, bringing gifts for Mahpari. He expressed sympathy for her ordeal and sent her back to her father's palace with his respects.

Soon after, the royal palace was set for a feast to celebrate the princess's wedding. Khorshid Shah, his brother Farokhruz, Samak, and Shaghal arrived with a retinue of ayyars, all formally dressed for the banquet. As they entered, they willingly surrendered their weapons to the king's servants as a guarantee of peace.

The guests took their assigned seats, Khorshid Shah on the king's right, his brother beside him. On Faghfur Shah's order, the ceremony began. Musicians and exotic dancers performed while beautiful servants plied the guests with food and wine. After two hours, everyone present was intoxicated in a pleasurable trance.

Mehran judged that the opportune moment had arrived. He nodded to Faghfur Shah, who stood up and left. As soon as the king had left the hall, Mehran removed his hat as if he were feeling overheated, and stroked his beard with his fingers. This was the signal. Dozens of guards armed with swords and daggers burst into the room and fell upon the ayyars, slaughtering them.

Samak realized that the banquet had been a trap by Mehran. He reached for a dagger strapped to his left thigh and began fighting back. But the attackers were too many and too well armed. Samak fell to the floor, grievously wounded, while ayyars were slain all around him. Only Shaghal, Khorshid Shah, and Farokhruz were spared. On the vizier's orders, soldiers bound them hand and foot and dragged them from the banquet hall.

Mehran stood triumphant amid a sea of blood. As his guards began cleaning up the mess, the vizier selected a group of men and told them: "Go to the ayyar headquarters. Kill whoever is guarding it and take anything you find of value as a reward for yourselves. Then set the place on fire." To the remaining guards, he said: "Take the carcasses to the desert and leave them there to feed the dogs and wolves."

SECTION 2

The People's Defenders

8

THE GRAVE ROBBER

THERE was a grave robber named Mehruye who lived with his wife on the outskirts of the city. He made his living by selling what he could salvage from the dead. When he heard that the ayyars had been massacred at Faghfur Shah's palace and their bodies dumped in the desert, he hitched his mule to his cart and hurried to the site.

It was already dark when he arrived. Moonlight shone on the pile of corpses. A few stray dogs were feeding on the exposed carcasses. Mehruye began stripping the dead ayyars of clothes, hats, sashes, bracelets, and anything else of value. All of these he threw into the cart.

A glint in the moonlight caught his attention. It was a silver necklace shining on an ayyar's throat. Mehruye pulled out his dagger and began to cut the chain. Suddenly the man's eyes opened. Mehruye screamed and jumped back but found himself held in place by an iron grip. "Who are you?" the man croaked. "Where am I?"

Mehruye, shaking with fear, answered: "I am Mehruye. And you are dead in the desert!"

"I am not dead," answered the hoarse voice. "I am Samak the ayyar. Give me water."

Mehruye had seen Samak before in town and knew him by reputation as a good and generous man. He was relieved that he was not speaking with a corpse. He rushed to his cart, brought back a jug, and poured a little water into Samak's mouth.

Soon Samak felt a bit stronger, and asked Mehruye to lift his head. Mehruye saw that Samak was bleeding from many wounds. "We have to get you out of here," he said. Mehruye dragged bodies out of the way until the path to the cart lay clear. Then he half-lifted, half-pulled Samak's body to the cart, with difficulty, for he was a small man and slightly built. His original plan of a profitable adventure forgotten, he rode the mule as fast as it could go until he reached home.

Mehruye called his wife, Samana, to come out and help him bring Samak into the house. Surprised to see a wounded man in the cart instead of the expected load of goods, she asked: "Who is this?"

"This is Samak the ayyar," said Mehruye. "God has blessed us with this chance to save his life."

Samana quickly started washing the blood from the young man's body and binding his wounds with cloth to stop the bleeding. "We need a surgeon," said Mehruye. He mounted his mule and rode off.

When Samana had finished binding Samak's wounds, she gazed upon him with worry. His face was pale from blood loss. "What more can I do for you?" she asked.

Samak said in a voice so soft that she had to lean down to hear him: "I would like some dove soup."

It was midnight when Mehruye returned with a surgeon. By then, Samana had boiled several doves in water with minced onions and a little rice and was spoon-feeding Samak the broth.

Mehruye did not reveal his patient's identity, but the surgeon immediately recognized Samak. "Thank God you are alive," he said. "I will do my best for you."

Samak said: "You are taking a great risk by helping me. For your own safety, tell no one I am here." They all agreed. "Thank you," said Samak, and he lost consciousness at once.

The surgeon worked with Mehruye and Samana's assistance, stitching and covering Samak's wounds. The sky was growing light by the time he finished. Mehruye took the surgeon home and returned exhausted. Only then did he and his wife lie down to rest.

Samak remained at Mehruye and Samana's house for forty days, throughout which they served him devotedly, with regular visits from the surgeon.

As soon as Samak felt better, his first thought was to find a way to reward these people who had cared for him with such dedication. He said to Mehruye: "My friend, you have done so much for me. I have one more request. Would you bring me a dagger, a lasso, and a torch, and lend me your mule?"

Mehruye complied. Samak got dressed and waited until it was dark. Then he rode Mehruye's mule to the city.

Samak knew that in the bazaar there was a jeweler with whom Mehran the vizier had a long-standing secret arrangement. When one of the king's subjects angered the vizier by refusing him a favor or a bribe, Mehran would confiscate the offender's gold and jewels. Instead of depositing the seized valuables in Faghfur Shah's treasury, he would send them to his friend the jeweler, who would sell them and quietly return the proceeds to Mehran, keeping a percentage for himself.

Samak and Shaghal had long been aware of this abuse but had been unable to stop it, since the vizier was the king's trusted right hand. Now that Samak found himself alone and penniless, it occurred to him to reward the people who had saved his life at the corrupt jeweler's expense.

The bazaar was closed and its gates locked by the time Samak reached the city. He moved quietly around the bazaar's outer wall until he found the jeweler's shop. He waited until all the torches had been put out. Then he used the dagger Mehruye had given him to cut a hole in the back wall of the shop, just wide enough to enter.

After making sure that no one was in the shop, Samak selected ten small sacks of gold and left the shop the same way he had entered it. He then rode the mule back to Mehruye's house.

The next morning, Samak gave five gold sacks to Mehruye and three to Samana as a reward for the good care they had taken of him. When the surgeon came for his regular visit, Samak gave him the remaining two sacks. "One sack is for your services," said Samak. "The other is to pay for the medicines and herbs you have given me throughout my illness." The surgeon gratefully accepted the reward.

As it happened, to reach his next patient that day, the surgeon had to pass through the jewelers' bazaar. Noticing a crowd gathered around the largest and best-known jeweler's shop, he stopped to see what was going on.

"Ten sacks of my gold have been stolen!" cried the jeweler, while the crowd debated who might have done the job. "This is the work of the ayyars," said some. Others argued: "There are no ayyars in this town anymore. Mehran has seen to that."

One man muttered under his breath that the jeweler's loss was no great tragedy since he was a thief himself. This accusation provoked a heated response from the jeweler's defenders that turned into a physical quarrel. It was the surgeon's bad luck that, just as he arrived, one of these men was shoved right into him and knocked him down. The two sacks of gold Samak had given him fell out into the road where all could see them.

"That's my gold!" cried the jeweler. The crowd encircled the surgeon and held him until the magistrate arrived with the guards. The jeweler denounced the surgeon to the magistrate and convinced him that he was the thief. The guards took the surgeon away in chains, followed by the jeweler and a crowd.

When they arrived at court, the jeweler bowed to Mehran the vizier. "Your Excellency!" he said. "This man broke into my shop last night and took ten sacks of gold worth one thousand dinars each. We found two of the sacks on him."

Mehran looked coldly at the surgeon. "Where did you get these?" he asked.

The surgeon replied: "I found them lying in the road on my way to the bazaar. Perhaps the thief dropped them as he fled."

Mehran ordered the court executioner: "Whip this man until he tells the truth."

The executioner began to whip the surgeon. Despite the torture, he did not betray Samak but only repeated: "I found the sacks in the road!" until blood ran down his back. At last the surgeon collapsed, unconscious. Mehran ordered him thrown into the dungeon.

• • •

When the surgeon opened his eyes, he saw a dozen prisoners sitting around him, staring at him with concern. "What did you do to deserve such a brutal whipping?" asked their leader. The surgeon recognized him as Shaghal, the chief of the ayyars.

"I know you," said the surgeon. "But I don't know these others."

Shaghal explained that these were the ayyars who had been left to guard their headquarters. Rather than sacrifice themselves fighting against unwinnable odds, they had surrendered to Mehran's soldiers. Shaghal assured him: "Anything you have to say to me, you can say in front of these men."

"Then I will tell you what I did not tell the vizier," said the surgeon, and he told Shaghal how Samak had rewarded him.

Shaghal was overjoyed to learn that Samak was alive. He said: "If I know Samak, he will find a way to free us all from this dungeon."

The story of the theft at the jeweler's shop and the surgeon's arrest spread through the city. When Mehruye heard the news, he rushed home and told Samak. Samak was stricken: "It's because of me that this good man is in prison." He resolved to free the surgeon before he could be subjected to more torture.

As soon as night fell, Samak headed to town and waited outside the prison wall until the street became dark and quiet. Then he lassoed a crenellation at the top of the wall and climbed to the top of the battlement.

Two guards were stationed beside the dome of the prison's roof. Samak crept up behind them and swiftly dispatched them with his dagger. He then climbed to the top of the dome where there was a small hatch. Samak opened the hatch, tied one end of his lasso to an iron bar, and descended the rope into the darkness of the prison.

The floor of the dungeon was covered with prisoners, two or three men sleeping under each blanket. Shaghal, who had been sitting up awake in anticipation of Samak's arrival, waved to him.

Samak's face lit up on seeing his master alive. He hurried to unchain Shaghal, but Shaghal pointed to the surgeon: "Release this man first," he said. "He is a doctor and has patients waiting for him. I am not so important."

Obeying his master, Samak went to the surgeon and freed him first. He thanked him for his discretion and courage, then tied the lasso around the surgeon's waist, climbed the rope to the top of the dome, and pulled the man up after him.

"Do you have a safe place to hide?" asked Samak. The surgeon assured him that he did. Samak advised him to go there, and lowered the man carefully down the exterior wall of the prison.

Once the surgeon was out of sight, Samak descended the rope and untied Shaghal and the ten ayyars who were with him. One by one they climbed the rope and down the exterior wall of the prison until they were all outside. Dawn was just breaking. Samak led the men quickly through the still-empty streets until they reached the grave robber's house.

Mehruye was startled to see Samak arrive with so many ayyars. "Dear brother," said Samak: "I must ask you to hide these people."

Mehruye gulped. He went inside the house and opened a trap door in the floor. The ayyars descended the ladder one by one and arrived in a basement piled with loot from Mehruye's grave robbing.

Samak frowned when he noticed an unpleasant smell. Looking around, he saw that the odor was coming from piles of bloodstained clothing. "Take these clothes away and burn them!" he ordered. Mehruye hastily removed the bloody garments and returned with clean blankets to keep the ayyars warm. Samak accepted them with thanks.

Samana served hot meals for everyone. From that night, Mehruye's cellar became the ayyars' temporary refuge.

9

THE PRINCE OF MACHIN

WHEN the vizier Mehran was informed that twelve prisoners, including Shaghal, the chief of the ayyars, had escaped, he was furious and blamed the jailers for their incompetence. But he could not dwell long on the incident, for by then his mind was occupied with more pressing matters.

After the night of the royal banquet, Mehran had reason to feel satisfied. He had successfully prevented Khorshid Shah's marriage to Princess Mahpari, imprisoned him and his brother, and massacred the ayyars of Chin. Soon afterward, he met with Shirafcan and told him: "Our next step is to arrange your marriage to Mahpari."

Shirafcan answered: "Your wish is my command. Of course, you realize that the princess is the only child of Faghfur Shah, so once I marry her, the kingdom of Chin will pass to me—and you."

Mehran said: "Faghfur Shah will never let you marry his daughter. Therefore, we must eliminate him in such a way that no one suspects who did it."

Shirafcan was startled. He exclaimed: "Eliminate the king! How?"

Mehran said: "I will send a message to Armen Shah, the ruler of Machin, who is no friend of Faghfur Shah. I will tell him, 'Faghfur has become a weak ruler and is making appalling decisions. I, Mehran, his vizier, and Shirafcan, his greatest hero, will help your army capture Chin. We will give you Princess Mahpari for your son Gezelmalek to marry, and send Faghfur to you in chains. Our one condition is that you leave Chin for Shirafcan to rule.'"

Shirafcan protested: "But you said Mahpari would be my wife!"

Mehran said: "Before the army of Machin enters the city, we will hide Mahpari, and tell Armen Shah and Prince Gezelmalek that she was killed. As soon as their army has left, and you are governor of Chin, you will marry her." Shirafcan understood, and appreciated Mehran's cleverness.

The next day, the letter was written, sealed with the vizier's stamp, and given to Mehran's trusted servant Shabkhiz to take to Armen Shah. Shabkhiz rode day and night until he reached Machin. The domes and minarets of the walled city came into view at a distance. Behind the city rose snow-capped mountains, beyond which lay the vast northern steppe. Shabkhiz rode into the city and through the streets until he reached the royal palace gate. He said to the guards: "Tell the king that a messenger from Mehran, the vizier of Chin, is here to see him."

When Shabkhiz was brought into the court, he bowed to Armen Shah, kissed the letter, and handed it to a guard to give to the king.

Armen Shah handed the letter to his vizier, Shahran, and said: "Read it." The vizier read it out loud.

After the letter had been read there was silence. Armen Shah sat in deep thought. It was his son, Gezelmalek, who spoke first. Dressed in red, the prince was a strikingly handsome, well-built youth with flashing dark eyes, pale skin, and high cheekbones. He bowed and said: "Dear father, we have dreamed for a long time of taking over the land of Chin. Allow me to go there with our army, bring back Faghfur Shah in chains, and take Mahpari as my wife."

Armen Shah turned to Shahran. "Wise vizier, what do you think of this suggestion?"

Shahran responded: "Your Majesty, I am not sure we should trust Mehran's offer."

Gezelmalek, who had heard of Mahpari's legendary beauty, had become excited by the possibility of marrying her. "O venerable father!" he said. "This is too good a chance to miss. If Mehran's offer is sincere, wonderful. If not, I can still capture the citadel with our great army and take Mahpari as my wife."

Armen Shah said: "I won't start a war for the sake of a woman. We have daughters of noble families here in Machin, any of whom would make you a fine wife." Stroking his beard thoughtfully, he added: "On the other hand, if Mehran and Shirafcan are willing to open the gates of Chin for us to conquer with little bloodshed, that is a rare opportunity."

Gezelmalek suggested: "We can find out easily enough if Mehran is true to his word. I will send an envoy to bring Mahpari to me before I reach Chin. If Mehran fails to send me the princess, I will occupy Chin's territory with our army, using Mahpari as an excuse."

Armen Shah said: "My son, I see how badly you desire to have Mahpari as your wife. I have some doubts about this plan, but I will let you proceed in the hope that Mehran will keep his word."

Within a few days, Gezelmalek and an army of thirty thousand warriors began their march toward Chin. Armen Shah ordered his vizier to answer Mehran with a letter saying: "We are honored by this offer from the great vizier and the hero Shirafcan, and are happy to satisfy your desire. Based on your assurance, we have sent our own son Gezelmalek to do what is needed." The letter was written and stamped with the seal of Armen Shah and handed to Shabkhiz to take to Mehran.

The army of Machin continued their march until they entered the territory of Chin. Gezelmalek, carried away with the power of being in command of such a large army, ordered his men to plunder and burn the villages along their path.

When news of Machin's aggression reached Faghfur Shah, he became outraged and ordered Mehran to find out why Armen Shah had invaded their territory. Mehran, who was well aware of what was happening, pretended to know nothing. He suggested they send a messenger to Armen Shah asking him to explain his actions.

Faghfur Shah ordered Mehran to send a letter to Armen Shah, saying: "From Faghfur Shah, the ruler of Chin, to Armen Shah, the ruler of Machin. We are troubled that your army has attacked our territory and wish to know your reason. We remind you that every past ruler of Machin paid annual tribute to Chin until our father, Piruz Shah, decided to waive the tribute because of his friendship with Your Highness. When we succeeded our father as ruler of Chin, we followed his policy. Given this precedent of friendship, we are surprised and distressed by your attack on our land and demand Your Highness to call your army back immediately." The letter was sealed, stamped, and sent with a delegation to the approaching army.

As soon as the envoy had left, Mehran called Shabkhiz and said: "I want you to deliver a secret message to Gezelmalek ahead of Faghfur Shah's envoy." Shabkhiz bowed and announced his readiness.

Mehran said: "Tell Gezelmalek that an envoy is on his way with a letter from Faghfur Shah. He should reply harshly, demanding, 'Send me your daughter immediately. If you refuse, I will massacre every citizen of Chin.' "

Shabkhiz left with all speed, reached Gezelmalek's army, and delivered Mehran's message. Hearing it, Gezelmalek became frustrated and said: "Your master promised me the princess Mahpari. If he is sincere, let him send her to me immediately. If he is unable to do so, let him send me his personal wealth and fortune as a show of good faith." Shabkhiz rode back to deliver Gezelmalek's secret reply to Mehran.

The next day, Faghfur Shah's envoy arrived at the army camp bearing the king's letter. Gezelmalek, wishing to make a good impression on his future father-in-law, ordered the entire delegation welcomed and brought into his royal pavilion.

Gezelmalek's pavilion was made of crimson canvas, held up by twelve ornate columns and fixed to the ground with decorated golden stakes. Inside the tent sat Gezelmalek, dressed in his formal royal outfit, on a throne covered with gold and precious jewels. He was flanked by his generals, with bodyguards, servants, and slaves standing behind them.

The delegation was welcomed and placed on seats that had been prepared. Gezelmalek ordered food, music, and entertainment for the guests. He then asked the envoy if he was carrying a message from Faghfur Shah. The envoy stood up, took out Faghfur Shah's letter, kissed it, and handed it to the vizier Shahran to read to Gezelmalek.

When the letter had been read, Gezelmalek ordered the royal clerk to write down his reply to Faghfur Shah. "What happened between our fathers in regard to tribute was their affair and has nothing to do with us. Had you asked for taxes from my father, he would have either paid you or faced you with his sword in the field. Perhaps you have a false sense of security because no one has attacked your territory for so long. Understand that your enemies left you alone out of fear for the safety of their sons and royal family members held hostage by your daughter's witch nurse. Now that the witch is dead, you are the one who should be afraid. I have entered your territory with a large army. I demand that you send me your daughter Mahpari, along with treasure equivalent to ten years of tributes and taxes. If you do, I will honor you as my father-in-law and return to Machin, causing no further harm in your territory. If you refuse, I will attack and plunder your kingdom without mercy." The royal clerk finished the letter, stamped it with Gezelmalek's seal, and gave it to the envoy to take back to Faghfur Shah.

When the king heard Gezelmalek's response, he became alarmed. Remembering his broken promise to Khorshid Shah and the massacre at the wedding banquet, Faghfur Shah thought: "Perhaps this misfortune is my curse because I murdered the ayyars." He turned to Mehran and said: "The tone of this prince's message is arrogant, but a marriage alliance with Armen Shah might not be a bad thing. It would be preferable to a war with Machin that could devastate our kingdom."

Hearing this, Mehran was troubled. It had not occurred to him that the king might be so weak as to agree to Gezelmalek's demand.

After leaving the king, Mehran summoned Shirafcan and said: "We have a problem. If Faghfur Shah hands over his daughter, Gezelmalek will simply go back home to Machin with his army and his bride, and our opportunity will be lost. To prevent this, I suggest we kidnap the princess and hide her away. We will send Gezelmalek treasure and several beautiful young maidens to show our good faith. When he arrives with his army, we hand him Faghfur Shah in chains and tell him Princess Mahpari is dead. Then we ask him to name you governor of Chin." Shirafcan agreed to this plan.

Mehran instructed his servant Shabkhiz: "Go to the royal compound tonight and figure out a plan to kidnap Mahpari."

Shabkhiz immediately left, saying: "Your Excellency's wish is my command."

All this happened while Samak was in Mehruye's house recovering from his injuries.

• • •

Once Samak and the ayyars were settled safely in Mehruye's cellar, Samak asked the grave robber to find out where Khorshid Shah and Farokhruz were being kept. Mehruye went into town and returned with the news: "The prince and his brother are being held in a house that is guarded by many watchmen and watchdogs."

Samak equipped himself with weapons Mehruye had taken from the dead warriors—bow and arrows, sword, dagger, and a lasso. Shortly after dusk, he said goodbye to everyone and left the house.

The place where the royal prisoners were kept was a well-built stone house with a pleasant courtyard filled with fruit trees, surrounded by high windowless walls. Guards were posted on the rooftops, keeping watch on all sides.

As soon as Samak came near the mansion, the dogs started barking. Samak retreated, took off his weapons and garments, and hid them in a corner of the street. He waited until the dogs were quiet. Then, in the darkness, with his dagger between his teeth, he crawled on hands and knees until he found a hole at the bottom of one of the courtyard walls, through which sewage flowed into a covered cesspool outside. Samak used his dagger to widen the hole enough to squeeze through.

Standing up, he found himself in an outhouse within the courtyard. The walls were made of adobe, and a wooden door to the courtyard was locked from outside. Samak cut a hole in the door, reached his hand through, and broke the lock with his dagger. Opening the door, he emerged quietly into the courtyard and crept through the shadows from tree to tree until he reached the building.

As he approached, he heard Khorshid Shah and Farokhruz's voices inside. A guard was posted outside the door. Samak threw a pebble to attract the guard's attention. When the guard turned toward the noise, Samak jumped on him from behind, clapped a hand over his mouth, and stabbed him in the heart. He lowered the dead guard silently to the ground, opened the door, and entered the room.

Khorshid Shah and Farokhruz were startled to see a filth-smeared man enter with dagger in hand. He said in a friendly voice: "It's me, Samak!"

Khorshid Shah exclaimed: "Samak! I saw you killed at the banquet! How did you come back to life?"

Samak said: "I'll tell you the whole story once we're out of here." He untied their hands and feet and led them through the courtyard and out the hole in the wall into the side alley. Then they headed for Mehruye's house.

"Where are you taking us?" Khorshid Shah asked.

"To the house of Mehruye the grave robber," began Samak, then stopped short on seeing that they were not alone. Ahead of them, he saw a man concealed in shadow at the end of the alley. Samak ran toward him, but when he reached the spot, no one was there. Samak searched down one alley, then another, until he finally gave up.

Samak returned to his companions and they continued on their way. They did not know that they were now being followed at a distance by the stealthy stranger, who was none other than Mehran's slave Shabkhiz.

10

STONE ALLEY

SHABKHIZ followed the three men until he saw them enter Mehruye's house. Then he rushed to the vizier's palace.

"Have you figured out a plan to kidnap Mahpari?" Mehran demanded.

Shabkhiz bowed and said: "O great vizier, the guard around the princess's quarters has been increased tenfold on the orders of Faghfur Shah, and I could find no way in. But I have important news for you." He told Mehran how he had stumbled on Khorshid Shah, Farokhruz, and Samak in the darkness and followed them to the ayyars' hideout.

"Samak!" cried Mehran. "It's impossible. I saw him killed at Faghfur Shah's palace with my own eyes. And Khorshid Shah and his brother are being held in a house that is as securely guarded as any dungeon. You must be mistaken."

Just then, a messenger arrived with the news that Khorshid Shah and Farokhruz had escaped from their prison.

Mehran turned to Shabkhiz. "Now I believe you," he said. "Yesterday, when I was informed of the escape of Shaghal and ten ayyars, I should have taken it more seriously." He rewarded Shabkhiz with several gold pieces for his cleverness.

The next morning, Mehran went to the royal palace to see Faghfur Shah. He found the king already upset, for he had been told of Khorshid Shah's escape from prison.

Mehran said: "Your Majesty, all these escapes are the work of Samak the ayyar, who cheated death at the royal banquet. First he killed my son, then he kidnapped your daughter and freed the witch nurse's prisoners. Now he has embarrassed Your Majesty by breaking important captives out of prison at the very moment an army is marching on our kingdom. If the enemy discovers that one man can defy you in this way, they will lose all respect for you, and your reign is as good as over. We must destroy Samak and the ayyars once and for all before the enemy reaches our city."

Faghfur Shah asked: "What do you need from me?"

Mehran said: "I know where the ayyars are hiding. All I need is Your Highness's order, and I will send Shirafcan with a detachment of soldiers to finish the job."

Faghfur Shah replied: "Let it be done."

It happened that the order to organize an attack on Mehruye's house was overheard by a palace guard who was a close friend of the grave robber. At the first opportunity, he found an excuse to leave his post and rushed to Mehruye to warn him.

The ayyars immediately understood that they needed to find a different hiding place. But where? Suggestions were made and dismissed until Samak spoke up: "I have a solution."

Everyone became silent, waiting for Samak to continue. Samak said: "There is a place in the city called Stone Alley. It is carved through solid rock and leads to a dead end with only one entrance. We could hold off an army from there."

The ayyars agreed and set out for Stone Alley, along with Mehruye. His wife, Samana, moved to a friend's home to hide.

The entrance to Stone Alley was in a poor neighborhood at the bottom of a hill, tucked away beside the intersection of two roads. The alley was dimly lit, with a few small openings for air and light to enter. Farokhruz, a skilled archer, asked his brother's permission to guard the entrance. Khorshid Shah agreed. The ayyars settled in to wait.

It did not take Shirafcan and his soldiers long to locate them. After finding Mehruye's house empty, they stormed through the neighborhood, questioning everyone, until someone revealed that the ayyars had gone to Stone Alley.

No sooner had the soldiers come within sight of Stone Alley than Farokhruz began shooting arrows. Any soldier who approached within a hundred yards of the entrance was felled instantly. By nightfall, fifty of Shirafcan's men lay dead.

A crowd had gathered admiring Farokhruz's skill. Some local residents began running food, blankets, and torches into the alley for the ayyars. Shirafcan's soldiers were helpless to stop them for fear of Farokhruz's arrows.

Early the next morning, Shirafcan ordered the soldiers to gather wood and build a fire outside the entrance. His plan was to cut the ayyars off from the public's help until heat, hunger, and thirst forced them out of hiding.

The soldiers began gathering and piling wood. Farokhruz could not prevent them from lighting the fire, which soon turned into an enormous inferno.

Inside Stone Alley, the ayyars began to suffer from the heat and smoke. Samak realized they could not stay where they were. Shirafcan's plan had succeeded.

Samak said to Shaghal: "We can't let Khorshid Shah and Farokhruz fall back into Mehran's hands. As soon as you hear me shout, take the two princes and run as fast as you can through the smoke. Lose yourselves in the crowd. Take them somewhere safe."

Samak pulled out his dagger and, with a shout, ran out of the entrance. Shirafcan, standing on the other side of the fire, was caught by surprise as Samak burst out of the smoke and flames. Before Shirafcan could defend himself, Samak's strong hand plunged the dagger into his heart so deeply that its tip came out his back.

Soldiers fell upon Samak. He fought back fearlessly, killing seven of them before they managed to subdue and tie him up. Meanwhile, more soldiers hurried to barricade the entrance, trapping the remaining ayyars and Mehruye inside Stone Alley. Shaghal had already taken advantage of the chaos to slip through the smoke with Khorshid Shah and Farokhruz. They merged into the crowd of onlookers as Samak had suggested.

Samak was taken in chains to Faghfur Shah's court and brought before the king and the vizier. Mehran demanded: "Where are Khorshid Shah and Farokhruz?"

Samak answered: "I don't know."

Mehran ordered the executioner to whip Samak ten times. The man whipped Samak until blood streamed down his body, but he said nothing. Mehran ordered: "Whip him ten times more." Samak withstood this too in silence. He then looked up at Mehran and said: "You can kill me, but I can't tell you where Khorshid Shah is, because I don't know. What I do know is what you have been doing behind His Majesty's back."

Mehran became afraid that Samak might know about his secret communications with Gezelmalek. He ordered the executioner: "Whip him again!" The whipping continued until Samak fell unconscious, covered with blood.

Faghfur Shah had heard Samak's words and wondered if his vizier was in fact hiding something from him. The king ordered his guards: "Keep this prisoner close by. I wish to interrogate him myself when he wakes up." The guards took Samak to a hall in the royal compound and chained him there.

When Princess Mahpari heard that Samak had been arrested and was in the royal compound, her heart leapt with hope that he might have news of her beloved Khorshid Shah. She immediately summoned her two most trusted guards and ordered: "Take me to him in secret."

The guards brought the princess to a private veranda off Samak's chamber, where she waited until the guards brought him out. By then he had regained consciousness, and they had washed the blood off him, but he was still in chains.

When Mahpari saw Samak, she said to the guards: "Remove his chains. He is a friend and will not harm me."

The princess offered Samak food and wine. Once he had eaten and drunk and was feeling better, she said: "Tell me, where is Khorshid Shah?"

While the guards stood watch outside, Samak told the princess the whole story, from the attack on the ayyars at the royal banquet up to the events at Stone Alley. The private conversation between Mahpari and Samak continued past sunset and into the night.

• • •

When the ayyars found themselves barricaded inside Stone Alley, they retreated to the end of the alley to escape the fire's heat. In desperation they began to dig under the stone walls with their daggers. The ground was soft and they made fast progress. As they kept digging, the ground became damp, and water started seeping into the tunnel around their ankles. All at once, the crumbling rock wall that they had been patiently chipping at with their daggers collapsed. Water flooded the tunnel waist-deep, so quickly that it nearly knocked the ayyars off their feet. They scrambled back in haste—not one of them knew how to swim. Now they were caught between fire and water.

"I can swim," said Mehruye. "Let me go." The ayyars stood back to let Mehruye go forward. He waded into the tunnel, took a deep breath, and submerged himself in the dark cold water.

Mehruye found himself in an underground water channel. He swam, holding his breath as long as he could, until he saw light ahead. He swam toward the light and surfaced, gasping, at the bottom of a deep well. Iron rungs were set into the walls above him. He climbed up toward daylight and emerged into a large, well-manicured garden surrounded by high walls. Birds were singing in the trees.

"I'd better find somewhere to hide until dark," he thought. Looking around, he spotted some dense bushes and hid behind them.

After sunset, when the garden had grown completely dark, Mehruye emerged from his hiding place and began looking for a way out.

He saw a faint light and headed toward it. Approaching, he saw a veranda tucked away behind trees. In the glow of candles a man sat on elegant cushions, deep in conversation with a beautiful young girl. Mehruye was startled to recognize Samak.

Suddenly he was grabbed from behind by a guard who had noticed him in the dark. Mehruye's hands were tied and he was brought to the veranda.

Samak jumped up and hugged Mehruye with joy. "Your Highness, this is a friend," he said. The guards untied Mehruye and Samak introduced him to Mahpari.

Mehruye gratefully accepted the food and wine the princess offered. Samak asked him: "How did you get out of Stone Alley, and how on earth did you get into the royal compound?" Mehruye told Samak and the princess everything that had happened.

Hearing the story, Samak became worried about the fate of the ayyars trapped in Stone Alley. Mahpari, whose heart was full of love for Khorshid Shah, the prince of Persia, was concerned about what had happened to her beloved.

Samak asked Mahpari's permission to leave the compound with Mehruye and bring back news. Mahpari immediately consented. She gave Samak and Mehruye food to take to their friends, and had her guards escort Samak and Mehruye out of the royal compound through a secret passageway.

11

SURRENDERING THE PRINCESS

THE next morning, Faghfur Shah told his guards: "Bring me the prisoner Samak." He intended to ask Samak to explain his accusation of the vizier. But when the guards went to fetch Samak from his prison, they found no trace of him.

Hearing the news, Faghfur Shah's first suspicion was that Mehran had kidnapped or silenced Samak to prevent him from revealing what he knew. The vizier spoke up quickly, saying: "I assure Your Majesty I had nothing to do with this! This is how Samak works—turning people against each other, sowing doubt and mistrust. He escaped rather than tell Your Majesty what he has done with Khorshid Shah." Mehran's stomach was churning at the thought that Samak, who had killed his son Qabiz, was again free to interfere with his plans.

Just then, the court's chamberlain announced that two soldiers had arrived with an urgent message. Faghfur Shah ordered: "Show them in."

The two soldiers, covered with dust and mud, entered and prostrated themselves before Faghfur Shah. They told him that the army of Machin, under Gezelmalek's command, had reached the Plateau of the Zebras and was advancing on the capital.

Faghfur Shah became afraid, for the Plateau of the Zebras was not far. Forgetting about Samak, he turned to his vizier. "What do we do now?"

Mehran said: "Your Highness, there is no time to waste. When you did not demand taxes from the rulers of Machin, they mistook your generosity for weakness. Gezelmalek is not coming as a friend to request your daughter's hand in marriage. He is coming with an army. If you give in to his threat and send him the princess, you will only earn his contempt. You must face him on the battlefield."

Faghfur Shah called in his army generals. When they arrived, he said: "The army of Machin, headed by Gezelmalek, the son of Armen Shah, has entered our territory and reached the Plateau of the Zebras. We must face them and stop their aggression." He added: "If the army of Machin were headed by Armen Shah himself, I would go to face him myself—but since it is not a king who is leading their army, it is more appropriate for one of our generals to take command."

Shiruyeh, son of the recently slain Shirafcan, stood up and announced: "My father would have been the first to volunteer to serve Your Highness. Now that he is gone, please let me take his place and lead the march against the enemy at the head of my father's army."

Faghfur Shah asked: "How large is your army?"

Shiruyeh responded: "Twenty thousand warriors. Ten thousand cavalry and ten thousand foot-soldiers."

Faghfur Shah thanked him for his readiness and said: "You shall lead the march."

Three more generals immediately volunteered to join the war, bringing an additional twenty thousand men. Within several days, an army of forty thousand soldiers had gathered under these four generals' command and they began the march toward the Plateau of the Zebras to face the enemy.

• • •

Khorshid Shah, Farokhruz, and Shaghal were in the crowd of onlookers at Stone Alley when they saw Samak captured and the entrance barricaded. Shaghal suggested: "I have a friend who lives on the outskirts of the city. Let us take refuge in his house."

Shaghal's friend welcomed all three men with open arms. He was honored to learn he was hosting the prince of Persia and his brother. He made his guests comfortable and served them delicious food and wine.

The next day, news spread through town that Chin's army was marching to face the army of Machin. Khorshid Shah said to Shaghal: "We should join the army as ordinary soldiers, without revealing our identities. That way we will not put this good man in danger by staying longer in his house." Shaghal and Farokhruz agreed. Shaghal's friend set about obtaining the armor, weapons, and horses they would need.

Khorshid Shah was looking out a window at the street, waiting for their host to return, when he recognized a man passing by. It was one of the loyal soldiers who had accompanied him from Halab to Chin. They had been separated after the witch nurse kidnapped Farokhruz. Khorshid Shah opened the door and called: "Jomhur!"

Jomhur turned. When he saw the prince, he fell on his knees crying with joy and excitement. Khorshid Shah lifted him to his feet and led him inside the house.

After both men had told each other all that had happened to them, Khorshid Shah said to Jomhur: "I want you to return to Halab and deliver a letter to my father the king."

Jomhur said: "Your Highness, I am dedicated to you. Your wish is my command."

Khorshid Shah wrote a letter to his father Marzban Shah, recounting the adventures that had befallen him and Farokhruz.

He concluded: "Kind father, if you could see us now, you would feel terrible that we are homeless with nothing but the clothes on our backs. Perhaps you would consider sending an army to bring us home as soon as possible."

He gave the letter to Jomhur and hugged him goodbye. Jomhur kissed the prince's hand and set out for home.

Shortly after Jomhur had left, Shaghal's friend returned with armor, weapons, and horses. Khorshid Shah, Farokhruz, and Shaghal thanked him, dressed themselves for battle, and rode off to join the army of Chin. Helmets covered their faces so no one would recognize them.

Meanwhile, Samak had been searching for his friends, asking about them everywhere with no luck. Finally, he remembered Shaghal's friend who lived on the outskirts of town. He reached the house shortly after Khorshid Shah, Farokhruz, and Shaghal had left. Shaghal's friend welcomed Samak and told him that the three men had left to join the army. Within a few hours, Samak was on horseback, likewise armed and outfitted, riding to catch up with them.

• • •

Soon after the army of Chin had begun its march toward the Plateau of the Zebras, the vizier Mehran wrote to Gezelmalek, saying: "O great prince, I have induced Faghfur Shah to send an army to face you. The army is weak and the generals have no combat experience. You will have no problem defeating them. Meanwhile, I beg you to have patience while I make arrangements to send Mahpari to you so that Your Highness may start to trust my words. The princess and victory will soon be yours." He then sealed the letter and sent it in secret with a dependable envoy. Gezelmalek received the letter one day before the armies of Chin and Machin arrived at the Plateau of the Zebras.

The two armies settled into opposing camps facing each other across the battle plain. The four generals of Chin gathered together. Samour, the oldest among them, suggested: "Before we fight, let us ask Gezelmalek if there is a way to avoid this bloodshed." The others agreed, and Samour rode toward the army of Machin with an escort of fifty soldiers.

Gezelmalek ordered his men to welcome Samour and bring him to his pavilion. When the general arrived, he bowed to Gezelmalek and said politely: "The people of Chin and Machin have been friendly with each other for many years. We are wondering what has caused Your Highness to attack our territory and start a war with us?"

Gezelmalek responded: "We did not come to fight, but to seek Princess Mahpari's hand in marriage. We have heard that a prince from Persia has asked to marry her and that Faghfur Shah has consented. We cannot imagine why he would give his only daughter to a foreigner when we are available. We have come to prevent this wedding and take the princess as our queen. If Faghfur Shah does not agree, we have brought our army to take Mahpari away by force."

Samour said: "Your Highness has been misinformed. Khorshid Shah and his brother were arrested and put in prison. They have escaped, and no one knows where they are, but I assure you that the princess is still available for marriage. If Your Highness wishes, we will convey your message to Faghfur Shah. If he consents, there is no need to fight. If not, then let our armies face each other in the battlefield." Gezelmalek accepted this offer. Samour returned to his camp, and the four generals wrote a letter to Faghfur Shah, sealed it, and sent it with an envoy.

• • •

problems, and now I'm sure of it. What a stupid father I have, to put power in the hands of someone like you!"

The princess turned to her African manservant and said: "Throw this scoundrel out!" The faithful servant strode to where Mehran sat, ordered him to get up, and, grabbing the vizier by the arm, showed him to the door with enough force that he lost his turban on the way.

Discouraged, the vizier returned to Faghfur Shah with tears in his eyes. He reported what the princess had said, using harsher words than she had actually spoken. Faghfur Shah became extremely upset. He asked Mehran: "What should I do?"

Mehran took advantage of this opportunity and said: "Your Highness, forgive me for speaking bluntly. A young woman's emotions and passions should not cause the destruction of a kingdom. You are a king. Your people depend on you to take a strong hand for the greater good. If your daughter refuses to obey your order, tie her up and send her to Gezelmalek by force. This will show him your friendship and he will repay you with loyalty."

Faghfur Shah protested, but the vizier eventually persuaded him. The king told Mehran: "All right. You have the authority to send my daughter to Gezelmalek with twenty maidens, twenty slaves, and several chests of gold and precious jewels."

12

REFUGE AMONG WARRIORS

AFTER a few days resting and recovering in the meadow with Khorshid Shah, Farokhruz, and Shaghal, Samak remembered his promise to the princess. He said goodbye to the others and left for town to bring Mahpari the news that her beloved was alive and well.

Since the ayyar headquarters had been destroyed, and Mehruye's house was being watched by the king's guards, Samak went to Ruhafza's house in hopes that she would be there to receive him. He found the door open. Entering, Samak saw Ruhafza sobbing in despair. "Dear mother, what has happened?" he asked with concern.

Ruhafza said: "My son, they have taken away the princess. And in the cruelest way!" She described how soldiers had forced their way into Mahpari's chamber, overpowered the princess, bound her hands and feet, and carried her out.

Samak exclaimed: "Who would do such a thing?"

Ruhafza responded: "It was that bastard Mehran the vizier. He is sending her to Gezelmalek against her will."

Samak, pale with anger, said: "Dear mother, do you know where the princess is now?"

Ruhafza responded: “They have taken her away in a caravan guarded by one hundred soldiers under the command of a general named Sanjar.”

Samak said: “I must warn Khorshid Shah. We have to stop that caravan before it reaches Gezelmalek’s army.” He hugged Ruhafza goodbye and rode back as fast as he could toward the meadow where he had left the others.

It was after midnight when Samak arrived. His three friends were asleep on the ground with their daggers in their hands. Samak saw a rare chance to play a trick on his master. Mischievously, he stole up to Shaghal and quietly removed the dagger from his hand. Shaghal leapt up in panic, ready to defend himself against the intruder. Then he recognized Samak in the moonlight.

Samak laughed and said: “My dear master, the princes are young and haven’t had much experience sleeping alone in the wilderness. But what’s your excuse for leaving no one awake to stand watch?”

Shaghal thanked Samak for the lesson and said: “This place is so peaceful that I had no fear of being attacked, even by wild animals.” Master and apprentice then hugged each other and awakened the two princes.

When Khorshid Shah heard that Princess Mahpari was being taken to Gezelmalek, he jumped on his horse, saying: “We have to stop this!” Samak, Shaghal, and Farokhruz mounted their horses and galloped after the prince.

The three rode all night until they reached the top of a hill with a good view of the main road. They dismounted, hid their horses behind a boulder, and took positions with their bows, waiting for the caravan to come into sight.

Two hours after sunrise, they spotted a dust cloud in the distance. Soon they had a clear view of the approaching convoy.

A hundred mounted soldiers escorted a carriage followed by twenty mules laden with bags and chests of treasure.

When the convoy came within range, Farokhruz began shooting arrows, killing soldiers one by one. Before long, half of them lay dead or wounded, while the rest took cover behind rocks and returned fire.

General Sanjar, worried about Princess Mahpari and the treasure he was carrying, called one of his soldiers and said: "Ride as fast as you can to General Shiruyeh. Tell him we are under attack by bandits and to send reinforcements immediately."

The soldier rode off, taking a winding path through the hills so that no one would see him. He was rounding a curve when Samak, who had been watching from above, jumped down on him, knocking him off his horse, and stabbed him with his dagger. Samak then removed the soldier's armor and helmet and put them on himself.

Samak let some time pass, then rode back to General Sanjar and bowed to him. The general, mistaking Samak for the soldier that he had sent, asked: "What message did General Shiruyeh give you?"

Samak responded: "The general said you should leave everything and rejoin the army immediately."

"What?" exclaimed Sanjar. "Leave the princess and the treasure?"

"Those are the general's orders," said Samak firmly.

Sanjar, glad to be relieved of the responsibility, shouted: "Follow me!" And he rode off, cutting through the hills toward Chin's army camp, followed by his soldiers.

As soon everyone was gone, Khorshid Shah and the others emerged from their hiding places behind the rocks and descended to the road. The prince ran to the carriage. It contained a large ornate chest. He broke the lock and lifted the lid.

Princess Mahpari sat up inside. Her face lit up with joy on seeing Khorshid Shah. Then she saw Samak and thanked him too for her rescue.

Khorshid Shah said to Samak: "Sleeping outdoors in the wilderness will not be safe or suitable for the princess. Where we can find shelter?"

Samak answered: "In Bograi Valley, not far from here, lives a community of warriors under the command of Arghonun. They are good and trustworthy people. Arghonun is an old comrade and friend of the ayyars. He will surely welcome us."

Shaghal thanked Samak for remembering Arghonun and blamed his old age for not having thought of it first. Samak led the way, guiding the twenty mules laden with treasure.

Throughout the journey, Mahpari rode shoulder to shoulder with Khorshid Shah, her eyes full of love as he told her stories of his life in Halab with his parents. It was the first time they had been able to spend together since the day the king had promised Khorshid Shah her hand. Khorshid Shah could imagine no greater happiness than to have Mahpari for his queen. He told himself that the hardships he had endured to reach this point were worth it, and that he would endure a thousand times more for the chance to share his life with her.

It was late in the afternoon when they reached Bograi Valley, a place of splendid natural beauty. Arghonun, the grey-bearded, barrel-chested leader of the valley, sat atop a rock with a group of his warriors, watching the sunset.

Samak and his friends dismounted. Samak went to where Arghonun was sitting and bowed to him. Arghonun got up and embraced Samak, and said: "You used to come here often when you were younger. You must be busy these days. You've stayed away so long, our younger warriors have had no chance to learn about the ways of the ayyars."

Samak apologized for his long absence and said: "O great honor of humanity, my friends and I have come to ask you for shelter. If this request does not suit you, we will turn around and leave the way we came."

Arghonun said: "Samak, you know me better than that. I would never push away a hand that reaches out to me for help, even if I have to protect you against the whole world."

Samak thanked Arghonun. He said: "My master Shaghal and I are here with three noble guests: the crown prince of Persia, his brother, and the princess of Chin."

Arghonun welcomed them. Samak then told him the whole story in detail, starting with Khorshid Shah and Farokhruz's arrival in Chin, all the way up to the events of that day.

Arghonun said: "Dear Samak, I would have welcomed your friends even if you had told me they were thieves and murderers, because it is you who brought them here. To have such important dignitaries here is an honor that I welcome with all my heart." He hugged them all and ordered several of his warriors to take their possessions to a safe place in the valley.

Arghonun sent Mahpari to his own house to stay with his wife and daughters while the men sat together in the moonlight, eating, drinking, and enjoying each other's company. Shortly before midnight, Arghonun's men showed the three visitors to a house that had been prepared for them. There they rested and slept in comfort, safe in Bograi Valley.

• • •

Among Arghonun's warriors was one he had severely punished in the past, who had long carried a secret grudge against him. When this man learned who Arghonun's guests were and the events that had brought them there, he decided to go to Faghfur Shah back with me for her safety. I fear that if Gezelmalek learns she is here, he will send his army to attack Bograi Valley."

Before Khorshid Shah or Arghonun could respond, Shaghal jumped to his feet and cried: "O prince, do not trust this vizier! His snake's tongue started all this trouble and bloodshed. If we hand the princess to him, you can be sure he will deliver her into the enemy's hands." Turning to Mehran, he continued: "Your lies and deceit might fool Faghfur Shah, but you're not in his court now. If it wasn't for the honor of the prince and the great Arghonun, I'd cut you to pieces right here."

Mehran ignored Shaghal's outburst. To Arghonun he said calmly: "O great master, whatever this man says, he is excused. I have come to deliver the king's message and to bring him your answer."

Arghonun replied: "I respect Faghfur Shah very much. If His Majesty makes peace with Khorshid Shah, I will gladly follow his commands. Until then, I will protect the prince and his friends as I would protect anyone who comes to me for shelter. This includes the princess Mahpari."

Everyone looked at Khorshid Shah to see what he would say. The prince, mindful of the importance of a good relationship with his future father-in-law, looked straight at Mehran and said: "If Faghfur Shah will give me his daughter's hand in marriage as he promised, I will join his army and fight on the side of Chin with all my strength."

The vizier said: "I assure you that this is the king's intention."

Arghonun went into thought for a while and then said: "There is a fortress called Shahak built into the top of the mountain above this valley. It is so strong and well guarded that no stranger can approach it. If Faghfur Shah takes an oath to keep his promise to Prince Khorshid Shah, we will place Princess Mahpari in that fortress for her safety. Then we will join forces with your army, defeat Gezelmalek in combat, and push him out of our land and back to Machin." He turned to the prince and asked: "Is this solution acceptable to you?"

Khorshid Shah agreed. Mehran would have preferred to take Mahpari back with him, but he saw that it would not be wise to push further. He bowed and left Bograi Valley.

When Mehran reached Faghfur Shah's palace, he reported the entire discussion and what had been agreed. The next morning, one of Arghonun's warriors sent by Khorshid Shah arrived at the royal court and was seated in a special place they had prepared for him. After greeting the envoy with food and wine, Faghfur Shah said: "You can tell the prince of Persia that he has our oath to place our daughter's hand in his hand in marriage as we have promised."

The king then turned to his vizier and said: "Tell the four generals who are leading our army, 'Khorshid Shah is alive and well and has saved our daughter from being sent to Gezelmalek for marriage. Now that the princess of Chin is reunited with her future husband, we appoint him as deputy governor to lead our army in battle against the army of Machin. We instruct you to treat him as your king and to follow his commands from the moment he arrives with Arghonun and his warriors.'"

Mehran wrote down the king's orders and dispatched an envoy to the generals, while Khorshid Shah's ambassador returned to Bograi Valley.

Once the messengers had gone and Mehran was alone, he sat down and wrote a letter to Gezelmalek describing everything that had happened. At the end, he added: "The army of Chin will be easily defeated by your soldiers because everyone here is afraid of Your Highness's superior might. As for Princess Mahpari, I have used my power to place her in the fortress of Shahak, which is well protected on a mountaintop above Bograi Valley.

After Your Highness has triumphed over the army of Chin, you can go there and the princess will be handed over to you."

Mehran then sealed and stamped the letter and gave it to a trusted messenger to take to Gezelmalek in secret.

13

A CLASH OF CHAMPIONS

WHEN Khorshid Shah heard the message from Faghfur Shah, he turned to Arghonun and said: "Are you ready to join the army of Chin for war?"

Arghonun said: "I will follow your command."

Khorshid Shah sent a messenger to Arghonun's house with a letter for Mahpari, informing her of Faghfur Shah's decision, and asking her to get ready to move to Shahak Fortress.

The messenger soon returned saying that the princess wished to see Khorshid Shah.

When Khorshid Shah entered Arghonun's house, he found Mahpari crying. He held her head against his chest and asked the reason for her sadness. Mahpari said: "I don't want to be separated from you again. Please take me with you!"

Deeply moved, Khorshid Shah said: "You are the comfort of my heart. I won't take you into a war zone. You will be safest in Shahak Fortress until I return. I promise I'll be back soon."

Mahpari said: "My beloved prince, if the whole world were a fortress built for my protection, I would rather be outside it with you. But since it is your wish, I will go to Shahak Fortress. I will sit at the window watching the valley until I see you coming up the path."

Khorshid Shah pulled Mahpari into his arms and said goodbye with tears in his eyes. Then he returned to Arghonun and told him that the princess was ready to leave.

Arghonun appointed two maidens to serve the princess, and twenty warriors to escort her and her treasure safely to the fortress.

A sentinel on watch at Shahak Fortress spotted the party below when they were still a great distance away. He immediately informed the fortress guardian, whose name was Mugavgar, that twenty warriors were approaching.

Mugavgar dispatched a guard to find out who the intruders were. The warrior in charge of the escort party told him: "We bring an important guest with a message for the fortress guardian."

Mugavgar had the bridge lowered to allow the visitors to enter. The escort leader delivered this message: "His Highness Faghfur Shah wishes to place his daughter Princess Mahpari and her considerable dowry under your protection, while her future husband, Khorshid Shah, prince of Persia, is at war with the invading army of Machin. Once the army of Machin has been defeated, the prince will come to claim his future wife and her fortune." Mugavgar greeted the princess warmly and took her into the fortress along with her maidens and treasure. The escorting warriors rode back to the valley.

Within two days, Arghonun had gathered an army of twelve thousand warriors under Khorshid Shah's command. When their force reached Chin's army camp, Faghfur Shah's four top generals bowed down to pay homage to their new leader. They took the prince straight to a royal pavilion they had raised for him.

As Khorshid Shah passed through the camp, he shone with regal splendor. Every soldier who caught sight of the prince felt ready to follow him and wished for his blessing. By nightfall, the entire army of Chin was singing his praises.

The next day, Samak, who had heard the news that Khorshid Shah was now leading Chin's army, arrived at the camp and went straight to the prince's pavilion. He found Khorshid Shah sitting with Arghonun and other friends. They embraced Samak, welcomed him, and drank wine to one another's health to celebrate their reunion.

The next morning at sunrise, Khorshid Shah ordered the generals to attack. Horns were blown, drums were beaten, and the army began to advance—armored foot soldiers marching in front, mounted warriors riding behind them.

Gezelmalek, hearing the sound of horns and drums, ordered his army to meet the enemy. The two great armies clashed: two thousand warriors from Chin battling three thousand from Machin. Two hundred men were slain on each side before the foot soldiers withdrew, allowing the cavalry to come forward and line up facing each other.

Farokhruz asked and received Khorshid Shah's permission to fight. He spurred his horse, rode to the middle of the battlefield, and shouted for an opponent.

A husky champion from Gezelmalek's side rode toward Farokhruz and shouted: "Who are you to dare stand in front of me? Tell me your name so I can decide whether you are worth killing, or let Khorshid Shah come face my sword himself!"

Farokhruz shouted back: "You worthless scum, how dare you speak the name of Khorshid Shah? He is a king with fifty thousand warriors at his command, and I am one of them! Let's see how much of a man you are." Saying that, Farokhruz lifted his spear above his head and charged at the opposing warrior, who likewise charged toward him.

The two champions battled until both their spears were broken. Then they drew their swords and continued fighting until, with one swift move, Farokhruz plunged his sword through the other warrior's shoulder straight down through his heart. He fell on the ground dead.

The shout of delight from Chin's army reached the sky, while the other side fell silent with despair. They had lost one of their greatest heroes.

One by one, five more warriors stepped forth from Machin's army to battle Farokhruz. All were slain.

Gezelmalek realized that the loss of his best warriors was weakening his army's morale. He decided to face Farokhruz himself.

As Gezelmalek rode forward, his greatest champion, Qatran, who had once defeated fifty warriors single-handed, bowed down to him and asked permission to fight. The prince granted this. Qatran immediately turned his horse and rode toward Farokhruz.

When Khorshid Shah's generals saw Qatran coming, clad from head to toe in shining gold armor, on a golden-armored horse, they pleaded with the prince to call Farokhruz back. "Your brother has exhausted himself. He cannot fight Qatran in this condition."

Hearing these words, Khorshid Shah became heavy-hearted. He knew the generals were right. But he also knew that if he called Farokhruz back, his men might think he was afraid and become demoralized. He could see no way out of this dilemma.

While the prince struggled with the decision, Samak bowed down to him and said: "Your Highness, permit me to stop this!" He galloped to the center of the field and shouted: "Qatran! They say you're a hero who can defeat a hundred warriors single-handed. Aren't you ashamed to challenge a man who is exhausted after six battles in a row!"

Qatran shouted back at Samak: "Who are you to dare speak to me about heroism?"

Samak said: "I am Samak the ayyar!"

Hearing this name, Qatran stopped, for he had heard of Samak's reputation and courage. He said: "For your sake, I will give your man time to rest. But he won't escape me, for I will return tomorrow morning!" His armor glowed in the golden rays of the setting sun as he turned his horse around and rode back to his side. Farokhruz did the same. The trumpeters blew their horns, calling for both armies to break for the day.

14

SAMAK AND ATASHAK

FAROKHRUZ'S heroism had lifted the spirits of the entire army of Chin. Now that there was a break in the fighting, Khorshid Shah invited Farokhruz, Samak, Shaghal, Arghonun, and the four generals to his pavilion to celebrate the day's victories. They ate, drank, and talked of Farokhruz's exploits until they were so drunk that their laughter could be heard from far away.

Some warriors suggested that Farokhruz was more than a match for Qatran and that Samak should have let the combat continue. When one remarked that Samak had been lucky to escape with his life after confronting Qatran, Samak, who was a little tipsy, felt annoyed and said: "Qatran is big, all right, but he's not as strong as some of you may think. If the prince permits me, I can prove it by bringing him here trussed up like a pheasant."

Shaghal said: "Samak, my son, we've all heard the tales of Qatran's strength. Don't make idle boasts about something that's impossible."

Samak said: "Wait and see!" He bowed to Khorshid Shah, put on his armor, took his weapons, and left the pavilion. Outside, everything was dark except for torches carried by the night watchmen and the soft glow of candles inside the tents.

Samak moved quietly through the darkness to the Machin army camp. He darted from one tent to another so stealthily that the sentries did not see him. The shadows inside Qatran's tent revealed the giant warrior sitting with several generals, drinking wine and enjoying one another's company.

Samak waited patiently until he heard the sound of snoring from inside the tent. Qatran's comrades put out the candles and left, closing the entrance drape behind them. Samak moved around to the back of the tent, silently cut a hole in the fabric, and entered.

Qatran had drunk a great deal—he was sound asleep on the floor. Samak moved to his side and swiftly tied his hands and feet together with his lasso. Before the warrior could speak, Samak pushed a ball of cloth into his mouth, saying: "Take a good look, so you'll remember Samak the ayyar the next time you see him!" Then he wrapped Qatran in his bedcovers and dragged him out of the tent.

Qatran's horse was tied to a stake outside the entrance, ready to ride. With difficulty, because Qatran was so heavy, Samak lifted the bundled-up warrior up onto his horse. He then mounted it himself and rode quietly through the darkness of the camp toward the Chin army's campground.

Unfortunately, for all the pains Samak took to remain silent, Qatran's stallion scented a mare in heat that was tied outside one of the tents, and began to neigh loudly. Samak, seeing the sentries coming, realized he was about to get caught. He dismounted and ran off into the darkness.

The watchmen saw a bundle writhing on the ground beside the horse, and were astonished to discover Qatran inside. They untied him and removed the cloth ball from his mouth. Qatran did not say a word, but only mounted his horse and rode back to his tent. None of the watchmen dared ask him what had happened.

It was shortly after dawn when Samak returned to Chin's army campground. The draped entrance of Khorshid Shah's pavilion was open. Samak went inside and found the prince awake with the generals around him. Samak humorously described the night's adventures. Everyone laughed and made jokes, adding to the fun.

In the midst of their laughter came the sound of drums and horns from the Machin campground, warning the warriors to prepare for battle. Khorshid Shah said to Samak: "You must have made Qatran so angry that he can't wait until after breakfast to attack!"

On Khorshid Shah's command, trumpeters blew their horns and drummers beat their drums, calling the army to get ready for the second day of combat. The two armies lined up to face each other across the field.

Qatran rode out in his shining gold armor. He shouted to Chin's army: "Who will be first to taste death at my hand?"

The words had hardly left his mouth when a warrior from Khorshid Shah's army, clad in silver armor, rode his piebald horse toward Qatran and shouted: "Are you a man of combat or just a shouter?" He charged at Qatran, holding his spear high. Qatran readied his own spear. The warriors clashed on horseback until Qatran drove his spear through his opponent's heart and out his back, lifting him clear off his horse. The silver warrior rolled dead on the ground.

Qatran shouted again: "Farokhruz! Come and face me if you dare!"

A second warrior from Chin's army rode out into the middle of the field to challenge Qatran. He too was slain.

The fighting went on until eight warriors from Chin's side had been killed by Qatran. Each time a soldier was slain, Qatran shouted again for Farokhruz to face him. But Khorshid Shah would not allow his brother, who was sore and wounded from the previous day's fighting, to enter the field.

Khorshid Shah was about to ride out to fight Qatran himself when Samak rode out ahead of him and shouted: "Qatran! I stopped the battle yesterday because Farokhruz was tired. Today, I'm stopping it for your sake, since you have fought so many."

Qatran recognized Samak and shouted: "Are you the scum who came to my tent last night like a thief? Come face me so I can destroy you!"

Samak called back: "My code of honor as an ayyar won't let me fight someone who is already worn out. I'll let you live today, so you can recover your strength to face me tomorrow." Then he turned and returned to Chin's army.

Qatran, who was in fact tired and injured, also turned around and went back to his army. Horns and drums announced the end of the second day of the war.

That night, the leading generals of Chin's army gathered at Khorshid Shah's pavilion to mourn and honor the loss of several of their top warriors that day.

After each had had several drinks and their sadness was lessened, Samak stood up, paid his respects to Khorshid Shah, and said: "Your Highness, I promised to bring Qatran to you tied up. Last night, his damned horse prevented me. I won't make the same mistake tonight." Khorshid Shah laughingly gave Samak permission. Samak left the pavilion and headed for Qatran's tent in the darkness.

Samak knew that after the previous night's attempt, the Machin sentries would be more vigilant. Instead of heading straight for Qatran's tent, he took a long way around through the rocky terrain behind the camp.

To his surprise, he saw someone moving in the darkness. He hid behind a rock and watched. The man was sneaking toward Chin's army camp.

Samak silently followed, then swiftly grabbed him from behind, placing his dagger at his throat. He said: "If you want to stay alive, tell me who you are and what you're up to!"

Stammering in terror, the man said: "Please don't kill me! My name is Atashak. I am Qatran's servant. He sent me to abduct Samak the ayyar and bring him back tied up."

Samak said: "What do you have against Samak, that you would think of doing such a thing?"

Atashak replied: "Since last night Qatran has been very angry. Tonight, he summoned me and promised that if I bring him Samak, he will arrange for me to marry Delaram, a maiden in Armen Shah's palace whom I love."

Samak asked Atashak: "Tell me, what do they say in Machin about Samak and the ayyars?"

Atashak said: "I have been told that ayyars are to be feared and trusted. And that Samak always keeps his promises."

Samak said: "You went looking for Samak. You've found him. Since you know my reputation, you know that you can trust this promise: If you take an oath to be loyal to me, follow my instructions, and never betray me, I will put Delaram's hand in your hand. I give you the choice between me and Qatran."

Atashak realized with relief that Samak was not going to kill him. He immediately took an oath to be faithful to Samak and follow his commands for as long as he lived.

Samak took Atashak in his arms and told him he would accept him as a brother from that moment. He then said: "I want you to tie me up and take me to Qatran, just as he ordered. He'll probably want to kill me on the spot. Your job is to convince him that it will be better to keep me alive until morning, so he can hang me on a gallows in front of Chin's whole army to show his supremacy. Then take me to your tent for safekeeping, and we will discuss what to do next."

Atashak followed Samak's instructions. He tied Samak's hands behind his back, put a rope around his neck, and dragged him back to Machin's camp and into Qatran's tent.

When Qatran saw Samak tied up, he exulted: "Which one of us looks like a fool now?" He then said to Atashak: "Cut off his head."

Atashak bowed to Qatran and said: "If you permit me, I can suggest an even better way to execute this pitiful man. I will take him to my tent and keep him tied up all night. Tomorrow before dawn, I will set up a gallows in the middle of the field and we can hang him from it. Chin's army will get a shock when they line up for battle and that is the first sight they see." Qatran liked the idea, and he told Atashak to carry out this plan.

Atashak took Samak to his own tent and extinguished the candles so that no one outside could see their shadows. He then untied Samak.

Samak ordered: "Give me a set of armor like the Machin warriors wear." Atashak complied. Samak put on the armor, then said to Atashak: "Tonight, we are going to carry Qatran to Chin's army camp. The problem is, he's quite heavy. Can you think of a solution?"

Atashak thought for a moment, then said: "Behind Gezelmalek's pavilion there is an elephant-skin hammock that the prince uses to rest in the open air. It would make a good stretcher to carry Qatran."

Samak liked this idea. He told Atashak to go to the slave master and select thirty slaves to escort them through the camp. Atashak soon returned with thirty slaves, two mules, and the hammock. Samak and Atashak crept to Qatran's tent, looked inside, and saw Qatran sound asleep. Tired from the day's battles, and happy at the prospect of hanging Samak on the gallows the next morning, he had drunk one goblet of wine after another until he passed out.

The two men entered the tent and rolled Qatran up in the hammock, which they secured between two mules. Samak instructed the slaves to accompany them to the edge of camp, and to be sure not to awaken Qatran while he slept.

On the way through the camp, they were stopped several times by sentries. Each time, Atashak explained that his master Qatran wished to sleep at the edge of the battlefield so that he could be first to challenge the enemy in the morning.

Thus Samak and Atashak left Machin's camp and crossed the battlefield plain, carrying their captive and accompanied by thirty slaves. When they reached the camp of Chin, Samak removed his helmet, revealing his identity to the guards, and ordered: "Arrest these men!" The slaves were so confused by what was happening that they did not resist.

Soon after sunrise, a messenger entered Khorshid Shah's pavilion and informed the prince: "Samak is here with a gift for Your Highness."

Khorshid Shah told the guards to send him in. Samak entered and paid his respects to the prince and generals. Khorshid Shah asked him how he had passed the night.

Samak responded cheerfully: "I went to pay my respects to General Qatran and invited him to visit Your Highness's pavilion. He is outside, relaxing in his hammock, waiting for permission to enter."

Khorshid Shah, bewildered, said: "Show him in."

Samak went out and came back with Atashak and the two mules. They laid their bundle in front of Khorshid Shah and untied it, revealing the great warrior snoring in his hammock. Samak then told them the whole story of the night's events. By the time he finished, Khorshid Shah and the generals were laughing so hard that tears rolled down their cheeks.

Samak bent over Qatran and plucked two hairs from his mustache. Qatran awoke with a start. He blinked to make sure he wasn't dreaming. He tried to sit up, but found his hands and feet tied. Then he saw Khorshid Shah sitting on his throne laughing at him.

Qatran shouted for his guards. Samak said: "Hush! Your guards are sleeping. Don't wake them!"

Qatran turned and saw Samak, and Atashak beside him. He exclaimed: "Atashak! Where am I? What have you done to me?"

Atashak responded: "You are in the presence of His Highness Khorshid Shah, and lucky that Samak has not killed you!"

After the laughter subsided, Khorshid Shah became serious. To Samak, Arghonun, and the generals, he said: "I am new to your manners and customs. How do relations stand between you and the king of Machin? What should we do with this valuable warrior from the enemy's side? Detain him or release him?"

General Samour said: "Your Highness, Machin has paid Chin tribute for centuries. Now they have attacked us, and their prince Gezelmalek insults us with his arrogance. Qatran is their greatest warrior. I would keep him as a hostage."

Arghonun suggested: "Why don't we send him in chains to Bograi Valley as our prisoner?" All present agreed and Khorshid Shah accepted the suggestion. As for the thirty captured slaves, he awarded two each to the army's fifteen most deserving warriors as a token of appreciation.

15

THE TRUCE

THAT morning, as the army of Machin prepared for the third day of combat, Gezelmalek sent guards to Qatran's tent to find out why he had not shown up yet. Soon the whole camp knew that Qatran was missing, along with thirty slaves, two mules, and Gezelmalek's elephant-skin hammock.

Gezelmalek called the commander of the night guard and demanded an explanation. The commander bowed down and said: "Your Highness, the night before last, we found General Qatran tied up and wrapped in his bedcovers on the ground next to his horse. He wouldn't tell us what had happened."

Then another soldier stepped forward, bowed down and said: "Your Highness, last night Qatran's servant Atashak took Samak the ayyar prisoner. Now neither Atashak nor Samak are to be found."

Next, the slave master came to Gezelmalek and said: "Last night, Atashak came to me and requested thirty slaves to guard Qatran, saying that he wished to sleep in the open air at the edge of camp."

Gezelmalek shook his head and shouted: "How could such things happen under my command?"

Just then a spy rushed in, threw himself on the ground in front of the prince and said: "Your Highness, I come from the enemy's camp. Atashak and Samak delivered Qatran to Khorshid Shah this morning with thirty slaves. Qatran has been sent to Bograi Valley in chains with a guard of two hundred soldiers, and the slaves have been given to the soldiers of Chin."

Gezelmalek became so furious that he bit the back of his hand in anger. He said: "How is it possible that two men could abduct a champion like Qatran, and his slaves, out of an army of thirty thousand warriors and no one stopped them?"

Qatran's brother Qatour, who was a well-known hero himself, stepped forward, paid his respects to Gezelmalek, then said: "Your Highness, if you command it, I will go and do my best to free my brother."

The generals discussed the situation. Some felt that without Qatran they did not have sufficient warriors to win the war. The argument went on until Gezelmalek declared: "We will not withdraw, but we will ask for a temporary truce, and send a message to my father Armen Shah asking him for reinforcements." Everyone agreed.

Gezelmalek called for a scribe and ordered him to write a letter. "This message is from Gezelmalek to the king of the world, our venerable father, Armen Shah. We wish Your Majesty to know that we left Machin with our army and entered Chin's territory based on the vizier Mehran's promise that we would meet with little resistance and would be given Princess Mahpari in marriage. Unfortunately this was not the case. Mahpari was taken away by the prince of Persia, Khorshid Shah, who has brought a large army into war against us. His brother Farokhruz killed six of our champions in one day. Last night, our great hero Qatran was kidnapped and delivered into their custody by an ayyar named Samak. Now we are here on the battlefield outnumbered by the enemy. If you wish your loyal son to return alive, please send us more soldiers and experienced generals, for we are sorely in need."

The letter was sealed and stamped and sent to Armen Shah with an envoy.

That same day, Gezelmalek sent a message to Khorshid Shah asking for a truce in the fighting. Khorshid Shah accepted, and the two armies remained in their respective camps.

Gezelmalek's envoy rode for two days and nights and arrived at the court of Armen Shah. When the king heard his son's letter read, sadness and concern overtook him. He asked: "Have you seen this Khorshid Shah with your own eyes?"

"I have, O king," replied the messenger. "He is a young man of great purity, magnificent and royal."

Armen Shah was silent for a moment. Then he asked: "Who is this person Samak who can get the better of a champion like Qatran and kidnap him from the middle of an army?"

His vizier, Shahran, informed him that Samak was a young ayyar who had been trained by Shaghal, chief of the ayyars in Chin. "Ayyars!" said Armen Shah. "We would do well to get rid of both of them."

The next day, Armen Shah called together his generals and told them: "My son Gezelmalek went to Chin to marry the princess Mahpari, but he was betrayed. Now his army is on the verge of defeat by Chin's soldiers. O my generals, you know I have been good to you and generous all my life. Now it is your turn to have compassion for my son in his time of trouble. He did not want war with Chin. He thought he was going there to get married. He is young and inexperienced in the ways of war. What do you suggest?"

One of the generals bowed down to Armen Shah and announced that he was ready to join the war with his army of five thousand soldiers. Armen Shah thanked him. Two more generals followed, one with an army of five thousand soldiers and the other with an army of ten thousand. Armen Shah thanked both for their readiness. The next day, twenty thousand soldiers began their march toward Chin to join Gezelmalek's army.

When the army had left, Armen Shah called in his vizier Shahran and asked: "What is the best way to assassinate these ayyars from Chin, Samak and Shaghal?"

Shahran answered: "In the kingdom of Machin there are two men whom I would entrust with such a job. One of them is named Kanun. He is the leader of our ayyars. Unlike the ayyars of Chin, an unpredictable lot who claim to be defenders of the common people, we can trust Kanun to loyally serve His Majesty's interests. The other is a young albino called Kafur, whom we have called on in the past to kidnap or eliminate those who acted against the royal family." Hearing this, Armen Shah was pleased, and he ordered the vizier to bring both men to his court.

Kanun and Kafur were brought in and bowed down to Armen Shah. Kanun was middle-aged, with a graying beard and a calm, unsmiling demeanor. He had been waiting a long time for an opportunity to eliminate Shaghal, who was his counterpart and rival in Chin. He said: "If it is Your Majesty's wish, I will go to the battlefield and return with the heads of Shaghal, Samak, and Khorshid Shah as gifts for Your Majesty." Kafur, a slender youth whose extremely pale eyes and skin gave him an eerie appearance, assured Kanun and the king of his allegiance.

Armen Shah told Kanun: "If you succeed, I will reward you and make you my special chancellor. I will accept the heads of these ayyars, but take care that you bring Khorshid Shah to me alive. One does not kill the son of a king. It has been three months since my son Gezelmalek left. He sends me news every day. I know he is well, yet still I suffer from the separation. Imagine the anguish Marzban Shah will feel when he is told that his son has been taken prisoner far from home. Only a father can understand what is in another father's heart. Marzban Shah has never been our enemy before now. I have no wish to inflict on him the greatest grief a father can suffer."

Kanun bowed down and said: "Your wish is my command." Kanun and Kafur paid their respects to Armen Shah and left the court. Soon afterward, they set out from Machin toward Chin's territory.

• • •

For several days the armies of Chin and Machin remained idle in their camps, until one morning Khorshid Shah, impatient with waiting, ordered the horns blown and drums beaten to sound the attack. When Gezelmalek heard the horns and drums, he became anxious and immediately dispatched an envoy to Khorshid Shah with a message saying: "We did not come to Chin for war, but to request the hand of Princess Mahpari in marriage. Given the losses we have suffered, including our champion Qatran, we have sent word to our king, Armen Shah, requesting his permission to return home. We ask Prince Khorshid Shah to grant us more time and not attack us until we receive our father's answer."

Khorshid Shah responded: "We love peace and have no wish to be your enemy. We will respect your request for a truce until you receive an answer from your king." Gezelmalek's envoy bowed down to Khorshid Shah and left the pavilion to take this response back to his commander.

Samak, who had listened to the exchange, bowed down to Khorshid Shah and said: "O great prince, in my opinion, Gezelmalek and his generals are not to be trusted. Since peace is your wish, I would suggest that we keep our army watchful and ready to respond to a possible surprise attack." Khorshid Shah thanked Samak for his warning and gave these instructions to his generals.

That evening, Samak took Khorshid Shah and Arghonun aside and said: "There is something I have been meaning to ask you. How is Princess Mahpari being safeguarded with so many of your warriors away from Bograi Valley?"

Khorshid Shah replied: "She is safe and in good hands at Shahak Fortress, as Arghonun suggested."

Hearing this, Samak became anxious. Khorshid Shah saw his reaction and asked: "My friend, why do you look troubled?"

Samak responded: "O great prince, we did so much to save Mahpari from the hands of the spiteful vizier Mehran. Now you have put her in the worst place imaginable!"

Khorshid Shah asked in surprise: "Why do you say that?"

Samak said: "Don't you know that the guardian of Shahak Fortress is no one but Mugavgar, the son of Mahpari's witch nurse Shervaneh? That witch killed and imprisoned all the princess's suitors for one reason—to save Mahpari for her son!"

These words hit Khorshid Shah like a sledgehammer. For a moment he could not focus. Then he turned to Arghonun and demanded: "Did you know this?"

Arghonun bowed down and said: "I swear I had no idea until this moment!"

Samak too bowed down and said: "O great prince! Give me your permission to go to Shahak Fortress and take your future wife out of that place however I can." Khorshid Shah, now gripped by fear for Mahpari's safety, thanked Samak and gave him permission to go.

SECTION 3

Machin

16

AN IMPREGNABLE FORTRESS

Now that Samak had the prince's permission to try to get Mahpari out of Shahak Fortress, he thought about how to get inside. Knowing that the fortress was occupied by renegades who did not recognize the authority of Faghfur Shah, he decided to present himself as an envoy from Arghonun, since the warlord was a bit of a renegade himself. Arghonun agreed and gave Samak his ring. Samak placed it on his finger and set out accompanied by his new servant Atashak.

After riding for two days and two nights, they arrived in Bograi Valley. Samak's first stop was to ensure that the prisoner Qatran was being held securely. Arghonun's guards assured Samak that the warrior was well guarded and that no one could get close to him.

Samak and Atashak then crossed the valley and rode up the slope toward Shahak Fortress, until it became so steep that their horses could go no farther. Since it was getting dark, they dismounted, tied up their horses, and lay down to rest. The next morning, they continued up the trail on foot.

Shahak Fortress sat atop the mountain's highest peak, overlooking the entire valley. The fortress was so high that the top of its tower was often hidden by clouds, and the trail that led up to its massive iron gate was so narrow that only one man could pass at a time. Samak remarked to Atashak: "No army could capture this fortress."

As the two men reached the gate, a sentinel who had been observing them since they had first appeared on the mountain called out: "Who are you? What do you want?"

Samak responded: "I am Samak, with a message from Lord Arghonun for the fortress guardian. This is my friend Atashak."

The sentinel called: "What is your proof?"

Samak raised his hand, saying: "Here is Lord Arghonun's ring."

When Mugavgar, the fortress guardian, was informed of the visitors, excitement gripped him. "Samak, who murdered my mother!" he exclaimed. "Fate has delivered him into my hands."

Mugavgar had grown up alongside the princess Mahpari and had loved her since childhood. His mother, the witch Shervaneh, had been her nurse. Since he was not from a royal family, he had no hope of marrying her. For years he had waited patiently, burning with love and frustration, while his mother did everything in her power to make her son's wish possible.

When the princess reached the age of marriage, Shervaneh had imposed the three challenges as a way to eliminate all rival suitors. Every time a prince or nobleman was mentioned as a candidate to marry Mahpari, the witch lured him to Chin to get rid of him. Even if a suitor survived the first two challenges, he was sure to be eliminated by the final riddle. The witch's plan had been to wait until Faghfur Shah became so discouraged that he was willing to accept any suitor. At that point, she would give her son the answer to the talking cypress riddle so that he could pass the challenge and marry the princess.

When Mugavgar saw Mahpari brought to Shahak Fortress for safe keeping, he was overjoyed by this stroke of good fortune and started working to earn the princess's trust. He housed Mahpari in an exquisite suite in the fortress's highest tower, with a magnificent view of the valley, and assigned two maidens and a servant to attend to her. When he saw that the princess was still sad and lonely, he arranged to bring her favorite handmaiden Ruhafza and her faithful African manservant from Faghfur Shah's palace to the fortress to keep her company.

Mugavgar had received the news of his mother's death at Samak's hand only two days before Samak and Atashak appeared at the fortress's gate. When the sentinel informed him who was below, Mugavgar's sorrow hardened into determination to take revenge. He told the sentinel: "Let Arghonun's messengers enter the fortress, and bring them to me."

Samak and Atashak were brought in. Mugavgar welcomed them warmly and asked about Khorshid Shah and Arghonun. Samak told him that Khorshid Shah had been placed in command of Chin's army, and that Qatran, Machin's greatest hero, had been captured and taken prisoner after two days of combat.

Startled by this news, Mugavgar exclaimed: "Qatran captured! What champion of Chin could perform such a feat?"

It occurred to Samak that if he took credit for Qatran's capture, this might make Mugavgar more cautious and his task even harder. He said: "Khorshid Shah pulled him down from his horse, threw him on the ground and tied him up right on the battlefield."

Mugavgar, impressed, said: "Prince Khorshid Shah must be a formidable warrior." He then asked Samak what message he had brought from Arghonun.

Samak said: "Lord Arghonun sent me and my companion Atashak to reinforce your fortress's defenses and fill its storerooms with food and wine and water that he will send from Bograi Valley. He wants to make sure it is impregnable, and ready to give safe refuge to him and his warriors in case Chin's army falls to Gezelmalek." He then showed the ring to support his claim.

Mugavgar recognized Arghonun's seal. He kissed the ring and said: "I will obey Lord Arghonun's command." He called the warehouse master and ordered him to show the visitors the available storerooms.

As soon as Samak had left, Mugavgar began thinking about the best way to kill him.

• • •

Samak had chosen a cover story that provided an excuse to learn the layout of the fortress and where Mahpari was being kept. While the warehouse master led him on a tour of the fortress's storerooms, Samak heard a sad love song coming from an open window in the tower above. He called up: "What a lovely voice!"

Ruhafza, who had been singing to the princess, was startled to hear Samak. She looked down from the window and saw him walking away with Atashak and the warehouse master. Excitedly, she told Mahpari what she had seen. Mahpari ordered Ruhafza: "Go follow him!"

Ruhafza hurried down and followed the three men at a distance. Samak, having noticed her, turned to the warehouse master and said: "My friend and I are tired from the journey. Is there a place we can rest for the night and finish the tour tomorrow morning?"

The warehouse master took Samak and Atashak to the visitors' quarters. As soon as he was gone, Ruhafza came out from hiding and went straight to Samak. Samak hugged her with joy and said: "My wonderful mother and friend, I'm so glad to see you! Tell me, is the princess all right? I hope Mugavgar has not tried to take advantage of her?"

Ruhafza assured him: "He hasn't dared. He has only come to visit her once, and I was with her the whole time." Anxiously, she added: "Samak, he asked about his mother, the witch nurse Shervaneh, and I told him you had killed her. I'm sorry I've put you in danger!"

Samak said: "Don't blame yourself, my dear mother! He was bound to find out. Go back to Mahpari and tell her that Samak sends his respects, and that I have come here for her sake and Khorshid Shah's. Tell her to send a message to Mugavgar, for you to deliver, saying, 'Mugavgar, we have known each other since we were children. We played together and drank milk from the same bosom. All my life I have been in love with you, but I never had the courage to reveal it. When my father promised me to Khorshid Shah, I was miserable but I could not change his mind. Now, at last, I have found my way to you in this fortress. I only want to belong to you. I am afraid that Samak, who killed my dear nurse and your beloved mother, has come to take me away. I beg you to prevent this by killing him and his companion, secretly, so that no one will know you are responsible. I will tell you how to do this. Then bring their heads to my chamber so that you and I can celebrate together.'"

Atashak, hearing this, cried: "Samak, what are you saying? I trusted you, I have put my life in your hands!"

Samak laughed and said: "My dear friend, I promised you that I would go with you to Machin and put Delaram's hand into yours. You can be sure that once we have accomplished our goal here, I will do exactly that."

Ruhafza hugged Samak, went back to Mahpari and relayed Samak's message. Seeing the princess's worried expression, Ruhafza reassured her: "Dear princess, you don't know Samak the way I do. He always knows what he's doing. Remember how he brought Khorshid Shah to you and saved you from being delivered into the hands of Gezelmalek? We must trust him and do exactly as he says. As impossible as it sounds, we have to believe that somehow he will take us out of this place."

Mahpari listened to her words carefully, then said: "All right. Go and tell Mugavgar exactly what Samak instructed you to say."

Ruhafza went to Mugavgar and said: "I have come to you with a wonderful message to replace the sad news I gave you last time."

Mugavgar said: "I see you smiling! What is this good news you have brought me?"

Ruhafza said: "The princess has sent me to tell you that she has a complaint to make. Since she arrived here, you have visited her only once. She has always liked you, ever since you were children together. The only reason she came to this fortress was so that she could be in your arms. She had hoped that you loved her too. Why this coldness?"

Hearing this, Mugavgar became excited, and asked: "When did she say these sweet words to you?"

Ruhafza replied: "Last night, when I was singing to her, I saw tears in her eyes, and asked what was making her so sad. She said she was disappointed because she left her father's royal palace to come here, and you have been ignoring her. She is afraid that Samak has been sent here by Khorshid Shah to bring her back. She wishes me to remind you that it was Samak who murdered your mother, and now he means to take her away from you as well. She asks you to kill Samak and his companion secretly. She will tell you the best way to accomplish this so that no one will know you are responsible. Then she can stay here and be yours."

Mugavgar was overjoyed. He asked Ruhafza eagerly: "How does she suggest I kill them?"

Ruhafza said: "Now that I know the princess can count on you, let me go ask her."

Mugavgar felt as if he had just been given the whole world. Ruhafza left him, went straight to Samak, and repeated the conversation.

Samak told Ruhafza: "The princess should say to Mugavgar, 'Organize a feast to welcome your guests, and invite everyone in the fortress. During the celebration, keep filling Samak and Atashak's wine goblets until they are completely drunk. When they go back to their quarters to sleep, send two trusted guards to cut off their heads and throw their bodies from the fortress walls. Bring their heads to me. The next day, tell everyone that Samak and Atashak left early in the morning. I will then move into your quarters and we can be together.' "

Ruhafza went back to Mahpari and reported everything Samak had said. The princess wondered: "Has Samak lost his mind?" Ruhafza admitted that she too was concerned, but that surely Samak knew what he was doing.

Mahpari said: "All right, take the message from me to Mugavgar as Samak instructed."

After Ruhafza delivered the message, Mugavgar invited everyone in the fortress to gather in the banquet hall for a feast to honor their new guests.

Samak told Atashak: "Get ready for an evening of fun!"

Atashak replied: "I'm not going with you to get killed!"

Samak said: "Atashak, have a little faith, or you'll never make a good ayyar. Stick with me and see what happens to Mugavgar and anyone who tries to kill us!"

"Why don't you go by yourself and eliminate everyone first? Then I can join the party later after they're dead," Atashak suggested.

Samak laughed and said: "Atashak, it's time for you to start enjoying life. Be happy! You worry too much."

Atashak retorted: "No matter what you say, I'm not going to a banquet to get drunk and then get my head cut off!"

"We have to go, or Mugavgar will send his guards to kill us here and now," Samak said. "Don't worry, I don't get drunk no matter how much wine I drink. I've won many bets from the ayyars this way. If you like, I'll drink from your goblet as well as mine."

Atashak said: "What's your secret? Do you pour the wine down your shirt instead of into your mouth?"

Samak explained: "My father was a winemaker. Once, when I was still a toddler, I fell into a vat filled with fermented grapes. By the time they pulled me out, I'd swallowed so much wine they had to hang me upside down to get it out of me. I was so sick, they recommended that from then on, as a cure, my mother should pour a little wine into everything I ate. She did that until I was seven years old. Then my father died. My mother took care of me for two more years, until she died and I was left completely alone. That's when Shaghal found me, in the street, eating garbage from a trash heap. He felt sorry for me and took me in. Ever since then, I've gone on drinking wine as medicine. That's why I don't get drunk."

Samak took out a small sack, gave it to Atashak and said: "Inside this sack is a strong sleeping powder. When I give the signal, go around the table and put a little powder into each wine jug without anybody seeing you. I'll create a diversion to make your job easier. Do that, and I'll take care of the rest." Atashak took the sack of powder and hid it in his clothing.

• • •

The banquet hall was at the edge of the fortress overlooking the gorge. When Samak and Atashak entered, they saw Mugavgar sitting surrounded by sixty warriors. All stood up to welcome the guests, who were then seated at the head of the table next to Mugavgar.

Dancers and minstrels entered and began to play. Wine was served, goblet after goblet. Soon everyone was drunk except for Atashak, who had drunk very little, and Samak, who had drunk Atashak's wine as well as his own, but was only pretending to be tipsy.

When the time was right, Samak stood up and, acting drunk, said to Mugavgar: "Get rid of these dancers and minstrels. I'll give you a real show!"

Mugavgar followed Samak's request and sent the dancers and minstrels away. Samak gathered everyone around him and began a dagger-throwing performance that amazed and entertained them with his skill and cleverness. While their attention was distracted, Atashak covertly poured sleeping powder into every jug of wine on the table.

Samak finished his performance, turned to their hosts and said: "Now let's fill our goblets and drink to your wonderful hospitality!" All of them drank. Within minutes they started to swoon, and one after another fell to the floor unconscious.

Samak said to Atashak: "Let's start with our host." They carried Mugavgar to the wall and pushed him out through a loophole. His body fell into the gorge and disappeared from sight. They did the same for every one of Mugavgar's warriors until the two friends were alone in the banquet hall. Samak said to Atashak: "Now the animals and birds can continue the feast."

The next morning, Samak and Atashak gathered all the women and children of the fortress and sent them away. Then they went to Mahpari's suite to see her. They were let in by her African manservant, who gladly opened the door for Samak as a friend of the princess.

Mahpari and Ruhafza were overjoyed to see Samak and rushed gratefully into his arms. Samak told them the story of the previous night's events. Mahpari thanked him for saving her life. Samak said: "The one you should thank is Khorshid Shah, because it's his good luck that we are alive!"

Samak asked Ruhafza and the African servant if there was anyone besides them in the fortress. Ruhafza indicated the princess's two other handmaidens, and answered: "Just those of us whom you see here."

Samak said: "Then I will go back to Khorshid Shah and tell him I have left Shahak Fortress in the capable hands of one man and four women. The storerooms are stocked with enough food to feed you for a year. It would take an army to breach its walls, so you are safe here—as long as you don't make the mistake of opening the gate to anyone who is not me or Khorshid Shah." He then said goodbye and departed with Atashak.

Several nights later, Samak and Atashak arrived at the Chin army campground. Samak found Khorshid Shah sitting in his pavilion with Farokhruz, Shaghal, Arghonun and the generals. Seeing Samak, they all got up and hugged him one by one. When Samak had finished telling them everything that had happened, Khorshid Shah hugged him again, and they went on drinking and enjoying each other's company until midnight. Then they all returned to their own quarters to rest.

17

REINFORCEMENTS

THE next day, shortly after noon, the sky behind Machin's army darkened, and the ground shook with the thunder of approaching warriors. Khorshid Shah asked what was happening. His scouts told him that a large army had arrived from Machin to reinforce Gezelmalek's position.

Soon afterward, a man came to Khorshid Shah's pavilion with a message for the prince. When he was shown in, Khorshid Shah recognized Sureh, one of his personal servants who had accompanied him from Halab.

Sureh said to the prince: "Your Highness, I come from Machin, where I have spent these past months as a spy. Armen Shah has sent an army of twenty thousand soldiers to help his son, Gezelmalek. And something else, for Your Highness's ears alone. . . ." He moved closer to the prince and whispered in his ear: "Following secretly in the footsteps of Machin's army are two ayyars named Kanun and Kafur. They plan to capture you alive and bring you to Armen Shah, along with the heads of Samak and Shaghal."

When night fell, and Khorshid Shah was alone in his pavilion with Farokhruz, Samak, and Atashak, he said: "Samak, I am alive because of you, and you are alive because of me. I must warn you that Armen Shah has sent two ayyars from Machin, named Kanun and Kafur, to bring him your head and Shaghal's head, and take me prisoner."

Samak said: "I'm flattered to hear that His Highness Armen Shah values my head that much. I have heard Kanun's name before. I wish I could be here to meet him myself, but I am obliged to go to Machin to fulfill a promise I made to my friend Atashak. Meanwhile, I urge Your Highness to be careful and watch out for their traps."

After saying goodbye to the prince, Samak went to Shaghal's tent and repeated the warning he had heard. Shaghal became serious, and said: "Kanun is a dangerous opponent."

Samak replied: "My master, you know I must go to Machin, because I promised Atashak I would fulfill his heart's desire." He added: "While I am gone, be vigilant and watch over Khorshid Shah. Although he is a prince, with all his education, he is still young. He is a foreigner in the midst of this army, and not familiar with the tricky ways of the ayyars. Don't be lulled into thinking that just because everyone here is his servant, he is safe. Look out for him. Even if he speaks harsh words to you in anger, don't blame him. Remember that he is both a king and a child."

Shaghal assured Samak that he would protect the prince with his own life.

Shortly before midnight, Samak and Atashak left the camp and rode toward Machin.

The next morning, Khorshid Shah gathered the generals in his pavilion and said: "Now that our enemy's ranks have been increased by twenty thousand soldiers, we must tell Faghfur Shah that if he wishes to continue the war, he too should send more soldiers." The generals agreed. A letter was written and dispatched to the king's palace in Chin.

When Faghfur Shah received the letter, he asked his vizier Mehran for advice. Mehran, privately disturbed by the news that Samak had captured Qatran and had slain Mugavgar, thought to himself that at this rate, the war would soon be over and Gezelmalek defeated. This would bring him little benefit. It was past time to put an end to the activities of this troublesome ayyar who kept thwarting his plans.

Mehran said to the king: "Your Majesty, I suggest we send ten thousand warriors and arms to ensure Gezelmalek's defeat. I ask your permission to lead this army and personally deliver your message of support to Khorshid Shah."

Faghfur Shah agreed and ordered Mehran to do this immediately.

While the army was being assembled and weapons brought from the warehouses, Mehran wrote a secret letter to Gezelmalek. "Faghfur Shah is sending ten thousand additional warriors to Khorshid Shah. I have persuaded him to place me in command of this army, which I recommend that you send a force to intercept. I will lead our army toward the battlefield in such a way as to expose us to your attack, so that you can easily win victory with almost no losses on your side, and then take me prisoner." Mehran signed and sealed the letter and dispatched it via trusted messenger to Gezelmalek.

• • •

As the truce wore on, thousands of soldiers sat idle in the opposing camps of Chin and Machin, awaiting orders to fight. One of Chin's generals, whose name was Siahgil, took a group of his men into the mountains to hunt.

They were in the foothills when Siahgil spotted a gazelle heading down toward the meadow. He called out to his men: "I'll take this one!" and rode after the animal. The gazelle changed course and galloped back up the hill. Siahgil chased it, but the gazelle was faster. By the time he reached the crest of the hill, it was nowhere in sight.

Scanning the landscape for his prey, Siahgil was surprised to spot, instead, a lone horseman riding along the mountain. He galloped toward the rider, shouting: "You there! Halt!"

The man (who was Mehran's envoy, carrying the vizier's secret message to Gezelmalek) slowed down.

Siahgil caught up with him and demanded: "Where are you going? State your name and business!"

Mehran's envoy recognized Siahgil as a general from Chin. He knew that if he told the truth about where he was going, he would be arrested. So he lied and explained: "I am carrying a message from Faghfur Shah to Khorshid Shah."

Siahgil said: "Follow me." He led the envoy back to their camp, directly to Khorshid Shah's pavilion.

The envoy said to Khorshid Shah: "Your Highness, Faghfur Shah wishes me to tell you that his vizier Mehran is on his way to you with ten thousand reinforcements. He advises you to prepare sufficient space for these men in your campground."

Khorshid Shah was happy to hear this, but asked: "Did the king not give you a letter with his seal?"

The envoy invented a lie on the spot and said: "I committed the message to memory, in case I was intercepted by spies from Machin."

Khorshid Shah was satisfied by this response. He ordered Siahgil to take a group of four thousand soldiers to welcome Mehran and his army and escort them to a suitable place in the campground. Siahgil obeyed Khorshid Shah's command.

The next morning, before dawn, Mehran's envoy left the camp, taking care to avoid the sentries, and rode across the battlefield to Machin's army campground. He was taken straight to Gezelmalek's pavilion.

After he read the secret letter from Mehran, Gezelmalek ordered General Salim, who was one of Machin's most experienced military leaders, to take twelve thousand men on a shortcut through the mountains above Chin's campground and attack Mehran's army of reinforcements as the vizier recommended.

Mehran, meanwhile, had provided his army with hundreds of wine barrels, and he encouraged the men to drink as much as they could along the way. By the time they reached the mountain pass where General Salim's Machin warriors were waiting, most of the Chin soldiers were drunk and unready for battle. The slaughter was horrendous. Within an hour, all ten thousand of Mehran's men were either dead or captured.

Salim's army set out toward Machin's camp transporting the captured arms and prisoners, including Mehran.

They were spotted by General Siahgil's scouts, who were themselves on their way to meet Mehran's army. Siahgil dispatched an envoy to warn Khorshid Shah. The general had only four thousand soldiers under his command, but he bravely gave the order to attack.

A bloody combat took place, with casualties mounting quickly on both sides. Siahgil's warriors, outnumbered and exhausted, were at the point of defeat when Khorshid Shah's reinforcements arrived. Eight thousand soldiers under the command of General Saum joined the fight against Salim's Machin army. Shortly after that, they were reinforced by another group of warriors under the command of General Shiruyeh. The battle continued until it was too dark for the two armies to fight. They pulled apart to regroup and to get ready to fight again the next morning.

That night in Khorshid Shah's pavilion, Farokhruz saw that his brother was worried about the next day's battle. He asked permission to lead the fight. Khorshid Shah granted it. Farokhruz took four thousand men and set out while it was still dark.

The next morning, the two armies faced each other: Chin's army on the slopes, Machin's army led by General Salim below them in the field. Farokhruz ordered the archers to begin the attack, with each man shooting three arrows into the Machin ranks. Within a short time, six thousand Machin soldiers and horses were slaughtered. Farokhruz then ordered his men to encircle Machin's remaining warriors and attack with their spears and swords. By noon, the entire Machin army was either massacred or captured. Siahgil fought his way through the battle to reach Salim. The two warriors fought hand to hand in bloody combat until Siahgil seized Salim, tied him up, and threw him into the group of captured Machin soldiers.

Farokhruz ordered the prisoners Salim had taken from Chin's army freed. Among them was Mehran. On Khorshid Shah's instructions, Farokhruz had General Salim interrogated to find out how he had known so much about the Chin army's movements.

With Mehran at Farokhruz's side, Salim made no attempt to hide the truth but forthrightly told Farokhruz everything that had happened since the beginning. As a close friend of Gezelmalek, he was aware of the secret communications between the prince and Mehran. He now revealed all the vizier's tactics and conspiracies, saying: "Mehran is responsible for this disaster that has come between our two kingdoms. He started this war by inviting Machin's army to invade Chin in the first place." To prove his claim, Salim told Farokhruz's men to look inside his boot. There they found the letter from Mehran that had been delivered to Gezelmalek a few days earlier, which Salim had kept.

Mehran protested: "These are lies! I never wrote that letter! This enemy general from Machin is trying to discredit me."

When Farokhruz read the letter, he realized that everything Salim had said was true. He turned on Mehran and shouted:

"Traitor! Bastard dog! Do you realize how many thousands of lives have been lost as the result of your vicious schemes? And you have the nerve to deny it?" He ordered Mehran tied up and sent to Khorshid Shah.

When the vizier was brought before him, Khorshid Shah asked him why he had acted so dishonestly. Mehran had nothing to say.

Arghonun suggested that they detain Mehran and Salim in his family stronghold in Bograi Valley, where Qatran was already being held prisoner. Khorshid Shah agreed and ordered them sent there with an escort of two hundred soldiers.

When Gezelmalek heard that twelve thousand warriors of Machin's army had been lost and Salim and Mehran captured, he went into a rage, not knowing what to do next.

At that point, Kanun and Kafur, who had been in hiding, came forward and found their way to Gezelmalek's pavilion. They told the prince: "If Your Highness commands it, we will go to Bograi Valley and use our skills to release Mehran the vizier, Qatran the great warrior, and General Salim from captivity, even though this is not the mission we were sent here to carry out." Gezelmalek calmed down somewhat and ordered them to proceed.

The two ayyars began by investigating what commodities were most sought after in Bograi Valley. When they learned that wine was in scarce supply there, they came up with a plan.

18

IN THE ENEMY'S CITY

SAMAK and Atashak reached Machin tired and hungry. Samak had lived all his life in Chin, and this was his first time in a foreign land. Atashak had been born and grown up in Machin and knew the city well. They went to a caravansary to eat and spend the night.

After two days of rest, they spent the third day walking around the city. Atashak showed Samak around the various neighborhoods, shops, and places of interest.

On the fourth day, they went to the city's main public bath and enjoyed a massage followed by a thorough head and body wash. In the bathhouse, they struck up a friendly conversation with an older man who was happy to answer Samak's questions about Machin.

Samak asked about the ayyars of the city. The old man explained that Machin's ayyars backed the nobility and the ruling class. This was the opposite of the situation in Chin, where the ayyars protected the public from oppression by the nobility.

Samak asked the old man: "Who is the leader of the ayyars here?" The old man replied that the leader's name was Kanun, and that he was out of town for an important mission. Samak already knew what Kanun's mission was, so he asked the old man if the leader of the ayyars had any relatives in town. The old man replied that Kanun had two sons, Behzad and Razmyar, both strong warriors.

After leaving the bathhouse, Samak asked Atashak to take him to Kanun's home, which was the ayyar headquarters. Samak told the two guards posted outside the door: "We have come to see Kanun, the leader of the ayyars."

The guard replied that Kanun had gone hunting and would not be back for a month. Samak then asked if his sons were in. When the guard said yes, Samak said: "Please go tell them that two visitors from out of town are here to see them."

Samak and Atashak were shown into the ayyar headquarters and taken to see the two brothers, Behzad and Razmyar.

Samak told them: "My friend and I are travelers from Bukhara who wish to serve the ayyars. First, we went to Chin, but we were told that Shaghal, the head of the ayyars there, had gone to war. So we have come to Machin to offer our allegiance to Kanun."

Behzad and Razmyar welcomed the visitors and offered them food and wine. Samak noticed that the young girl who brought the food was extraordinarily beautiful, and that her dark eyes seemed to watch him with unusual focus and intensity. He dismissed this thought and told himself that this was no time to get distracted.

After they had drunk several goblets, Samak stood up and said: "We are strangers in town. I'm afraid if we enjoy your hospitality much longer, we'll be too drunk to find our way back to our caravansary." The brothers insisted that Samak and Atashak stay with them in the ayyar headquarters. Samak thanked them and they were led to a comfortable place to sleep.

Samak and Atashak remained in Kanun's home for three days. On the third day, Atashak asked Samak: "Have you forgotten the reason we came to Machin? You promised me that you would put Delaram's hand in my hand."

Samak responded: "My dear friend, love has made you impatient. I don't even know where your beloved Delaram lives. Give me some time to inform myself before we jump into action."

Atashak said: "Delaram lives in the royal palace, in the building that houses the wine cellar. She is the king's wine attendant. What more information do you need?"

Samak said: "All right! We will go tonight."

That night, Samak and Atashak put on their armor and left the ayyar headquarters. Behzad and Razmyar, who had been suspicious of them since they arrived, decided to follow them to see what they were up to.

Atashak led the way to Armen Shah's palace compound. On Samak's request, Atashak took him to the part of the outer wall that was closest to the wine cellar building.

Samak and Atashak waited in the darkness outside the wall until shortly after midnight, when the city was quiet. Samak handed Atashak his lasso and said: "Throw it and catch a crenellation at the top of the wall."

Atashak tried several times, but was unable to throw it high enough. Samak took the lasso and showed him the proper way to throw it. Atashak said admiringly: "Ah, that's the difference between an ordinary person like Atashak and a great ayyar like Samak!"

Behzad and Razmyar were watching from the shadows. When they heard Atashak speak Samak's name and realized who their two visitors were, they became happy that they had followed them. Behzad told Razmyar: "Our father traveled a long way to kill Samak, and here he has come to us!"

Razmyar said: "This Atashak is Qatran's servant. How did he end up serving Samak?" The brothers decided to find out what these two were up to, then kill them both.

Samak tested the lasso's strength, then climbed it to the top. Atashak followed fearfully, as it was his first time scaling a wall.

One of the guards posted on the battlement heard a sound, turned, and spotted Atashak just as he reached the top of the wall. The guard rushed toward Atashak, unaware that Samak was hiding behind the crenellation. Samak grabbed him from behind and put his hand over his mouth to stop him from shouting. He whispered into the guard's ear: "If you scream, you will die. Agreed?" The guard nodded and Samak released his hand.

The guard asked: "Who are you?"

Samak answered: "I am the angel of death. Tell me where I can find the maiden Delaram, and I will spare your life."

The guard said: "What kind of angel are you, that you need to ask about a human being's whereabouts?"

Samak smiled, liking the guard's cleverness. "I'll make you a bargain. I'll let you live if you promise to stay quiet tonight and not give us away." The guard agreed. Samak asked him to point the way to the wine cellar.

The guard pointed to a dome and said: "Behind that dome. That's where you will find Delaram."

Samak and Atashak left the guard and climbed down from the roof until they reached the wine cellar. They peered through a small opening in the closed door and saw a chamber lit by candles, with musical instruments hanging on the walls. Delaram lay asleep on a bed of cushions. Atashak said to Samak: "That's her! That's the maiden who captured my heart."

Samak unlocked the door from outside. He said to Atashak: "Go in and bring her out."

Atashak, trembling with excitement, replied: "I'm too nervous."

Samak said: "All right, I'll go in first." He quietly opened the door and entered the chamber. The room was lined with elegant musical instruments, many covered with gold leaf and precious jewels. Samak chose several, carefully placed them inside a chest that was sitting against one of the walls, and brought the chest out to Atashak.

Atashak asked in confusion: "What are you doing?"

Samak replied: "These will make good souvenirs for Khorshid Shah." He then went back inside the chamber, went to Delaram and gently shook her.

Delaram opened her eyes. Seeing a strange man clad in armor, she opened her mouth to scream. Samak said: "Don't be afraid! I won't hurt you. My name is Samak and I have come to take you to Atashak, who is madly in love with you."

When Delaram heard Atashak's name, she became calmer. She knew that Atashak was in love with her, because he had often told her so, but she had never considered him as someone that would interest her. She made a sudden lunge to escape. Samak held her down and quickly tied her hands and feet together.

Delaram said: "You don't have to tie me up. I'll go with you wherever you want."

Samak replied: "I'd like to take your word for that, but I have no choice." He took a cloth and covered her mouth.

He brought Delaram outside to Atashak. Seeing her bound and gagged, Atashak became nervous and said: "Please don't tie her up like that! She might suffocate."

Samak assured him: "My friend, you have many things to worry about. I promise that's not one of them." He tied the lasso around the chest of musical instruments and told Atashak to pull it. Atashak tried, but he could not pull the chest.

He told Samak: "I'm not strong enough."

Samak said: "Is there anything you *can* do?" and pulled the chest himself.

Samak threw the rope up and lassoed a crenellation on the battlement above them. He tested it to make sure it would hold, then climbed the rope to the top of the wall and pulled the chest up after him.

Looking down from the battlement, he saw Atashak below, kneeling on the ground, kissing Delaram's tied-up hands and feet and begging her forgiveness. Samak threw a pebble at Atashak's head and said: "An apology is not what your beloved needs from you!" He tossed the end of the lasso down to Atashak. "Tie her with this and I'll pull her up."

Atashak jumped to his feet and tied Delaram to the end of the lasso. Samak pulled her up to the top of the battlement.

Atashak looked up, expecting Samak to throw the rope down to him next. Instead, Samak looked down from the battlement and ordered: "Now go and take Delaram's place at her job!"

Atashak became alarmed and exclaimed: "What are you saying? I don't know how to serve wine! They'll kill me!"

Samak said sternly: "If you have so little confidence in yourself, how can you deserve to be with this girl the king trusts so much that he's willing to drink wine from her hand? It doesn't seem like a good match to me. I think I'd better leave you here."

Atashak, now completely terrified, begged Samak: "Don't leave me here. I'll do anything you ask!" Samak started laughing. He threw down the lasso and pulled Atashak up. When Atashak reached the top, he said reproachfully: "O brother! Is this what you call helping me?"

Samak laughed again and said: "O brother, I was only testing you. You know I'll protect you forever."

Atashak thanked him and said: "You had me scared! Let's get out of here before you change your mind."

Samak said: "We can't go back the way we came."

Atashak asked: "Why not?"

Samak replied: "Those two brothers, Behzad and Razmyar, have been following us ever since we left the ayyars' compound. I expect they're waiting for us below and planning to kill us. I didn't mention it before, since you were nervous enough to begin with. We'd better go down a different part of the wall." Atashak agreed.

They moved to another part of the battlement, Samak taking care to avoid being spotted by the guards, until they found a place where the ground below them lay in complete darkness. Samak tied one end of the lasso to a crenellation and carefully lowered first Atashak, then the chest of musical instruments, then Delaram, and finally descended the rope himself and pulled the lasso down after him.

Once they were outside the royal compound, Atashak asked Samak: "Where do we go now?"

Samak said: "O brother! I thought you knew your way around this town. I see you're more lost here than I am. Pick up your beloved and follow me!"

Samak picked up the chest and started walking. Atashak followed, carrying Delaram, and wondering where Samak was going.

Samak stopped at the entrance to an alley. He turned to Atashak and said: "Leave Delaram with me. Go into that alley and knock at the first door on your left. Say: 'It's me, Atashak, and I'm here with Samak the ayyar.'"

Surprised, Atashak asked: "You know the people in that house?"

Samak replied: "It's Khomar's house."

Atashak became even more surprised and said: "I'm a native of this town and I don't know Khomar. How do *you* know him, and how do you know where he lives?"

Samak laughed again and said: "Khomar is the old man we met in the bathhouse. When I told him we were strangers here, he gave me his address and invited us to stay with him."

Atashak followed Samak's instructions and went into the alley. While he was gone, Samak untied Delaram and reassured her that she was safe.

Atashak found the door and knocked, saying: "It's me, Atashak." The door was opened by the old man from the bathhouse. He stared at Atashak without recognizing him. Atashak repeated: "I am Atashak, Samak's servant."

Khomar laughed then and said: "Forgive me, I did not recognize you with clothes on. Where is Samak?"

Samak's voice said from the darkness: "Here I am, Khomar! Is your invitation still good?" Khomar looked in the direction of the sound and saw Samak in the dim moonlight standing with Delaram. Khomar smiled, walked toward Samak and gave him a hug, then helped Samak and Atashak bring Delaram and the chest into his house.

Khomar's wife and daughters took Delaram to the women's quarters to make her comfortable. Khomar took Samak and Atashak to a large room where they sat drinking and eating while Delaram slept, and Samak told him the whole story from the time they left the bath house. After that, they were all tired and went to sleep.

19

THE BROTHERS

BEHZAD and Razmyar waited all night outside the royal compound. When the sky grew light and Samak and Atashak had not returned, they went back home. There they changed their clothes, then returned to the palace to try to find out what had happened to Samak and Atashak.

In the palace garden, Behzad and Razmyar encountered Armen Shah's vizier, Shahran, looking distressed. He told them that the king's wine attendant, Delaram, had vanished in the night along with several valuable musical instruments, and added: "Since your father, Kanun, is out of town, I count on you two to help us catch the thieves."

Behzad and Razmyar assured the vizier that they would. They did not mention that Samak had already been their guest, out of fear that the king would blame them for letting him slip through their fingers. They returned to their headquarters, gathered the ayyars, and told them what had happened. The ayyars split up into groups of ten and spread out through the town, questioning every man and woman as they searched for Delaram and the stolen instruments.

Khomar returned from his morning errands looking worried and told Samak that the city was filled with search parties of ayyars looking for Delaram. Samak said: "There's nothing to worry about. Let's relax and celebrate." Khomar called for wine, and they started drinking. Two of Khomar's sons, Saber and Samlud, soon joined them. Atashak, after a few drinks, started enthusiastically telling everyone about Samak's exploits.

Samak said: "Atashak, don't admire me too much, or you'll build up my ego! Most of what I've done has been in the dark, when it's easy to hide. Now, a *real* challenge would be to go in broad daylight to the ayyar headquarters and seize Kanun's sons, who are leading the search for me."

They all stared at Samak. Atashak asked: "Are you serious?"

Samak responded: "I'm dead serious."

Atashak said: "Everyone in town is looking for you. You'll be captured the moment you step outside."

Samak said: "Atashak, you don't know me yet. Wait and see!" He told Khomar to borrow some clothes from his wife and daughters. Khomar went to the women's quarters of his house and came back with a dress, a scarf, a shawl, and a pair of shoes.

Samak got dressed, called for Delaram, and told her: "Make me look pretty!" Delaram put rouge on his cheeks, collyrium in his eyes, kohl on his lashes, and dabbed him with a few drops of musk.

Samak left Khomar's house and walked to the central bazaar. The people he passed saw a tall, solidly built woman, with feminine charm and beauty that could be perceived through her veil. Samak meandered through several bazaars, looking for Kanun's two sons, until he ran across Behzad in an alley.

As Samak passed Behzad, he brushed his shoulder against the warrior's as if by accident, and continued on his way, leaving a fragrant trail of musk. After a few steps, Samak glanced back at Behzad, who was mesmerized. Behzad told himself: "If that woman looks back a second time, I'll know that she bumped into me on purpose, and that she wants me." Notice that one glance from a beautiful woman was all it took to make this warrior forget the purpose that had brought him to that alley.

After Samak took a few more steps, he looked back again. This time he winked at Behzad. Behzad was hooked, and began following the enticing woman and her intoxicating scent. Samak kept going, looking back every now and then to charm Behzad. When Samak reached the entrance to the alley, he stopped and fanned his face with his sleeve as if he were overheated. This gave Behzad time to catch up to him.

Samak, in a soft and sweet voice, asked coyly: "What do you want? Why are you following me?"

Behzad became more excited. He asked: "O lovely lady, would you like to share your beauty with me for an hour or two? My home is nearby. I can serve you a cool refreshing drink and we can get out of this heat."

Samak replied: "I'm not the kind of girl you seem to think! I don't speak to strangers in the street."

Now Behzad felt sure he had her. He told himself that her soft voice and flirtatious eyes did not match her stern words. He said: "Beautiful lady, I would never compare you with any other woman or look at you the way other men do. I am only inviting you to relax and have lunch with me as my guest. Afterwards, you can go wherever you want."

Samak thought: "I'd better not stretch this any further, or the bow might break!" He smiled and said: "You are such a persistent man, it wouldn't be fair for me to ignore your friendliness. Where do you live?"

Behzad replied: "Behind the wheat sellers' bazaar."

Samak said: "That's far to walk on such a hot day. My house is closer and no one is there now. Why don't we go there?"

Behzad could think of nothing but having this woman in his arms. He said: "As you wish! I want you to be happy."

Samak walked in front, Behzad following him, until they reached Khomar's alley. From the second-story window of the house, Atashak and Khomar saw Behzad and Samak approaching. Khomar rushed downstairs, unlatched the entrance door, and hurried back upstairs.

Samak opened the door and led Behzad inside into the courtyard. As Behzad stepped close to take him in his arms, Samak turned and removed the scarf from the lower portion of his face. When Behzad saw his beard, he jumped back in alarm. "Who are you?" he demanded.

Samak responded: "Don't you recognize your friend Samak? Last night you and your brother followed me to the royal compound. You've been looking for me all day. Here I am!"

Behzad drew his sword, but it was too late. Samak spun him around and held him tight. Atashak and Khomar's sons hurried in and tied Behzad up, all the while expressing amazement at how Samak had caught him.

Samak said: "The scent of a lioness traps fearless lions. Now watch and see how I'll catch Behzad's brother!"

Samak took off his female garb and asked Khomar to bring him a cloak and a hat. He put on the cloak, placed the hat on his head, and pulled it down to cover his eyebrows. Then he asked for a cask of good vintage wine and a small golden cushion. When these were brought to him, Samak placed the cushion on his head, the wine cask on top of it, and left the house, staggering as if he were drunk. He set out for the bazaar in search of Razmyar.

Samak found Razmyar in the potions and herbs bazaar. Lurching as he walked, balancing the wine cask on his head, he came toward Razmyar, saying in a drunken voice: "O great ayyar! I've been looking for you everywhere. This wine is so good, you're the only one in town who can appreciate it. Come, let's finish this cask together!"

Razmyar looked at Samak suspiciously. He was about to refuse, when Samak lifted the cask from his head and offered him a taste. Razmyar took a sip and had to admit the wine was excellent. Samak, slurring his words, said: "It would be a great honor for me to tell people I drank with Razmyar, the greatest hero in Machin."

Razmyar's ego swelled on hearing this. He thought: "It would be silly to pass up such good wine when it comes so easily." He said: "I have important business, but I won't refuse your kindness. I'll come with you for a short while." They walked together until they reached Khomar's house.

One of Khomar's sons, watching the alley from the second-story window, called to the others. They were amazed to see Samak return with Razmyar after such a short time.

Samak entered the house with Razmyar and led him to the terrace. Razmyar was startled to see his brother Behzad tied up on the floor. He cried: "My brother, who did this to you?"

Behzad responded: "The same man who brought you here!" As Razmyar turned, Samak grabbed him. Atashak and Khomar's sons rushed in, bound Razmyar hand and foot, and laid him next to his brother.

Now that the brothers were captured, Atashak took Samak aside and asked him: "May I now have Delaram, as you promised?"

Samak said: "Atashak, this is a thing that can't be rushed. It's not as easy as you think. Consider the prince of Persia and the princess of Chin. Look how long they've been in love, and how long they've waited for the proper moment when they can hold each other's hand in marriage. If they can be patient, so can you. Or do you think you're more important than they are?"

Atashak admitted that he was not.

Samak explained: "I promised you Delaram would be yours, and she will be. But you must not touch her until I find out how she feels about being married to you. To marry a woman who has no interest in you is like trying to grab fire with your hand. You could get badly burned."

Atashak said: "I hear your wisdom and will follow your command."

They spent the rest of the day enjoying each other's company while celebrating Samak's triumph in a foreign city.

20

ENEMY AGENTS

Bograi Valley was a large territory controlled by the Bograi family. When Arghonun left to join Khorshid Shah in war, he left the valley in the hands of his uncle Lord Bograi, the family's elderly patriarch. It was to Lord Bograi that he sent the prisoners of war—the champion Qatran, general Salim, and the vizier Mehran—to be guarded.

Shortly after placing the prisoners under guard according to his nephew's instructions, Lord Bograi was informed that two men had arrived in the valley with a considerable cargo of wine barrels. After paying their respects to Lord Bograi, the merchants requested his permission to sell their wine to the valley's residents.

The "wine merchants" were, of course, Kanun and Kafur.

Lord Bograi, accepting their story, ordered the wine barrels evaluated and weighed in order to determine a fair price. While this was being done, he invited the merchants to join him for food and wine.

As they sat eating and drinking, Kanun remarked that he was happy to see the splendors of Bograi Valley first-hand, since he had heard so much about it. Lord Bograi immediately summoned a servant, Samron, and told him to take the newcomers around to show them the valley.

Samron took Kanun and Kafur on a horseback tour of the valley, pointing out various sights. Kanun noticed a stone castle perched atop a green and lushly forested hill. The main entrance had two guards posted on either side of a massive iron gate; the lower level of the castle had no windows or other openings.

Kanun asked Samron: Who lives in that castle?" Samron replied that it was the residence of Lord Bograi's nephew, Lord Arghonun, but that since Arghonun was away at war, it was temporarily being used to house prisoners.

Kanun remarked: "It might have been built for that purpose. It looks impregnable!" Samron agreed.

Kanun could guess who was imprisoned in the castle. To make sure, he asked: "What prisoners could be so dangerous as to be worth these pains in such a secure and well-governed valley?" Samron explained that they were two warriors from Machin by the names of Qatran and Salim, as well as Faghfur Shah's vizier Mehran.

Kanun said nothing more. He had his answer.

After spending the rest of the day being guided through the valley, Kafur and Kanun were taken to a guest house to sleep and rest.

Shortly after midnight, Kanun awakened Kafur. The ayyars slipped out of the guest house and headed for Arghonun's castle in the light of the full moon. Climbing the hill, they separated, taking separate pathways around the castle wall so that they approached the entrance from opposite sides.

When Kanun came within twenty yards of the entrance, he let out a wolf howl. The two guards turned toward the sound. This placed their backs to Kafur, who had crept up on the other side of the gate. Kafur jumped the closest guard from behind and swiftly dispatched him with his dagger. He then let out a wolf howl of his own. As the other guard turned toward Kafur, Kanun leapt on him from behind, and ended the man's life before he had time even to cry out.

Kanun and Kafur dragged the guards' bodies into the shadows, removed their armor and helmets, and put them on themselves. They opened the gate and entered the main courtyard.

The castle was quiet, everyone asleep. Kanun and Kafur explored until they found an iron trap door set into the ground, locked with a large padlock. Kafur used the tip of his dagger to pick the lock. He lifted the trap door, exposing steep stone steps.

Kanun and Kafur descended the steps into a basement originally built to store the castle's food supplies. Qatran, Salim, and Mehran lay asleep on the stone floor. They awoke with a start. Kanun said: "Do not be afraid. I am Kanun and my friend is Kafur. We have come from Machin's army camp to free you and take you back to Prince Gezelmalek."

The three prisoners were happy to hear these words. Kanun and Kafur used their daggers to break the chains on the men's feet, but left their hands chained while they led them up out of the basement into the courtyard. Kanun cautioned them: "Act as if you are still prisoners."

Sure enough, two guards were waiting in the courtyard above. They had heard noises and come to investigate. Seeing Kanun and Kafur emerge from the trap door with the prisoners, the guards drew their swords in alarm. Kanun smoothly explained that he and Kafur had been sent by Lord Bograi to bring the prisoners to be executed at dawn.

The guards believed Kanun's story so completely that when Kanun asked for three horses to be brought from the stables, they hurried to obey. So it was that Kanun and Kafur rode out of Bograi Valley, headed for Machin's army camp with the three prisoners, before dawn had broken.

By the time the sun rose in the sky, all five riders were tired. Kanun guided them to a meadow out of the line of sight of the main road and let the prisoners rest while he and Kafur took turns guarding them.

In the afternoon they mounted their horses and continued their journey. They rode long into the night over mountainous roads. Near midnight they reached a peak from which they could see an army campground with dozens of tents, horses, and hundreds of sleeping soldiers. Although the camp was lit only by moonlight and a few watchmen's torches, General Salim's experienced eye quickly told him that this was a division of Khorshid Shah's army under the command of generals Siahgil and Saum of Chin.

"This is good luck for us," said Qatran. "I won't go back to Prince Gezelmalek empty-handed." He told Salim and Kanun to ride down the slope on the right-hand side of the hill, while he and Kafur rode down the left-hand side, leaving Mehran the vizier alone on the peak. As soon as the four warriors reached the campground, they drew their swords and began to slaughter the sleeping soldiers.

The men of Chin woke up in confusion amid shouts and alarms to find many of their comrades already lying dead. They rushed to grab weapons, not knowing whom to fight. The four attackers shouted: "Long live Armen Shah! Long live Gezelmalek!" as they galloped through the camp, slaying all about them. So great was the chaos that warriors of Chin attacked each other in the darkness, unable to tell friend from foe.

In the tumult of the battle, Qatran and Siahgil came face to face. The two warriors fought on horseback until Qatran's spear knocked Siahgil from his saddle. Qatran dismounted and was starting to tie up Siahgil as his prisoner when Saum charged at him on horseback, swinging his sword. Qatran dodged and turned to face Saum on foot. What could have been a mighty combat between two champions went no further because at that moment, Salim rode up behind Saum and struck him with his mace so hard that the general and his horse both tumbled to the ground.

Salim jumped from his saddle. Together he and Qatran tied up the two Chin generals and slung them over two horses. "Let's go!" shouted Qatran. He rode from the battlefield, followed by Kanun, Kafur, and Mehran, leaving chaos behind them. Hundreds of men lay dead, the soldiers of Chin's army leaderless and not knowing who had attacked them or that the battle was already over.

The next morning, Khorshid Shah was notified about the night ambush and that his generals Siahgil and Saum had disappeared. He raged and blamed himself for not having kept the entire army on alert. His frustration increased when he realized that the attackers had been only a handful of people. He was still trying to figure out who these men could have been when the servant Samron arrived from Bograi Valley bringing the news that Qatran, General Salim, and Mehran the vizier had escaped from Arghonun's fortress.

Khorshid Shah called Arghonun and Shaghal to his pavilion and demanded to know how such a thing could have happened. Samron recounted the story of the arrival of the two wine merchants in Bograi Valley and the prisoners' escape and disappearance that same night. Shaghal exclaimed: "Kanun is behind this. This is the kind of trickery we can expect from the ayyars of Machin!"

Meanwhile, Kanun, Kafur, and the freed prisoners arrived at Machin's army camp and went straight to Gezelmalek's pavilion. Gezelmalek was delighted to learn of their escape and of the previous night's surprise rout. Following Qatran's suggestion, he ordered the captive Chin generals, Siahgil and Saum, sent directly to Armen Shah in Machin, guarded by two hundred soldiers.

Mehran bowed to Gezelmalek and said: "Your Highness, I am no warrior. My presence here is of little use. I beg you to send me to Machin as well to serve His Majesty your father." Gezelmalek agreed and the convoy started their journey toward Machin.

Qatran, eager for battle, asked Gezelmalek if he would order the army to resume the combat. Gezelmalek agreed.

The next morning at dawn, horns and drums were sounded, calling the army to line up for battle. When Khorshid Shah heard the call, he ordered Chin's army to line up as well. Within a short time, both armies came face to face.

The first warrior to enter the battlefield was Qatran, in full armor and riding an armored gray horse. He rode up and down before the row of Chin's warriors, brandishing a spear, and shouted: "O Khorshid Shah! Are you so afraid of us, that you abduct our heroes while they sleep? A cowardly fox can surprise a sleeping lion. Are there no lions in your forest, only foxes?"

Qatran continued these taunts until one of Khorshid Shah's warriors rode into the combat arena on a black horse, shouting: "A lion wouldn't brag so much!" Qatran took one look at the warrior and laughed out loud. He raised his spear and struck the warrior in the chest, knocking him off his horse.

Qatran turned again to the line of soldiers and shouted: "Where is Samak, the thief who kidnaps people in their sleep? Come out, if you dare face me now that I am awake!"

A second warrior entered the field and met the same fate as the first. Within a short time, sixteen warriors from Chin's army had been felled by Qatran. No one else dared come forward.

Qatran shouted: "O Khorshid Shah, send me a warrior who can withstand me longer than a minute! Where is your beloved Farokhruz? If he is afraid, why don't you fight me yourself and show me what kind of man you are!"

When Khorshid Shah saw no one else moving to fight Qatran, he spurred his own horse to attack. Farokhruz blocked his way, saying: "You won't enter the battlefield while I am alive. Better for a thousand of us to get killed than for you to lose one hair from your head. Out of all of us, you're the only one that can't be replaced." After saying that, Farokhruz rode toward Qatran, shouting: "Who are you to think you're worthy to stand before Khorshid Shah? Let's see how much of a fighter you are!"

The two warriors lifted their spears and began battling, but neither could defeat the other. When darkness fell and both were still standing, they decided to cease their fight until next morning.

21

RESCUE FROM TORTURE

WHILE the armies of Khorshid Shah and Gezelmalek faced each other across the battlefield, the convoy led by Mehran the vizier began its journey toward Machin.

Samak was at home in Khomar's house when his host rushed in to tell him the news he had just heard in town—Mehran and two hundred soldiers were on their way to Machin with two captured generals of Chin. Armen Shah had sent his own vizier, Shahran, with a delegation to welcome them at the city gates. Hearing this, Samak became concerned. None of what he had heard sounded like good news for Khorshid Shah. He said: "I need to see this with my own eyes."

Khomar warned Samak that it was too dangerous for him to go out in public when everyone was looking for him. Samak responded: "Don't worry. Fetch me an old robe, a hat, and a donkey." Khomar returned with the items Samak requested.

Samak put on the old robe and hat, placed a peasant's saddlebag on the donkey's back, and rode the animal to Machin's main gate, where the welcoming party was bringing the newcomers into the city. Acting like a peasant, Samak took the donkey's bridle in his hand and stood unnoticed in the crowd watching the procession.

The two viziers, Mehran and Shahran, appeared first at the head of the procession, dressed in fine robes and waving to the crowd from horseback. After them followed Saum and Siahgil, chained to their horses with heavy shackles, their bodies covered with dried blood. Seeing those two great Persian generals in that condition brought tears to Samak's eyes. Overcome by rage and sorrow, he left the scene and returned to Khomar's house.

Samak called Khomar's two sons, Saber and Samlud, to him and said: "Go quickly to the palace. Tell me everything you see and hear." The two brothers hurried to the king's palace. They joined the crowd of nobles in the royal court, where Armen Shah sat proudly on his throne awaiting the procession's arrival.

The viziers Shahran and Mehran soon arrived at the court. Mehran bowed down to the king. Armen Shah welcomed him and seated the vizier in a place of honor near his own throne. The guards brought generals Saum and Siahgil into the court in chains, barefoot, bareheaded, and covered in blood.

Mehran spoke up: "Your Majesty, these men are enemies of Machin. I believe their actions against Your Highness justify the most severe punishment."

Armen Shah frowned and said: "If my son Gezelmalek wanted these generals executed, why did he send them to me alive?"

Mehran answered: "The prince did this out of respect for Your Majesty's greatness, so that you could personally order and witness their execution."

Armen Shah looked with pity at the two chained generals, and said: "It is not in our interest to put an end to the lives of these two great Persian heroes. They have suffered hardships to be where they are. We will keep them prisoner until we are free of the problems that we are presently facing."

Mehran said: "I wish Your Majesty nothing but joy and happiness! I am your lowly servant and always available to eliminate anything that might disturb Your Greatness."

Armen Shah said: "As a matter of fact, there is something that troubles me. A week ago, my wine attendant Delaram vanished and cannot be found. Two sons of Kanun, the ayyar who freed you from your detention, have gone missing as well."

Mehran turned pale. He said with agitation: "Your Majesty, I swear by your crown that the man responsible for these disappearances is none other than Samak the ayyar. He is a danger to society. It was Samak who kidnapped the great warrior Qatran out of an army of thirty thousand soldiers. If Samak is now in this city, Your Majesty can be sure he will seek a way to release these two Persian generals from captivity."

Armen Shah said: "Dear Mehran, have no fear on that account. We have a prison here in Machin that no one can break into. My jail keeper and his guards are so vigilant that not even birds can fly over the prison undetected." The king ordered the jail keeper, whose name was Tarmashe, to be brought to him.

Within a short while, Tarmashe arrived at the royal court. A massive, powerfully built eunuch, he gave the impression of being sexually drawn to neither men nor women—he considered both his enemies. Tarmashe bowed deeply to the king.

Armen Shah pointed to the two chained generals and told Tarmashe: "These men were captured from Faghfur Shah's army. I want you to guard them with special attention. There is an ayyar at large in this city who I believe kidnapped my wine maiden Delaram and Kanun's sons. He may attempt to free these prisoners as well."

Tarmashe bowed again and said: "No one has ever escaped from my prison and no one will. Your Majesty can be sure that if all the ayyars and night-crawlers of the world came together, they could not remove even one stone from inside its walls." He then took the generals away, escorted by two dozen royal guards.

It was Tarmashe's custom to welcome every new prisoner with fifty lashes on the back. As a result of this treatment, some died within days of their arrival, while those who lived took long painful months to recover. Saum and Siahgil were no exception. Upon reaching the prison, Tarmashe took the generals to the torture chamber, tied their hands and feet to the walls, and ordered his men to give them fifty lashes.

After the first lash, Siahgil shouted: "We are soldiers, not thieves! Why are we being tortured?"

Tarmashe laughed and answered: "To me a soldier is the same as a thief. My rule is my rule." And he ordered the guards to lash them even harder.

Blood streamed down the two generals' backs. On the third lash, Saum fainted. Still the guards went on whipping him. Siahgil screamed with pain on each stroke until he too passed out.

Khomar's sons Saber and Samlud, who had seen the generals taken away by Tarmashe, rushed home and relayed the sad news to Samak. When they told him about Tarmashe's reputation and his prison, Samak wept in despair.

Then he made himself calm. Once his mind was clear, he asked: "What measures are they taking to find me? And by the way, where is Mehran staying?"

Saber reported: "Before we left the court, we heard Mehran advise Armen Shah to place extra guards at every intersection and alley, as well as at the city gates, and announce a curfew throughout the city. Anyone who appears on the streets after dusk will be arrested."

Samlud added: "Mehran is so afraid of you that he begged the king to house him within the royal compound, with a special detachment of bodyguards to watch him day and night."

Samak said: "Afraid of me? I can't imagine why."

Samak thanked Khomar's sons for their good work. Then he thought for a long time. When the sun dipped below the horizon, he turned to Atashak and said: "We'll bring back the generals tonight. Get ready."

They waited until after midnight to leave the house. Saber and Samlud guided Samak and Atashak through a warren of culverts, ditches, and sewers, keeping to the shadows and out of the night watchmen's sight until they reached the main city prison.

Samak saw that the prison walls were built of solid stone with no windows or openings anywhere. He said to Saber and Samlud: "Stay out of sight while Atashak and I look around."

Saber and Samlud hid in a ditch while Samak and Atashak explored the darkness looking for a way into the prison. After an hour, they still had found no leads. Samak lassoed himself onto the roof of a nearby house and pulled Atashak up after him. The two crept across the rooftops until they reached a building about two hundred yards from the prison. Samak suddenly became attentive and started exploring the rooftop in detail.

"What is this place?" asked Atashak in confusion.

Samak replied: "By the look of it, I'd say it used to be a bathhouse." He continued exploring until he discovered a dust-covered skylight. It was a thin, translucent layer of onyx. Samak removed the onyx and the two lassoed down into the main hall of the bathhouse below.

The bathhouse was abandoned and in disrepair. Samak lit a torch from the wall, and with its light he soon located the well that had once provided water for the bath. He instructed Atashak: "Wait here. I'll go down and see if it's still connected to a water channel." He tied one end of his lasso to a nearby column and, carrying the lit torch, lowered himself into the dry well.

On reaching the bottom, Samak noticed a large stone set into the floor. He placed the torch in a wall holder and moved the rock to one side. A draft of cool air blew up from a hole under the stone. Samak lowered the torch down into the hole and saw its light reflected in the moving water below. It was an underground water channel flowing from the direction of the prison.

Samak shouted up to Atashak: "Wait for me!" He dropped down through the hole and landed waist-deep in cold, rushing water. He waded up the channel, against the current, until the torchlight revealed an open shaft above him. Bracing hands and feet against the shaft's damp stone walls, he climbed to the top. The top of the shaft was blocked by a large stone slab. Samak used all his might to push the slab aside, and climbed out into the prison's courtyard.

Moonlight spread across the empty courtyard. Samak crept through the shadows until his ears made out a faint, distant moan. He followed the moaning and soon found a man lying on the ground, badly beaten and covered with blood. Seeing Samak, the man croaked from a dry throat: "Water!" Samak was shocked to recognize Siahgil.

"Siahgil!" Samak cried. "What have they done to you?" He looked around in the dark until he spotted a ewer hanging on a wall. He brought it back and poured some water into Siahgil's throat, cradling the general's head in his arms. After a few minutes, Siahgil regained enough of his strength to look up at Samak and rasp: "Who are you?"

Samak responded: "O great general, I am your servant Samak."

Siahgil was happy to hear this, but asked in bewilderment: "What are you doing in this place?"

Samak said: "All I can tell you is that I was guided here by God. Do you know where the jailer is?" Siahgil explained that he had been unconscious and did not even know his own whereabouts.

He thought Saum must be in the same prison, but he could not say where.

Samak crept down the corridor until he found a prison guard dozing at his post. He drew his dagger, leapt on the guard and swiftly dispatched him.

Samak then searched until he found Saum lying on the floor, almost drowned in his own blood. Samak placed a hand on the general's chest and heard him croak: "Water!" Samak poured water into his mouth, patiently, a little at a time. Soon Saum's eyes opened. Seeing Samak, he asked: "Are you a man or an angel?"

Samak introduced himself and promised to explain everything once they were in a safe place. He lifted Saum in his arms and carried him to where Siahgil was lying. "I'll take you out one at a time," he said. Lifting Siahgil on his back, he climbed down the shaft, through the water channel, and pushed the general up through the hole onto the dry floor of the bath-house well.

The lasso was dangling just as he had left it. Samak tied Siahgil to the lasso's end and called to Atashak above: "Pull it up!" Atashak tried, but struggled helplessly with the general's weight until Saber and Samlud fortunately arrived to help. Together they pulled Siahgil up into the abandoned bath-house hall.

Once Siahgil was safe, Samak returned to the prison and brought Saum back the same way. It was nearly dawn by the time the four rescuers and the wounded generals were reunited on the rooftop beside the broken bath-house skylight.

They now faced a new challenge: How to transport the prisoners to safety without being seen, with the entire city on alert?

22

NEW FRIENDS

WHILE Samak, Saber, and Samlud tried to think of a place to take the wounded generals, Atashak suddenly remarked: "My godmother lives in this neighborhood!"

Samak wondered aloud: "If that's so, why didn't you mention her the night we abducted Delaram?"

Atashak said: "I'd been away from the city so long, I didn't think of her. I guess I was so excited to be with Delaram, my mind wasn't working properly."

Samak said dryly: "Thank God Delaram isn't with us now." He continued: "Do you think you could find her house in the dark from the rooftops?"

Atashak responded: "I'll try."

Samak lifted the injured Saum onto his back, while Khomar's sons carried Siahgil between them. They followed Atashak across the rooftops in the moonlight, taking care to stay out of sight of the streets and courtyards below, until Atashak exclaimed: "That courtyard there! That's my godmother's house."

Atashak advanced to the edge of the rooftop and tossed pebbles down into the courtyard until an old woman stepped out and looked up. She jumped back in fear and shouted: "Who are you? What do you want? I'll call the guards to arrest you!"

Atashak whispered loudly: "Mother! It's me, your godson Atashak!"

The old woman frowned and asked suspiciously: "What would Atashak be doing on my roof at this time of night?"

Atashak stepped into the moonlight so his godmother could see his face. He said: "I'll explain later. Right now, please open the door to the roof. I have friends with me, and two of them are hurt."

The old lady rushed inside. Moments later, she unlocked a door that opened onto the rooftop. A flight of steps led into the house below. As soon as she saw the two wounded generals, she stepped aside to let the men pass.

Samak, Saber, and Samlud carried the wounded men down the stairs into a back room, followed by Atashak and his godmother. They laid the generals on blankets that the old lady quickly arranged on the floor. By this time, the night's darkness had given way to the faint light of dawn.

Once everyone was safe inside, the old lady asked Atashak to explain. Atashak said: "Dear mother, this is Samak the ayyar. And these men are two great generals serving Prince Khorshid Shah, whom we have just freed from Tarmashe's dungeon."

The old lady was about to reply when they heard a knock at the front door. She said quickly: "That must be my son Sorkhvard, back from his night's work. All of you stay quiet while I let him in. I will take him directly to his room so that he does not know you are here." Saying that, she crossed the courtyard to the front door of the house.

Samak peered around the edge of the doorway, curious to see who might be arriving at such an early hour. He saw the old lady open the front door on the far side of the courtyard. A slim young man entered, clad in a large hat and dark cloak. He opened his cloak, letting its contents—a number of garments, hats and shawls—fall to the floor. In a cheerful, pleasant voice, Sorkhvard said: "Mother, this is all I was able to gather tonight. Bring me some food—I'm starving!"

The old lady guided Sorkhvard to his room, near the front door, and hurried to the kitchen. Soon she emerged with a tray holding several loaves of flat bread, a bowl of stew, pickled vegetables, and cookies, which she took to Sorkhvard's room. Samak stepped further out into the courtyard to get a better look. The door to the bedroom was ajar. Through it, Samak saw the youth sitting on the floor. His mother placed the tray in front of Sorkhvard, sat down on the floor across from him, and they began eating together in a comfortable, casual way.

Samak found himself fascinated by the grace of Sorkhvard's movements. He thought: "This young man seems nimble and does things at night, like an ayyar." Seeing Sorkhvard wolf down three loaves of bread with stew in quick succession, Samak added to himself: "He also seems to have quite an appetite."

When the meal was finished, mother and son rinsed their hands. Sorkhvard leaned back against the wall, stretched out his legs on the floor, and remarked: "Mother, I heard something interesting last night. Armen Shah's guards are searching the city for an ayyar named Samak from Chin. People say he is a dangerous trickster who kidnapped the king's wine maiden and the sons of Kanun."

"Ah," remarked the old lady. "The guards are out in force! So that's why you were able to do so little hunting."

"Yes, but that doesn't matter," said the youth impatiently. "This Samak—if he's done the things they say, what a hero he must be! I'd give anything to meet him."

Overhearing this, Samak felt his heart beat faster, and wondered why.

"Why on earth would you want to meet such a person?" asked the old lady.

"O mother!" exclaimed Sorkhvard. "If I ever met Samak, I would beg him to accept me as his apprentice."

She asked sternly: "Are you sure that's what you would do? Wouldn't it be more profitable to turn him in to the king's constable for a reward?"

Sorkhvard exclaimed: "O mother! You have raised me to never reveal secrets to anyone. How could I betray a man like that? I swear, if I find Samak I will become his slave for the rest of my life!"

The old lady smiled, took Sorkhvard's face between her hands and said: "You make me so proud! Any mother would dream of having such a son. As a matter of fact, I happen to know where Samak is at this very moment." She left Sorkhvard's room, walked across the courtyard, opened the door to the room where Samak was hiding, and told him: "My son Sorkhvard wishes to meet you."

Samak stepped out into the courtyard. Sorkhvard stared in astonishment. Then he rushed to Samak and threw himself on the ground at his feet.

"Come on, that's no way for friends to meet!" said Samak. He reached out a hand, pulled Sorkhvard to his feet, and hugged him. Sorkhvard stiffened and ducked away awkwardly. Samak saw that the youth was blushing, so excited to be in Samak's presence that he could barely speak.

Sorkhvard turned to his mother, kissed her hands, and said joyfully: "O mother! Why didn't you tell me right away that Samak was here, instead of letting me babble on like a fool? What is this great hero doing in your house?"

The old lady said: "I'll let the great hero answer your questions himself. He arrived not long before you did."

Samak said: "Dear Sorkhvard, it's a long story that I will tell you later. Right now, I am concerned about my companions." Gesturing to the room behind him, Samak added: "These men are generals of Khorshid Shah's army. They've been badly treated and we must see to their wounds. And these are my Machin friends Atashak, Saber, and Samlud."

Sorkhvard and his mother hurried to heat up some water. After carefully washing the blood off the generals' bodies, Sorkhvard brought a jar of ointment and applied it to their wounds, then covered them with poultice. While Saum and Siahgil slept, Samak told the story of the night's excursion into Tarmashe's prison.

Sorkhvard brought a large earthenware jug of wine and they all drank to celebrate the rescue of the generals. By now, the sun had risen in the sky and the courtyard was filled with sunlight.

Samak turned to Saber and Samlud and said: "This might be a good time for you two to return to the royal court and see what's going on over there." They agreed and left the old lady's house immediately.

• • •

Shortly after Khomar's sons arrived at the palace, Tarmashe rushed in, threw himself on the floor before Armen Shah's throne, and said: "Your Highness, I beg your forgiveness. Have mercy on me! The generals have escaped."

The king jumped up in rage and shouted: "What? How is this possible?"

Tarmashe, pale and shaking with fear, responded: "O great king! The prison gate is intact and I can find no tunnel or hole anywhere. Yet my guard has been slain and the prisoners are gone. I cannot figure out what happened."

Armen Shah shouted angrily: "Did they fly away, or melt into the ground? Did jinn or fairies carry them off?" Tarmashe was unable to answer.

The silence was broken by Mehran the vizier, who bowed to the king and said: "Your Majesty, this is why I recommended that we execute the generals yesterday. With Samak around, nothing and no one is safe." He added: "If Your Majesty wishes, I will personally visit this prison and investigate to discover how the prisoners were taken away."

Armen Shah agreed. Mehran left for the prison with Tarmashe and several trusted courtiers.

Saber and Samlud hurried back to Samak and told him what they had seen and heard. Samak listened carefully, then turned to Sorkhvard's mother and said: "Bring me some beeswax, a handful of coal dust, and some flour."

Saber and Samlud wondered why. Samak told them: "So that you can meet your new Hindu slave. We're going back to Armen Shah's court. I'll make sure this Tarmashe pays for what he did to these brave men."

The old lady brought the requested items. Samak heated the beeswax, mixed it with coal dust, and rubbed it on his face and hands until his skin was dark. He then had Sorkhvard dust white flour onto his hair, mustache and eyebrows. Finally, he put on a used robe and shawl and wrapped a turban around his head. When he was finished, anyone would have taken him for a middle-aged Hindu.

Samak followed Saber and Samlud, acting like their slave, and the three men headed toward Armen Shah's palace.

They arrived just in time to see Mehran, Tarmashe, and their entourage returning from the prison discouraged. On Samak's suggestion, Khomar's sons maneuvered through the crowd of courtiers until they found themselves alongside Mehran. Saber tapped the vizier on the shoulder and whispered: "O vizier! Last night, after midnight, I saw Tarmashe leave the prison by the front gate."

Samlud added: "And I saw him meet two men who gave him a purse full of coins and took the prisoners away with them."

After saying this, Saber and Samlud melted back into the crowd.

When Mehran and Tarmashe reached Armen Shah's throne, the king demanded: "Did your investigation shed any light on this mystery?"

Before Tarmashe could reply, Mehran spoke up: "Your Majesty, the prison is indeed secure, as you said. I do not believe the prisoners could have escaped without the cooperation of Tarmashe himself. I have heard from a trusted source, which I cannot reveal, that he was well compensated for his help."

Hearing this, Tarmashe dropped to his knees. "Your Majesty! I swear by your head that this is false!"

Mehran snapped: "How dare you swear by His Majesty's head? We know you sold those prisoners. Confess, or it will be worse for you!"

Tarmashe looked around the court in terror at the sea of hostile faces. He cried: "It's not true!"

Armen Shah ordered the guards to whip Tarmashe until he revealed the truth.

The guards looked at each other. No one wanted to volunteer for the job. They could foresee that if Tarmashe was pardoned, the jailer would make sure whoever whipped him would pay dearly for it later.

Samak whispered into Samlud's ear. Samlud spoke up: "Your Majesty! If others are too afraid of this man to whip him as he deserves, let my Hindu slave do it."

Armen Shah gestured his agreement. On Samlud's command, Samak rolled up his sleeves, stepped forward, took the whip in hand, and began lashing Tarmashe with as much mercy as he had shown the generals. By the fifth lash, Tarmashe's clothes were in tatters, his back streaming with his own blood. He screamed: "Stop! I'll confess!"

On the king's command, Samak stopped lashing him. Tarmashe, in agony, admitted that on the night before, two men had indeed come to the prison and taken away the two generals. Under further prompting from the vizier, Tarmashe identified the men as two butcher brothers from the bazaar and said that they had paid him four hundred golden dinars.

Armen Shah ordered the butchers brought to the court. Within a short time, the guards returned with two husky men—identical twin brothers, with bloody hands and aprons, and no idea why they were there. The brothers knelt in front of Armen Shah's throne. The king demanded: "What have you done with the Persian generals?"

The brothers looked at each other in astonishment and did not know what to say. Finally, one of them dared to ask the king what he meant.

Tarmashe, in terror that he would be lashed again, screamed: "Tell them how you came to the prison last night and paid four hundred dinars for the prisoners!"

The brothers swore on the head of Armen Shah and on their honor that they were innocent. Tarmashe grabbed the whip and lashed them until blood ran down their backs, but still they swore they knew nothing.

The king turned to Mehran the vizier and asked his advice. Mehran said: "Let the brothers be taken to the bazaar and hanged in front of their own shop, so that the people see what punishment awaits those who disobey the royal command."

The constable and guards placed ropes around the two brothers' necks and took them to their shop in the butchers' bazaar. A crowd had gathered there, crying and weeping for the brothers, whom they knew as good, generous, and honest citizens.

While the executioners set up a gallows, the crowd's mood began to change from sorrow to anger. The constable realized he was in danger of facing a riot. He already felt unhappy about his assignment, for he had received generous gifts from the butcher brothers in the past. He climbed onto the gallows and faced the brothers, saying: "O free souls! His Majesty commanded your execution and I have no power to disobey him. But if you tell the honest truth now in front of all these people, I will go to the king and plead for mercy."

One of the brothers spoke up, saying: "O great constable! We swear to God that we are innocent. You know us, you know we are good people."

The other added: "If we had done what we are accused of, we would reveal it now, to free our souls before we die."

When the constable heard this, he realized that if he went ahead with the execution, he would never be able to forgive himself. He told the executioners: "Wait for me until I return. I will go to the king and ask him for a pardon. I pray it will be granted." Saying that, he mounted his horse and rode toward the palace through the crowd, which by now was cheering for him.

At the palace, the constable bowed before the throne of Armen Shah and said: "Your Majesty! I am sure the butcher brothers are innocent. The whole city is crying for them and cannot believe they committed this crime. Perhaps Tarmashe accused them for his own reasons. God knows I only wish well for Your Majesty. I fear that if these men are executed, the town will turn against you and we will have a riot."

Mehran the vizier, whose own suspicions had been growing, ordered Tarmashe brought again before the throne. He demanded sternly: "Tarmashe, if the butchers are innocent, do not let their deaths be on your conscience! Withdraw your false accusation. I think I know who really helped the prisoners escape. His name is Samak the ayyar, he is my sworn enemy, and I will not rest until he is captured."

When Tarmashe heard this, he turned to the king and said: "O great king! Forgive me. I could not stand the pain of the whipping, so I invented the story to end my suffering. I swear to God the two brothers are innocent."

Armen Shah shouted: "You are a disgrace! It's bad enough that you let my two prisoners escape. You would have had me execute these innocent men and turn my people against me?"

On the king's orders, the constable returned to the bazaar and announced the royal pardon. The crowd cheered and celebrated. The constable brought the two brothers to the court, where Armen Shah welcomed them and gave each of them gifts and a robe of honor. When the brothers left the palace, the road was lined with crowds cheering for them all the way back to the bazaar.

Tarmashe bowed once more to the king, and to Mehran the vizier, and begged their forgiveness. "Your Majesty, if you spare my life, I swear I will devote all my strength to finding and capturing this man Samak who broke into my prison." The king granted his request.

• • •

Tarmashe left the court and went straight back to the prison to investigate again, accompanied by a detachment of guards.

As thoroughly as they searched, they could find no sign of how Samak might have gained entrance. Then Tarmashe looked down into the well and asked for a rope.

Tarmashe tied the rope around his waist and lowered himself down into the well. When he saw the stream of running water, a suspicion began to form. He followed the stream. By the time he reached the abandoned bathhouse, he was certain that this was how the prisoners had escaped. He blamed himself for having overlooked the well, and wondered: "How could this ayyar, who is not even from this town, find a flaw in my prison so quickly?"

Tarmashe returned to the court and told the king about the passageway. "Samak! I knew it!" exclaimed Mehran.

Armen Shah ordered: "Let all the gates of the city be closed. No man or woman shall be allowed to leave until Samak, the generals, Delaram, and the sons of Kanun are found."

Samak, resting in Sorkhvard's house with Atashak, Siahgil and Saum, became cheerful when he heard the news. He said: "Now it's time to find Mehran the vizier and bring him back here, trussed from head to foot." Everyone laughed, and they began celebrating with food and wine.

While they were enjoying each other's company, Samak suddenly felt a sharp pain in his abdomen. The pain was so intense that he fell to the floor, groaning and rolling in agony. Neither Atashak, Siahgil, Saum, Sorkhvard nor his mother knew what to do to relieve Samak's pain and cure him.

SECTION 4

Falaki Fortress

23

AN OCEAN OF WARRIORS

On the morning after Farokhruz and Qatran fought their first battle, the two armies lined up once again to face each other across the field of combat.

The first to ride out was Qatran. Brandishing his spear, he shouted at Khorshid Shah's army: "Farokhruz! Where are you? Are you afraid of my crushing mace? Afraid to face a warrior greater than yourself? Is that why you are hiding in the middle of your army?"

Farokhruz cantered into the battlefield, shouting: "A warrior proves himself by deeds, not foolish insults! Let's see what you're made of!" He charged at Qatran with his spear.

The warriors battled fiercely until both their spears broke. Next, they used their maces, but still neither could defeat the other. Then they drew their swords and fought until the sun went down. When it became too dark to continue, they stopped fighting, and both armies went back to their camps to rest.

Khorshid Shah sent a message to Faghfur Shah: "O great king, thousands of warriors are now facing each other across the battlefield. With sorrow I inform you that your vizier Mehran, whom you sent for our support, betrayed us and caused much loss and anguish. He secretly arranged for the army of Machin to attack and plunder the convoy you sent us. With God's help we were able to defeat the enemy in combat. We captured Mehran, along with General Salim and Gezelmalek's greatest warrior, Qatran, and sent them to Bograi Valley in chains. Alas, enemy agents delivered them from captivity, and Qatran has returned to combat. We remain confident of victory, but these events have shaken the army's morale, and we wonder what will happen next."

When Faghfur Shah received this message, he dispatched couriers to every province of Chin, ordering his governors to send as many reinforcements as they could muster. Within days, forty-five thousand warriors from throughout Chin had gathered in the capital. On the king's orders, the doors to the royal storehouse were opened, and the warriors were supplied with arms.

As the army prepared to leave for the battlefield, the sound of distant drums and horns stopped everyone in their tracks. It was a horde so vast that the approaching thunder of men and horses shook the ground. When Faghfur Shah heard it, he turned pale and shivered in fear on his throne. His first thought was that one of the princes the witch nurse imprisoned had come back with an army to take Mahpari.

Scouts rushed into the royal court and told the king that a huge unknown army was setting up camp outside the city. Dignitaries and generals gathered at the palace to ask Faghfur Shah what they should do.

The king wrung his hands and bemoaned the situation: "With our army and our best warriors out fighting against Machin, how can we defend the city?" He ordered his adjutant, Nasur: "Go and find out who these people are and what they want with us!"

Nasur rode out of the city with fifty men. A mile away, they rode to the top of a steep hill and saw the valley below filled with soldiers setting up tents. Nasur looked out across the sea of warriors and saw, on the ridge of a plateau overlooking the valley, a man with a long white beard and hair, wearing a white silk robe and fine linen turban, seated on a white, long-maned Arabian horse covered with shining gold embroideries. A jeweled canopy and banner held above his head identified him as the commander. His face glowed in the sunlight. To Nasur he looked like a holy man.

The number of soldiers in the valley seemed to be increasing every moment. They were setting up tents and pavilions as if they planned to stay for a long time. Nasur's scouts returned saying that the army was neither from Chin nor Machin, nor any place they knew.

Soldiers, tents, and horses spread out as far as Nasur could see. It seemed to him as if all the people of the world had come together. As he watched, a pavilion of red satin was raised on the spot where he had seen the white-bearded man on the white horse.

Nasur rode toward the pavilion, accompanied by his entourage. A hundred yards away, they were stopped by a group of guards who politely ordered them to dismount, surrender their weapons, and behave with reverential silence. They did as they were told. The head guard asked them who they were and what their purpose was. Nasur responded: "We have been sent by Faghfur Shah, the king of Chin, to inquire who you are and your purpose in coming to this city."

The guard told them to wait. He soon returned, saying to Nasur: "You may enter the pavilion alone."

Nasur was led to the pavilion. Inside, it was decorated with gracious artifacts of master craftsmanship. The man with the white beard sat on a golden throne, surrounded by seven beautiful maidens and generals on elegant seats. Slaves, attendants, and royal guards stood at respectful attention, protecting the pavilion's occupants.

Nasur bowed upon entering, continued bowing as he approached the throne, kissed the ground, and offered polite greetings. He said: "Your Highness, with your permission, I have come to deliver a message from Faghfur Shah, the ruler of Chin."

The elder man gestured his permission. Nasur continued: "The king sends his greetings and asks where Your Highness and your army have come from; whether you are just passing through or planning to stay; and, finally, whether you are enemy or friend, so that we may respond appropriately."

The white-bearded man gestured to the guards to seat Nasur close to his own throne. When Nasur was seated, the man said: "O citizen of Chin, your king is not wise! He has no knowledge of how to rule a country." He looked at Nasur carefully to make sure he was listening, then continued: "A king should know what is happening in his domain. He should have trustworthy guards controlling every road, and ambassadors to report on events in the surrounding regions. What kind of ruler allows an army to reach his city gates before it occurs to him to wonder if they are friend or foe? That is no way to rule a kingdom! A ruler so neglectful deserves to be dethroned."

Nasur bowed and said: "Your Highness! Your remarks are wise. Our king, Faghfur Shah, is a peace lover who never attempts to conquer other lands, so we have no enemies and were not expecting to be attacked. This is why we were unaware your army had entered our territory until you reached our city gates and we heard your drums and horns. At that point we became concerned, fearing we might be under attack by a foreign army."

The man with the white beard said: "We are loyal subjects of our reigning prince Khorshid Shah, son of Marzban Shah, supreme ruler of Persia. I am the king's grand vizier Haman. Three years ago our prince journeyed from Halab to Chin to seek the hand of Faghfur Shah's daughter in marriage. He has not returned. Now the king has sent me to bring Khorshid Shah back—or, if any harm has come to him, to turn Chin into a vast cemetery."

Nasur said: "O great vizier! The prince is well and unharmed. He is engaged to the daughter of our king, Faghfur Shah, and is now commanding Chin's army."

At these words, everyone in the pavilion cheered with joy. Haman told Nasur to convey his reverences to Faghfur Shah and to inform him that he and his army of one hundred and thirty thousand men stood at Khorshid Shah's service.

Nasur stood up, bowed to the vizier, and left the pavilion with his entourage. When he reached the city, Nasur found the gates locked and reinforced from inside, with catapults at the ready and archers posted atop the walls. "Let us in!" he shouted. Recognizing Nasur, the guards opened the gates. Inside, citizens of Chin were setting up barriers and traps on every street to repel the invaders. Nasur cried: "Remove the barricades and replace them with flowers and decorations, for the army camped outside our walls is our own ally!" He continued shouting the same message, spreading joy throughout the city, until he reached the king's palace.

When Nasur entered the royal court and saw Faghfur Shah sitting in despair with dignitaries gathered around him, he went straight to the king, bowed and said: "I have great news for Your Majesty. The army outside our city walls is none other than the army of Marzban Shah, come to serve their crown prince Khorshid Shah. The grand vizier Haman sends his reverences to Your Majesty and lets you know that his army is at the prince's service."

Faghfur Shah exclaimed with joy and turned to his confidants, saying: "Thank God I did not execute Khorshid Shah when my vizier Mehran suggested it! You see how wise I was!"

Now that Faghfur Shah knew that the army outside the city was friendly, he decided to go and greet them himself. The king assembled an entourage of two thousand courtiers, noblemen, and attendants, and set out for Marzban Shah's army camp.

The vizier Haman rode out to welcome the delegation, accompanied by his leading generals. When Haman saw Faghfur Shah, he dismounted from his horse and ordered his generals to do the same. Seeing the vizier and his group approaching on foot, Faghfur Shah started to dismount from his own horse. But Haman rushed forward and kissed the king's stirrup, preventing him from dismounting. He then took the bridle of Faghfur Shah's horse and led it toward the pavilion with the others walking behind them.

Haman led Faghfur Shah to his throne and invited him to sit, while he remained standing. Faghfur Shah said: "Dear grand vizier! We are equal and I do not wish to be treated exceptionally. Please be seated and let us enjoy each other's companionship!" Haman followed the king's orders and sat on a seat next to him.

Faghfur Shah said: "Please tell us the purpose of your visit."

Haman paid his respects to the king and said: "Your Majesty, His Royal Highness Marzban Shah has sent me, and part of his army, with a personal letter to you." He took a sealed letter out of his robe and handed it politely to the king. Faghfur Shah kissed the letter, removed the seal, and returned the letter to the grand vizier so that he could read it out loud for everyone to hear.

Haman read: "In the name of the Lord of the Universe, this letter is from Marzban Shah, king of Persia and ruler of Halab, who is distressed and heartbroken by the absence of his only son, to Faghfur Shah, the supreme and just ruler of Chin. When you receive this letter, you will know that our son is the crown prince of Persia, a wise, educated, and powerful young man named Khorshid Shah. It was his destiny to fall in love with your daughter Mahpari and follow his heart's desire to journey to Chin to seek her hand in marriage.

"His departure darkened our days and took away our comfort. It was three years ago that he left us. Since then, we have been informed that our son has endured great anguish and hardships in order to unite with princess Mahpari. Although it grieves us to hear of his suffering, we do not feel it is advisable to blame Your Majesty, but must consider it his destiny.

"We demand that you immediately deliver Khorshid Shah, the light of our eyes, along with your daughter Mahpari, to our grand vizier Haman. If the head of our son is short by even one hair, we have commanded our troops to burn Chin to ashes. As God is our witness, if the hundred and thirty thousand warriors we have sent are not enough, we will send another three hundred thousand to raze your kingdom to the ground so that no one will ever know there was once a place called Chin."

When Faghfur Shah heard this letter, he thanked God once again that he had done no harm to Khorshid Shah. He told Haman: "O Grand Vizier! There was no need for my beloved brother to send us such a harsh message. I pray that even the wind does not blow dust on his face. Khorshid Shah is my own dear son, the light of my eyes. Our land has been attacked by the army of Machin, led by Gezelmalek, the son of Armen Shah, who wants my daughter Mahpari for himself. We have sent her to Shahak Fortress to be safe, and Khorshid Shah has voluntarily taken command of our army in the war against Machin."

When Haman heard this, he jumped up and ordered his generals to prepare the army to move. Faghfur Shah said: "O great vizier! You have traveled so far. Stay and rest with us a while. Let us show you our hospitality. We have also gathered about forty-five thousand warriors who can accompany you to help Khorshid Shah."

Haman said: "Your Majesty, we have not been sent here for sightseeing. Our orders are to find Khorshid Shah and place ourselves at his service. To delay or rest for even one moment while our beloved crown prince is under pressure in a war zone would be a disobedience to our king. How far away is the army?"

Faghfur Shah answered: "The battlefield is two days and nights' ride from here. It will take you more than twice that time, since you also have foot soldiers." Hearing this, Haman ordered his generals to strike camp immediately. Soon after that, the army was on its way to join Khorshid Shah.

24

VICTORY AND DEFEAT

AFTER Farokhruz and Qatran fought for the second day and neither was able to defeat the other, the two armies retreated to their camps.

Gezelmalek was resting in his pavilion when an envoy from Machin arrived with a letter from Armen Shah. Gezelmalek unsealed the letter and gave it to one of his confidants to read out loud. The letter said:

"My dear son, we are sending you this letter to let you know that while you have accomplished little on the battlefield, unfortunate events have taken place here in Machin. After we dispatched the leader of our ayyars, Kanun, to bring us the heads of Samak and Shaghal who have caused so much trouble, Samak entered the city under our noses and kidnapped our wine bearer Delaram, along with several valuable musical instruments. Adding insult to injury, he somehow lured or abducted Kanun's two sons—they have not been seen since. The captured enemy generals Siahgil and Saum, who the turncoat vizier Mehran brought to us as prisoners, escaped from Tarmashe's prison before spending even one night there. We have no doubt that the one responsible for all these setbacks is Samak the ayyar."

Hearing this, Kanun was shaken and disturbed to learn that his sons had been captured, and he worried for their fate.

At that moment, a scout rushed into the royal pavilion to tell Gezelmalek that a vast army of one hundred and thirty thousand warriors sent from Halab was approaching. Gezelmalek jumped to his feet and demanded: "How far away?" The scout responded that with so many foot soldiers, it would probably take the army a week to reach the battlefield.

Gezelmalek trembled and turned pale. He said to his generals: "We cannot defeat such a large force. Perhaps we should return to Machin right away."

The generals consulted among themselves, and then Qatran spoke for them: "Let us wait until this army of Halab arrives, so that we can judge whether we have the capability to face them. If their numbers are indeed too formidable, then we will retreat and return to Machin."

Kanun spoke up: "Your Highness, may I make a suggestion? Allow me to go to Shahak Fortress and bring back Princess Mahpari. Whether you then take her back to Machin or use her to negotiate, it can only be an advantage to have her in our custody."

Gezelmalek, pleased by this suggestion, told Kanun to go immediately and bring back Mahpari. Kanun bowed to the prince and assured him he would start the journey right away. Kanun called for paper and ink and wrote a letter on the spot, saying:

"In the name of God, this letter is from Faghfur Shah to his daughter Mahpari, the queen of the world. My dear daughter, I have wonderful news. Marzban Shah, the king of Halab, has sent one hundred and thirty thousand reinforcements to his son Khorshid Shah. I have seen these soldiers with my own eyes. There is no doubt that with their help, Khorshid Shah will demolish the army of the brash and aggressive young prince Gezelmalek, and the war will soon be over. I wish you to begin your journey back home right away to be ready for your marriage with Khorshid Shah when he returns from combat. The bearer of this letter is a confidant whom His Highness Marzban Shah has personally entrusted with your safety. Please follow his guidance and every instruction."

Kanun sealed the letter with a forged stamp that was a copy of Faghfur Shah's and said to Gezelmalek: "Lend me Kafur and five stout warriors, and we will bring back Princess Mahpari." Gezelmalek agreed and the group started their journey toward Shahak Fortress.

Kanun, Kafur, and the five warriors rode nonstop, taking a long detour so that anyone watching from the fortress would think they had arrived on the road from Chin. As they climbed the mountain, Shahak Fortress loomed above them so high that its top was lost in clouds.

The seven riders stopped at the fortress gate. Kanun shouted: "We come from Chin with a letter from Faghfur Shah to his daughter, Princess Mahpari." The princess's handmaiden Ruhafza and her African servant, the castle's only male occupant, came down to the gate, opened a small hatch, and asked to see the letter. Kanun handed the letter through the hatch.

Ruhafza took the letter to Mahpari, who read it and frowned, saying: "Samak told us not to open the gate to anyone but him or Khorshid Shah."

Ruhafza said: "This letter has your father's seal on it. Shouldn't we at least go down to the gate and hear what they have to say?"

Mahpari agreed and they went together to the gate. Ruhafza called from inside: "Reveal your identity!"

A voice responded: "As the great king has explained in his letter, I have been entrusted by Marzban Shah to escort his future daughter-in-law, Princess Mahpari, to her father so that she can get ready for her marriage to Khorshid Shah. My name is Shahdahr and I know the prince well."

When Mahpari heard these words, her heart beat faster with excitement. She asked Ruhafza: "What do you think we should do?"

Ruhafza replied: "The person behind the gate does seem to truly be your father's messenger. It is for you to decide!"

Mahpari thought for a short while, until the prospect of being reunited with her beloved overwhelmed her doubts. She ordered the gate opened and let Kanun and his entourage in.

The moment Kanun saw Mahpari, he was struck by her beauty and grace, and thought: "No wonder kingdoms have gone to war over her." He said to Mahpari: "Your Highness, we have no time to waste. Let us leave right away."

Mahpari looked past him and wondered: "Is there no carriage for me to ride in?"

Kanun answered: "O queen of the world! Your father has informed me that you are well able to ride a horse, and that given the situation you would prefer speed to comfort. When we reach Chin a carriage will be waiting to take you into town."

Mahpari, Ruhafza, and the manservant quickly dressed for travel, packed their belongings, and within a short while were mounted on their horses. Kanun told two of his five warriors to stay and guard the fortress along with Mahpari's two handmaidens, and the rest set out on their journey.

The eight riders rode until they reached a meadow and decided to rest there. As Kanun climbed down from horseback, he noticed a dust cloud in the far distance. He frowned and stared at it. The dust cloud was coming closer.

Mahpari, noticing his fixed attention, asked: "What's the matter?"

Kanun did not answer, but went on staring at the approaching dust cloud, wondering if they were about to be attacked by bandits. By now Kafur the albino was staring too. As they watched, the dust settled, revealing a zebra. Kafur laughed: "A thirsty zebra looking for water!" The zebra looked up, was startled to see people in the meadow, and immediately bolted. This made both Kanun and Kafur feel calmer and cheerful.

After a short rest and food, they mounted their horses again and rode until it became dark. They found a place to rest behind some rocks.

Kanun took two containers of water from his horse. One was filled with pure drinking water, the other doctored with a powerful sedative. He drank from the first container, and handed it to Kafur to share with the three accompanying warriors. He then handed the second container politely to Mahpari to drink and share with Ruhafza and her manservant.

Minutes later, Mahpari, Ruhafza, and the servant all lay on the ground unconscious.

Kanun drew his dagger and swiftly cut the African servant's throat. He was about to kill Ruhafza as well, but thought: "Surely no harm will come my way from this maiden." With the warriors' help, he and Kafur bound Mahpari and Ruhafza hand and foot, put them on their horses, and continued the journey in the dark.

They rode all night and reached the vanguard of Machin's army camp shortly after dawn. They were met by guards who accompanied them to Gezelmalek's pavilion.

The prince, who had just awakened and arisen from his bed, saw Mahpari unconscious and slung over the saddle of her horse. His heartbeat quickened. For a moment he thought that he was still in a dream. The first sight of her inflamed his passion into an overwhelming desire. "All the sacrifice and pain I've gone through for her was worth it," he told himself. He struggled with his feelings, for he desperately wanted to hold this girl in his arms, but he said to Kanun: "Thank you. The princess will not be safe here on a battlefield. Take her straight to Machin to my father's palace. I will join her there when I am able."

Kanun bowed to Gezelmalek and said: "Your Highness! With your permission, I do not think it would be wise to send the princess to Machin while Samak is at large in that city. I am sure he would soon learn she is there and make it his mission to abduct her."

Gezelmalek asked anxiously: "Then where should we take her for safe keeping?"

Kanun responded: "There is a fortress between here and Machin, located well off the main road. It is called Falaki Fortress, because it is set so high that it appears to reach the firmament. Not even a thousand Samaks could enter that fortress. All the armies of the world gathered together would not be able to take it. The fortress master, Edkhan, is a friend of mine and loyal servant of your father Armen Shah. I believe this is the safest place to send the princess until Your Highness decides whether to continue the war or to retreat."

Gezelmalek liked Kanun's suggestion and told him: "Leave right away before the princess wakes up." He then added: "Once you have delivered her, you have my permission to return to Machin to find your sons and kill Samak."

Kanun bowed to Gezelmalek, took Mahpari and Ruhafza along with Kafur and fifty stout warriors, and headed for Falaki Fortress.

After Kanun and Kafur had left, Gezelmalek marveled at the two ayyars' heroic cleverness in getting Mahpari out of Shahak Fortress. He and his generals drank wine to celebrate their triumph long into the night, until the distant sound of horns and drums put an end to their celebration.

"What is happening?" demanded Gezelmalek. A scout rushed into the tent with the news that the army from Halab was approaching.

• • •

Across the battlefield in the Chin army campground, the sound of the approaching army was heard in Khorshid Shah's pavilion as well. Khorshid Shah jumped to his feet and told his generals: "Let us go welcome them!" They agreed and rode out together to greet the newcomers.

When the grand vizier Haman and his soldiers saw Khorshid Shah coming to greet them, they cried out with joy. All dismounted from their horses, shouting: "Long live Khorshid Shah! Long live the crown prince!" Khorshid Shah rushed into the vizier's arms and the two men embraced, unable to hold back their tears.

One by one, the generals who had come with Haman approached and kissed their prince's hand. Haman ordered Khorshid Shah's favorite horse brought, and helped him mount. Haman then mounted his own horse and they headed for Khorshid Shah's pavilion, where Farokhruz joined them.

Khorshid Shah seated Haman next to his throne and eagerly said: "O vizier, tell me, what news from Halab?"

Haman said: "O great prince, since you left three years ago, your father has missed you greatly. In the first year, he spent much of his time drinking wine with his generals and closest friends. After that, he became solitary and stopped appearing even for ceremonies and games. Your mother, the queen, was also very sad. I am sorry to tell you that she became very sick and passed away."

When Khorshid Shah and Farokhruz heard their mother was dead, they cried out in anguish and wept together.

Haman, also in tears, continued: "Marzban Shah's days and nights are now so dark, and he is so desperate to see you, that he wanted to lead the army to Chin himself. I convinced him to send me instead, for he is needed in Halab. I promised him I would not return without you."

Haman added that he had brought Khorshid Shah a quantity of goods sent by his father. Khorshid Shah told the vizier to keep and spend them as he thought best for the army's needs. Haman and the others then left the pavilion to give Khorshid Shah time to mourn.

For two days Khorshid Shah stayed alone in his tent, drinking wine to forget his sorrows. Then he called in his confidants and generals and said: "Now let us make battle plans and discuss how we will defeat Gezelmalek's army."

At dawn the next morning, the drums were beaten and the horns blown to call Khorshid Shah's army for combat. The sun had not yet risen above the horizon when the two armies lined up to face each other on the battlefield.

The first to ride out from the ranks was a warrior from Halab named Hormozgil. After asking Khorshid Shah's permission to begin the combat, he spurred his armored horse and rode toward Gezelmalek's army with a piercing battle cry. He threw his spear into the ground, removed his helmet, and shouted: "I am Hormozgil, an ordinary soldier. I serve Marzban Shah and my prince Khorshid Shah. Let's see if there is a man among you brave enough to face death at my hands!"

A warrior from Gezelmalek's army rode out, shouting: "I'll show you what a real man is!"

Hormozgil called back: "Tell me your name, so I'll know who I've killed!"

The warrior responded: "I am Qatour. Our great hero Qatran is my brother, and I serve Prince Gezelmalek!"

Hormozgil pulled his spear from the ground and charged toward Qatour, who drew his own spear and rode toward him. As the two warriors approached, Hormozgil hurled his spear at Qatour so hard it pierced his breastplate. Before the warrior could pull it out, Hormozgil was upon him. Still on horseback,

Hormozgil grabbed the spear, pushed, and twisted it until its tip emerged from Qatour's back. The Machin warrior fell from his horse, dead.

Hormozgil shouted: "Who's next? I'm just getting warmed up! Come, show me what passes for a hero in Machin!"

Qatran, shocked by his younger brother's death, howled in grief and anger and charged toward Hormozgil. He found his path blocked by one of his own warriors, named Kalsavar, known as the greatest spear thrower of Machin. Kalsavar said: "Qatran, you are too upset to fight. Let me put an end to this braggart!" Saying that, he drew his spear and rode toward Hormozgil.

Hormozgil charged at Kalsavar and the two warriors fought on horseback until both their spears broke. They then drew their swords out and went on battling, but neither could defeat the other.

Khorshid Shah watched until he could stand no more. All his sadness—at his mother's death, his father's grief, his long separation from Mahpari—burst out in a cry of rage. He spurred his horse, ignoring those who tried to stop him, and charged toward the enemy lines.

The white-bearded vizier Haman shouted to his men: "Let's follow our great leader!" He galloped after the prince.

The two armies plunged into battle, thousands of warriors fighting hand-to-hand. Kalsavar the spear-thrower was hit in the chest by an arrow and fell from his horse dead. Warriors were struck down, men and horses rolling in the dust, until the battlefield was red with blood.

Gezelmalek, feeling his own death near, turned his horse around and galloped from the field. The army of Machin followed him and was soon in full retreat.

25

THE MISSING PRINCESS

KHORSHID Shah had no wish to pursue the retreating army of Machin. Happy about his victory, but heartsick thinking of all it had cost, he returned to his pavilion, followed by his closest generals and the vizier Haman.

Khorshid Shah said: "Now that the war is over, it is time for us to take Princess Mahpari out of Shahak Fortress and bring her back to Faghfur Shah."

Shaghal, the grey-bearded head of the ayyars of Chin, stepped forward and said: "O prince, if young Samak were here, he would surely volunteer. Since he is not with us, I would be happy to go."

Farokhruz spoke up: "My brother, there is no need to send ayyars on such a straightforward mission. Mahpari is your princess and will soon be your queen. Let me go as your emissary."

Khorshid Shah agreed to this, and Farokhruz left with Samron and three soldiers. Farokhruz and his companions rode day and night until they reached the base of the mountain. As they rode up the steep trail that led to the fortress, they were startled to see rocks and boulders rolling and hurtling down the hillside toward them. They narrowly dodged the avalanche. Farokhruz shouted: "Stop throwing rocks! I am Khorshid Shah's brother with a message for Princess Mahpari!"

A voice from the fortress shouted: "To hell with you and Khorshid Shah! We are soldiers of Armen Shah. Mahpari is not here!"

Farokhruz shouted: "What are you saying?"

The voice responded: "I told you, the princess is not here! Now get out of here, or you'll get more of the same!"

Farokhruz was crushed. Instead of easing his brother's pain as he had hoped, now he had to add to it. He returned to Khorshid Shah and told him how they had been greeted at the fortress.

Khorshid Shah was thunderstruck. He summoned Shaghal and Arghonun. Hearing Farokhruz's report, Shaghal cried out: "Kanun is behind this! I'd stake my life on it."

Devastated, Khorshid Shah said to Shaghal and Arghonun: "It was your idea to put Mahpari into Shahak Fortress in the first place. Are you telling me that after all the trouble Samak took to get her out of the hands of that witch's son, she has been taken again—and we don't even know where?"

Haman the vizier said consolingly: "O prince, in war and in life, no victory lasts forever. If this Samak was clever enough to get into that fortress, it's to be expected that another ayyar might do the same. Have faith. You were patient and suffered for three years to be with your beloved. Let us not waste time in regrets, but go now to Machin and demand her return from Armen Shah. We will go in force, so that the king can see with his own eyes the army that drove his son from the battlefield, and consider the price to be paid if he refuses."

Khorshid Shah agreed with the vizier's suggestion. A message was sent to Faghfur Shah explaining the necessity and requesting that additional provisions be sent from Chin to equip their two hundred thousand men and horses for the journey. The combined armies of Chin and Halab then gathered their belongings and set out for Machin.

• • •

While the armies of Khorshid Shah and Haman stretched for miles along the road to Machin, Kanun, Kafur, and their entourage were riding through a dense forest with their prisoners, Mahpari and Ruhafza. The two women had wept for a long time after realizing that their captors had murdered the African manservant. By now, their grief and terror had hardened into stoic resolve.

As they climbed the hill, the forest thinned and above the tree line turned into a rocky slope. At its top sat Falaki Fortress. On the other side was a sheer cliff that dropped straight down to the sea, so that the fortress could be seen by ships ten miles away.

A watchman saw the small group of about fifty warriors approaching from a distance. He reported it to Edkhan, the fortress guardian, who sent down two guards to find out who the newcomers were.

The sentinel on duty recognized Kanun as soon as his group neared the gate. Kanun shouted: "Tell Edkhan that I come from Prince Gezelmalek with a valuable consignment: Princess Mahpari, the daughter of Faghfur Shah, king of Chin!" He continued: "The prince is at war fighting Faghfur Shah's army, and he wishes the princess to be guarded so well that not even the wind will blow in her direction."

A guard took Kanun's message to Edkhan, and returned with several servants and maidens. The gate was opened to let in the newcomers. Kanun told the guards that he had to attend to an urgent matter in Machin, and promptly left with Kafur and the soldiers.

The maidens and servants escorted Mahpari and Ruhafza into the fortress and untied them. Edkhan, who had been watching from a window, came down to welcome the princess, but Mahpari was so angry she would not even look at him.

Edkhan ordered the guards to take the princess and her handmaiden to Shahdar, a secluded residence in the fortress tower. He told them: "Once you have made proper arrangements for our guests, all of you must leave except for one manservant and two maidens to attend to the princess's needs. No one else is to go near Shahdar as long as the princess is there."

Meanwhile, Kanun and his followers rode nonstop until they reached Machin. Kanun went straight to the ayyar headquarters to find out what had happened to his two sons.

He was told that not long after he and Kafur had left Machin, two strangers had arrived saying they had come from Bukhara to join the ayyars. Behzad and Razmyar had welcomed them as guests. On the third night, all four men disappeared without a trace. No one had seen Behzad or Razmyar since.

The ayyars confirmed what Kanun already knew from Armen Shah's letter to Gezelmalek—Delaram, the king's wine maiden, was also missing, along with several musical instruments from the royal court. Mehran the vizier had arrived with generals Siahgil and Saum as his prisoners only to see them vanish overnight from Tarmashe's prison, and Armen Shah had imposed martial law throughout the city until Samak the ayyar was found.

Kanun spent the night in solitude, unable to sleep for anxiety about his sons. In the morning he awoke, got dressed, and went to the royal court, where he paid his respects to Armen Shah.

The king asked Kanun for an account of his activities since he had left Machin and for news from the battlefield. Kanun related all that had happened, including his abduction of Princess Mahpari and her transfer to Falaki Fortress. He concluded: "Your Majesty, when I left Prince Gezelmalek, he was safe and well, but an army of one hundred and thirty thousand soldiers sent from Halab was approaching."

Armen Shah turned pale. Before he could ask more, a guard rushed in and announced that Prince Gezelmalek had entered the city and was on his way to the court.

Armen Shah jumped down from his throne and strode to meet Gezelmalek as he entered. The king embraced his son with relief. Gezelmalek's clothes were dusty from the road, his face streaked with the dried blood of battle. Armen Shah asked: "My son, what has happened? Where is the army?"

Gezelmalek kissed his father's hand. Burning with shame and rage, he told Armen Shah of their defeat and flight from the battlefield. Qatran, who had entered with him, bowed his head while Gezelmalek narrated these events.

After the prince finished speaking, a silence fell over the court.

The vizier Shahran bowed to the king and said: "Your Majesty! Since Khorshid Shah has defeated our army, we should expect that demands will follow."

At that moment, a scout entered with the news that an army of two hundred thousand warriors led by Khorshid Shah had entered Machin and settled in Zafron Plains, just one day's march from the city walls. Hearing this, Armen Shah and all present in the court shivered with fear.

Shahran said: "Your Majesty, we cannot defend ourselves against such a large force. I recommend that we dispatch swift messengers to each of our states and order them to send as many reinforcements as they can right away."

Mehran, the vizier from Chin, who had been listening quietly, now bowed to the king and said: "Your Majesty, if I may make a suggestion? We should prepare for the assault by building barricades throughout the town. Close the city gates and post soldiers on the walls. This will buy us time to negotiate while we gather an army."

Through all this, Sorkhvard had been standing listening quietly in a corner of the king's court. Now he slipped out, unobserved among the crowd of noblemen flowing in and out of the palace, and went straight home.

• • •

Samak tossed and turned in bed, sweating with fever and plagued by uneasy dreams. All week long he had been suffering from the mysterious abdominal pain that resisted every remedy.

In his dream, a lovely young woman leaned down and kissed his forehead. The cool touch of her lips brought Samak such relief that he wondered if she were an angel. Then he opened his eyes and saw Sorkhvard sitting at his bedside.

Samak asked: "My friend, did you kiss my forehead just now?"

Sorkhvard looked embarrassed, and admitted that he had. Then he told Samak the wonderful news he had heard at court.

Samak was so excited to hear that Khorshid Shah was on his way to Machin that he sat straight up in bed. He realized that he felt better. His fever had broken during the night.

"I think I feel well enough to drink a little wine," Samak said. Sorkhvard quickly brought some.

As Samak sipped the wine, Sorkhvard caught him up on the news of the past week. Samak was reassured to hear that Siahgil and Saum were back on their feet; Atashak, Delaram, Saber, Samlud, and their father Khomar were safe; and Behzad and Razmyar were still captive, despite the king's guards searching the city for them.

Sorkhvard called his mother to heat water for Samak's bath. He sat at Samak's side, sponging his back with hot water. Samak sighed: "My dear friend, I feel my strength returning."

After his bath, Samak went back to bed to rest. He told Sorkhvard to keep him informed of any news of Khorshid Shah. Sorkhvard left the house right away.

26

A BRAVE ENVOY

ONCE Khorshid Shah and his army were settled on the outskirts of Machin in Zafron Plains, the grand vizier Haman came to the prince's pavilion. After paying his respects, Haman said: "O Prince, before I left your father, Marzban Shah, he gave me a message to convey to you in a moment when I find Your Highness relaxed and calm. He wishes you to know that if you shed a drop of innocent blood, it will haunt you throughout your life. Therefore, you should wage war only when there is no alternative. If Your Highness will permit me to make a suggestion, now that we have driven Gezelmalek's army from the field, I suggest that we send a message to Armen Shah demanding the release of Princess Mahpari. If he obeys, there will be no further need to fight. If he refuses, the bloodshed will be his burden. In either case, we will have followed your father's command."

Khorshid Shah agreed. Haman called for the royal scribe and dictated a letter to Armen Shah.

When the letter had been written and sealed, General Shiruyeh bowed to the prince and said: "Your Highness, I must tell you there is a risk that the messenger we send to Machin with this letter will not return alive."

Haman asked his generals: "Is there one among you who knows Machin and their customs and is willing to take this risk?"

A general from Halab named Khordasb, who was known to be subtle and well-spoken, stepped forward and said: "Your Highness, I will go and, if God wills it, bring back Armen Shah's response."

Haman gave the letter to Khordasb, who left immediately for Machin with an entourage of two hundred guards.

When Khordasb arrived at the city gate, he saw catapults and other defenses being erected all around the walls. His guards shouted: "An envoy is here with a message from Khorshid Shah to your king!" Soon thereafter, the gates were opened and Khordasb and his entourage were led into the city.

Sorkhvard hurried home and told Samak that an envoy from Khorshid Shah had arrived. Samak got out of bed and announced: "I'm going to the palace."

Sorkhvard became alarmed, and said: "Samak, it's not safe for you to leave this house. Tarmashe and the king's men are searching the city for you. They have spies and informants everywhere. Mehran the vizier is with the king. He knows you by sight. To go to the royal court would mean your death."

Samak said: "My friend, don't worry! If the divine force is on my side, a thousand enemies can't hurt me. All I need is an army officer's uniform. Go fetch one for me, and I'll do the rest."

Sorkhvard left the house and soon returned with a Machin army officer's uniform. Samak was impressed that he had acquired one so quickly. "You seem to be a natural at ayyars' work," he remarked. Sorkhvard glowed with the praise. Samak took off his own clothes and put on the officer's hat, turban, shoulder belt, and sword. When he was finished, anyone would have taken him for a soldier in the king's army.

Samak left the house and went straight to the palace. No one stopped him. In the tumult and anxiety throughout the city, most people were thinking only about saving their own lives and families.

A crowd of thousands had gathered outside the palace, fearing an invasion by Khorshid Shah's army. A group of Machin soldiers pushed through the crowd, clearing a path for Khordasb and his entourage to enter the palace. Samak joined the Machin guards, shouting: "Make way!" He thought: "This envoy Khordasb is a brave man, to put himself into the hands of the enemy."

Once they were inside the palace, Khordasb dismounted from his horse and continued on foot. Samak leapt in front of him, helping to push the crowd aside to clear his path. Khordasb glanced at Samak and saw only a bold young army officer, energetic and vigilant in his duty.

When Khordasb entered the royal court, he was struck by its magnificence. The hall was vast, hung with elegant silks and gold-brocaded satin. Exquisite candles and oil burners decorated the walls and columns. Generals and dignitaries sat in their seats, and two slaves stood at attention behind each one. On a platform in the center of the court stood a throne covered with gold, silver, and precious jewels, lined with elegant embroidered cushions and pillows. The viziers Shahran and Mehran sat in golden seats. Khordasb was led to an empty seat beside the throne. Samak elbowed his way forward and took up a guard's position behind Khordasb, standing with a hand on his sword hilt.

Once Khordasb and his entourage had taken their seats, a curtain of embroidered Kashmir silk parted. Servants and maidens entered in orderly procession. All were young and beautiful, dressed in silk and satin robes and wearing golden shawls. Next came Prince Gezelmalek and the royal entourage. Last to enter the court was Armen Shah, wearing an extravagantly embellished royal robe and a silk turban. All present rose to their feet and stood motionless while the king walked to his throne. He took his seat, made himself comfortable, then gestured to everyone to be seated.

By this time, Sorkhvard, Saber, and Samlud had also entered the court and pushed their way to the fringes of the crowd. They were astonished to see Samak on the platform so close to the vizier Mehran, and they prayed he wouldn't be recognized.

Hors-d'oeuvres, pastries, and fruit juices were served. Once everyone had eaten, servants brought ewers for the guests to wash their hands before drinking wine. Samak bent down and whispered in Khordasb's ear: "Your Excellency, I advise you to be on your guard."

A wine bearer filled a goblet and placed it in front of Khordasb. The general rose to his feet and politely told Armen Shah: "Your Highness, in Persia it is not our custom for messengers to drink wine before we have delivered our message and received a response."

Armen Shah said: "Speak your message, or if you have a letter, give it to us!"

Khordasb bowed to Armen Shah, and took from the folds of his robe a cylinder wrapped in silk. He kissed it, touched it to his forehead, and then placed it on the arm of the throne. Armen Shah gave him permission to return to his seat. Khordasb responded: "In Persia it is not our custom to sit while our king's statements are being read."

Armen Shah gestured to Shahran to read the letter. Shahran broke the seal, unrolled the letter and read aloud for all to hear:

"In the name of the Creator of Life, this letter is from Khorshid Shah, son of Marzban Shah, king of Persia, and Haman, his grand vizier, to Armen Shah, ruler of Machin. Be aware that we have come to your kingdom for no other reason than to take Princess Mahpari of Chin back to her own land. We have no wish to continue a war that has already cost thousands of brave soldiers' lives. Although we consider the abduction of the princess a crime, we are willing to forgive those responsible on condition that she is returned to us safe and unharmed. In this way, we can keep our friendship with you and peace between our kingdoms."

A murmur spread through the hall. Shahran went on reading: "Should you refuse this demand, expect an attack from our army of two hundred thousand warriors, as well as Faghfur Shah's army of eighty thousand that is on its way to join us. We will show no mercy to a single life in your kingdom—the blood of thousands of innocents will be on your head. We are giving you a clear warning. The choice is in your hands."

After the letter had been read, there was silence in the throne room. All eyes were on the king.

Armen Shah sat with lowered head, thinking: "If I give them Mahpari, my son will be devastated. He is so headstrong he might even kill himself. But if I refuse, it could be the end of my kingdom."

Gezelmalek, who was standing next to his father's throne, stepped forward, grabbed the letter, and tore it into pieces. He said: "What is there to think about? We would be cowards to give in to this demand." He turned to face Khordasb, and said: "Do you think there are no men in Machin or in Chin, that we would give away our women to foreigners from Halab? I took Princess Mahpari like a man. Go and tell your king that if he wants her, he'll have to take her the same way!"

Khordasb responded: "Dear prince! You are young and speak from your heart without thinking. Let kings deal with kings. A king knows what it is to rule a kingdom. You have yet to learn. Your army fled the battlefield after only a taste of our heat. You cannot imagine the inferno that will consume this city and claim thousands of innocent lives if you continue this war. To abduct a princess is one thing—my compliments to you if you believe you did so bravely. To keep her is another matter."

Enraged, Gezelmalek wrenched a jewel-encrusted golden arm from his father's throne and hurled it at Khordasb. Quick as lightning, Samak stepped forward and batted it aside with his sword. The arm missed Khordasb and hit the floor. Gezelmalek turned angrily on the presumptuous soldier, but the vizier Shahran said: "Your Highness! This man is only a messenger. His mission is to deliver a letter and bring back our response. It is beneath your greatness to throw things at him in your father's presence."

Khordasb bowed to Armen Shah, saying: "Your Majesty, we hold you in high respect. We will not take offense at the prince's behavior in this royal setting, but await your answer."

Armen Shah thought for a moment, then said: "It is our custom in Machin that messengers stay here as our guests for as long as needed to give us time to prepare a proper response."

Khordasb bowed to the king and said: "I am at your command."

The reception master escorted Khordasb and his entourage out of the throne room. Samak went with them, fulfilling his self-assigned role as a Machin army guard protecting Khordasb. They were shown to guest quarters within the royal palace compound.

As soon as they were alone, Khordasb drew Samak aside and asked: "Who are you?"

Samak introduced himself. Khordasb smiled and said: "I am glad to meet Samak the ayyar! Your name is known in Marzban Shah's kingdom. Jomhur and Khorshid Shah mentioned you in their letters. I happen to know that His Majesty wishes to reward you with one hundred thousand dinars in appreciation for all you have done for his son."

Samak responded: "His Majesty is too generous. I have done nothing yet that is worthy of his greatness, and certainly nothing that deserves a reward. I am only an ayyar—my purpose is to help others, not to achieve personal wealth. A piece of bread is enough to make me happy."

Khordasb placed a hand on Samak's shoulder and said: "Your heroism is worth more than money can buy. My prayers go to your parents who brought you up like this."

Samak thanked Khordasb, then he revealed that the generals Siahgil and Saum were in hiding and that their situation was not safe. He suggested: "These guest quarters could be a good place to hide the generals. They could disguise themselves and leave with you and the rest of your party when you return to Khorshid Shah." Khordasb agreed.

Samak left the guest quarters, went to Sorkhvard's house, and returned with Siahgil and Saum dressed as slaves. Khordasb was happy to receive them and thanked Samak for his good work. Next, Samak went to Khomar's house and ensured that Delaram was comfortable and that Behzad and Razmyar were still safely tied up. Leaving Atashak and Sorkhvard to guard them, Samak returned to join Khordasb in his guest quarters in the royal palace.

27

THE WEDDING THIEF

SAMAK nosed around the palace, but he could find no clue where Mahpari was being kept. He returned to Khordasb and said: "This war over the princess has cost so many lives already. We might prevent more bloodshed if we could find the princess and take her back to Khorshid Shah ourselves."

Khordasb said: "How can we find out where she has been taken when we're being watched and guarded day and night?"

Samak said: "There is one person who will know where the princess is being held—Tarmashe, Machin's prison master."

"Where is he?" Khordasb asked.

Samak smiled: "As a matter of fact, I just heard that Tarmashe is personally going around town looking for me and the escaped prisoners Saum and Siahgil. I could make his job easier."

Shortly after sunset, Samak left the guest quarters and joined the Machin guards combing the streets for the fugitives after curfew. He went from one alley to another, asking every guard he met: "Have you seen Tarmashe?" Their directions eventually led him to a group of women celebrating a wedding.

As Samak watched the women playing music, singing, and dancing in their colorful dresses, he spotted Tarmashe in their midst. He was pulling the wedding guests aside one by one, making each one remove her head covering and show him her face, to make sure that none was Saum, Siahgil, or Samak in disguise.

Samak had to smile at the prison master's diligence. He stood near the entrance to the alley as if he were a guard keeping an eye on the wedding party. In fact, the one he was keeping an eye on was Tarmashe.

The women entered a house, singing and dancing around the bride. Tarmashe entered with them. Samak stepped forward, but the door to the house was closed in his face leaving him outside in the alley.

Samak bent down and peered through the keyhole. Inside, he saw the women remove their head coverings, veils, and shoes, and place them by the front door as the party became more relaxed.

Suddenly Tarmashe appeared in front of the keyhole, blocking his view. Samak quickly stepped aside as Tarmashe emerged from the front door carrying a sack. Samak waited a moment, then followed him.

Samak tailed Tarmashe through dark narrow streets, from one alley to another, until they were alone. He stole up behind Tarmashe, locked an arm around the prison master's throat, and wrestled him to the ground. Women's clothing, veils, and shoes spilled out of the sack. Samak sat on Tarmashe's chest, grabbed him by the throat, and shouted: "What are you doing with these clothes, you thief?"

Tarmashe struggled to pry Samak's strong hands from his throat. Unable to breathe, and taking Samak for one of the king's guards, he gasped: "Stop strangling me! I'm taking these garments to keep them safe so no one else steals them."

Samak pressed Tarmashe's throat harder and said: "How dare you lie to me!" He rolled the prison master face-down, took out a rope, tied his hands behind his back, and gagged him with a heavy cloth. Then he dragged Tarmashe through a series of dark alleys until they reached Khomar's house.

Atashak opened the door. Sorkhvard, Delaram, Khomar, and his sons were relieved to see Samak, and they were even happier when they saw Tarmashe tied up. Samak told Sorkhvard to take the sack of dresses back to the wedding house where they belonged.

After Sorkhvard had left, Samak turned to Tarmashe and demanded: "Where is Princess Mahpari?"

Tarmashe replied that he did not know.

Samak told Samlud: "Go fetch a stick to help him remember." Samlud returned with a thick club.

Samak began beating Tarmashe with all his might until the jailer screamed: "Stop! Don't kill me! I'll tell you where Mahpari is."

Samak stopped. Tarmashe asked for water. After drinking, he said: "Mahpari was taken to Falaki Fortress."

Samak asked: "Where is Falaki Fortress?"

Tarmashe answered: "At the top of a sheer rock cliff above a thick forest. It's hard to reach and impossible to get into."

Samak said: "You'll take me there. If I find out you've been lying to me, I'll chop you into pieces on the spot." He told Saber, Samlud, and Atashak to keep Tarmashe tied up and guard him.

All night long, they took turns watching Tarmashe, but he was only pretending to be asleep and eavesdropped on their conversation. By the time dawn broke, Tarmashe knew that Delaram and Kanun's sons were in the house and that the generals were with Khordasb in the royal guest quarters.

Early that morning, Samak left Khomar's house with Tarmashe as his prisoner. Samak tied the bridle of Tarmashe's mount to his own to make sure he would not escape.

As they approached the city gate, Tarmashe turned to Samak and said: "Last night you could have killed me, but you let me live.

I beg you one more favor. The road to Falaki Fortress is hard, I am not dressed for traveling, and I am hurt from the beating you gave me. If you let me stop at my house to get proper clothes and ointment for my wounds, I will be a better guide and less of a burden to you." Samak agreed, and they went to Tarmashe's house.

Samak followed Tarmashe inside and stood watching while his maidservant helped him dress for the journey. But Tarmashe was cunning, and at a moment when Samak's attention was diverted, he whispered in his servant's ear: "Tell the king that I am taking Samak the ayyar to Falaki Fortress. Kanun's sons and Delaram are in the house of Khomar, and the generals are in the guest quarters of Khorshid Shah's envoy." Samak did not realize that Tarmashe had spoken to the maidservant.

When Tarmashe was dressed, he mounted his horse and rode with Samak to the city gate. The guards, recognizing Tarmashe, opened the gate for them. Samak and Tarmashe rode out of the city and headed for Falaki Fortress.

• • •

Tarmashe's maidservant hurried to the palace and asked to see the king. When Armen Shah and Mehran the vizier heard what she had to say, they immediately dispatched two groups of well-armed soldiers. One group went to the palace guest quarters and arrested Khordasb, Saum, and Siahgil. The second group stormed Khomar's house, arrested the old man and his sons, Saber and Samlud, and freed their prisoners, Behzad and Razmyar. Delaram hid in the basement, but the soldiers soon found her as well.

News of the release of Behzad and Razmyar echoed through town. Kanun was delighted to be reunited with his sons. Armen Shah wanted to execute generals Khordasb, Saum, and Siahgil in reprisal, but his vizier Shahran convinced him that with Khorshid

Shah's army at the gates of the city, it would be wiser to keep them as hostages.

Atashak and Sorkhvard escaped the round-up, for they had the good luck to be away from Khomar's house when the soldiers arrived. When they heard the news, Sorkhvard jumped on his horse and rode out of town after Samak. Atashak, a less gifted rider, did his best to follow, but Sorkhvard left him in the dust.

Samak was resting by a lake with his prisoner when he saw Sorkhvard coming. He knew immediately that something bad must have happened. Sorkhvard arrived breathless, dismounted, and told Samak the terrible news.

Samak shouted at Tarmashe: "You did this! I was a fool to turn my back on a liar like you for even a moment. Now you'll pay for your crimes!" Samak shoved a ball of cloth into Tarmashe's mouth and, with Sorkhvard's help, tied him by the ankles and hung him upside down from a thick tree branch.

Atashak caught up, lamenting: "Samak, did you hear? They have taken my Delaram!"

Samak said to Tarmashe, hanging from the tree: "If the king had harmed one hair on the heads of the generals or any of our friends, I'd cut your throat right on this spot. But they're still alive, so it's not for me to end your life. I'll leave that up to nature." Leaving Tarmashe hanging there, Samak mounted his horse and continued toward Falaki Fortress, accompanied by Sorkhvard and Atashak.

28

SORKHVARD'S SECRET

The lake where Samak had left Tarmashe hanging from a tree was fed by a river that ran through a dense forest. Samak, Sorkhvard, and Atashak rode through that forest, following a road that became narrower as it rose uphill, and finally they emerged onto a steep, rocky slope. They rodc on, climbing the precarious, winding mountain trail until they came within sight of Falaki Fortress.

The fortress stood so high that parts of it were hidden behind clouds. Banners flapped in the wind above the battlements. A waterfall crashed down the cliff from the fortress into the river below and flowed into the forest. Catapults and formidable defenses could be seen silhouetted against the sky.

Samak took in the fortress, then turned to Atashak and Sorkhvard and said: "I don't think we're going to get in through the main gate." He sent them around the mountain to look for a side entrance, while he went around the other way.

Samak climbed over rocks and cliffs until he reached a wooded slope below the fortress. His ears picked up the sound of people singing and chopping wood. Below him, a dense evergreen forest sloped steeply downhill. Samak followed the sound to a clearing where a woodcutter and his two young sons were cutting logs.

When they saw him, they stopped singing and stared frozen as if he were a ghost.

"Hello," Samak said.

The woodcutter responded warily: "These woods are forbidden."

Samak said: "I don't want to cause you any problems. I am here to study the fortress." As the woodcutter and his sons stared, Sorkhvard and Atashak came out of the woods. Samak heaved a discouraged sigh. Turning to Sorkhvard, he said: "Ah, if only I had a friend to help me!"

Sorkhvard said: "Master, what are you talking about? Atashak and I are your friends."

Samak said: "A friend is someone who is there to help you when you need it. What would help me now are some pieces of gold."

Sorkhvard looked stricken, for his pockets were empty. Atashak spoke up, saying: "I have gold! Remember the day you told me a man should never leave home with empty pockets? I've followed your advice ever since." He took a purse from his pocket, handed it to Samak, and said: "There are two hundred dinars in this purse. It's all yours."

Samak took the bag from Atashak, kissed it, and handed it to the woodcutter. The old man's eyes went wide when he saw the gold glittering inside. He had never seen so much wealth in his life. He said: "O great man! Why are you showing me this gold?"

Samak asked: "Are these your sons?"

The man nodded. "I am Razmoq, the woodcutter of this fortress. These are my boys."

"I can see they're working as hard as you are. How many people live in the fortress?"

Razmoq answered: "Four hundred men and one hundred women."

Samak remarked: "That's quite a stack of logs you're building up there."

The woodcutter replied that the fortress master had told him to fill the storehouse with as much firewood as it could hold.

Samak said: "I hope you're well paid, at least!"

"We get three loaves of bread a day, one sheep per month, and new clothes twice a year. At the end of the year, if the fortress master is satisfied, we get a bonus of ten dinars."

Samak said: "Ten dinars isn't much for such a hard-working family. I want you to keep this purse as my gift to you."

Razmoq clutched the purse tighter, but looked suspicious. "Why would a great man like you bother with someone like me?" he asked.

Samak said: "My friends and I are building a fortress. We've heard there's no fortress stronger or better designed than Falaki, so we came a long way to study it. We just need you to take us inside."

Razmoq said: "Impossible. The fortress has twelve towers and all of them are guarded day and night. The fortress master, Edkhan, sleeps in a different tower every night."

Samak said: "Surely you and your family are allowed to go in and out?" Razmoq acknowledged that they were.

Samak thought, then said: "I have an idea. Each of us can carry a load of logs on his back and go in with you. If anyone asks why we are so many, you can say you hired extra help to fill the warehouse quickly."

Razmoq, who wanted to keep the money, said: "That could work. Tonight would be a good night to do it, because Edkhan is staying in a tower that faces away from the fortress entrance."

Each man took a load of logs on his back. Razmoq led them out of the woods and to the fortress's main gate. The gatekeeper called: "Who goes there?"

Razmoq answered: "Razmoq the woodcutter, with my sons and three helpers." The gate was opened and they entered the fortress.

Razmoq led them to the warehouse, where they unloaded the wood, then took them to his lodging in the fortress. Razmoq's wife and two young daughters were waiting. By then it had grown dark. "Who are these strangers?" his wife asked. Razmoq explained that he had hired them to help fill the warehouse.

Razmoq's wife prepared lamb stew with bread. After they had eaten, each man took a spot on the floor, laid down, and went to sleep.

Samak woke up shortly after dawn. Everyone else was asleep. Samak crouched by Razmoq's side, shook him gently awake, and said: "There is a princess in the fortress, isn't there?"

Razmoq, still half asleep, yawned and said: "Yes. Mahpari, the princess of Chin, is in the tower of Shahdar."

Samak asked: "Does anyone see her?"

Razmoq responded: "No one is allowed into Shahdar. Only two maidens who go to serve the princess every day."

Samak walked over to Sorkhvard, who was still sleeping quietly, and shook him by the shoulder. Sorkhvard awoke with a start.

Samak said: "Sorkhvard, get up. I need you to dress like a girl and go to Mahpari."

Sorkhvard looked alarmed and tried to persuade Samak that this plan would never succeed. Samak said: "Sorkhvard, you're the only one of us who doesn't have a beard or mustache. You have to do it." He told Razmoq to go and fetch one of his wife's dresses, a shawl, and a pair of her shoes. Razmoq quickly brought what Samak wanted and gave them to Sorkhvard.

Sorkhvard went into a room to dress and stayed there for a long time. When he emerged, his eyes shyly downcast, he looked to all the world like a beautiful maiden. Samak felt his heart lurch with desire, to his confusion. He said cheerfully: "You see, Sorkhvard? This will work."

The sunrise had just lit up the battlements when Sorkhvard approached the gate of Shahdar. The guards, taking him for a maiden, let him pass. Inside, Mahpari was having breakfast with her confidante Ruhafza, served by two handmaidens.

Sorkhvard greeted the princess and Ruhafza. Mahpari, surprised to see a new face, asked: "Who are you?" Sorkhvard indicated by private gestures that Mahpari should send the two servant girls away. As soon as they were gone, he revealed that he was a messenger sent by Samak.

"Samak!" Mahpari exclaimed. "Where is he?"

Sorkhvard responded: "Your Highness, he is here in this fortress. He sent me to tell you he will take you out of here and to Khorshid Shah."

Mahpari was overcome with excitement. "Please send him to me right away!" she said. Sorkhvard bowed, returned to Samak, and delivered the princess's message.

When Samak heard that Mahpari had asked for him, he told Sorkhvard: "Take off your dress. I'll wear it myself."

Sorkhvard objected: "But, Samak, you have a beard and a mustache. You'll be caught."

Samak said: "The guards saw you go in once today. They won't look so closely the second time. Hurry up. I don't want to keep the princess waiting." Saying this, Samak took off his own shirt in order to put on the dress.

Sorkhvard saw that Samak was impatient. With no place to change, he had no choice but to take off his dress right in front of Samak. In that moment Samak noticed on Sorkhvard's chest, bound by a cloth, a pair of breasts as round as pomegranates.

Samak reached out his hand in wonder, and said: "What are these?"

Blushing, Sorkhvard said: "O Samak! Sometimes, from the way you were looking at me, I thought you might have already guessed my secret. You are the only one who knows, apart from my mother and father. I am not a man but a girl."

Samak said: "My dear Sorkhvard! The first morning I was in your house, when I watched you eat breakfast with your mother, I felt my heart drawn to you. I said to myself, 'This person is dressed like a man and talks like one, and yet . . .' I pushed that feeling from my mind. When I saw how clever you were at doing ayyars' work, I convinced myself that you were a man and what I felt was friendship. It was difficult for me, because every time I looked at you, I had to resist the desire to take you in my arms. Now that I know you are a woman, I can tell you that I am in love with you. I want you as my wife."

While Samak was saying this, Sorkhvard blushed. As soon as he finished, she kissed his hand and said: "My beloved Samak, you are my master and I am your devoted maiden."

Samak was thrilled to hear these words. He pulled Sorkhvard into his strong arms and kissed her. Razmoq's wife and daughters, who had witnessed the conversation, watched with tears in their eyes. Atashak, standing nearby, reproached him: "Samak, remember what you told me when I wanted to embrace my Delaram? You said it wouldn't be right while Khorshid Shah and Mahpari have to wait. The same should go for you and Sorkhvard."

Samak was about to tell Atashak to be quiet but he said instead: "Atashak, you're right. Sorkhvard and I will also wait until that time." Having said that, he put on the maiden's dress and shoes, covered his face and mustache with a shawl, and headed for Shahdar.

• • •

Inside Shahdar, Mahpari waited impatiently with Ruhafza. She had sent away her two handmaidens for the day. When the princess saw Samak coming, she ran to him and hugged him like a brother. Ruhafza embraced him like a son. All three sat down together, and Samak told them of Khorshid Shah's victory and what had happened since. He recounted the events leading up to the arrest of Khorshid Shah's envoy Khordasb, the two generals, and Khomar and his sons. Mahpari then told Samak how Kanun had deceived her and Ruhafza, killed her loyal servant, and brought them here to Falaki Fortress.

Samak said: "You will soon be out of this place. I will work out a plan with Razmoq the woodcutter and his family. Wait here until I return." Samak put his shawl back on, left Shahdar, and went back to Razmoq's house.

Samak explained the situation to the woodcutter, and said: "We must leave the fortress, but if we all go at the same time it will cause suspicion. Do you know a place outside the fortress where Mahpari and Ruhafza can hide?"

Razmoq thought for a minute and said: "There is a cave where I store wood on rainy days. I could take them there and give them bread and water to eat until you come. But I cannot be responsible for their safety."

Samak returned to Shahdar and told Mahpari: "Your Highness, I have found a way. It will mean you must forget about being a princess and become an ordinary person for a day or two."

Mahpari responded: "I trust you and will do whatever you say."

Samak said: "In that case, follow me!"

Samak, Mahpari, and Ruhafza left Shahdar dressed as three handmaidens and went straight to Razmoq's house. There, Mahpari and Ruhafza put on Razmoq's sons' clothes. That afternoon, Razmoq left the fortress with Mahpari and Ruhafza dressed as his two young boys.

The path through the woods to the cave was rocky, and Mahpari's feet soon began to chafe and bleed in her ill-fitting shoes.

The woodcutter noticed her discomfort and carried the princess on his back until they reached the cave. He rolled aside a boulder to reveal the entrance and took the two women inside. There he gave them each a blanket, a container of water, and a loaf of bread.

It was after sunset by the time Razmoq returned home to the fortress. The friends ate a simple dinner, and everyone went to sleep in the places they had slept the previous night.

29

TRAIL OF A LION

When Tarmashe had not returned after three days, Armen Shah sent a messenger to Falaki Fortress to inquire after him. The messenger arrived soon after Razmoq had taken Mahpari and Ruhafza out of the fortress to hide them in the cavern. He asked Edkhan, the fortress master, if Tarmashe had arrived with Samak.

Edkhan replied: "No one has entered this fortress within the past week." He sent for his first lieutenant, whose name was Benkhan, and ordered him to take two hundred soldiers and search the surrounding forests for Tarmashe and Samak.

Samak, in Razmoq's house inside the fortress, noticed the unusual activity and said to Razmoq: "Our presence is putting you and your family in danger. We won't stay here any longer." He told Atashak: "Go to Khorshid Shah and tell him we've found Mahpari. Tell him the forest is filled with soldiers and that he should send a group of trusted warriors to take her from the cave where she is hiding. Razmoq will show you the way."

Razmoq's wife gave Sorkhvard several flat loaves of bread and a container of water. Sorkhvard embraced her and thanked her for her hospitality. Then she and Samak left to explore the fortress for a new place to hide.

Samak soon found a hay warehouse, and inside it a locked iron door. He broke the lock with his dagger and entered an empty room with a trap door in the center of the floor. Samak lifted the trap door, climbed down a ladder, and found himself in a basement containing four large vats on platforms set against the four walls. Each vat was filled to its brim with gold coins.

Samak climbed back up and told Sorkhvard: "I've found us a perfect place." They climbed down the ladder, Samak closing the trap door behind them.

In the basement, Samak lit two torches on the walls. The flames reflected off the coins, filling the chamber with warm golden light. They lay down together on the cold stone floor, away from the world outside.

• • •

Meanwhile, Atashak rode through the forest along the river path that Razmoq had shown him, continuing without rest long into the night. He reached Khorshid Shah's army camp on Zafron Plains shortly after sunrise. The prince welcomed Atashak warmly. Atashak told him of his and Samak's adventures since they left the army camp, and that Princess Mahpari was now hiding in a cave outside Falaki Fortress.

Khorshid Shah called in a powerful and trustworthy warrior named Kirmun, and said: "Take five hundred soldiers to Falaki Fortress and bring back my beloved Mahpari." Kirmun and his men left immediately with Atashak on the river path by which he had come.

Meanwhile, at the fortress, Edkhan's lieutenant Benkhan and two hundred soldiers fanned out through the woods, looking for any sign of Samak or Tarmashe. The roar of a lion stopped Benkhan in his tracks.

Benkhan gestured to his men to stay put, for it had long been his dream to hunt the king of the forest. Calming his horse, he advanced quietly in the direction from which the sound had come. Soon an enormous lion came into view behind the trees.

The lion let out a ferocious roar upon seeing Benkhan. Benkhan drew his sword and spurred his horse, but the mare instead backed up in terror. As the lion sprang, Benkhan swiftly exchanged his sword for his bow and let fly. His arrow skewered the lion through the left eye. Roaring with pain, the lion tumbled to the ground and fled. Benkhan gave chase.

The wounded lion zig-zagged through the dense forest, Benkhan in pursuit, until the forest ended at the edge of a lake. The lion plunged into the water and began swimming to the other side. Benkhan was about to follow when he noticed someone hanging upside down from a tree.

Abandoning the lion hunt, Benkhan rode toward the hanged man. His hands were tied behind his back, his mouth gagged, his swollen face covered with dried blood. Benkhan cut the rope with his dagger, and the man fell to the ground. He removed the gag and wiped the blood from the man's face. "Tarmashe!" he exclaimed. The two had met once in Machin, years before.

Benkhan lifted Tarmashe's head and poured a little wine into his mouth. Soon Tarmashe began to revive. Benkhan said: "We were expecting you at Falaki Fortress. What happened?"

Tarmashe answered in a voice so weak that Benkhan had to bend down to hear him: "Tell Edkhan to guard the princess. Samak is coming for her."

Benkhan immediately sent a soldier to convey the warning to Edkhan.

By the time the soldier returned several hours later, Tarmashe's wounds had been dressed and he was on his feet. The messenger reported: "The princess and her handmaiden have escaped. I've never seen Edkhan so angry. We are to search the woods around the fortress until we find them."

Word spread among Benkhan's search party of two hundred men that Tarmashe had been found and that Samak and the princess were at large.

Mahpari and Ruhafza, hiding in their cave, heard the sound of riders coming up the hillside. "The boulder!" they exclaimed. Working together, they rolled the boulder back into place to conceal the entrance. They held their breath in the darkness, waiting.

Outside, they heard a horse neigh, and men's voices.

Moments later, the boulder rolled aside. Soldiers peered in and saw the princess and her handmaiden huddled together in fear, looking like two young boys.

The soldiers brought the women down to Tarmashe and Benkhan. Tarmashe demanded: "Who brought you here?"

Ruhafza answered quickly: "Some men. I don't know who they were."

Tarmashe said: "I know perfectly well who took you out of the fortress. You can tell me, or you can tell Edkhan. One way or another, you'll talk." He turned to Benkhan and said: "Samak can't be far away. Keep searching the woods for him."

Tarmashe brought Mahpari and Ruhafza to the fortress. Edkhan, seeing Mahpari in ragged clothes, declared angrily: "Look at you! Is this how a princess of Chin behaves? You bring shame on yourself and your noble family. I could have chained you in a dungeon. Instead I put you in Shahdar, a place fit for kings and queens, where you had every comfort and privacy. This is how you repay me!" He shook Mahpari, shouting: "How did you get out of the fortress? Who helped you?"

"I don't know!" cried Mahpari. "Soldiers came and took us away. What were we supposed to do, fight back?"

"You lie to my face! Do you think I won't lay a hand on you because you're a woman? I'd rather be punished by the king than let a girl like you humiliate me." Edkhan pushed Mahpari to the ground. He ordered Tarmashe: "Beat her until she tells the truth."

Tarmashe drew Edkhan aside and reminded him: "She is a princess of royal blood. Her servant, on the other hand . . ."

Edkhan understood. Pointing to Ruhafza, he ordered the nearest guard: "Make her talk."

The guard picked up a club and struck Ruhafza, knocking her to the ground. He hit her again and again until Mahpari screamed: "Stop! I'll tell you what you want to know."

At a gesture from Edkhan, the beating stopped. Mahpari told them all that had happened, from Sorkhvard and Samak's first visit to Shahdar until Razmoq took them out of the fortress and to the cavern.

"Where is Samak?" Edkhan demanded. Mahpari answered truthfully that she did not know.

Edkhan ordered the soldiers: "Tie their hands and take them back to Shahdar. Guard them day and night."

He took Tarmashe and a group of soldiers to Razmoq's house. The woodcutter's wife and daughters screamed as the soldiers kicked in the door. Edkhan grabbed Razmoq's wife, shouting: "Is this how you thank me for my kindness? By betraying me and helping my prisoners escape? Where is your husband?"

Razmoq's wife, weeping in fear, said: "O great master, I know nothing. My husband and sons are cutting wood for you right now outside the fortress."

Tarmashe advised Edkhan: "She is lying. I would take these dishonest women to the wall and throw them to their death."

Razmoq's wife cried louder, saying: "Have mercy! Please spare me and my daughters. We've been here in our house the whole time. We have no idea what is happening outside."

She was so convincing that Edkhan relented. He ordered the soldiers: "Take these women to the fortress gate and tell them never to return." Then he turned to Tarmashe and ordered: "Go with Benkhan. Find the woodcutter and his sons and make him tell us where Samak is hiding." Tarmashe left right away.

30

MASSACRE IN A CANYON

RAZMOQ had been watching from the woods when Benkhan's soldiers took Mahpari and Ruhafza out of the cavern. He knew he would soon be exposed and that they would come for him and his family next. He hurried back to his two sons and told them: "We must leave the forest. Our only hope is to go to Khorshid Shah's army camp and ask for his protection. I pray no harm will come to your mother and sisters. How I wish I had never taken that ayyar's gold!"

Razmoq and his sons began running along the river path that led to Chin's army camp, the same route Razmoq had shown Atashak. They soon ran into Atashak on his way back to Falaki Fortress with Kirmun and five hundred soldiers.

Razmoq told them that Mahpari had been recaptured and taken back to the fortress. Kirmun absorbed this bad news, and asked: "How many soldiers are guarding the fortress?" Razmoq answered: "Four hundred. But at least two hundred are outside now searching the woods."

Kirmun said: "We should take advantage of this situation and attack the soldiers while they are outside the fortress. What is our best chance to approach without being seen?" Razmoq replied:

"Below the fortress is a deep canyon near a waterfall. You and your men could camp there out of sight."

Kirmun ordered Razmoq to lead them there. He then turned to Atashak and said: "Since you are not a warrior, there is no need for you to take part in this battle. You have already done a great service to Khorshid Shah. You are free to go if you wish." Atashak thanked him and left immediately for Machin.

Kirmun and his army followed Razmoq, reaching the canyon just before dusk. It was just as Razmoq had described it. They settled there to plan their attack.

Not far away, Tarmashe and Benkhan rode with a group of soldiers searching the woods for Samak. Tarmashe suddenly stopped and silenced Benkhan. In the darkness they could hear the faint sound of someone whistling.

Tarmashe gestured to Benkhan to stay where he was. Dismounting, he crept silently through the woods in the direction of the sound. As he reached the river, he saw in the moonlight a man whistling while his horse drank water.

Tarmashe jumped the man from behind, forced him to the ground, and tied his hands behind his back before he could defend himself. Tarmashe demanded: "Who are you? What are you doing in these woods?" The man replied that he was a hunter from Machin tracking a herd of deer.

Tarmashe asked: "Do you know who I am?"

The man shook his head. Tarmashe punched him in the face so hard his nose bled, and shouted: "You're a liar! Anyone from Machin would know I am Tarmashe."

The man said quickly: "Tarmashe! Forgive me, I didn't recognize you in the darkness!"

Tarmashe snarled: "Another lie! I'm going to beat you until you tell me the truth." Picking up a stick, he began beating the man without mercy. The man realized that if he did not speak he was going to die. He shouted: "Stop! I'll tell you the truth. I am a soldier in Khorshid Shah's army."

Tarmashe stopped beating the man. He demanded: "What are you doing here? Tell me the truth and I will set you free." The soldier confessed everything, including that he was part of an army of five hundred soldiers camped in the canyon below.

When the man finished, Tarmashe said: "Thank you for your honesty. Now I will set you free. A brave soldier would have died rather than betray his army as you have done." He drew his dagger and cut the soldier's throat.

Tarmashe wiped his dagger on the dead soldier's clothes, resheathed it, and went back to tell Benkhan what he had learned.

Benkhan suggested: "That canyon has only one entrance. Let us build a large fire to seal the soldiers inside. Then we can rain boulders and hot tar on them from the fortress above."

Benkhan's two hundred soldiers spent the night felling trees and gathering them into a pile outside the canyon's entrance. They set the trees ablaze and returned to the fortress to wait.

Kirmun and his army were awakened by smoke pouring into the canyon. Rushing to the entrance, they found their way blocked by the blaze. As they searched frantically for a way out, boulders and hot tar began raining down on them from the fortress above. The fire spread through the canyon. Kirmun's men died in agony with no chance to defend themselves. By noon, not a man nor a horse remained alive.

• • •

On Edkhan's orders, all the fortress's residents joined in the search for Samak. Fortunately for Samak and Sorkhvard, the hay warehouse they had chosen as a hiding place remained undisturbed.

For two days and two nights they were alone, unaware of what was happening outside.

At sunrise on the third day, Samak and Sorkhvard were awakened by noises in the chamber above. They immediately extinguished the torches and hid themselves in a nook out of sight.

The trap door opened and a man climbed down the ladder carrying a torch. Samak saw that he was young, dressed in a handsome silk robe and hat decorated with precious stones and silver tassels.

The young man checked all four vats of gold to make sure that they had not been disturbed. He was about to leave when Samak leapt from hiding and grabbed him by the throat. The man cried out: "Who are you? What do you want?"

Samak said: "My name is Samak. All I want from you is information."

The young man's eyes shone with excitement. He fell on his knees and said: "Samak the ayyar! O great hero, it's been my dream to serve you!"

Sorkhvard stepped out from the nook. The man's eyes widened further on seeing a beautiful young woman. He explained: "My name is Neyal. I am the treasurer of the fortress, Edkhan's servant."

Samak said: "We have been hiding here for three days. What is going on outside?"

Neyal told them of Tarmashe's rescue from the hanging tree, the recapture of Princess Mahpari and her companion Ruhafza, and the massacre of five hundred soldiers sent by Khorshid Shah. Hearing of these dire events, Samak became more and more disturbed.

Neyal warned: "Edkhan's army and everyone in the fortress are searching for you. You won't have a chance unless I help you." He added: "I could hide you in my own house. Of course, by doing that, I would be risking my life."

Samak understood that Neyal wanted something in return. He said: "If you help us, once I have returned Princess Mahpari to Khorshid Shah, I will ask the prince to make you the keeper of this fortress."

Neyal said: "That's a handsome offer. But I have no interest in being a commander. I will gladly do anything you ask, if only you will take me as your apprentice!"

Samak laughed and said: "I can't refuse that!"

Neyal said: "I will go prepare my home for your arrival, and return at nightfall." He climbed the ladder, closing the trap door behind him, leaving Samak and Sorkhvard once again alone.

"That was a piece of luck!" Samak said. Sorkhvard was less certain: "We're trusting him with our lives, just because he flattered you and said he wants to be your apprentice. How do you know he won't go straight to Edkhan?"

Samak assured her: "Dear Sorkhvard, don't worry. I have good instincts about people."

Neyal returned a few hours after nightfall, carrying a bundle of servants' old clothes. Samak and Sorkhvard put them on and followed Neyal to his lodging in the fortress. They became tense when they saw soldiers standing guard, but the soldiers accepted them as Neyal's servants and let them pass.

Once inside Neyal's house, all three breathed a sigh of relief. They sat and enjoyed a delicious dinner with vintage wine, their first meal in days.

After dinner, they sat and talked until dawn. Neyal asked question after question about Samak's life and adventures. Samak answered enthusiastically at length, not noticing that Sorkhvard was silent and did not share his good mood.

At sunrise, Neyal stood up and declared: "It's time for me to go to Edkhan. Would you like me to bring Tarmashe back with me, if I can manage it?"

Samak grinned and said: "Do whatever you think would please me as your master!"

When Neyal arrived at the commander's quarters, he found Tarmashe, Benkhan, and several officers reporting to Edkhan. Neyal listened while they described their lack of success in finding Samak.

Neyal spoke up: "Have you checked the treasury? That would be a good hiding place. It's hidden away in a hay warehouse and hard to find." When they replied that they had not, Neyal said to Tarmashe: "I can show you the way there."

Tarmashe agreed and followed Neyal. As they passed Neyal's house, the young treasurer remarked: "I left home this morning before breakfast. Would it be all right if we stop for a moment to eat something?" Tarmashe, who was hungry himself, agreed.

Samak and Sorkhvard, seeing Neyal and Tarmashe approaching, climbed to the second floor and waited. Neyal brought Tarmashe inside and they sat down to eat some bread and goat cheese with cucumbers.

While they were eating, Samak and Sorkhvard crept silently down the staircase behind Tarmashe. A sixth sense warned Tarmashe. He turned and saw them, drew his dagger and jumped to his feet. As Samak and Tarmashe grappled, Sorkhvard spun Tarmashe around and punched him in the face so hard he staggered. Blood gushed from Tarmashe's mouth. He fell to his knees, spitting out two broken teeth. Neyal tackled him to the floor and tied him up with a rope. Samak, with nothing left to do, stared at his beloved Sorkhvard in awe at her strength.

Samak said to Tarmashe: "That's twice I've spared your life, and twice you've made me regret it. Weren't your crimes in Machin enough, that you had to add to them here?" He added: "Now Khorshid Shah will decide your punishment."

They threw Tarmashe into a room and locked the door. Samak sat down in the breakfast seat that Tarmashe had occupied and said: "Good food should not go to waste." For the rest of the day they continued to eat, drink, and share stories, while they waited until nightfall to pay a visit to Shahdar.

31

LOVERS REUNITED

As midnight approached, Samak said to Sorkhvard and Neyal: "Now it's time for us to go get the princess."

They left the house and walked quietly to the base of Shahdar. Finding the door locked, Samak said: "I'll need a lasso." Sorkhvard smiled and removed a lasso that she had wrapped around her waist.

Samak tossed the lasso several times until it caught on a crenellation. He pulled to make sure it was sturdy, then climbed the lasso to the building's roof. From the rooftop he looked down into a series of rooms surrounding a central courtyard until he saw the one in which Mahpari and Ruhafza lay sleeping. The women's feet were tied together. A candle burned nearby.

Samak quietly dropped down into the courtyard and stole into the princess's room. He gently shook Ruhafza awake, then Mahpari. The women were overjoyed to see him.

"How many soldiers guard this room?" Samak asked.

Ruhafza responded: "Just one outside the door."

"Find an excuse to call him in," Samak said. He hid behind a curtain.

Ruhafza shouted for the guard until he opened the door. "We're thirsty," Ruhafza said. The guard went out and returned

When Edkhan and his warriors heard the thunder of hooves and saw the dust cloud rising from the path below, their first thought was that Neyal had returned with reinforcements. By the time they realized that the army was Khorshid Shah's, it was too late. They were caught outside the fortress, outnumbered ten to one. Soon Edkhan's army was crushed and scattered, the fortress surrendered, Edkhan and Benkhan taken as prisoners.

When Mahpari learned that the fortress was now occupied by Khorshid Shah's army and that the prince himself was on his way there, she exclaimed: "O Samak, take me to him!"

Samak bowed to her and said: "O lovely princess! You are the queen of the world. You should return to Shahdar and wait there like a queen until Prince Khorshid Shah comes to take your hand in his hand."

Mahpari understood. She and Ruhafza returned to their quarters in Shahdar. With Ruhafza's help, Mahpari put on her royal outfit and made herself up to look more beautiful and radiant than any princess of Persia who had ever lived. She waited at her window, watching the path below, until she saw the dust clouds of two hundred soldiers approaching. Mahpari shivered with excitement as she recognized Khorshid Shah's banner.

Samak and Sorkhvard rode out of the fortress gate to meet the prince, with Tarmashe tied up and slung over a horse's saddle. Khorshid Shah embraced Samak and thanked him for all he had done. He asked who the people with him were, whereupon Samak explained that Sorkhvard was his beloved partner and Tarmashe his nemesis.

At that moment, several of Khorshid Shah's soldiers arrived escorting Razmoq and his two sons with their hands tied. They had been discovered hiding behind the rocks under the waterfall. Samak told the soldiers to untie them, and explained to Khorshid Shah that Razmoq had helped him get into the fortress and had taken care of the princess.

Khorshid Shah was pleased and asked Samak to suggest an appropriate reward. Samak bowed and said: "If it is Your Highness's will, Razmoq would make an excellent fortress keeper, since he has lived here all his life and is a trustworthy man." Khorshid Shah approved of this plan.

Samak pointed to Tarmashe and said: "If the prince commands it, I believe this man should pay for his crimes."

Khorshid Shah said: "You know his crimes better than I do. I leave it to you to decide a fair punishment."

Samak told the soldiers to take Tarmashe into their custody. The soldiers followed Samak's command and took Tarmashe away.

By now Khorshid Shah's longing to see Mahpari was so intense that he could wait no more. He said to Samak: "Take me to her."

Samak and Sorkhvard led the prince to Shahdar, where Mahpari was waiting. Khorshid Shah entered the princess's chambers. The sight of her took his breath away. Mahpari threw herself into his arms and the lovers embraced.

The moon rose and spread its light through the courtyards of Falaki Fortress. Khorshid Shah called for food and wine, and he invited Samak and Sorkhvard to join them. Ruhafza played the harp and sang for the lovers. The five friends ate, drank, and enjoyed each other's company long into the night as they recounted all that had happened since Khorshid Shah and Mahpari said goodbye to each other in Bograi Valley so long ago.

• • •

The next morning, Neyal was summoned to the hall where Khorshid Shah sat with Mahpari at his side. Samak instructed Neyal to take all the gold out of the treasury chamber, load it onto several mules, and deliver it to the prince's army for safe keeping.

Next to arrive were Razmoq and his family. Samak told them that the prince had named Razmoq commander of the fortress and that Shahdar would be their new home. Razmoq and his wife, sons, and daughters thanked Samak, kissed Mahpari and Khorshid Shah's hands in gratitude, and promised they would be devoted to them for the rest of their lives.

Once these arrangements had been made, Samak asked Khorshid Shah's permission to return to Machin, as he was concerned about his friends and the three generals who had been taken prisoner. The prince gave his consent. Samak thanked him, and added a word of warning: "Your Highness may wish to remember that Kanun and his two sons are at large. I suggest you stay on your guard for further hostile actions."

They all said goodbye and embraced one last time. Khorshid Shah, Mahpari, and Ruhafza left the fortress with the army, heading back toward the camp of Chin. As for Samak, he set out for Machin, accompanied by Sorkhvard and Neyal, with their prisoner Tarmashe riding in a box fastened on top of a mule.

PART II

SECTION 5

Zafron Plains

32

KINGS BARGAIN, AYYARS DIG

THE journey to Machin took Samak and his friends a day and a night. At sunrise on the second day, they saw the minarets of the town appear in the distance. By the time they reached the city gates, the sun had begun to drop in the sky. The mule carrying Tarmashe in a box limited their speed.

Samak proposed to Sorkhvard and Neyal that they enter the town separately in disguise, since they were wanted fugitives. Sorkhvard's mother's house, as well as Khomar's, would certainly be under surveillance. Sorkhvard suggested that they meet in the butchers' bazaar and make further plans from there. Samak said: "An excellent idea! I know two butcher brothers who have a shop there. They recently received robes of honor and other gifts from the king thanks to Tarmashe. They will be happy to see him again so they can thank him for their good fortune."

Sorkhvard separated from them and rode through the city gate first. Neyal followed, riding on horseback and leading the mule carrying Tarmashe as if he were a merchant with a box of goods to sell in town.

The last person to enter the city was Samak, who had covered his hair and beard with ashes to disguise himself as an old man. As he passed through the gates, he noticed a group of well-armed soldiers who struck him as more alert and formidable-looking than the usual city guards. He noticed that they wore green sashes.

Once inside the city, Samak went straight to the butchers' bazaar and stood outside the shop belonging to the twin brothers, scanning the crowd until he spotted Sorkhvard. He exchanged a signal with her so that she knew it was him.

Neyal emerged from the back of the shop, where he had just delivered the box containing Tarmashe. The three friends made eye contact and came together. Neyal reported: "The brothers asked me what was in the box. I told them it was a gift from Samak the ayyar."

Samak sensed someone coming up behind him. He turned swiftly, his hand on his dagger, ready to attack. Then he saw who it was. "Atashak!" They embraced.

Atashak warned Samak: "Samak, it's not safe for you to be here. Armen Shah has appointed a new constable named Surkhkafar with special orders to capture you. His guards are everywhere in town."

"Do they wear a green sash?" Samak asked.

Atashak was amazed: "How could you possibly know that?"

Samak smiled and said: "Atashak, you should know by now that it's my job to know things." He told Atashak the good news that Khorshid Shah had captured Falaki Fortress and been reunited with Mahpari. Then he asked about the situation of their friends who had been arrested thanks to Tarmashe's information.

Atashak said: "The generals are alive. They are prisoners in the royal palace. I don't know what happened to Khomar and his sons." Then he burst out: "But, Samak, they have taken my Delaram back to Armen Shah's wine cellar! I did not even get to embrace her once before we were parted. It's like a wound in my heart that never heals."

Samak said: "I promised you that I would put her hand in your hand. I don't forget my promises."

He then asked Atashak where he had been staying. Atashak said: "In the home of the brothers who own this butcher shop. It's the most beautiful and comfortable place you can imagine. We eat like kings there every night. It's very secure, with hiding places everywhere and plenty of room for all of us. I have told them all about you and they would be delighted to have you as their guest."

The end of the day was approaching. Samak waited as the bazaar grew dark and the shops closed one after another, the shop keepers going home. Atashak found an opportunity to take Samak to the butcher brothers and introduce him along with Sorkhvard and Neyal. The brothers were happy to meet Samak, and they invited him and his friends to stay in their home for as long as they wished.

When all their employees had said goodbye and left the shop, the brothers locked the entrance from inside. The bazaar was empty, the butcher brothers, Samak and his friends were the only ones left.

Samak said: "Now it is time to open your gift."

The brothers pried open the box. Inside, squatting in the uncomfortable position he had been forced into, was Tarmashe. The butcher brothers were delighted to see in such a state this jailer who had had them brutally whipped, and over the years had abused many citizens who had fallen out of the king's or some other official's favor. "What shall we do with him?" they asked.

Samak said: "I am not from Machin. You who have lived here all your lives can judge what this man deserves."

The twins looked at each other. Each understood what was in his brother's mind without needing to say a word. They led Samak outside into the bazaar, which was dark and empty of people. There stood a gallows.

The first brother said to Samak: "This is the gallows that was built to hang us. The vizier Mehran ordered it left there as a warning to anyone who might defy the king."

They took Tarmashe out of the box, put a rope around his neck, and stood him on the gallows. The second brother said: "Tarmashe, jailer of Machin, for years you tortured and abused innocent prisoners. You accused us falsely to the king to save your own skin. You are a man without honor, a thief, and a disgrace to your office, an enemy of the people of this city. Do you have anything to say for yourself?"

Tarmashe said with scorn: "Who are you to lecture me? You who have the best stall in the marketplace and built a palace with your riches. What do you know of a jailer's life? I did my duty, nothing more."

The butchers hanged Tarmashe from the gallows. His body quivered a few times and he died.

Atashak wrote on a placard: "Retribution to the people's bitter enemies!" They left it hanging on Tarmashe's chest to be seen by everyone when the bazaar opened in the morning.

The two brothers led Samak and his friends to their home. Its modest doorway opened into a splendid central courtyard. A brook ran through a beautifully landscaped garden. In its center stood a pavilion exquisitely decorated with mosaic tiles and a fountain flowing into a fish pond.

The butcher brothers invited Samak, Atashak, and their friends to make themselves comfortable on cushions placed on carpets around the fountain. Minstrels soon arrived with oud, harp, ney, tanbur, and tombak. The friends enjoyed a delicious meal to the accompaniment of three female dancers and a musical performance worthy of a king's court. They drank to each other's health and celebrated their recent accomplishments until the sky above the courtyard began to lighten with the first rays of dawn.

• • •

Meanwhile, Khorshid Shah and Mahpari returned to the army camp in Zafron Plains. The vizier Haman greeted them warmly, delighted to meet Mahpari for the first time. He looked at Khorshid Shah and said: "O my prince, I once told your father I had seen in the stars that it was your destiny to follow your heart's desire and marry a young princess from a foreign land. I know now that your good fortune is our kingdom's fortune."

The prince and princess were led to Khorshid Shah's pavilion, which had been decorated in honor of Mahpari's arrival. There they celebrated the princess's safe return with a feast.

When the meal was finished, Haman bowed to Khorshid Shah and said: "O prince, since there is no longer any reason to continue this war, I suggest we write to Armen Shah and offer peace." Khorshid Shah agreed. Haman called in the court scribe and dictated the following letter:

"From Khorshid Shah, the prince of Persia, to Armen Shah, king of Machin. Our purpose in coming to this region was to marry the Princess Mahpari and fulfill our promise to her father. Despite the hardships we have suffered and the many innocent lives lost in this war, we are willing to make peace with you on condition that you immediately release our emissary and two generals who you are holding prisoner. Should you decide to do otherwise, we will attack your territory and kill ten thousand of your soldiers for each prisoner you hold. Let it be known that we have given you this warning to prevent further bloodshed."

When the scribe had finished, Haman read the letter to the prince. Khorshid Shah approved and asked who would be willing to take the message to Armen Shah. Hormozgil stood up, bowed to the prince and said: "I will take it and bring back his response."

Haman handed him the letter, and Hormozgil left for Machin with two hundred soldiers.

It was nightfall by the time Haman and the last retainers departed from the pavilion, leaving Khorshid Shah and Mahpari alone together. As they sat in each other's arms, exchanging caresses and words of love, their desire mounted and became overwhelming. The princess stopped Khorshid Shah with a kiss, saying: "O my beloved prince! Don't you want to follow the royal ceremonies?" Khorshid Shah agreed, and they slowed down the pace of their courtship, continuing with conversation and sweet kisses through the night.

The next morning, Khorshid Shah sent a messenger to Faghfur Shah in Chin, requesting that he send a trustee to arrange for his daughter's wedding.

When Hormozgil and his soldiers arrived in Machin bearing the message from Khorshid Shah, they were taken straight to Armen Shah's court. The king was in a rage, since news had reached him of the seizure of Falaki Fortress and plunder of its treasures. As Hormozgil approached down the corridor, he could already hear the king's voice shouting and berating those around him.

Hormozgil noticed as he entered the court that no arrangements had been made for the polite reception or greetings that a king's messenger would customarily receive. The noblemen around the king were pale and shivering in fear. Hormozgil knelt in front of Armen Shah, took out the letter, kissed it, and placed it on the step of the throne. Armen Shah gestured angrily to his vizier Shahran to read the letter. Shahran took the letter, opened its seal, and read it aloud.

As soon Shahran was finished reading, Gezelmalek, who had been seething like a wounded lion, grabbed the letter from the vizier's hand. He tore it into pieces and threw them at Hormozgil, shouting: "We don't bargain with thieves and murderers. Your insults mean nothing to us. Go and tell your Khorshid Shah we will execute the prisoners and massacre your entire army!"

Shahran, who was a wise vizier, bowed to Gezelmalek, then said to Armen Shah: "Your Majesty, please allow us time to consider Khorshid Shah's letter before we respond. Killing prisoners will solve nothing, but it would reduce our options and increase the fire of hatred between the two nations."

Armen Shah went into deep thought. He knew their army was no match for Khorshid Shah's. Yet he shared his son's sense of outrage. He was especially upset by the loss of his nation's gold treasures, which he had believed to be safe in Falaki Fortress. After a moment, he turned to Hormozgil and said: "We will consider your letter and give you our response when we are ready. Until then, you will stay in the palace as our guest. Generals Khordasb, Siahgil, and Saum will join you in your quarters."

Gezelmalek exploded with anger. He shouted: "I can't believe I'm hearing this from my father. Look at what these criminals have done to us! They stole our nation's gold. They kidnapped the woman for whom we sacrificed fifty thousand men. We have lost so much, and what are we left with? Four prisoners! Now you want to return them too and end up with nothing in our hands. Do you want us to become servants and vassals of Halab, so that from now on they can do as they want with us? I would rather die than bring such disgrace upon our name."

Armen Shah ignored his son's outburst. He signaled to Shahran, who followed his command and escorted Hormozgil out of the court.

Kanun, who was in the court and had been listening, chose this moment to step forward. He bowed to Armen Shah, then turned to Gezelmalek, paid his respects, and said: "Dear prince, we should not let anger cloud our judgment. There are other ways than war to achieve our goals. Remember that it was not an army but an ayyar named Samak who took Mahpari from Falaki Fortress. I promise you I am no less than he in ayyari. Let kings and viziers treat messengers of other nations according to their custom, and let me bring you the princess and Khorshid Shah with their hands tied behind their backs. Then the world can decide who is cleverer, the ayyars of Chin or the ayyars of Machin."

Hearing these words, Gezelmalek cooled down a bit. He took off his royal armband and placed it on Kanun's arm, giving him a look that Kanun understood.

Kanun bowed to the prince and king and left the court. He mounted his horse and rode directly to a modest house on the outskirts of the city, which was no more than a shack. There a skinny old man with gray hair and white beard looked up from his gardening to see Kanun.

Kanun said: "I need you for an important mission."

The old man, whose name was Khatur, went on gardening and said nothing. Kanun told him about all the actions Samak had carried out against the ayyars of Machin, from kidnapping Kanun's sons to abducting Mahpari from Falaki Fortress, and explained the promise he had made to Gezelmalek. He then said: "I want you to go to Khorshid Shah's army camp on Zafron Plains and dig a tunnel under his pavilion."

Khatur was silent for a long time. Then he said: "To dig such a tunnel surrounded by thousands of enemy soldiers is something only a fool or madman would do."

Kanun said: "I'll give you as many helpers as you want. Ten, twenty, a hundred."

Khatur said: "Even if it were possible, I retired from ayyari a long time ago. Perhaps when I was twenty years old I would have been crazy enough to try this kind of thing. At my age, it's out of the question."

Kanun smiled and said: "My old friend, I knew you wouldn't be able to resist this challenge."

The next morning, Kanun arrived at Khatur's house with horses, tools, and a dozen experienced diggers hand-picked from the ranks of the ayyars. Khatur was ready. They mounted their horses and headed for Zafron Plains toward Khorshid Shah's army camp.

Meanwhile, at the king's palace, Armen Shah and the vizier Shahran met to discuss how they should respond to Khorshid Shah's ultimatum. Armen Shah said: "Gezelmalek is right. If we surrender to these people, our honor is gone and we are kings no longer." He suggested to his vizier that if they called upon all their vassals throughout Machin, within ten days they might assemble an army capable of resisting Khorshid Shah.

Shahran thought for a moment, then said: "Since this is the course you are determined to follow, we must find a way to buy time and placate Khorshid Shah. If he attacks the city before our armies arrive, we are lost." Armen Shah asked the vizier what he suggested.

Shahran said: "Let us keep his envoy here as long as possible, then send him back with a proposal to return the prisoners one at a time, in exchange for their weight in gold that was taken from Falaki Fortress. I believe Khorshid Shah will agree to this. This will save face and buy us time until our army comes together and we are in a position to defend ourselves." Armen Shah agreed to this plan.

While Hormozgil waited in the royal guest quarters, fast riders were dispatched in all directions bearing letters from Armen Shah to the rulers of city-states throughout the kingdom of Machin, telling them that the capital was under attack from a foreign army and asking them to send as many soldiers, horses, weapons, and foodstuffs as they could gather.

quarters for the king's reply until, on the fifth day, he was brought to the court. He was seated on the messengers' platform and treated with courtesy in front of the dignitaries and noblemen of Machin. Shahran presented Hormozgil with a letter for Khorshid Shah. Hormozgil thanked the king and vizier, bowed, left the court, and rode with his soldiers back to Khorshid Shah's camp.

On hearing Armen Shah's proposal to exchange the prisoners for their weight in gold, Khorshid Shah and Haman agreed to accept it. Both were relieved that there would finally be an end to the fighting and bloodshed. It was the eve of Khorshid Shah's wedding, and preparations for the feast had already begun. Khorshid Shah went to Mahpari, embraced her, and told her that the war was over.

The day after the wedding, Armen Shah's emissaries brought Khordasb to the camp and returned to Machin with a heavy bag of gold in exchange. Two days later, a similar exchange was repeated for Saum, and two days after that, for Siahgil. The wedding feast went on for seven days and seven nights, during which Khorshid Shah and his generals and noblemen celebrated each prisoner's return and rewarded them for their loyalty throughout their long ordeal.

During this time, Khorshid Shah's scouts began bringing reports of massive armies seen marching toward Machin from various directions. By the time the last prisoner exchange had been completed and the wedding feast ended, a total of one hundred sixty thousand soldiers from various city-states of Machin had gathered outside the city walls.

Khorshid Shah said to Haman: "We offered peace, but it seems the only way we will end this war is on the battlefield." He ordered his generals to prepare the men to fight.

The din of kettle drums and trumpets, neighing of horses and warriors' cries resounded through Zafron Heights as Khorshid

Shah's army gathered on the plain. At dawn, a distant sound like thunder was heard and the sun dimmed by another approaching army's dust. It was an ocean of warriors flooding toward the plain from Machin, a greater fighting force than anyone then alive in that region had seen in their lifetime. At the head of the army, flanked by warriors bearing Armen Shah's banner, rode Gezelmalek and the king himself. Armen Shah had come to lead his army.

The earth shook as the two armies lined up to face each other. The dust had not yet settled when the first warrior rode out from Khorshid Shah's ranks. His name was Chapmar, Farokhruz's stepbrother from Iraq on his father's side, who had come with Marzban Shah's army from Halab. Chapmar rode up and down between the two armies. His stallion stamped the ground and snorted with eagerness for battle. Chapmar shouted: "Who is brave enough to fight me? Come out if you dare, and I'll show you what happens to enemies of Khorshid Shah!"

A warrior built like a mighty tree trunk rode out from Machin's army and shouted: "Where is your prince—hiding behind your skirts? Stop prancing and I'll show you how a real man fights!"

The two warriors lifted their spears and charged at each other. They clashed on horseback, battling with spear and shield until both their spears were broken. The Machin warrior threw his broken shaft aside and drew his sword. Before he had time to strike the first blow, Chapmar had notched an arrow to his bow and let fly. His draw was so powerful that the arrow pierced his opponent's shield, skewered him through the chest and came out his back. The warrior fell from his horse, dead on the spot.

A second warrior rode out from Machin's ranks with a savage war cry and charged at Chapmar with his spear. Chapmar took his time, drew with careful aim, and shot while the warrior was still some distance away. The arrow pierced the man's armor, killing him before he had even come within spear's range. A roar went up from the Machin army. The next warrior rode out to fight, and met the same fate, until Chapmar the archer had killed seven men in a row.

Out of Armen Shah's army rode a husky knight, clad in black armor and riding a black stallion. The black knight charged toward Chapmar, dodging and weaving so expertly that Chapmar's first arrow missed, and his second as well. The distance between them was closing quickly. Chapmar rode alongside one of the fallen warriors, leaned down from the saddle and grabbed the spear from the dead man's hand just in time to meet the black knight's charge. The two warriors fought spear to spear until Chapmar was knocked from his saddle. On the ground, Chapmar drew his bow, but his opponent's spear skewered his arm. Blood poured from the wound. The black knight turned on horseback, drawing his sword to charge again. Chapmar staggered to his feet, but his arm had no strength to lift either sword or bow.

Farokhruz, who had been anxiously watching his older brother Chapmar fight, saw his death coming. He galloped into the field, getting in between Chapmar and his opponent just as the black knight swung his sword in a blow that would have taken off Chapmar's head. It slashed Farokhruz's horse instead. The horse crumpled under Farokhruz, sending him tumbling to the ground.

The black warrior circled again and saw who he had unhorsed. His eyes gleamed with the glory that would be his if he could defeat Khorshid Shah's brother. As Farokhruz tried to get out from under his fallen horse, the warrior let out a cry and charged on horseback with drawn sword to finish him off.

A thrown mace struck the black knight in the chest so hard it knocked him from his saddle. It was Hormozgil, galloping into the field to save Farokhruz. As the black knight staggered to his feet, Hormozgil leapt on him from his horse, knocking him on his back in the dirt. He drew his sword and severed the black knight's head with one blow.

Now Hormozgil held the field. While Farokhruz pulled the wounded Chapmar out of the combat zone, Hormozgil mounted his horse and rode up and down before Armen Shah's ranks, calling for a new opponent.

The first warrior to ride out in answer to Hormozgil's challenge was clad from head to foot in armor of shining silver. He lifted his spear and charged toward Hormozgil. His piebald mount was also armored, with reflecting mirrors mounted on its forehead. The mirrors flashed sunlight into Hormozgil's eyes, blinding him as he charged. That didn't save the silver warrior. Hormozgil's spear struck him in the chest so hard that he fell from his horse. He lay unconscious in the dust, his armor shining no longer.

One after another, five more warriors rode out to fight Hormozgil, but he took each one down with his spear. It was the first day of the combat, and fourteen warriors from Machin's side had fallen.

Hormozgil hurled his spear toward Armen Shah's ranks. It planted in the dirt, quivering before them as a challenge. Hormozgil shouted: "Gezelmalek, is this the army your father gathered under cover of his lies? Come out and face me like an honest warrior!"

This was too much for Gezelmalek. He rode forward and shouted: "I should have killed you in my father's court. I'll shut your mouth once and for all!" He drew his sword and charged Hormozgil. The two mighty warriors battled on horseback, swords and shields clashing and glinting in the sun, until their mounts glistened and sweat was streaming down the horses' backs. They fought until the sun was low in the sky, and still neither one had gained an advantage over the other. At last the day turned into night, and the trumpets blew to call a halt

Samak assured the brothers he would be careful. He thanked them for their hospitality and, covering his face so as not to be recognized, left the house.

Samak made his way through streets and back alleys, keeping to the shadows and rooftops, until he arrived at Mehran's residence. It had high walls and a front gate guarded by two well-armed warriors. Samak noticed that they wore green sashes.

Samak crept around the building but saw no outside opening. A tall tree overlooked the side alley, its uppermost branch overhanging Mehran's wall. Samak took out his lasso and threw it to catch the branch. Using the rope, he climbed the wall and dropped silently onto the roof. He was in.

Samak reconnoitered the rooftop and saw a guard sitting against a wall. The man was African, powerfully built, and appeared to be napping. Samak crept up behind him and locked his arm around the man's throat. The guard opened his eyes and tried to scream, but Samak tightened his grip so that he could make no sound. He demanded: "Have you seen any strangers or intruders around here the past two nights?" The guard shook his head no. Samak said: "One last question. Which room does Mehran the vizier sleep in? Answer truthfully and I'll let you live." The terrified guard pointed to a room in the courtyard below. Samak saw lamp light coming from the window.

"I hope for your sake that you've told the truth," Samak said. He tied the guard's hands and feet with rope. As Samak did this, the cloth over his face accidentally fell away, revealing his features. The guard's eyes went wide and he exclaimed: "Samak the ayyar!"

Samak was startled to be recognized. Before he could ask the guard how he knew him, the man said: "Praise God! I've been praying that fate would bring me into your path. I saw you once in Chin. My brother and I came as eunuch slaves from Africa. He was given to Princess Mahpari and I was given to the vizier

Mehran. My brother was with the princess at Falaki Fortress when Kanun the ayyar abducted them and cut his throat. His murder broke my heart. I've prayed day and night for an opportunity to avenge his death. I know you are Kanun's sworn enemy. I told myself that if I ever saw you again, I would throw myself at your feet and be your loyal servant forever."

Samak, moved by the man's story, asked him his name. The eunuch responded that his name was Anbar. Samak said: "Anbar, I accept your offer. Kanun has many crimes to answer for. It will be my pleasure to help you achieve your heart's desire." Tears of joy rolled down Anbar's face. He promised to be faithful to Samak, whatever he might ask.

Samak said: "I'm afraid the first thing I must ask of you is to betray Mehran, your master from Chin. He too has much to answer for. Three of my friends went on a mission to abduct him and did not return. Do you know anything about that?"

Anbar answered: "If anyone was captured here in the last few days, I didn't hear of it. But I do know that there are three people in chains in the cellar who are friends of yours."

Samak was excited and followed Anbar, who led him to the cellar, taking a route out of the other guards' sight. There in chains were Khomar and his sons Saber and Samlud.

After their initial joy at being reunited, Samak became serious and said: "My friends, if I take you out of here tonight, it will alert Mehran and the guards, and make it harder to do what needs to be done next. Please be patient one more day. I promise if I am still alive tomorrow, I will come back for you." Khomar and his sons assured Samak that they would gladly do whatever he required of them.

With Anbar's help, Samak left the house the way he had come, by the roof, giving Anbar instructions to prepare everything needed for him to return to accomplish his mission.

34

SAMAK FEARS FOR HIS FRIENDS

On the second day that the armies of Khorshid Shah and Armen Shah lined up to face each other, Hormozgil was the first warrior to ride out into the field. He rode up and down the ranks calling for an opponent.

From the right flank of Machin's army rode a tall, heavily armed warrior, who shouted: "It's time you met your match!"

Hormozgil shouted back: "You must want to be killed!"

The warriors charged at each other and clashed on horseback, fighting spear to spear. The combat went on until Hormozgil drove his spear through the tall warrior's thigh with such force that it penetrated his horse's belly. Mount and rider fell together. A cheer went up from Khorshid Shah's army.

A second Machin warrior entered the field. He lasted no more than a minute before he too was felled by Hormozgil's spear. One by one, five more warriors came to challenge Hormozgil, but all were conquered.

Seeing that no one else was coming forward, Hormozgil rode to the front line of Machin's army and shouted: "Where is your prince Gezelmalek, that braggart who wants to fight with champions? Is he afraid to show his face?"

These words enraged Gezelmalek, who was watching from a hilltop where he and his father sat on horseback. He spurred his horse to ride downhill and attack Hormozgil, but Armen Shah restrained him and said: "My son, a prince should not risk his life in battle. You don't see Khorshid Shah coming out to fight, do you? You proved your bravery yesterday. Let our warriors do the job we pay them for."

Before his words were out, a new warrior had ridden into the field. His name was Iluq. He and his brother Tiruq were famed among the great champions of Machin. Hormozgil was tired after battling seven warriors in a row, his spear and shield damaged. Letting out a cry, Hormozgil hurled his spear at Iluq as he charged, hoping to end the fight before it began. Iluq nimbly dodged it and the warriors clashed, Hormozgil drawing his sword to meet Iluq's.

They battled on horseback, their swords clanging, until the blades were as dull as wood saws. Both threw aside their swords and drew their maces. The two great warriors fought at close combat, neither able to land a decisive blow. At last Iluq saw his opportunity. He reached out, grabbed Hormozgil's belt, and pulled him from his saddle.

As Hormozgil fell, he grabbed Iluq and pulled him down with him. The two warriors rolled and grappled in the dirt near their horses' stamping hooves. Hormozgil glimpsed Iluq's dagger strapped to his thigh. He drew it from its sheath and stabbed Iluq with his own dagger, first in the side, then in the chest, again and again until his opponent went limp and fought no more. Hormozgil threw Iluq over his own horse's saddle and slapped its rump, sending it back toward Khorshid Shah's front lines. He knew that a prisoner of Iluq's fame was worth his weight in gold.

Iluq's brother Tiruq rode out from Machin's ranks and shouted: "You ignoble bastard, you've taken down a hero who's worth a thousand of you. I'll make you pay for him!" Raising his spear, Tiruq let out a battle cry and charged.

Hormozgil saw Tiruq galloping toward him on a fresh horse. He was tired and on foot, blood streaming from many wounds, with no weapon but Iluq's dagger. He readied himself for an unequal battle.

As Tiruq arrived, Hormozgil tried to dodge the spear's blow and grab the shaft, but exhaustion slowed him. Tiruq's spear struck him to the ground. Leaping down from his horse, Tiruq followed up his advantage. He raised his spear again and skewered Hormozgil through the thigh. A cry of horror went up from Khorshid Shah's ranks as they saw their champion fall.

Hundreds of Machin soldiers shouted in bloodlust, urging Tiruq to finish off this enemy who had killed twenty of their friends in two days. Tiruq could have ended Hormozgil's life with one thrust of his spear. But he knew that to kill him would doom his brother Iluq. Instead, he threw the vanquished champion over his horse's saddle and brought him back through the army lines to Armen Shah.

Gezelmalek seethed watching this, for he would have liked to see Hormozgil dead, but Armen Shah reminded him: "Tiruq did right. A prisoner is more valuable than a corpse."

The trumpets blew, calling an end to the day's fighting. The men returned to their tents.

Khorshid Shah, concerned for Hormozgil's life, thought immediately of offering Iluq in a prisoner exchange. He rode to the surgeon's tent where Iluq had been taken, but he was informed that Iluq had died of his wounds.

Khorshid Shah took the news grimly. He ordered the soldiers present: "Keep this to yourself. If the enemy finds out he's dead, they might kill Hormozgil in retaliation. Tie him up as if he were still alive, and guard him in a tent. Let no one in."

• • •

When Samak returned to Mehran's house on the second night, Anbar was waiting for him on the rooftop as arranged. He took Samak down to the cellar, where they freed Khomar and his sons. The five of them crept through the palace, following the plan that Samak and Anbar had worked out the night before.

Khomar's sons stood watch in the courtyard while Samak stole into the room that Anbar had told him was Mehran's. It was a large chamber with vaulted ceilings, decorated with silk curtains and ornate cushions. In its center stood a magnificent bed in which the vizier lay sleeping. Samak climbed on top of him and before the startled Mehran could cry out, he gagged him with a cloth and tied his hands and feet with rope. Anbar and Khomar carried in a chest from the kitchen that had been used to store meat. With the eunuch's help, Samak stuffed Mehran inside and locked it. All five of them carried the box up to the roof, lowered it down into the street with a rope, and climbed down after it. Until now, Samak's plan had gone without a hitch.

They carried Mehran around the corner to the spot where Samak had arranged for the butcher brothers to be waiting. The plan had been for them to bring a cart and to hide Mehran's box in it as part of a meat shipment to the bazaar. But the butcher brothers were not there.

Samak became concerned. "We can't wait here," he said. He told Khomar and his sons to split up and meet back at the butcher brothers' house. They of course knew the way. Samak and Anbar carried the chest containing Mehran through the streets, at great risk of being spotted and questioned by a guard. They were lucky and arrived at the butcher brothers' house without incident.

A servant let Samak and Anbar in the back. Samak questioned the servant and learned only that the butcher brothers had left to meet him as arranged. The brothers' wives came downstairs. When they saw that the butchers had not returned with Samak, they too became worried.

Samak opened the box, lifted out Mehran, and untied his gag, saying: "Mehran, you know who I am. If you want to live, tell me where my friends are."

Mehran spat distastefully, and said: "You can be sure that if you harm one hair on my head, your three friends will suffer worse. I understand that one of them is female. I'm surprised that someone as famous for his honor as Samak the ayyar would send a girl to fight his battles."

Samak would have liked to beat Mehran to a pulp, but he held back. He also noticed that Mehran had spoken of three friends, not five. He wondered what had become of the butcher brothers.

There was a knock at the door. The servant opened it and Khomar and his sons entered, breathless and agitated. Samak knew the moment he saw their faces that something terrible had happened. Khomar said: "Samak, I wish I didn't have to tell you this news, the worst possible. Khorshid Shah and Mahpari have been captured. They were taken from the camp and are prisoners in the royal palace."

35

NEWLYWEDS ABDUCTED

All this time, Khatur and his twelve helpers had been patiently digging their tunnel under the Chin army camp, extending it by a few feet every day. Khatur monitored the progress with regular visits to the surface, estimating the distance and making adjustments as needed to ensure that the digging continued in the correct direction.

It was during the second day of combat that Khatur told the diggers to start digging straight upward. They dug upward until they broke through the ground. Khatur had judged the distance so accurately that the digger who poked his head up through the opening found himself not only inside Khorshid Shah's pavilion but directly under the prince's bed.

Khatur sent word to Kanun, who soon arrived with his young albino sidekick Kafur. When Kanun saw the opening, he said to Khatur: "Ah, my friend, you haven't lost a step. Sometimes age is superior to youth."

The soldiers who would normally have been on guard inside the tent had all gone to the battlefield. Khatur told the diggers to take advantage of this opportunity to enlarge the opening under the bed. When all was ready, the ayyars retreated into the tunnel and waited for nightfall.

At the end of the day, after the trumpets blew to announce the end of battle, Khorshid Shah returned to his tent dejected, worried about his captured friend Hormozgil. Mahpari joined Khorshid Shah at his pavilion and did all she could to lift his spirits. The newlyweds shared dinner and wine, then went to bed together and fell deeply asleep in each other's arms.

Soon after midnight, the ayyars Kanun, Kafur, Khatur, and a fourth helper emerged silently from the opening and surrounded the bed. As one, they pounced on the sleeping prince and princess, and swiftly gagged and bound them before they could cry out for the guards. They pulled Khorshid Shah and Mahpari through the tunnel and out into the dry river bed, where their helpers waited with horses. They wrapped Khorshid Shah and Mahpari in rugs so that, from a distance, they would appear to be rug merchants carrying their wares. From there they rode straight to Machin and delivered their prize to Armen Shah's palace, which in the king's absence was as securely guarded as any fortress.

It was just after dawn when Kanun arrived at Armen Shah's army camp pavilion and informed the king and prince of his mission's success. Gezelmalek was delighted and wanted to ride back to the city right away. He imagined the pleasure of seeing Khorshid Shah a chained prisoner at his mercy. His heart beat faster at the thought of freeing Mahpari from her shackles and bringing her back to his pavilion. But Armen Shah told his son firmly: "Your place is on the battlefield."

Gezelmalek argued: "We started this war for the princess Mahpari. Now at last we have her. We don't know what the enemy might do next to free her and Khorshid Shah. She ought to be here, close to us, where our army can guard her."

Armen Shah understood his son's desire all too well. He said: "Wait until we win the war before you claim the spoils of victory. Remember that if by God's will we don't prevail, our kingdom, our crown, our lives, and the lives of your mother and sister will be at the enemy's mercy. We can expect the same courtesy from them that we show to Khorshid Shah and his queen now. To bring the princess into an army camp would be inappropriate. It might be misunderstood."

Gezelmalek said: "I still want to go to town to make sure she is being kept safe under close watch. And that she is well treated."

Shahran the vizier, who had been listening, bowed to the king and said: "Your Majesty, if I may make a suggestion, there is a fortress in the area known as Twelve Canyons that would be ideal. It is built high on a mountain that no army or intruder can reach, and it is not too far from the city. The royal prisoners will be safe there."

Armen Shah agreed with this suggestion, and Gezelmalek reluctantly gave in.

The king called in Tiruq. He stood before the king, a brutal mountain of a man. His praises resounded throughout the camp after his defeat of the great Hormozgil the day before. The king ordered: "Tiruq, you are the greatest of my warriors. Prince Khorshid Shah and Mahpari are now our prisoners in the royal palace. I want you to take them from Machin to Twelve Canyons Fortress. Take fifty of your best men. We can expect that the enemy will try to free them." Tiruq bowed to Armen Shah and left the pavilion.

Early that morning, when the princess's maidservant went into Khorshid Shah's tent to serve Mahpari, she was surprised to find the bed empty. She alerted the other servants and guards. They soon discovered the hole under the bed. The guards, with increasing alarm, followed the tunnel to the dry ditch. The horses' hoof prints told the rest of the story.

Shock and outrage echoed through camp as the news spread that Khorshid Shah and Mahpari had been abducted. Many wanted to attack Armen Shah's army immediately in retaliation. The vizier Haman ordered everyone to stay calm while he dispatched a messenger to Faghfur Shah informing him of the terrible news. He sent another to Armen Shah demanding an explanation.

• • •

When Samak heard of the abduction, he was so distressed that for a long time he could not speak. His friends waited anxiously. They had never seen Samak at such a loss.

The vizier Mehran, even with his hands and feet tied, could not keep himself from gloating. He hated Khorshid Shah and was delighted that Princess Mahpari, whose father he had served and developed contempt for, was in the enemy's hands. His glee became so annoying that Anbar finally put the gag back in his mouth and returned him to the box in which they had brought him.

At length, Samak pulled himself together and said to Khomar: "Are you sure they're being held in the royal palace?" Khomar confirmed that this was what he had heard.

Samak said: "I have been to the royal palace once before with your sons. It won't be so easy this time." Saber and Samlud acknowledged that the days when they had been welcome in the royal court as respected citizens of Machin were past.

Samak turned to Anbar and said: "Anbar, have you ever been inside Armen Shah's harem?" Anbar responded that he had often gone there in his capacity as Mehran's servant. Eunuchs like himself were the only men allowed to enter the harem. Samak said: "If you showed up this afternoon escorting six wives of dignitaries whom your master Mehran ordered you to bring to the palace, would the guards let you in?"

Anbar considered and replied: "The guards know me. The danger is that if the news of my master's abduction has already reached the palace, my appearance may arouse suspicion."

Samak said: "It's a risk we'll have to take." He looked at the butcher brothers' wives, who sat with a maidservant, anxiously holding each other's hands. He said: "I promised you I would do everything in my power to find and bring back your husbands. Right now, I must ask you to get dressed in your best outfits. You are about to meet the queen and princess of Machin."

Half an hour later, the butchers' wives were ready in elegant dresses of embroidered silk, scented with exotic perfumes, their eyes rimmed with kohl. The young maidservant had likewise put on her most formal outfit to escort her mistresses on the royal visit. Samak expressed his admiration. He then asked the maidservant: "Can you make me look as beautiful as your mistresses?" An hour of hard work ensued with the help of the maid and the butchers' wives. By the time they were finished, Samak, Saber, and Samlud matched the three women in elegance, if not in beauty. Samak presented them for Anbar's inspection. Anbar made a few adjustments and pronounced them ready.

When they arrived at the royal palace, Anbar took them as far as the courtyard of the royal compound, then he entered the harem alone to request permission to present the dignitaries' wives to the queen and princess.

While they were waiting in the courtyard, a formidable-looking warrior arrived fresh from the battlefield. Samak saw him talking to the guards and urged the maidservant to get close enough to eavesdrop. The maid returned reporting that she had heard the warrior tell the guards that Armen Shah had sent him to take the royal prisoners into his custody. He had shown a scroll with the king's seal to prove it. This warrior was, of course, Tiruq.

Samak said: "Then we have no time to lose." Anbar returned and told them that he had received permission for the visit. Six individuals, all appearing to be women, followed Anbar into the palace and through a series of courtyards and corridors until they reached the harem.

The queen of Machin and the princess Mahaneh sat on silk cushions, attended by handmaidens and eunuch slaves. A minstrel maiden played the sitar and sang a love song. In the center of the room was a reflecting pool. Samak saw that Mahaneh was young, no more than twenty years old. She was strikingly beautiful, with a slender figure and a face like the full moon. Her long black hair shone like polished onyx. She moved with the grace of a gazelle. Her mouth was like a rose, her teeth white as pearls. Her high cheekbones, long eyelashes, and dark, intelligent, flashing eyes arrested Samak's gaze so that he found it hard to look away.

Anbar introduced the newcomers. Samak and the others paid their respects and sat politely on cushions that were placed in front of the queen and princess. Samak felt his heart pound on being seated so close to Mahaneh. If a breeze had blown through the princess's hair at that moment, its scent would have enchanted the world. Samak told himself that even an ascetic Sufi mystic, seeing this girl, would forget his vows.

At a signal from Samak, Anbar leaned forward and whispered to the queen: "Your Majesty, our guests wonder if they could speak to you in private. They have information they are eager to share, for no one's ears but yours and the princess's." The queen became curious, and she instructed the handmaidens, musicians, and slaves to leave the room.

When the queen and princess were alone with Anbar and their guests, the queen said: "What is this information?"

Samak said: "Your Majesty, I can tell you the exact whereabouts of Samak the ayyar." With that, he removed his face covering, revealing his beard and a wide grin. Before the queen or the princess could scream, Samak said: "We are here to take back Khorshid Shah and Mahpari. If you help us, no one will get hurt, and I promise to show you every courtesy. If you scream for the guards or oppose us in any way, I assure you that each one of us is prepared to die for the sake of the prince and princess, and we'll take as many with us as we can, starting with you."

The queen and princess were silent. Samak turned to Anbar and told him: "Go and bring Tiruq. Tell him the queen wants to see him right away."

Anbar left and returned soon afterward bringing Tiruq, who was obliged to leave his weapons outside with the guards before entering the queen's presence. Samak hid beside the doorway. As Tiruq entered, Samak struck him from behind with a heavy ceramic pot so hard that the warrior was instantly knocked unconscious. Saber and Samlud hurried to tie him up.

Mahaneh, who had been watching Samak with keen interest, now spoke up and said: "I know where they are being kept, and I can take you to them." Samak warned her of the consequences if she was trying to trick him. The princess arched her eyebrows—she did not seem afraid of him.

Samak told Saber and Samlud to stay in the harem with the butcher's wives and handmaiden, to guard the queen and Tiruq, and not to let anyone enter. Then he and Anbar followed Mahaneh. She led them down a series of corridors, down a stone staircase, and they finally arrived at a locked door guarded by a formidable, heavily-armed eunuch.

Mahaneh said to him: "I wish to see the prisoners."

The guard looked uncomfortable and said: "O Princess, I am your servant, but your father the king gave strict instructions that no one may enter here without a written order and his royal seal."

Samak and Anbar sprang on the guard, forced him to the ground, gagged him, and tied his hands and feet with rope.

Samak took the guard's keys and unlocked the door. Inside the cell, Khorshid Shah and Mahpari were sitting on straw, their hands tied and feet shackled. Their faces lit up on seeing Samak. Anbar untied Mahpari while Samak untied Khorshid Shah and, bowing to him, said: "My lord! It's my good fortune that I happened to pass by. As long as I'm alive, I will let no harm come your way."

The moment they were untied, Mahpari flung herself into Khorshid Shah's arms. "My beloved," he murmured, and held her tight. Tears came to Samak's and Anbar's eyes. Everyone in the room felt how much the prince and his queen loved each other.

Princess Mahaneh stood alone, tall and straight like a cypress, watching the royal couple embrace. Samak thought he noticed a strange expression on her face. He could not have guessed what she was thinking.

Samak said to Anbar: "What's the quickest way out of here?"

Anbar said: "A secret underground passageway leads from the harem to an alley outside the palace compound." Samak approved of this plan. All five of them hurried back to the harem where the others awaited. Anbar pulled aside a curtain, revealing a door that led to the secret passageway. The whole group followed Anbar down a flight of stairs and through the underground passage—Khorshid Shah and Mahpari, the butchers' wives and their handmaiden, Saber and Samlud carrying the tied-up warrior Tiruq, and finally Samak, escorting the captured queen and princess, with his eye on Mahaneh to make sure she didn't try to escape or give them away. They emerged up a flight of stairs and into an alley outside the palace. It was late in the day; night was already settling over the city.

Samak sent the butchers' wives and maiden home, accompanied by Saber and Samlud, whom he instructed to guard the vizier until he returned. Samak, Anbar, and the others then continued through the streets until they arrived at the city's outer wall.

Samak took out his lasso, threw it until it caught a crenellation, and scaled the wall to the top. Gazing into the distance, he saw in the moonlight a small grove about half a mile outside the city. He told Anbar to fetch seven horses and meet him in this grove at sunrise. Then, with Khorshid Shah's help (for the prince was by now familiar with this kind of work), Samak pulled the rest of the party up after him one by one, and down the lasso on the other side of the wall.

The hardest job was carrying the tied-up warrior Tiruq. He refused to go quietly, thrashing and straining against his bonds with such determination that Samak feared he would break them. But eventually he gave up trying, and Samak and Khorshid Shah were able to share his weight as they carried him to the grove. There they camped for the night.

It was a clear moonlit night, the sky above Machin bright with stars. Mahpari lay sleeping in Khorshid Shah's arms, Mahaneh next to her mother. Samak kept watch while the others slept, breathing in the cold fresh mountain air to stay awake.

Shortly after dawn, Anbar arrived at the grove with seven horses. They headed for Khorshid Shah's army camp with the three prisoners tied up on three horses, led by Samak, Anbar, Khorshid Shah, and Mahpari.

The entire army soon rejoiced as news of the prince and princess's triumphant return spread through the camp. Haman the vizier was so excited that he walked to Khorshid Shah's mount, kissed the prince's boot, and led him directly to his pavilion. There they celebrated with wine and delicious food and toasted Samak's latest marvelous accomplishment. Samak suggested to the prince that Anbar be given to Mahpari as her personal servant. Khorshid Shah agreed immediately.

The queen and princess of Machin were taken to Mahpari's pavilion, where they were treated as honored guests, under close watch to ensure they would not escape.

Khorshid Shah sent an emissary to the enemy's camp informing them that they had taken Tiruq prisoner and offering him in exchange for Hormozgil. Armen Shah and Gezelmalek were apoplectic at the news but had little choice but to agree. The prisoner exchange took place soon thereafter. Hormozgil's return was cause for more rejoicing in Khorshid Shah's pavilion. The celebration resumed that evening and continued long into the night.

The only one missing from these festivities was Samak. He had asked Khorshid Shah's permission to return to Machin, as he was worried about the fate of his five friends. This being granted, Samak said his goodbyes and left immediately.

36

BATTLE OF PRINCES

ONLY one day after having sent Tiruq to the royal palace to take charge of their hostages, Armen Shah, Gezelmalek, and Shahran were stunned to see him returned in shackles as the enemy's prisoner. Tiruq bowed low to the king and, burning with shame, recounted how he had been fooled by Samak the ayyar.

When the king heard that Samak had not only freed Khorshid Shah and Mahpari, but had taken his own queen and daughter prisoner, he shouted in rage and hurled his crown to the ground. Gezelmalek screamed: "They took Mahpari, after all we went through to get her! I will kill every one of those bastards! Get my horse ready! I'll fight Khorshid Shah right now!"

The vizier Shahran restrained him and said: "Your Highness, don't let anger make you do something you might regret. Now more than ever, we must think clearly. Your mother and sister should be our first concern."

Armen Shah agreed with the vizier's wise words. As Shahran picked up the crown and replaced it on the king's head, Armen Shah turned to his son and said sternly: "That is the last time I wish to hear Mahpari's name on your lips. She is married to Khorshid Shah now and is the queen of Persia. To go after her further would only bring disgrace upon our kingdom. Put her out of your mind once and for all."

Gezelmalek, seething with anger, said: "They have Mother and Mahaneh! We should attack their camp with our entire force and take them out of there."

Shahran said: "Such a battle would cost many soldiers' lives and endanger your mother and sister. I suggest a peaceful solution." Armen Shah asked his vizier what he had in mind. Shahran explained: "If it is Your Majesty's wish, I will personally carry offerings to Khorshid Shah as wedding gifts and express our desire for peace. I will then ask for the return of the queen and princess. Once we have them back, we can contemplate our next move." Armen Shah agreed to this plan.

Shahran bowed to Armen Shah and Gezelmalek, left the pavilion, and ordered one hundred thoroughbred horses, one hundred bags of gold, and one hundred slaves gathered as royal gifts from Machin. Kanun, upon hearing that Shahran was going to the enemy's camp, went to him and said: "Your Excellency, you engaged me to assassinate Samak the ayyar. It is my shame that I have not succeeded, while he has done so much damage. Please let me accompany you in disguise as your attendant. If I can get a look at this Samak with my own eyes, I will be sure to recognize him in the future and not miss a chance to kill him."

Shahran agreed to this. A messenger rode to Khorshid Shah's camp to request permission for the vizier to visit.

While Armen Shah and his entourage awaited the response, a great cloud of dust appeared on the horizon. A rumble like thunder shook the ground, becoming louder as the dust cloud approached. A scout rode back to inform Armen Shah: "Arkalak the mountain warrior is coming with an army of thirty thousand to join Your Highness!" As the troops reached the camp, Armen Shah and Gezelmalek were thrilled to see that Arkalak had brought not only men and horses, but catapults and sixty war elephants. A cheer went up from the Machin army. With this force on their side, they felt they could not lose.

The messenger returned and informed Armen Shah that Khorshid Shah was ready and waiting to receive Shahran.

Shahran crossed the battlefield leading a procession of a hundred horses, slaves, and bags of gold. Incognito among the attendants, so that he could observe freely, was Kanun.

When Shahran arrived at camp, the vizier Haman walked toward him and gave him a warm hug of welcome as soon as he dismounted from his horse. Haman escorted the vizier to Khorshid Shah's pavilion. Shahran kneeled in front of the prince, congratulated him on his marriage, and mentioned that he had brought gifts from Armen Shah.

Khorshid Shah thanked the vizier and gestured to an empty seat beside his own. Once Shahran was seated, a royal banquet began, with delicious food, wine, minstrels, and exotic dancers. As the entertainment drew to a close, Khorshid Shah glanced at his vizier, signaling that he was ready to hear their visitor's proposal. Haman turned to Shahran and informed him that he had the prince's permission to speak.

Shahran rose from his seat, bowed to Khorshid Shah, and spoke: "Your Highness, Armen Shah sends his greetings to you and Faghfur Shah. Our parents and grandparents were always on good terms with each other. This war, in which we have both lost so many soldiers, began over the princess Mahpari. Now that she is your queen, that matter is done and ended. The king hopes you will accept these wedding gifts as an expression of his sincere desire for peace." He gestured to the chamberlains, who opened the pavilion curtains for Khorshid Shah to view the gifts. Shahran added: "The only remaining issue is that our queen and princess are still in your custody. We hope that you will now release them. Surely we can agree that an army camp is no place for noblewomen, who should not be exposed to public view."

Khorshid Shah gave the gifts only a brief, disparaging glance, and said: "Dear vizier, I am disappointed to hear a wise man speak like this. I am equally surprised that a prudent king like Armen Shah can so easily forget the harm you have caused us. It was your army that attacked our domain of Chin. It was your agents who kidnapped my promised wife from Shahak Fortress and imprisoned her until God brought her back to me. You kept my ambassador and my dearest generals in a dungeon. As if these insults were not enough, you burrowed under my pavilion in secret and abducted my queen Mahpari and me in our sleep. Is she not also a noblewoman who should be kept out of public view?"

The prince continued: "We have no interest in your gifts. Take them back to your king. You can reassure him that his wife and daughter are not in shackles. They are comfortable and enjoying the hospitality of my queen Mahpari. We will return them to you in exchange for five citizens whom I have been told are in your custody, friends of Samak the ayyar. For their sake I will give up our royal prisoners. Bring this offer to your king. If it does not suit him, let him send his great burrowers to make another tunnel and take back his wife and daughter that way."

Shahran bowed and left the pavilion. Outside, Kanun had used this time to gain information about Samak and his whereabouts, but all he had been able to learn was that Samak was not in the camp and had gone back to Machin. Kanun asked Shahran's permission to go to Machin to try to capture Samak before he caused new problems. This the vizier granted. Shahran then mounted his horse and returned to Armen Shah's camp, taking the rejected gifts with him.

Soon thereafter, scouts came to Khorshid Shah with the news that a large army of reinforcements was arriving from Chin.

A dust cloud appeared in the distance, and the ground trembled with the thunder of men and horses. The vizier Haman went to welcome the new arrivals and escorted them to Khorshid Shah's pavilion. The leaders, two generals by the names of Azarjush and Irmun, bowed to the prince. Azarjush explained that they had been sent by Faghfur Shah to help with the siege of Machin, and he expressed joy at seeing the prince and princess safe and well.

Shahran returned to Armen Shah's pavilion and reported Khorshid Shah's response to the king and Gezelmalek. Armen Shah stroked his beard and said: "Five commoners in return for the queen and princess is not a bad exchange. We should accept it."

Gezelmalek disagreed and said: "We have Arkalak and his army of elephants. Now is the time to attack, while they are overconfident and gloating." The three of them discussed the possibilities and finally agreed with Gezelmalek. Armen Shah summoned the generals to gather in his pavilion and told them to get the army ready to fight.

• • •

Early the next morning, Khorshid Shah was surprised to hear the drums beaten and trumpets blown in Machin's camp. "So Armen Shah wants to continue this war," he said. He called his generals to his pavilion and ordered them to prepare for combat. As the morning mist lifted, the two armies lined up to face each other, weapons and armor glinting in the sun, two vast rivers of men and horses.

Irmun, the newly arrived general from Chin, rode to Khorshid Shah and asked his permission to be the first one to fight. This Khorshid Shah granted. Irmun thanked the prince, and spurred his horse across the field toward the Machin ranks, calling for a combatant. A heavily armored champion rode toward him. The two warriors battled until both their spears were broken, then with swords until they fell from their horses, then on foot until Irmun's dagger found its mark. His victory lasted only a moment, as his dying opponent plunged his own dagger into Irmun's throat. A cry went up from the assembled armies as they saw both warriors fall dead.

Moments later, a young warrior named Harrar rode out of Khorshid Shah's army on a black stallion. "Who will fight me?" he shouted. A Machin warrior answered the challenge, but he lasted only a few minutes before he was run through by the young man's spear. Eight more warriors entered the field. One after another, all fell. Harrar raised his invincible spear high and shook it in the air, shouting: "Gezelmalek! Come and face me! How long will you let other men fight your battles for you?"

Gezelmalek, resplendent in his red armor, rode to Armen Shah's side and said: "Father, let me fight!"

Armen Shah said: "My beloved son, this is our warriors' job. Let our army be our shield. Better to lose ten thousand soldiers than have one hair taken from your head."

Gezelmalek's face burned. He said: "You don't understand. You can't feel my pain. I'll fight with or without your permission. Win or lose, no one will say I was afraid to fight for Mahpari!" With that, he rode into the field and straight at Harrar, letting out a terrible war cry. The young warrior met Gezelmalek's spear with his own. The two battled on horseback until Gezelmalek's spear shattered. Tossing it aside, Gezelmalek drew his sword, lifted it high and brought it down with tremendous force on Harrar's head. Harrar raised his shield to protect himself, but Gezelmalek's sword broke the shield in two, sliced through Harrar's helmet and split his skull. Blood streamed down the young warrior's face. He turned his horse and rode back to the Chin army's ranks.

Gezelmalek pranced in triumph, brandishing his sword. The sight of the red prince on horseback struck fear into the hearts of Chin's soldiers. With his pale face and black hair, he looked like a man possessed with the power of a demon. He shouted: "Khorshid Shah! Come fight me! Let's settle this war once and for all!"

Farokhruz looked at Khorshid Shah and saw that his brother was about to ride to meet the challenge. He blocked his way, saying: "I won't let you risk your life against an idiot like Gezelmalek while I'm alive."

Khorshid Shah said: "My dear brother, you are the best and bravest of men. But I am the one Gezelmalek challenged, not you."

Farokhruz said: "I am your shield. I swear it to you and on Marzban Shah's head!" And he spurred his horse toward Gezelmalek.

When Gezelmalek saw Farokhruz riding toward him, with his gleaming armor and noble bearing, he thought: "This must be Khorshid Shah." Lifting his spear, Gezelmalek charged at Farokhruz, who dodged. The two princes battled on horseback until suddenly Gezelmalek thrust his spear straight at his opponent's heart. Farokhruz raised his shield to block the blow, but Gezelmalek cleverly lowered his attack at the last moment, so that his spear skewered Farokhruz's thigh and came out the other side with enough force to penetrate his horse's belly. Blood poured from the wound. Farokhruz realized he could fight no longer. He turned his injured horse and rode back to the Chin army ranks.

Exultant, Gezelmalek shouted after him: "So this is the great Khorshid Shah everyone talks about! So easily defeated!"

Khorshid Shah could hold back no longer. He spurred his mount and charged toward Gezelmalek. He shouted: "I am Khorshid Shah! Here I come to end your life and give your father Armen Shah eternal pain!"

When Gezelmalek saw Khorshid Shah riding toward him with his armor shining like the sun, he felt a shiver of fear run through him. He shouted back: "I will fight you! But let me exchange my horse for a fresh one. The animal is exhausted."

Khorshid Shah said: "Go on then, prolong your life by a few minutes! I'll wait for you right here."

While Gezelmalek rode to exchange his horse, the news spread through Chin's army camp that Khorshid Shah was about to fight Gezelmalek. Mahpari, hearing this, turned pale with fear. She said to her servant: "Anbar, I can't stay here in my pavilion. I need to be near him and see him fight, even if he doesn't know I'm there. Fetch me men's armor and a helmet." Anbar ran out and returned with several sets of armor and helmets, which he helped Mahpari try on until they found one that fit.

During all this, Princess Mahaneh had been watching. Now, as Mahpari left the tent wearing a man's armor, Mahaneh drew her aside and said: "Dear sister, I love Khorshid Shah. I admired his nobility and courage before I ever met him. The first day I laid eyes on him, in the palace dungeon, and saw him embrace you, it was like a burning arrow shot into my heart. I yearn for him day and night. I want you to know that if Khorshid Shah takes me as his wife, I would treat you as my beloved sister and never do anything to cause you a moment's unhappiness."

Mahpari stood still for a moment, then replied: "O my dear, I had no idea you were suffering. I must tell you, Khorshid Shah promised me when we got married that he would never take another wife." Then she went outside the tent to where Anbar was waiting, mounted her horse, and rode to the combat zone.

Mahaneh waited until Anbar and Mahpari had left the pavilion. Then she scooped up the armor they had left and ran to her mother the queen, who was resting. Mahaneh shook her awake, saying: "Mother, we have to leave this place."

Soon thereafter, the queen and princess rode away from Mahpari's pavilion, wearing men's armor and riding two horses, looking from a distance like Chin warriors. With most soldiers at the front lines, awaiting the battle between Khorshid Shah and Gezelmalek, Mahaneh and her mother easily reached Machin's army camp without being stopped.

Meanwhile, Gezelmalek, returning to camp to exchange his horse for a fresh one, had an inspiration on seeing Arkalak's elephants being tended by their keepers. He thought to himself: "Khorshid Shah has never fought against elephants." He ordered a war elephant to be made ready for combat.

When Armen Shah saw what his son was doing, he became enthusiastic, and ordered: "Send in two more elephants, one on each side to guard him."

Gezelmalek mounted a seat on his elephant's back. Twenty drivers surrounded the animal and guided it onto the field. Gezelmalek felt invulnerable as he rode atop it. On either side of him rode another elephant, each surrounded by twenty drivers.

A roar of outrage rose from Chin's ranks as they saw how Khorshid Shah had been tricked. Mahpari, watching with Anbar, gasped in fear.

Khorshid Shah immediately covered his horse's eyes so it wouldn't be spooked by the sight of the elephants. He charged head-on at the elephant carrying Gezelmalek. The elephant reared to attack, but Khorshid Shah dodged nimbly aside, and with one slash of his sword severed the elephant's trunk. The animal let out a roar of pain so loud that the other two elephants took fright. The elephant drivers could not control them. All three stampeded back toward camp so fast that the Machin soldiers had to scramble out of their way to escape being trampled.

With that, both armies returned to their camps to rest for the evening.

When Armen Shah returned to his pavilion, he was pleasantly surprised to find his queen and princess waiting for him. This was some consolation for the disappointing outcome of the day's battles.

37

A WATCHMAN'S REWARD

Samak returned to Machin the same way he had left—under cover of darkness, using his lasso to scale the city wall. He made his way to the butchers' house, slipping through back alleys and over rooftops, taking care to stay in shadow.

Arriving at the butchers' house, Samak was greeted by Saber, Samlud, and their father Khomar. They brought him Mehran, still tied hand and foot. After removing his gag Samak said: "O vizier, I am sorry you had to wait so long in such uncomfortable circumstances. I am happy to tell you that Khorshid Shah and his queen Mahpari have been returned to their proper places in Chin's army camp, and furthermore, that Armen Shah's queen and daughter are now their guests. The only ones still not where they should be are the two brother butchers whose hospitality we are now enjoying, and my friends who went missing the other night in the vicinity of your house. Their names, in case it helps you remember, are Sorkhvard, Atashak, and Neyal."

Hearing this, Mehran understood that he was at Samak's mercy and that if he was to save his life, he needed to be clever. "I was a fool to join with Armen Shah," he said. "Faghfur Shah was incompetent, not worthy of his crown. Your Khorshid

Shah is a different matter. He will win this war. A vizier exists by a king's good graces. I have no right to expect mercy and have nothing to bargain with. The lives of a few commoners are of no importance to a king. So my fate is sealed. I ask only for a quick death."

Samak said: "Listen, Mehran, nothing can undo blood that has already been spilled. If you help me get my friends back alive, I will get on my knees and ask Khorshid Shah to spare your life. You have my word."

Mehran said: "In that case, I can tell you that three people were captured near my house by guards reporting to the city watchman, a man named Surkhkafar. But I warn you not to try to free them by your usual methods. Surkhkafar is no one to underestimate. He has sworn an oath to Armen Shah to capture and deliver you. He has placed the watchmen's headquarters in his own compound, a fortress within the town. I am told that before the war not even the king's tax collectors dared set foot there. The compound and streets around it are manned by his guards day and night. If you try to assault or infiltrate that place, you will fail. Your only hope is to lure Surkhkafar out of there and bring him to you. I can help you with this."

Samak had already heard some of this from the butcher brothers. This made him think that Mehran might be telling the truth.

Samak conferred with Khomar and his sons. He then returned, and dictated a message which Mehran wrote in his own hand. In the message, Mehran identified himself and paid his respects to Surkhkafar, saying that he had been abducted but had managed to escape, and he had met someone who knew the whereabouts of Samak the ayyar. He asked Surkhkafar to meet the informant at midnight at a certain place, adding: "Take the greatest care that you come alone, and bring no guards with you, or this opportunity will be lost."

Samak read the message several times, looking for some hidden trap, but he could find no fault in it. He sent Saber to deliver it to Surkhkafar at the watchmen's headquarters. Saber returned half an hour later reporting that the message had been delivered.

Shortly before midnight, Samak, Khomar, and his sons led Mehran to a neighborhood that was a warren of narrow, twisting streets. There they waited.

Mehran asked uneasily: "What are we doing here? This is not the meeting place we said."

No one answered. After a few minutes, the silence was broken by a beautiful singing voice wafting through the night. It was a woman singing from an open window in a nearby alley.

Khomar listened, then turned to Samak and said: "Five of Surkhkafar's guards have stationed themselves in the alleys surrounding the meeting place. If we go there we will be captured."

"That is unfortunate," Samak said. Turning to Mehran, he demanded: "Why did Surkhkafar disobey you when you told him clearly to come alone?"

Mehran, who had turned pale, stammered: "I don't know. Whatever gave you that idea?"

"A songbird," said Samak. Khomar led them down the street, around the corner, through a doorway, up a narrow staircase, then through a series of passageways connecting the buildings of that block in a manner no outsider could have guessed, until finally they arrived at a certain door on which Khomar knocked gently. It was instantly opened by an attractive middle-aged woman.

Saber, Samlud, and Khomar greeted her affectionately. Khomar said to Samak: "This is my sister. You have already heard her beautiful singing voice." She expressed pleasure at meeting Samak the ayyar and thanked him for his recent rescue of her brother and nephews. Samak said that on the contrary, it was he who should thank them. As for Mehran, he was growing paler by the minute.

On Samak's instructions, Saber and Samlud bound and gagged Mehran and left him for their father and aunt to watch over. The brothers then separated. Saber led Samak out a back way, down a staircase, and through more corridors, ending at a narrow doorway that opened onto a side alley. There they waited silently, Samak with his dagger drawn.

After a moment, the sound of their aunt's singing voice reached them.

"Now," said Saber. Samak burst through the doorway into the alley, startling a well-built, powerful-looking man who happened to be striding past at just that moment. The man, who was none other than Surkhkafar, whirled, drawing his dagger, but Samak, with the advantage of surprise, blocked the blow while driving his own dagger deep into Surkhkafar's side. At the same instant, Samlud came running up the alley behind Surkhkafar and tackled him to the ground. The three of them quickly dragged the constable into the doorway and out of sight.

Before long they heard shouts and running footsteps of guards in the alley and surrounding streets. Working quickly, Saber and Samlud bound and gagged the unconscious constable. Samak tore his own shirt and wrapped it tightly around the wound to stanch the blood flow. Soon the shouts and footsteps receded. From the guards' point of view, Surkhkafar had simply vanished.

Samak, Saber, and Samlud lugged Surkhkafar's massive body through the passageways and up the stairs until they reached their aunt's doorway. They pulled Surkhkafar inside and closed the door behind them. Their aunt exclaimed: "Surkhkafar! I never thought anyone could capture that man! I'd have said it was impossible."

Samak instructed the brothers to remove Surkhkafar's gag. The constable blinked and looked slowly around him at the people in the room, recognizing no one. His gaze rested for a moment on Mehran, bound and gagged. Then, turning to Samak, he said calmly: "You must be Samak the ayyar. I swore an oath to Armen Shah to bring him your head."

Samak said: "I could have killed you in that alley. I spared your life so that you can tell us what you've done with my friends—Sorkhvard, Atashak, Neyal, and the butcher brothers."

Surkhkafar said: "They are in my custody. But I won't tell you where." He studied Samak, then said: "No one has ever bested Surkhkafar in battle. You are the first."

Samak replied: "Surkhkafar, you speak like a man of honor. Yet when your friend Mehran the vizier told you to come alone tonight, you secretly sent your guards to surround the meeting place. Was that honest?"

Surkhkafar said coldly: "I take orders from no one. Mehran used a code phrase I had suggested he use in case of need. 'Take the greatest care' means bring armed force. The rest of the sentence is to be disregarded."

"Ah," said Samak. "That makes sense." He turned to the vizier, whose eyes bulged in terror as he tried to speak through his gag. "A forked tongue that's already cost so many lives deserves no last words. It will only find a way to do more damage." He drew his dagger and thrust it into the vizier's heart. Blood poured from the wound and soaked through the silk robe. Mehran keeled over dead, his eyes frozen wide open in astonishment.

The room had gone silent.

Samak turned to Khomar's sister and said: "Well! We'd better get these two out of here before they cause you and your family any more trouble."

Shortly before dawn, the guards at the main gate of the royal compound were surprised to see a rider gallop past on horseback and pitch an object that rolled toward them. By the time they had retrieved it, the rider was gone. The guards unwrapped the sack. Inside was the head of Mehran the vizier.

It was early morning when Samak, Saber, and Samlud reached Khorshid Shah's army camp with their tied-up prisoner. Samak was shown straight to the prince's pavilion.

Khorshid Shah was so excited to see Samak that he stood up from his throne and walked toward him with open arms. Everyone else present immediately stood up, following the prince's example. It was an extraordinary honor for the prince of Persia to greet a commoner with such humility. Samak bowed deeply to Khorshid Shah. The prince invited him to sit beside him. Samak told him the whole story, starting with his friends' disappearance and ending with Surkhkafar's capture and the execution of Mehran, for which he begged the prince's forgiveness.

Khorshid Shah ordered Surkhkafar brought in. Surkhkafar entered flanked by Saber and Samlud. Bound and manacled, his midriff wrapped in a blood-soaked cloth, Surkhkafar cut an imposing figure. His cold, dark-eyed gaze swept the room, somehow dominating the assembled warriors despite his abject condition. A murmur rippled through the pavilion as everyone marveled at how Samak could have captured such a powerful man.

Khorshid Shah said to Saber and Samlud: "I remember you from Machin. I owe you thanks for my queen's escape and safe return, and for much else." He looked at Samak, who confirmed that Saber and Samlud were like his own brothers and that he owed them his life. Khorshid Shah asked the brothers to name their reward. They replied that their only wish was to join the ayyars of Chin, whose leader Shaghal was Samak's mentor. This Khorshid Shah granted readily. Saber and Samlud walked to

Shaghal, bowed to him, and took their places behind him in the pavilion.

Samak asked Khorshid Shah's permission to interrogate Surkhkafar. This granted, Samak looked at the chained warrior and said: "You know who I am. I hope you have realized by now that you are in the presence of the great prince of Persia. The friends of mine whose whereabouts you refuse to reveal are his loyal servants. If you will not tell me where they are, tell him."

Surkhkafar said: "I have no doubt that your prince is a blessed one. He is fortunate to have a servant like you. Few men living could capture and bring me here alive the way you have done. You can tell your prince that Surkhkafar serves no one, not prince nor king. I swore an oath to Armen Shah to bring him your head. I will not submit to you as long as blood runs in my veins."

Samak ordered the servants to bring a bowl. With his dagger, he made a cut in Surkhkafar's wrist so that his blood dripped into the bowl. He said: "Now that blood is running out of your veins, you can tell us where you are keeping the prisoners."

Surkhkafar looked at Samak with scorn but said nothing. The bowl began to fill with blood.

Samak became frustrated and said: "I don't understand. You say you are no man's servant, yet you swore an oath to Armen Shah. What reward could he have offered to deserve such loyalty? I promise you Khorshid Shah will spare your life and repay you a thousand times over."

Surkhkafar said: "I have no fear of death and no need for gold. Since I am dying, I can tell you that it was not I who went to Armen Shah. He called me to his court and asked my help to capture you. In exchange he offered me the one thing no one else could give, not Khorshid Shah nor any other king in the world—the hand of his daughter, the princess Mahaneh. I love her and will gladly die for her. If this is how my life must end, so be it."

Samak exclaimed: "O my friend, if Princess Mahaneh is your heart's desire, you are luckier than you know. I took her from the royal palace just two days ago. She is Khorshid Shah's prisoner and guest here in this camp. If you take a vow to serve Khorshid Shah and never betray him, I promise to put your hand in Mahaneh's hand."

At first Surkhkafar did not believe what Samak was telling him. When he finally understood that his beloved princess was a prisoner in Khorshid Shah's camp, his eyes blazed. Turning to face the prince, he stated in a clear voice: "Khorshid Shah, since your servant has promised me the hand of the princess Mahaneh, I renounce my oath to Armen Shah and will serve you from this day on. You have the word of Surkhkafar."

Khorshid Shah accepted Surkhkafar's vow. A cheer went up from everyone in the pavilion. The prince ordered a tent set up for Surkhkafar in the camp among the warlords, with all the amenities befitting a general. He then ordered his guards to go to Mahpari's pavilion and advise Princess Mahaneh to prepare for her marriage to Surkhkafar.

It was when the guards arrived carrying Khorshid Shah's message that the maidservants in Mahpari's pavilion discovered that the captive princess and queen whom they had assumed to be sleeping were nowhere to be found. An investigation soon revealed the missing horses and armor, and then all became clear. A banquet had already been brought and wine poured at Khorshid Shah's pavilion when the guards returned with the news that Mahaneh and her mother had escaped to the enemy's camp.

Khorshid Shah was stunned. Surkhkafar, who for a brief moment had felt on top of the world, fell into a dark, brooding silence that made everyone around him uneasy. No one could predict what he might do. He seemed about to explode.

Samak said: "Surkhkafar, I promised you that I would put Princess Mahaneh's hand in your hand. I admit this is a setback. But I am not someone who gives up easily. When I promise to do something, I do it."

Surkhkafar stared Samak in the eye. At last he shrugged, lifted his glass and drained it. Seeing him drink, everyone in the pavilion relaxed. A royal celebration began, with toasts to Surkhkafar, Samak, Saber, and Samlud, and enchanting music, delicious food and fine wine, long into the night.

38

SAMAK IS CAPTURED

MACHIN resounded with the news that the vizier Mehran had been executed and the great hero Surkhkafar captured by Samak the ayyar. Some young ayyars of the city began to express desire to leave Machin and join Samak. Early one morning, a crowd of four hundred young men gathered at the city gate, telling Armen Shah's guards that they were going to join the king's army. Instead, as soon as they were outside the city, they headed for Khorshid Shah's army camp.

The patrols took the young men to the prince's pavilion, where they were warmly greeted. Samak hugged them one by one and introduced them to Shaghal, head of the ayyars of Chin. Khorshid Shah ordered his soldiers to arrange facilities for the newcomers and to furnish them with weapons according to Samak's instructions.

Meanwhile, Samak was eager to get back to Machin to release his five friends, especially his beloved Sorkhvard. Surkhkafar had given Samak directions to the watchmen's headquarters, where the prisoners were being kept, and precise instructions on how to get them out. Surkhkafar told Samak: "When you reach the watchmen's headquarters, ask for the commander, Jeldak. Tell him that Surkhkafar wishes him to deliver the fourteen boxes of jewels and gold coins along with the five prisoners. When you say this, squeeze his arm, so that he will know it was I who sent you."

Samak thanked Surkhkafar, took leave of Khorshid Shah, and headed for Machin. He entered the city disguised as an old peasant, as he had done before. He went straight to the watchmen's headquarters, an imposing stone compound within the city, and asked for Jeldak. When the commander came to the door, Samak took his arm and squeezed it as Surkhkafar had instructed. Jeldak, recognizing the signal, drew Samak aside and asked: "Who are you? Where is Surkhkafar? What has happened to him?"

Samak said: "I am Samak the ayyar. Surkhkafar has pledged allegiance to Khorshid Shah and moved to his army camp. He sent me to bring him the fourteen boxes of jewels and gold coins and the five prisoners you have been holding."

Jeldak became concerned and said: "You are too late for the prisoners. Armen Shah's general Tiruq came by early this morning and took them away. He had an order from the king himself, stamped with the royal seal. I could not disobey. By now they have surely reached their destination, Twelve Canyons Fortress."

Samak's heart dropped like a stone, but he hid his disappointment from Jeldak. Showing no reaction, he asked: "What about the treasure?"

Jeldak assured him: "The treasure is safe in a vault in our headquarters. If you plan to take all fourteen boxes to Khorshid Shah's camp, you will need mules. I would say four or five. I also wonder how you will get past the king's guards at the city gate without being stopped?"

Samak replied: "Get the boxes ready. I will return at sundown to pick them up." He left, distressed and worried about his friends' fate.

What had happened was this: A Machin spy serving in Khorshid Shah's pavilion had brought Armen Shah the news that

Surkhkafar had joined Khorshid Shah. The king was shaken to learn of this unexpected setback. The vizier Shahran, guessing that Surkhkafar might release the prisoners from the watchmen's headquarters, suggested to the king that they immediately move them to a more secure location. Armen Shah agreed to the vizier's suggestion of the Twelve Canyons Fortress where they had once planned to house Khorshid Shah and Mahpari.

For the mission they chose Tiruq, who had shown his power by wounding and capturing Hormozgil on the battlefield, and was eager to prove himself after the humiliation of having been outwitted and captured by Samak in the palace harem. Tiruq set out for Machin early that morning accompanied by one hundred soldiers, escorting the queen and princess Mahaneh, whom the king had instructed him to return to the royal palace. This accomplished, Tiruq proceeded to the watchmen's headquarters. There he took Sorkhvard, Atashak, Neyal, and the butcher brothers into his custody, and they traveled onward to the region in the mountains outside Machin known as Twelve Canyons.

The fortress was built of stone, strategically situated atop a massive rock at the convergence of the twelve canyons that gave the region its name. Its single gate was made of iron and set into the fortress wall at a considerable height, so that anyone wanting to enter could only reach the gate by climbing a ladder that had to be dropped down from above.

When Tiruq and his soldiers arrived at the fortress with their five prisoners, he called for the guardian. The fortress guardian, a wise and cautious man, insisted on seeing the king's written orders. Only after reading the letter and verifying Armen Shah's royal seal did he order the ladder lowered so that Tiruq could send up the five prisoners. Sorkhvard, Atashak, Neyal, and the butcher brothers went up one at a time, guarded by soldiers above and below, until the transfer was complete. Once this had been accomplished, the ladder was pulled up after them.

Tiruq warned the fortress guardian: "Watch out for an ayyar named Samak. He is cunning and will stop at nothing to take back these prisoners. Whatever he says, however he might try to trick you, at all costs don't let him into the fortress!"

The guardian said: "Thank you for warning me, but I don't need you to tell me my job. I've kept this fortress for thirty years and no one has gotten around me yet." Tiruq and his soldiers then rode back to Armen Shah's camp.

• • •

Samak left the watchmen's headquarters with a heavy heart, discouraged that he had arrived too late to rescue his friends. He went straight to Khomar's sister's home and knocked at the door, which she promptly opened. Samak was surprised to see her dressed up. He asked: "Dear aunt, are you going somewhere?"

The woman replied: "You know I am a singer. It happens I am on my way to sing at the ayyar headquarters. Their leader, Kanun, has returned to town and they are celebrating with a banquet."

Samak exclaimed: "Kanun! I've been a guest in his home once before and enjoyed his sons' hospitality. I understand that he has met several of my friends—unfortunately not to their advantage. I'd like to see him with my own eyes. This is too good an opportunity to miss."

The singer warned him: "Samak, you take too many risks. If Kanun and his ayyars ever suspect that I helped you capture Surkhkafar, my life will be over. I need to get along in this town just like everyone else. It's not easy for me now that everyone knows my brother and nephews are in the resistance. I almost didn't get this job tonight. It's only because I'm Kanun's favorite singer and he asked for me personally."

Samak suggested: "Surely you can use one more daf player tonight. If anything goes wrong, you can deny you ever saw me before. I promise I won't give you away."

After more argument and persuasion, Khomar's sister finally agreed. She took Samak into the house and helped him get ready with clothes, make-up, and an instrument, until he was completely convincing as a daf player.

They arrived at Kanun's home, which was the ayyar headquarters, shortly after sunset. Kanun sat on cushions with the digger Khatur and other senior ayyars, enjoying themselves with a delicious banquet and fine wine while a group of musicians played. Kanun introduced Khomar's sister to his associates as one of the best singers of Machin. She introduced Samak as a musician visiting from another town who had come along to accompany her.

Samak joined the other musicians at the end of the room and began to play the daf while Khomar's sister sang and danced. To her surprise, Samak was in fact not a bad player. Meanwhile, goblets of wine were emptied one after another as the ayyars sang along with the music.

In the midst of the festivities, a servant entered and spoke into Kanun's ear. Kanun responded: "Bring him in, let him join us!" Moments later, Samak was surprised to see Jeldak enter the room and pay his respects to Kanun and the ayyars.

Kanun gestured to Jeldak to be seated. He asked: "Jeldak, what brings you here tonight?"

Jeldak replied: "You may have heard that my master Surkhkafar broke his pledge to Armen Shah and joined the enemy's camp. I came to let you know that I have ten boxes of gold coins and jewels that Surkhkafar left with me at the watchmen's headquarters for safe keeping. Earlier today, Samak the ayyar came by in person to take them on Surkhkafar's instructions."

"Samak!" exclaimed Kanun. "Then he is here in Machin."

Samak's expression darkened as he overheard Jeldak betray his commander. He muttered to himself: "Ten boxes? What about the other four? You thief, even as a betrayer you are dishonest!"

Jeldak continued: "I bought time by sending him to get mules. I know you are loyal to Armen Shah, while Samak and Surkhkafar are in the service of the enemy. I came to warn you because I thought this treasure should go to our own king's camp rather than to strangers from Chin."

Kanun thanked Jeldak for thinking of him, and invited him to stay and enjoy the ayyars' hospitality. Later, they would go and retrieve the treasure. Jeldak gladly accepted.

Kanun filled a goblet of wine and passed it to Jeldak. He called to Khomar's sister: "A song to honor our guest!"

Khomar's sister stepped forward and sang. Samak bent his head while he played to avoid being recognized.

Jeldak watched the musicians appreciatively as he sipped from his goblet. "What a lovely singing voice she has," he began. Then suddenly he turned pale. The goblet dropped from his hand, spilling its contents at his feet.

Kanun exclaimed: "My friend! Are you drunk after only one sip?"

Jeldak, his face white, pointed across the room at the daf player and said: "That is Samak! Samak the ayyar! It's him!"

Samak froze. The musicians stopped playing and gaped at him. The ayyars around the room drew weapons and stepped to block the exits. Samak realized that he had no chance to escape. He offered no resistance as the ayyars fell upon him, bound him hand and foot, and stuffed a cloth into his mouth.

Kanun turned his cold gaze on Khomar's sister. Terrified, she could only stammer: "I . . . I . . ."

"Of course you had no idea," said Kanun, with unexpected gentleness. "You are not the first one in this town whom Samak has fooled. I will see to it that you are the last. You have brought a great prize to my doorstep. Sing on, my dove, for now we have even more to celebrate."

Khomar's sister knew there was no way she could help Samak. She put a smile on her face and resumed singing. The other musicians likewise resumed playing.

Kanun stood over Samak and said with satisfaction: "What a delightful evening this has turned out to be." He turned to Jeldak: "My friend, thanks to you, I can bring Armen Shah a gift that he will value more than ten boxes of gold and jewels—the head of Samak the ayyar."

As Kanun drew his dagger to cut off Samak's head, Khatur the burrower stopped him and said: "My friend, would it not be better to deliver him alive? Let the king have the pleasure of executing him before the entire city, as a lesson for future generations."

Kanun thought for a moment and replied: "You are right. To capture and deliver such an enemy alive is an even greater triumph." The ayyars took away Samak's lasso, dagger, and everything he was carrying (including sleeping potions, for he had not come empty-handed), and left him tied up on the floor.

Soon thereafter, Kanun's sons Behzad and Razmyar arrived. They exclaimed in delight at seeing their enemy Samak tied up at their feet. They took turns spitting on him, then they joined their father and the other ayyars celebrating while the musicians played.

At midnight the party broke up. Kanun gave a purse of coins as a reward to the singer who had delivered Samak into his hands. Khomar's sister thanked him profusely, and left in a hurry.

Kanun instructed Jeldak: "Go back to the watchmen's headquarters and prepare the ten boxes of treasure. I will send someone to pick them up later tonight." He amended this: "As a matter of fact, I'm sure the king will be just as happy with nine boxes. Keep one for yourself as a reward for your loyalty." Jeldak thanked him and left. It seemed to those standing closest to Samak that a groan emitted from the tied-up captive.

Kanun told Behzad and Razmyar: "My sons, stay here tonight and keep our guest company. Such an important person should not be left alone for even one moment. In the morning we will take him in shackles to Armen Shah."

SECTION 6

Twelve Canyons

39

AN AYYAR'S DAUGHTER

KANUN had a young daughter whose name was Ruzafzun. Along with her brothers, Behzad and Razmyar, she had been trained since childhood in combat and the tricks and techniques of the ayyars. By the time she was twelve, she was so fearless and clever in ayyari that her father began to fear for her life. He forbade her to pursue ayyari any further. She tried every way she could to get around him, but all paths were blocked. She could not join the ayyars of Machin, for no one dared defy Kanun.

When Samak first appeared in Machin and word of his endeavors spread, beginning with his capture of her brothers, Ruzafzun felt a longing like a pain in her chest. She had glimpsed Samak for just one moment, when she served him as her brothers' guest, and felt a connection with him although they had never spoken. Later, when Samak's name became notorious throughout the city, Ruzafzun's feelings for him increased rather than diminished knowing that he was her father's and brothers' sworn enemy.

When Ruzafzun heard that four hundred young men of Machin had defected and made their way to Khorshid Shah's camp to join the ayyars of Chin, she wept with frustration that she had not learned of it in time to join them. What most enraged her was that they would have the chance to meet Samak, which was her dream, while in Machin all doors were closed to her.

Ruzafzun had not been permitted to attend the banquet to celebrate her father's return. When she heard that Samak had been captured and was a prisoner in their home, her heart began to beat so hard with excitement that she was sure people could hear it from across the room. She waited until the last of Kanun's guests had gone, the house was quiet, and everyone was asleep. Then she slipped out of her bedroom and stole to the banquet room. Silently she pushed open the door and peered inside.

Samak lay face down on the floor, his hands and feet in shackles. As an added precaution, he had been tied by a rope to Behzad, and by a second rope to Razmyar. Each brother had wrapped the rope around his own hand to make sure their captive could not escape. By this time, both brothers were sound asleep and snoring on cushions, having drunk much wine throughout the evening.

Ruzafzun crept into the room, cut the ropes and shackles from Samak's hands and feet, and whispered in his ear: "Get out as fast as you can!"

Samak turned and was amazed to see that the one who had freed him was a beautiful young girl. "Who are you?" he asked.

Ruzafzun whispered: "Go and find out who I am! Right now there's no time—just get out of here!"

Samak bowed in appreciation, left the room, and disappeared into the darkness.

Ruzafzun slipped out the way she had come and waited in the hallway until she judged Samak had had enough time to get far away. Then, for the second time, she opened the doorway to the room where her brothers slept—and let out a cry of shock. "Father, come quickly!"

Hearing Ruzafzun's shout, Behzad and Razmyar jumped up from their sleep, and were bewildered to find Samak gone. They turned to Ruzafzun and demanded: "What happened?"

Ruzafzun shouted back: "Why are you asking me? You were supposed to be watching him!"

Moments later, Kanun arrived with Khatur, who was spending the night as his guest. The old digger exclaimed: "Impossible that he could have escaped by himself! Someone must have helped him."

Kanun looked at Behzad and Razmyar and shouted: "How could you have gone to sleep so deeply that he escaped without waking you up?"

Behzad said helplessly: "We were tired from the day's work. . . . After all that wine at the banquet, we must have passed out."

"I taught you better than that!" said Kanun angrily. He rang the alarm, awakening all the ayyars and servants who were sleeping in the house. Leaving Razmyar in charge to organize the others, the three men ran outside, fanning out in both directions.

In fact, Samak was hiding in an alley not far from the house. When Behzad paused to peer into that alley, Samak jumped him from behind and snapped his neck. Behzad fell dead on the spot.

Samak took Behzad's dagger from his hand, but as he was about to exit the alley, the sound of footsteps in the adjacent street froze him where he stood. He could hear two men approaching the mouth of the alley from either side. He was trapped with no escape route.

Samak waited in the darkness until he judged that the men were almost upon him. He jumped out, grabbed the first man (it was Khatur) and swiftly cut his throat. The expert digger fell, his blood soaking into the ground. As fast as Samak moved, before he could turn to face his next opponent, the wily Kanun had knocked him flat on his back, straddled him, and had drawn his own dagger. One glance at Behzad's body, which lay nearby, told Kanun that Samak had killed his son. Kanun's face contorted. He was about to thrust his dagger into Samak's heart when a dark figure leapt at him from behind like a cat and, to Samak's amazement, cut Kanun's throat in one swift move. Kanun's hand flew to his neck. Blood poured from the wound. With an incredulous look, he crumpled and lay there dead, in an alley a stone's throw from his own house.

Samak stood up and looked at Ruzafzun, quietly wiping blood from her dagger. He asked: "May I know the name of the person who has saved my life twice in one night?"

Ruzafzun said: "Since you insist, I can tell you that I am the daughter of the one whose life I just took to save yours." She added: "Now that my brothers and my father and his close friend are dead, I don't expect my mother will welcome me back home. I will probably be the second most wanted outlaw in Machin, after you. So if you'd care to return the favor and save *my* life, you could consider taking me in as an apprentice."

Samak bowed and said: "I am obliged to you. It would be my honor to have you join my team of ayyars."

Ruzafzun exclaimed with joy, threw her arms around Samak and hugged him. Then she said: "We're not safe here. My other brother Razmyar and the servants are looking in the wrong direction, but we'd better get out of the city fast."

Samak said: "The safest place I know of is Khorshid Shah's army camp."

This was exactly where Ruzafzun longed to go. She said: "We'll need two good horses. Follow me!"

Samak hurried to keep up with Ruzafzun. She led him to a stable, slipped in through a window, and a moment later unlocked the door from the inside. Samak was impressed by her quickness. The sky was still dark when they rode out the city gates and away from Machin toward Chin's army camp.

Shortly before noon, Samak and Ruzafzun reached Khorshid Shah's camp and were taken to the pavilion where the prince sat on his throne surrounded by his generals. He welcomed Samak and asked: "Who is this accompanying you?"

Samak responded: "Your Highness, this girl from Machin is more powerful than most warriors three times her size. She saved my life twice last night, and killed her own father and brother with very little help from me."

Khorshid Shah welcomed Ruzafzun and ordered the servants to set up a special tent for her close to Princess Mahpari's pavilion.

• • •

Meanwhile, in Armen Shah's camp, the king received the news that three of Machin's most senior ayyars had been killed. The messenger reported that fear of Samak and what he might do next had reached such a pitch in the city that citizens were on the verge of riot.

When Gezelmalek heard this, he shouted at Armen Shah: "O father, see what your softness has led to! Being a king doesn't just mean amassing wealth and giving gifts. If you had executed your enemies instead of using them as captives to bargain with, then people would fear you as they should. We have five traitors in our custody, citizens of Machin who betrayed you and joined the enemy. Execute them now in public as a lesson to others! They killed three of ours, we kill five of theirs. Do this and you will be respected."

Armen Shah listened to his son carefully. "Your suggestion is just," he said. He called in Tiruq, who had just returned from taking the five prisoners to the Twelve Canyons Fortress, and ordered him to go immediately and bring back their severed heads. He handed him a written order for the fortress guardian and his own ring with the royal seal. Tiruq bowed to the king, took the letter and the royal ring (which he put on his own finger for safe keeping), and set out for Twelve Canyons with two hundred soldiers.

After Tiruq left, Armen Shah turned to his vizier Shahran and said: "Send an envoy to Machin to inform Razmyar that I appoint him chief of ayyars in place of his father, and that I am counting on him to maintain order in the city. Treason will not be tolerated. Anyone who speaks or acts against the royal family will be arrested and executed."

40

THE ROYAL RING

SAMAK sat in Shaghal's pavilion with Ruzafzun and the other ayyars, trying to come up with a plan to free his friends from Twelve Canyons Fortress. Nothing anyone could think of seemed workable. Finally Ruzafzun offered: "Let me sneak into Machin's army camp and steal Armen Shah's royal ring. Then we can show it to the fortress guardian as proof that we have the king's order to hand over the prisoners."

Samak objected: "It's too risky. Since I kidnapped Qatran from the enemy camp, they've redoubled security. Armen Shah's and Gezelmalek's pavilions are impossible to get to."

Ruzafzun turned to Shaghal and said: "O great ayyar, I appreciate Samak's warning and value his advice. Please give me the chance to prove to him that I am his dedicated devotee and am not afraid to put myself in danger."

Shaghal reminded Samak: "My son, this young ayyar sacrificed her father and brother for the chance to serve us. The least we can do is let her try." Samak reluctantly assented. Shaghal said: "All right, my daughter. Go ahead and show us what you can do!"

That night, as darkness fell, Ruzafzun headed toward Machin's army camp. She took the long way around, thinking she would be less likely to arouse suspicion if she were seen coming on the road from Machin than from Khorshid Shah's camp.

As she approached the main road, she saw four mules laden with boxes led by a man riding ahead of them on horseback. They were headed toward Machin's army camp. Ruzafzun changed her plan and rode straight toward the rider. When they came face to face, Ruzafzun acted like a patrol from Machin's army, and demanded: "State your name and business!"

The rider said that his name was Jeldak and that he was carrying a cargo of wine as a gift for the king. Ruzafzun took a careful look at him in the moonlight, and noted that he matched Samak's description of Surkhkafar's commander, Jeldak, who had betrayed him.

Ruzafzun ordered Jeldak to get down from his horse. The commander stood by while she inspected the boxes. When Ruzafzun was finished, she turned to him and demanded: "Are you sure those nine boxes contain wine, and not gold coins and jewels?" Jeldak looked startled. Before he could react, Ruzafzun locked an arm around his throat and strangled him to death.

Ruzafzun thought to herself: "I set out to steal the king's royal ring, but fate had a different plan for me tonight." And she led the mules straight back to Khorshid Shah's army camp.

As Ruzafzun approached the ayyars' pavilion, she saw the light in Samak's tent still burning. She called his name softly. Samak came out of the tent, saw the mules laden with boxes, and said with a smile: "Do you need so many mules to carry just one ring?" Ruzafzun told him how she had taken the opportunity to kill Jeldak and take his treasure. Samak embraced her and said: "You are amazing!"

Together Samak and Ruzafzun unloaded the boxes from the mules and carried them inside Samak's tent for safe keeping. Samak used his dagger to pry open one of the boxes. Heaps of gold and jewels glittered in the lamplight. They caught their breath.

"That's a lot of treasure," Ruzafzun said. "Perhaps I should stay here tonight and help you guard it."

Samak and Ruzafzun stayed together in his tent for the rest of the night.

In the morning, they took the treasure to Khorshid Shah's pavilion. The prince was delighted by Ruzafzun's achievement, and he introduced her to his generals as the newest hero among the ayyars. Shaghal and the other ayyars surrounded Ruzafzun, congratulating her and praising her courage, initiative, and quick thinking.

Just then, one of Khorshid Shah's spies came running in and told the prince: "Your Majesty, Tiruq is on his way to Twelve Canyons Fortress to execute the prisoners and bring back their heads as a lesson to others. Armen Shah has given him the order with his royal seal ring."

When Samak heard this, he became anxious and asked Khorshid Shah for permission to go straight to the fortress to get there before Tiruq. Khorshid Shah granted this. Samak and Ruzafzun left immediately for Twelve Canyons.

They rode nonstop and continued past nightfall until they reached a hilltop that gave them a clear view in the moonlight of what they had been hoping to see. Camped in the valley below them was an army of two hundred soldiers that had set up tents for the night. A few guards stood watch, but the rest were sound asleep. "Tiruq," said Samak with satisfaction. "We're not too late."

Samak and Ruzafzun crept quietly down the hill into the enemy's camp, keeping out of sight in the shadows, until they reached a spot behind Tiruq's tent. "Cover me," whispered Samak. Ruzafzun notched an arrow to her bow. Samak carefully made his way through the darkness to Tiruq's tent. Drawing his dagger, he cut an opening into it and slipped inside without being seen by the guards.

Tiruq was snoring loudly in his tent, sound asleep. Samak lost no time and cut the warrior's throat on the spot. Tiruq's eyes opened wide, his body jerked for a few moments, then he was dead. Samak noticed the empty wine goblet at Tiruq's side, and said quietly to no one: "You shouldn't drink when you're on a mission."

Samak removed the king's royal seal ring from Tiruq's finger and put it on his own. He searched through Tiruq's belongings until he found the written order from Armen Shah. He took it, left the tent through the opening he had cut, and went back to the spot where Ruzafzun was waiting for him. He noted with approval that she still had her bow and arrow at the ready.

On their way out of camp, Samak detoured past a corral he had seen earlier. He and Ruzafzun picked out five horses and led them up the hill to where they had left their own horses. They mounted and continued toward Twelve Canyons in the moonlight, leading the five extra horses.

Day broke, and the sun rose. By the time Samak and Ruzafzun came within view of Twelve Canyons Fortress, the sun was blazing high in the sky. From a distance the fortress looked like a jewel on a ring, set high above the clouds in the center of the twelve canyons. "It's magnificent," Samak remarked. But then he saw what lay between them and the fortress. A vast army was stationed in the valley and along the ridges, sealing off the entire Twelve Canyons area.

Ruzafzun exclaimed: "How are we going to get around that?"

Samak studied the army before them. He estimated it at two thousand soldiers. He said: "We won't get around it." Ruzafzun looked in the direction Samak indicated, and saw a group of scouts riding toward them.

When the scouts arrived, Samak said boldly: "We're carrying an important order from Armen Shah. Who is your leader?"

"Qatush," said the soldier.

"Take us to him."

The scouts escorted Samak and Ruzafzun to the tent of their leader, Qatush. The general was small and compactly built with a trim beard. Samak handed him the written order and said: "Armen Shah has sent us to execute the prisoners in the fortress."

As Qatush read the order, Samak noticed that the general in his elegant silk robe could not keep his eyes off Ruzafzun. Although she was dressed as a soldier and dusty from travel, Qatush was clearly distracted by having a pretty girl in his tent. Samak took note of this aspect of the general's character.

When Qatush had finished reading, Samak showed him Armen Shah's seal ring. Qatush kissed the ring and told his soldiers to escort Samak and Ruzafzun to the fortress.

When they reached the base of the fortress and Samak saw the single door set into the fortress wall high above them, he thanked his luck. He turned to Ruzafzun and said: "We could never have gotten into this fortress if we didn't have the royal ring and the letter."

The head of the fortress guardian appeared in the window above the entrance gate. He demanded: "State your name and business."

Samak responded: "We have a message from His Majesty Armen Shah, for no one's eyes but the fortress guardian's."

A rope was lowered with a basket. Samak placed the letter and the royal ring in the basket and sent it back up.

A few minutes later, the ladder was lowered. Samak turned to Qatush's soldiers and said: "Go and tell General Qatush that we arrived safely at the fortress. We'll take it from here." Samak and Ruzafzun tied up their seven horses and then climbed the ladder into the fortress.

The fortress guardian welcomed them, asking: "His Majesty Armen Shah is well?"

Samak responded: "The king is well. He has sent us to bring back the heads of his prisoners to show the people of Machin how he rewards treason."

The fortress guardian smiled and said: "His Majesty is wise and knows how to keep his subjects happy." He then invited Samak and Ruzafzun to join them for food and wine. Samak accepted. He whispered to Ruzafzun: "Qatush will send soldiers after us as soon as he realizes what we've done."

As they walked through the fortress, Samak asked the guardian in a loud voice: "Where are the prisoners?"

Samak's voice echoed through stone passageways and reached the cell where Sorkhvard, Atashak, Neyal, and the butcher brothers were chained. Sorkhvard whispered excitedly to the others: "It's Samak!" The prisoners' mood lightened instantly. They marveled to themselves at how Samak could have managed to get into this impregnable fortress.

Moments later, the fortress guardian appeared outside the cell door with Samak. He pointed at the prisoners, saying: "There they are!"

Samak looked coldly at his friends and said: "Good!" He and Ruzafzun followed the fortress guardian into the main hall.

The fortress guardian ordered servants to bring food and wine. When the food was being served, Samak found a moment when no one was watching and poured sleeping potion into the wine beakers. He asked the guardian: "How many are you in the fortress?"

The guardian answered: "We are ten men, plus women and children."

Samak said: "Surely there's enough food and wine for everyone."

With Samak's encouragement, the guardian invited all ten men to join them. As the meal began, Samak and Ruzafzun took care to pour out their own wine goblets instead of drinking. Before long, all ten men and the fortress guardian lay unconscious on the floor.

Samak and Ruzafzun took the guardian's keys, hurried to the cell, and freed Samak's friends from their shackles. They embraced Samak joyfully. Samak introduced Ruzafzun and said: "Meet our newest member. It's to her as well that you owe your freedom, because she saved my life and has been my brave and steadfast companion since I left Machin." Hearing these words, Sorkhvard felt a pang of disquiet.

On their way out, Samak paused at the fortress's treasure vault. "Even in a hurry, it's better not to travel empty-handed," he said. He used the guardian's keys to open the vault and took several boxes of treasure and as many valuables as they could carry.

The five men and two women climbed down the ladder out of the fortress, mounted the waiting horses, and rode away fast.

As they rode, Ruzafzun drew up alongside Samak. Worried, she asked: "Samak, what will we do when we run into Qatush's army? They must have realized by now that they've been tricked. They'll never let us pass."

Samak said: "I've been thinking about that too. I don't have a plan yet. But God has helped us this far. Let's have faith!"

41

THE AYYARS OF TWELVE CANYONS

EARLY that morning, as the sun rose over Tiruq's camp, the guards discovered the champion warrior in his tent with his throat cut. The news rapidly spread among two hundred soldiers that their leader was dead and the king's seal ring missing. They could guess that this was the work of Samak the ayyar, whose name by now evoked an almost superstitious dread.

A messenger was dispatched back to Zafron Plains to bring the bad news to Armen Shah, while a fast rider named Shosham, who was from the Twelve Canyons area and knew it well, rode ahead to warn Qatush's army and the fortress guardian.

Shosham rode nonstop until he ran into Qatush's army patrol guarding the entrance to Twelve Canyons. He was taken directly to Qatush, whom he informed of Tiruq's murder and the theft of the royal ring.

Qatush turned pale and began shaking. He realized that the one who had shown him the royal ring must have been no one else but Samak the ayyar. He gave Shosham a detailed description of Samak and Ruzafzun, and told him: "Take a fresh horse. Ride straight to the fortress. Tell the guardian that anyone who comes with a royal ring and letter from the king is to be arrested on the spot. I'll send a detachment of soldiers to follow you, but don't waste a moment—leave now. Pray that you get to the fortress before Samak."

Shosham left Qatush's tent and rode toward the fortress. Focused on speed rather than caution, he had the bad luck to run right into Samak and his convoy, who had seen him coming from a distance and had hidden themselves behind rocks above the path.

They dismounted Shosham from his horse and searched him. Samak said: "My friend, I am guessing you have been sent by Qatush, and that you know who I am."

Shosham saw that lying would be of no use and said: "O great ayyar, I am at your mercy."

Samak said: "You are a good rider and seem to know this area well. If you want to save your life, guide us out of these canyons in a way that avoids the army checkpoints."

Shosham said: "I do know Twelve Canyons well. And I prefer to stay alive, so I will tell you the truth. Qatush's army is guarding every pass and every exit. You are seven against two thousand. In my opinion, even with me as a guide, your chances of getting out of this area alive are small. And if we are caught, I will be executed too for helping you." Seeing Samak's expression, Shosham added quickly: "But I have an idea that could keep you safe, at least for a while."

Samak asked him to continue. Shosham explained: "Twelve Canyons is home to a community of about twelve thousand ayyars. They live by their herds, farming and hunting, in a prosperous valley just over that ridge. Their leader is named Gurkuhi, and his brothers Kuhyar and Kushyar. They do not serve Armen Shah or any other king of a far-away city but follow their own ways as they always have. It's possible that Gurkuhi would give you sanctuary."

Samak said: "I had no idea there was such a large community of ayyars here. Lead us there!"

Shosham rode off the path, and the others followed him. After riding for an hour, they came to a green forested canyon. Under a huge ironwood tree, surrounded by a number of warriors, sat an older man on cushions atop a stone seat that had been elegantly carved into the rock. Shosham told Samak and the others to wait. He rode toward the tree, dismounted, bowed to the man on the stone seat, and offered his warm greetings.

The man, who was no one but Gurkuhi, asked Shosham: "Who are these people with you?"

Shosham responded: "O great chief of ayyars! I have brought you an ayyar from the city, whose name is Samak, in the hope that you might give him and his friends refuge."

Gurkuhi told the young ayyars to bring the new arrivals to him. As they returned with Samak and his friends, Gurkuhi got up from his seat, walked toward Samak, and embraced him. He said: "O great hero! Your deeds in the kingdoms of Chin and Machin are well known in this valley. I am honored to welcome you as my guest." He took Samak's hand, brought him to the stone slab, and offered him a seat next to his own. The rest of the company was likewise warmly welcomed. Gurkuhi ordered food and wine brought, and they enjoyed a delicious feast.

After they had all drunk several goblets of wine, Gurkuhi asked Samak: "I am wondering what has brought the great Samak in this direction?"

Samak responded politely: "It was the will of God to bring us into your presence!" He described how his five friends had been arrested in Machin and imprisoned in the Twelve Canyons Fortress, how he and Ruzafzun had infiltrated the fortress and gotten them out in time to prevent their execution, and finally how they had run into Shosham on the road, who had led them to Gurkuhi.

Gurkuhi listened to Samak's story with full attention. When Samak had finished, Gurkuhi said: "Now you are here and under my protection. It is our custom to offer hospitality to those who seek refuge in our domain, especially people of such impressive capabilities as you and your companions. You are my guests and may stay as long as you like. When you are ready to leave, we will help you and equip you for your departure so that, God willing, you may arrive at your next destination in safety."

Samak and his friends thanked Gurkuhi for his generosity and warm welcome. They continued to eat, drink, and enjoy each other's company until night fell.

The news of Samak's arrival soon made its way through Gurkuhi's valley and then out of the valley. A shepherd who was grazing his flocks near Qatush's army camp gave the information to the nearest patrol. When Qatush heard the news, he immediately sent a message to Armen Shah letting him know that Samak and his five friends had taken refuge with Gurkuhi.

When Armen Shah heard the messenger's report, he shouted in fury: "How much bad news must I receive in one day? Tiruq, our great champion, slain! Twelve Canyons Fortress fallen! The prisoners gone! How can one man do so much harm, and we with our army of thousands cannot stop him?"

The vizier Shahran bowed and said: "Your Majesty, I recommend that you place Qatush in command of Twelve Canyons. Let him take a letter from you to Gurkuhi with royal gifts, requesting that he hand over the fugitives."

Armen Shah said: "Let it be done."

Shahran wrote a letter from Armen Shah to Gurkuhi, sealed it with the royal stamp, and gave it to an envoy to take to Qatush along with fine garments, jewelry, and weapons as gifts for Gurkuhi.

Qatush put on his finest general's robe and hat and set out for Gurkuhi's meadow with a detachment of two hundred soldiers carrying Armen Shah's gifts. They found Gurkuhi sitting with

Samak and his friends under the ironwood tree, drinking wine and exchanging stories of past exploits and adventures.

Gurkuhi welcomed Qatush, who handed him Armen Shah's letter. Samak smiled at Qatush: "General Qatush, it's a pleasure to see you again."

Qatush glared at him. The general's gaze shifted to Ruzafzun, then to Sorkhvard and Samak's other friends, memorizing their faces. Samak had no doubt that Qatush would have liked to kill them all on the spot.

Gurkuhi unsealed the letter, then handed it to his brother Kuhyar to read. Kuhyar read out loud:

"From Armen Shah, king of Machin, to our respected subject Master Gurkuhi. We wish to let you know how pleased we are with you and your people, whom we are told are thriving under your wise leadership. We have been recently informed that a group of enemies of the realm, led by Samak the ayyar, have taken refuge in your domain. We have sent you our general Qatush to request that you hand over these fugitives to him in shackles. We trust that you will obey our royal command and accept these gifts as token of our appreciation. Should you refuse . . ." Kuhyar paused, then finished reading: "Should you refuse, it is you who will be brought to us in shackles."

Kuhyar looked contemptuously at Qatush, saying: "I thought Armen Shah was a wise ruler. Does he think my brother Gurkuhi is someone he can threaten and order around? We honor and respect our guests and will never give them up as long as blood flows in our veins. Not to you nor a thousand like you, not if he sends all the armies of the world to take them away from here."

Qatush said: "You speak like a child. Watch your words before they cost you your head."

Kuhyar pulled out an arrow, notched it to his bow, drew and aimed it at Qatush's heart, saying: "Out of respect for Armen

Shah, I will give you and your men one chance to leave this valley alive."

Qatush realized that he was in a delicate situation. He mounted his horse and left in a hurry, followed by his soldiers.

When Armen Shah received Qatush's message recounting how he had been received by the ayyars of Twelve Canyons, he flew into a rage. "Who is this Gurkuhi? How dare he defy and insult me!"

Shahran bowed and said: "Your Majesty, when insurrection goes unpunished it can quickly spread. We must put an end to Samak and those who support him. Our problem is that our soldiers have no experience fighting in the mountains. To attack someone like Gurkuhi will require different strategies and tactics than we are used to. I suggest we advise Qatush to gather an army of mountain warriors who know the terrain, and encircle and defeat Gurkuhi."

Armen Shah agreed. Shahran sent the messenger back to Qatush bearing the king's command.

Within three days, Qatush had assembled an army of ten thousand warriors from various mountain regions of Machin and was marching on Twelve Canyons.

• • •

When Gurkuhi learned that Qatush was on his way with an army, he gathered his own warriors to defend the canyon. Samak volunteered to join them along with his five friends, but Gurkuhi refused, and said: "You are my guests. Let no one say of Gurkuhi that he made his guests fight his battles for him!"

Samak thanked him and asked: "Would you at least permit my friends and me to watch the combat from a distance?" To this Gurkuhi agreed.

Early the next morning, the two armies lined up at the entrance to the canyon, ready for combat. The first warrior who rode out to challenge the enemy was Qatush's nephew, a powerfully built young man in shining armor, armed with fourteen different weapons. He rode back and forth in front of Gurkuhi's army, shouting: "Look at you shepherds and goatherds! Is there one of you who dares to face a real warrior?"

Kuhyar asked his brother's permission to fight. He rode out into the field and shouted: "Do you hate your life so much that you're in such a hurry to lose it?"

The two warriors battled on horseback with their spears. Then Kuhyar threw his spear aside, drew his sword, and struck Qatush's nephew in the head so hard that the blade cleaved his helmet and his skull in two. Qatush's nephew fell from his horse, dead on the spot.

A second warrior from Qatush's army rode forward and was likewise slain by Kuhyar. Eight more warriors attacked, one after another. Kuhyar slew them all without breaking a sweat. The combat continued until the sun went down and darkness settled over the canyons. Then the two armies retreated to rest.

That night, as Samak and his friends sat eating and drinking in the camp their hosts had prepared for their shelter, Samak began retelling the story of his capture by Kanun and how Ruzafzun had saved his life twice in one night. Sorkhvard, who had already heard this story, listened until she could take it no longer. She interrupted Samak, saying: "How much longer will we have to listen to you praise Ruzafzun? To jump someone from behind and cut their throat in a dark alley is something any thief or child of the streets can do. The real test of an ayyar is what he can do outside the city, in dangerous and unfamiliar terrain, in the mountains and canyons."

Ruzafzun looked straight at Sorkhvard and asked: "What test are you referring to?"

Sorkhvard said: "Well, for example, a real hero might sneak into the enemy's camp and leave a souvenir in Qatush's tent, so that he would wake up and be ashamed to realize his enemy had gotten close enough to cut his throat."

Ruzafzun laughed and said: "I like that idea! But in war, it's not worth risking your life for a childish prank."

Sorkhvard said: "You're afraid? I'm not! I'll take one of Samak's headbands and leave it on Qatush's pillow tonight."

Ruzafzun said: "Go ahead, I won't stop you! Do that, and you can call yourself a true ayyar. I'll retire and spend the rest of my life knitting and sewing at home. But if you don't, I hope you'll shut up once and for all and stop boasting about heroism in front of a real hero like Samak."

Sorkhvard's face flushed. She stood up and demanded: "Samak, give me your headband! I'll show her if I'm boasting."

Samak saw that the situation had gotten out of hand. He said: "Dear Sorkhvard, sit down. You're right, canyons and mountains in wartime are more dangerous than city streets. That's why I don't want you taking needless risks, especially after all the trouble we just took to get you out of that fortress."

Sorkhvard replied with heat: "I'd rather get captured or lose my life than sit here listening to that woman needle me, and you encourage her! I couldn't care less if you prefer her to me. I just hate to see you taken in by someone who doesn't deserve such admiration. I'll put an end to her bragging once and for all. If I'm not back by morning, at least you'll know that I wasn't afraid to risk death for you."

With that, Sorkhvard snatched Samak's headband, tied it around her forehead, put on her armor, and left the canyon.

Stealthily, in the darkness, she climbed behind the rocks along the hillside toward Qatush's army camp. Unfortunately, Qatush had posted sentries throughout the area, and one stationed high on the hill soon spotted her moving in the shadows. He lit his torch as a signal to the others. A second watchman spotted her as well, and likewise lit his torch. By the time Sorkhvard realized she was surrounded, it was too late. The soldiers fell upon her, tied her hands, and brought her to Qatush's tent, saying: "We caught him trying to sneak into camp."

Qatush demanded: "Who are you and what do you want here?"

Sorkhvard responded boldly: "You must be Qatush. I came here to give you a souvenir. The headband of Samak the ayyar." The general yanked the headband off Sorkhvard's head. Her long dark hair spilled down over her face.

Qatush laughed and said: "This Samak likes to surround himself with pretty women. I should have been an ayyar." He addressed the guards: "The safest place to keep her is right here in my tent." Following his instructions, the soldiers tied Sorkhvard to a post in the corner of the tent and blindfolded her. Qatush tied Samak's headband around his own forehead, saying: "I'll wear this until the day I capture Samak the ayyar and send him to Armen Shah in shackles."

Thus Sorkhvard became a prisoner again after only a week of freedom.

Samak waited all night for Sorkhvard to return. When the sun rose in the sky and he heard the morning war drums, Samak's worry turned into certainty that something had gone wrong.

The two armies gathered to face each other for the second day of combat. The first warrior to enter the field was a champion from Qatush's side. He rode his horse up and down in front of Gurkuhi's army. He shouted: "Kuhyar! We captured one of those outlaws you're hiding last night. Hand over the rest of them now, and you can still save your own life!"

When Gurkuhi heard this, he called Samak and asked: "What is he talking about?"

Samak confessed: "O great ayyar, last night Sorkhvard and Ruzafzun got into an argument about heroism, and Sorkhvard went to pay Qatush a visit to prove her point. Unfortunately it seems she may have gotten herself captured. It's my fault. I never should have let her go."

Gurkuhi became upset and told Samak: "I risk my people's lives and defy Armen Shah to keep you safe, and you go and deliver yourselves into the enemy's hands? You have embarrassed me and damaged my honor. I swore to protect you as my guests, but if anything like this happens again, I will wash my hands of you and deliver you to Qatush in shackles." Samak apologized and promised Gurkuhi it would not happen again.

Kuhyar rode out to face the warrior who had challenged him. He shouted: "You coward! You must have no honor if you think we would hand over our own people to strangers!"

Qatush's champion responded: "I'm from Twelve Canyons just like you! You're the one who's taken in strangers, brought war upon us all, and made an enemy of Armen Shah—for what? Samak the ayyar doesn't give a damn about you, even if he stays alive, which I doubt!"

Kuhyar shouted back: "If you knew the first thing about honor, you'd know that no ayyar would push away a hand that reaches out to him for help!" With that, Kuhyar charged at the warrior. They battled with spears on horseback until, in one quick move, Kuhyar drew his sword and thrust it through his opponent's chest with such force that the tip came out his back. The warrior fell from his horse and died on the spot.

Immediately, a second warrior rode out from Qatush's army. He raised his spear and charged at Kuhyar. Kuhyar hurled his spear with deadly accuracy, skewering the warrior in his saddle.

Ten more warriors came to fight Kuhyar. One after another, all were slain, until the total of warriors killed by Kuhyar in the first two days of combat stood at twenty-two. Trumpets were blown to announce the end of the second day's fighting. The two armies went back to their camps to rest.

42

RESCUED BY HER RIVAL

SAMAK was crushed by the loss of Sorkhvard. He could not stop blaming himself for having allowed her to go to the enemy's camp. That night, as he sat brooding apart from the others, Ruzafzun came to him and said: "It's my fault. I provoked her into going. I have to go after her."

Samak said: "You're not going anywhere." He told Ruzafzun how Sorkhvard's capture had angered Gurkuhi. "He and his people are risking their lives fighting a war for us, and we've made him lose face. If you're captured too, he'll wash his hands of all of us."

Ruzafzun said: "We can't just abandon Sorkhvard. Who knows what they might be doing to her?"

Samak said: "That won't matter to Gurkuhi if you get captured. He's a mountain man and doesn't see things the way we do."

Ruzafzun said: "If I don't come back, you can give me up for dead and tell Gurkuhi it was my fault. But you can't stop me from going, no matter what you say."

Samak realized that Ruzafzun was determined to go. With a heavy heart he told her: "Do what you feel is right."

Ruzafzun put on light armor and covered it with shabby clothes and an old farmer's hat. She said to Samak: "Tell Gurkuhi to make sure the camp is well guarded tonight." Leaving him wondering why, she snuck past Gurkuhi's sentries, and then headed for the enemy's camp.

As Ruzafzun approached the outskirts of the army camp, she began singing in a loud voice so the guards could hear her. She was counting on them assuming that anyone who acted so unafraid must be on their side.

She continued walking and singing until she reached the heart of the camp. She walked up to a pair of guards and said: "I have an important message for Qatush. Take me to him right away." The guards escorted her to Qatush's tent.

Qatush was sitting drinking wine with three of his warriors. As Ruzafzun entered, she saw Qatush's wine goblet stop on the way to his lips, and knew that he had recognized her. She noticed too that he was wearing Samak's headband. Ruzafzun bowed and said: "O great leader of these twelve canyons, you know me as an associate of the outlaw Samak. I am Ruzafzun, daughter of Kanun, chief of the ayyars of Machin. My father was loyal to Armen Shah all his life. Samak cut his throat and murdered my brother Behzad as if they were dogs in the street. I joined Samak and earned his trust, waiting for the day I could take my revenge. Today is that day. I put sleeping powder in the wine at Gurkuhi's feast and left Samak, Gurkuhi, and his brothers and guests unconscious on the floor of his tent as a gift to you and Armen Shah. On my way out of camp I cut the throats of four sentries who won't be missed until daybreak. Ten soldiers should be enough to get in and out with your prisoners tied up like lambs."

As Ruzafzun spoke, she noticed Sorkhvard tied to a post in a corner of the tent, blindfolded. Ruzafzun guessed that Qatush was planning to take her into his bed. She added: "That one you captured is Samak's woman. If you think I deserve a reward, let me be the one to cut her throat once you've finished with her."

Sorkhvard, hearing this, writhed and threw herself against her ropes, shouting: "Ruzafzun, you traitor! I'll kill you for this!"

Qatush, seeing Sorkhvard's reaction, believed it was genuine. He turned to the warrior sitting to his right and said: "Take two hundred men. Go to Gurkuhi's camp. If this girl ayyar has done what she says, you may not even need to fight your way out. You'll have Gurkuhi as a hostage and his people won't want him harmed."

The warrior bowed and left. Ruzafzun said to Qatush: "I don't expect my reward until they come back. While we're waiting, could I at least have a sip of wine?"

Qatush said: "Help yourself and come sit with us." He patted the empty cushion next to his own seat.

Ruzafzun went to the wine jug and filled a goblet for herself. As she did, she opened the medallion on her necklace and shook some sleeping power into the jug so deftly that neither Qatush nor the two warriors sitting with him noticed.

Ruzafzun knelt beside Qatush, raised her goblet, and drank to Armen Shah's victory. At the general's prompting, Ruzafzun told the story of her part in Samak's missions, beginning with the theft of the royal ring, and how they had infiltrated Twelve Canyons Fortress to free the prisoners.

As she talked, the three men continued drinking, refilling their goblets from the wine jug. Qatush's eyes rarely left Ruzafzun. At one point he interrupted her to remark: "The first time I saw you, you were dressed like a soldier. Today you look like a farmer. I can see you've got a nice body under those clothes. I bet if you put on a dress and some makeup, you'd be as beautiful as any princess or courtesan."

Ruzafzun looked down shyly and said: "I don't know anything about being pretty. I grew up with brothers. I only wanted to learn the ayyars' ways and make my father proud of me. But General, you are an elegant man. That's a beautiful robe you're wearing."

Qatush looked pleased. Ruzafzun resumed her narrative. She noticed the men's heads start to dip as they struggled to stay awake. By the time her tale arrived at Gurkuhi's canyon, Qatush and his two companions were sprawled unconscious and snoring on the rug.

Ruzafzun hurried to Sorkhvard's side, removed the blindfold and untied her wrists. She whispered: "Don't worry, sister. Samak and our friends are well and the canyon is as well guarded as ever. I'm not a traitor."

"I never thought you were," replied Sorkhvard.

Ruzafzun took Sorkhvard's hand, brought her out of the tent, and led her through the darkness to a corral she had spotted at the edge of the camp. She came out with a saddled horse, saying: "Dear sister, as much as Samak loves you and wants you back in his arms, I know that if he were here, he would tell you not to come back with me, but to ride straight to Khorshid Shah's army camp. Tell the prince everything that has happened and stay there in safety until the rest of us can get out of here and join you, God willing."

Tears welled in Sorkhvard's eyes. She hugged Ruzafzun and said: "Thank you for putting yourself in danger for me. I made a fool of myself. You deserve all the praise Samak gave you."

Sorkhvard mounted the horse and rode away. Ruzafzun stood guard until Sorkhvard disappeared over the crest of the hill. Then she went back to Qatush's tent. The three warriors were snoring as she had left them. Ruzafzun took off Qatush's robe and hat and put them on herself. The general was not much bigger than she was. She reached for her dagger, then hesitated. As much as she despised Qatush, it felt wrong to kill an enemy while he lay helpless. She left her dagger in its sheath, and Qatush's head on his shoulders.

Ruzafzun found Qatush's horse tied to a post outside his tent, where it was kept saddled and ready. She mounted and rode straight through the camp. In the moonlight, the soldiers who saw her riding Qatush's horse and wearing his robe and hat assumed she was the general.

Once Ruzafzun was safely out of the army camp, she spurred the horse to a gallop. As she approached Gurkuhi's canyon, she passed soldiers fleeing toward Qatush's camp, some wounded. These were the survivors of the army of two hundred Qatush had sent. Ruzafzun counted only eleven. When she reached the site of the battle, she saw with satisfaction that the rest had been slaughtered or taken prisoner.

Ruzafzun rode straight to Gurkuhi's tent where he and his brothers were gathered with Samak, Atashak, Neyal, and the butcher twins, trying to figure out why Qatush had ordered such an ill-conceived attack. Ruzafzun dismounted, went over, and sat next to Samak. Gurkuhi stared at her. He said: "I did not give you that robe and hat. Please explain to me how you got them."

Ruzafzun bowed and said: "O great commander, I received these because of your good fortune. Please forgive me for disobeying you." She then related all she had done that night, from leaving Gurkuhi's camp, to how she had tricked and drugged Qatush, freed Sorkhvard and sent her to Khorshid Shah's army camp.

When she had finished there was silence. Everyone looked at Gurkuhi to see his reaction. Samak braced himself. This was the second time he had gone behind Gurkuhi's back, and he feared the worst.

Gurkuhi said to Ruzafzun: "You had a dagger in your hand. Your enemy was unconscious at your feet. Why did you not kill him?"

Ruzafzun said: "O great leader, your brother Kuhyar had an arrow pointed at Qatush's heart, and he let him ride away unharmed. I followed his example."

Gurkuhi clapped his hands and ordered wine and a banquet brought in honor of Ruzafzun's accomplishments. He dispatched a messenger, saying: "Tell Qatush that in consideration for his losses, tomorrow will be a day of rest rather than combat. And return the general's hat."

It was noon by the time Qatush's men managed to rouse him. The general was groggy, with a headache which got worse as he listened to them narrate the night's events, including the loss of nearly two hundred soldiers, along with their prisoner Sorkhvard and Qatush's own cherished horse. By the time they got to the message from Gurkuhi, Qatush's head was aching so badly that he ordered them to leave his tent and let him go back to bed.

When Qatush woke up that evening with a clear head, he raged and swore revenge—against Samak, ayyars in general, and Ruzafzun in particular. He sent a messenger to Armen Shah, relating the dismal outcome of the war's first few days and requesting help.

• • •

Back in Gurkuhi's domain, Samak and his friends had spent the night celebrating Ruzafzun's heroic rescue of Sorkhvard. Samak woke up early, saw the sun rising in the sky, and felt a sense of peace and well-being. He decided to take a walk and explore the canyon.

After walking for about a mile, he came to a grove of fruit trees in the midst of a meadow with a little brook running through it. Samak walked among the trees, inhaling the cool fresh morning air. He was filled with gratitude to the one who had created a place of such beauty for all people and animals to enjoy.

He walked upstream, following the brook along the bottom of the canyon. Soon the brook became a river. The end of the canyon revealed the river's source—a great waterfall thundering down a solid rock wall as sheer as polished marble, so smooth that not even an ant could climb it.

On the other side of the river was an amazing sight, an open meadow heaped with mounds of gold and silver coins, jewelry, armor, and other treasures, carelessly piled here and there amidst an abundance of wildflowers.

Samak waded across the river. He walked among the incredible wealth, unable to believe his eyes. He was about to pick up a jeweled necklace to make sure it was real, when he was startled by what sounded like a woman moaning. He froze, listening. The sound was faint, almost lost amid the noise of the waterfall. He looked around to see where it might be coming from, and saw a door of solid iron set into the smooth rock wall, sealed with a massive padlock.

Samak was tempted to break the lock to find out what lay behind it. But he thought to himself: "This is Gurkuhi's canyon. This treasure must be his. It would be ungrateful to dig into his secrets when he has shown us such kindness and hospitality."

Samak left the place and walked back to camp. Ruzafzun asked him where he had gone. He answered: "For a walk." But he could not get what he had seen out of his mind. For the rest of the day, his thoughts kept returning to the mystery.

That night, as Samak sat eating and drinking with his friends, the wine loosened his tongue, and he told his friends what he had seen that morning.

Atashak said: "Samak, are you sure you weren't dreaming?"

Ruzafzun said: "I'd like to see this place. Samak, take me with you!" Atashak asked if he could go too. Before Samak could respond, Neyal and the butcher brothers also chimed in. All of them wanted to see this magical place.

Samak said: "One at a time! What would Gurkuhi think if he saw us all walking down the canyon together? Ruzafzun, you asked first, so I'll take you tomorrow. Atashak, I'll take you the day after." Everyone accepted this.

The next morning, Samak and Ruzafzun awoke before dawn and walked together up the canyon. They reached the meadow, passed through the grove of fruit trees, and arrived at the rock wall and waterfall. As they crossed the river, Ruzafzun exclaimed in wonder at the sight of the treasure.

Samak showed her the iron door. "This is where I heard it," he said. Ruzafzun pulled on the padlock to see if it would open. As she let it fall back against the door, it made a clanging noise. A female voice within called: "Who is there?"

Before Samak could stop Ruzafzun, she cried out: "O you on the other side of this door! Who are you? What is this place?"

The voice answered: "O you who have come this far! If you care about us, open the door and see the pain we are in!"

Ruzafzun said: "I would, but it's locked!"

The voice said: "Gurkuhi keeps the key under the cushion where he sits. Take the key, open this door and set us free!"

Ruzafzun turned to Samak, perplexed, and asked: "Why would Gurkuhi imprison people here?"

Samak said: "That's his affair and none of our business."

Ruzafzun said: "That was a woman's voice. She sounds young, and so sad! It feels wrong to just walk away and leave her there."

Samak said: "I know, I feel the same. But this is not the right time to act. We are Gurkuhi's guests and have no right to interfere in his secrets." Saying that, he took Ruzafzun by the arm and they returned to camp.

43

A CLAN DIVIDED

WHEN Armen Shah received Qatush's message telling him of Gurkuhi's defiance and the losses inflicted on his army, he called his generals to meet in his pavilion. The king ordered his vizier Shahran to read the message out loud. He then asked the generals: "What do you think we should do?"

It was Shahran who broke the silence. He said: "Your Majesty may remember that for many years, the region of Twelve Canyons was under the command of Turaj Khan, who ruled from his seat at Shadareh. When he passed away, his brother Gurkuhi claimed leadership of the twelve canyons, but Turaj Khan's son Shabdeez considered himself the rightful heir to his father's domain. It was a bitter argument and almost came to war. In the end they compromised. Gurkuhi and his brothers took their present place, while Shabdeez stayed in the largest canyon, Shadareh."

Shahran continued: "I believe Shabdeez would be receptive to an offer from us. I suggest we send a messenger with royal gifts and invite him to gather an army of warriors from the canyons loyal to him and join Qatush in the war against his uncle. With Gurkuhi eliminated, Shabdeez would become commander of all twelve canyons as his father was before him."

The generals congratulated Shahran for his excellent idea. Armen Shah agreed to the plan. Shahran bowed to the king, left the pavilion, and returned with two letters—one to Shabdeez, as he had suggested, and another to Qatush, explaining that with the army of Machin committed to the war against Khorshid Shah, the king was not in a position to provide additional soldiers, but that help would soon be on the way from Gurkuhi's nephew Shabdeez. The letters were sealed, stamped, and dispatched.

When Shabdeez received the king's letter and royal gifts, he could hardly contain his joy. A young man still in his twenties, with a handsome face and impulsive spirit, he had long been dreaming of an opportunity like this. At last he had the backing he needed to go to war against his uncles, Gurkuhi, Kuhyar, and Kushyar, and take back the portion of his father's kingdom that they had denied him. Shabdeez was not universally esteemed in the canyons. Some thought him noble, others said he was not to be trusted, and some thought him a coward. More than wealth or power, what he yearned for was to prove himself worthy of his father Turaj Khan's legacy.

Shabdeez ordered two warriors to go Twelve Canyons Fortress and toll the bells. This was the signal to gather the people of the region. Within hours, the great bells rang out from the fortress's highest rooftop and echoed throughout the canyons. Soon every man, woman, and child in Twelve Canyons knew that the war between Gurkuhi and Qatush would now involve them as well.

In Gurkuhi's canyon, his people heard the bells tolling. Gurkuhi told them: "It's my nephew, the traitor, who has turned against his own family. Have no fear. Shabdeez is an inexperienced hothead. My brother Turaj raised him in luxury like a prince. He's never tasted battle. If he wants an education, let him come. We are safe in this canyon and can hold off an army of any size."

Within a week, fifty thousand warriors gathered in Shadareh—brave men wearing their own armor. They carried spears, shields, bows, and maces. They rode horses ready for combat. When everyone was assembled, Shabdeez stepped out to address the soldiers. His words echoed throughout the canyon as his men relayed them down the warriors' ranks.

Shabdeez told them how Samak and his associates had sought refuge with Gurkuhi, and how his uncle had turned against Armen Shah. "This is the cause of the bloody war that has shattered the peaceful life of our lovely canyons. Gurkuhi is my uncle, but more important than family ties is loyalty to our king. My uncle was rash, foolish, and disloyal to defy Armen Shah and bring his wrath upon us. Our task now is to obey the king's command, demolish my uncles' army, and bring Twelve Canyons back into one single nation as it was in the time of my father Turaj Khan. I call upon every warrior, man, woman, and child in these canyons to fulfill the king's command, and show Armen Shah that his subjects in Twelve Canyons are loyal and brave." The crowd cheered and shouted their allegiance to Shabdeez.

Thus an army of fifty thousand warriors under Shabdeez's command set forth for Qatush's camp at the entrance to the twelve canyons. Qatush rode out to meet them leading ten thousand of his own soldiers. The earth shook with the rattle of armor and thunder of horses' hooves as the two great armies approached each other. Qatush rode ahead to greet Shabdeez, who was riding at the head of his troops. The two commanders rode up a hill and together watched the procession of warriors from above.

By the time all sixty thousand soldiers had settled into their camps, day had turned into night. Qatush invited the warlords of the canyons, including Shabdeez, to join him in his tent to discuss the best strategy to attack Gurkuhi.

After they had finished their meal and drunk some wine, one of the commanders suggested that the entire army should encircle Gurkuhi's canyon and close in, making the circle tighter and tighter until Gurkuhi and his forces were trapped within it.

Several commanders approved of this strategy. Others were quiet. Shabdeez said: "This would not be as easy as it sounds. The geography of the canyon does not work to our advantage."

Qatush agreed and said: "Gurkuhi is a clever commander. He knows his own terrain better than anyone, and he has many tricks up his sleeve. I think our main force should stay where it is, blocking Gurkuhi's passage out of the canyon. Then, each day, we send a different army to face him in combat until we have exhausted all of his war tactics."

This plan was accepted. The generals left Qatush's tent to rest for the next day's combat.

Early the next morning, eight thousand warriors under the command of General Niku moved to the front line.

When Gurkuhi heard that Niku and his men were assembling along the canyon, he ordered his army to line up in front of them. Thus the two armies came face to face with each other.

The sound of drums from both sides echoed throughout the canyon, announcing the beginning of combat. Samak rode to Gurkuhi and said: "Your people are at war because you gave me and my comrades shelter. Please give me permission to fight on the field rather than stay on the sidelines watching others risk their lives for me."

Gurkuhi said: "Samak, I have told you before to stay out of this fight. As long as you are with us, my men will do whatever it takes to protect you."

Samak said: "You are the chief of ayyars, so you must know that I am capable of more than just covert fighting. I can hold my own on a battlefield."

Gurkuhi said: "O Samak, I am sixty years old. I have spent enough time among people, good and bad, that I can tell their capabilities just by looking at them. I knew from the moment I saw you that as young as you are, you are a master of all trades. The point is that you came to us for refuge. So I will not let you risk your life in combat while I have a head on my shoulders. When I am dead, you can do as you like. Until then, you have my permission to watch the battle from a safe distance." Samak understood. He thanked Gurkuhi for his hospitality and rode back to join his friends.

The first warrior who entered the combat was Kuhyar. He rode out into the field and called for an opponent. A young and powerfully built warrior from Niku's army rode forth. He was known throughout the canyons as a fearsome fighter. Kuhyar hurled his spear with such force and accuracy that it penetrated the warrior's breastplate. The young man fell from his horse, dead before he hit the ground.

Kuhyar called for another opponent. He shouted: "Who wants to be next to die for my cowardly nephew Shabdeez, who is too weak to fight his own battles?"

The men of Niku's army looked at each other. Most of them did not have much combat experience. After seeing Kuhyar dispatch their champion, none of them wanted to be next.

Niku became frustrated and shouted at his warriors: "What happened to your courage? Are you wolves or sheep?" He spurred his horse and rode toward Kuhyar. "Kuhyar! You've lived a long time, but no one's luck lasts forever. To turn against Armen Shah was stupid. Hand over the prisoners and let's put an end to brothers killing brothers here in Twelve Canyons," he shouted.

Kuhyar said: "Niku, if you want the right to give me advice, you have to earn it. Come fight like a man and let's see what you can do! Or else turn around and go home and help your wife hand. He charged her, grabbed her belt, and pulled. Ruzafzun did the same. Both warriors fell from their mounts. Ruzafzun scrambled to her feet, drawing her dagger. The battle continued on foot. Intent on watching her opponent's every move, Ruzafzun failed to notice that Niku was guiding them closer and closer to his army line.

When they came within range, Niku signaled to the nearest warriors. Ruzafzun realized too late what was happening as the men ran toward her, grabbed her and tied her up. "Cowards!" she shouted.

Niku sheathed his sword. He didn't want to admit that a woman had come close to defeating him. He said to Ruzafzun: "You should be grateful my men saved your life." To the soldiers he said: "Take her to my tent and tie her up. I'll take care of her tonight."

Horns were blown announcing the end of the day's combat. Both armies returned to their camps to rest. Gurkuhi's soldiers left the field silent and dejected, while Niku's warriors celebrated their capture of two famous names from the enemy's ranks.

44

A DOUBLE RESCUE

GURKUHI called Samak and told him angrily: "Look what you've done to me! Again you've gone against my orders, and another one of your people has gotten herself captured. Now everyone will blame me for putting my guests in harm's way after they came to me for refuge."

Samak paid his respects and said: "O great leader, I am sorry that Ruzafzun disobeyed your orders. It was never our intention to embarrass you. What happened today was God's will and cannot be undone." He excused himself, said good night to Gurkuhi, and went to rejoin his comrades.

While sitting with his friends, Samak could not stop thinking about Ruzafzun. He had developed deep feelings for this girl who had sacrificed her father for his sake and risked her life again to save Sorkhvard. Finally he stood up and told the others: "I owe my life to Ruzafzun. I would rather lose it than leave her in the enemy's hands tonight."

Samak's friends became worried. Atashak said: "Samak, this is a different situation from when Ruzafzun snuck into Qatush's camp. There are thousands of soldiers guarding the canyon on both sides. At least let me come with you." The butcher brothers and Neyal also offered to join Samak on his mission.

Samak replied: "My friends, thank you. But I will have to move along exposed slopes with no place to hide. The more people in our party, the greater the risk that one of us will be spotted or captured. That would anger Gurkuhi even more. This is something I must do alone." After saying that, he put on his armor, picked up his weapons, and headed for Qatush's army camp.

Samak crept silently through the canyon in darkness. As he reached the outskirts of the enemy's camp, he saw the dark shapes of hundreds of tents. He heard horses and realized that a patrol of three soldiers was riding in his direction. Samak hid behind a rock.

As the soldiers approached, Samak heard them talking about the day's events. He waited until they had passed, then followed them on their patrol route around the camp. He counted on their chatter and the noise made by their horses to cover any accidental sound he might make. Also, by eavesdropping, he might learn where in camp Ruzafzun was being kept.

He got lucky. After ten more minutes on their circuit of the camp, one of the soldiers pointed to a tent in the distance that was lit from inside, and said: "We're wasting our time on patrol tonight. The only action will be in Niku's tent."

The others laughed. One said: "He won't get much sleep."

The third said: "Nice thought, but Qatush wants that ayyar girl for himself. I heard Niku get the order from Shabdeez."

The soldiers stopped their horses and continued talking with lowered voices. Samak listened intently. He heard one soldier say: "Niku won't send her to Qatush until morning. That's hours from now, if you get my meaning."

The other remarked: "I don't see Niku giving up his prize so easily." Samak felt his anger rise as the soldiers went on discussing which of the two generals, Niku or Qatush, would be first to possess Ruzafzun.

The soldiers looked toward the lit tent. Shadows could be seen moving inside. The first soldier said: "Niku's still drinking wine. We should come back later and hide behind his tent. Maybe we'll see some action then." The other two agreed and they continued on their ride.

Once the patrols were out of sight, Samak came out from behind his rock and made a careful reconnaissance of the tent the soldiers had pointed out. He crept toward it.

A thrill ran through Samak when he heard Ruzafzun's clear and angry voice saying: "Some hero! You couldn't beat me in a fair fight—you needed five soldiers to trap me. If you were a real warrior you'd be ashamed." Samak hid behind the tent to listen.

Inside the tent, Niku sat on cushions drinking wine. Two guards stood at the entrance. Ruzafzun was tied to a post. Niku drained his goblet, then tossed the dregs at Ruzafzun. He said: "I had my men rescue you out of chivalry. You were like a frightened lamb on the field. I did you a favor because I could see you were about to faint." He refilled his goblet.

Ruzafzun said: "Is this what a real man does? Throw wine in a woman's face when she's tied up? It would be one thing if you'd captured me fairly. Then I might admit you're stronger and obey you."

"How can you doubt I'm stronger? Look at you! You're like a helpless little bird in my hands." Niku drank, then added: "If Qatush hadn't insisted I send you to him, you'd be all mine." Again he threw the dregs from his goblet at Ruzafzun, and laughed.

Ruzafzun held her temper. She said with a challenging smile: "If you want to prove your strength, here's your chance. Untie me. We can wrestle. No weapons. If you win, I'll follow your commands, no matter what they are. If I win, you release me."

Niku's heartbeat quickened at the prospect. He was twice Ruzafzun's size. He was sure he could easily defeat her and then take her into his bed without much struggle. He ordered the two guards to leave the tent, close the entrance, and stay away until he called for them.

The guards followed his command. Once Niku was alone in the tent with Ruzafzun, he took his robe off, revealing the well-muscled, battle-scarred torso of a warrior. He untied the ropes binding Ruzafzun to the post, and he beckoned her to attack him.

The two wrestled. While Ruzafzun struggled to knock her opponent down, Niku's main idea was to undress her. Each time they grappled, he made a point of tearing at her garment. The feel of her lithe and strong young body against his excited him more and more.

Outside the tent, Samak heard the struggle and saw shadows moving. He took out his dagger, cut an opening in the tent wall, and slipped inside just in time to see Niku rip off what was left of Ruzafzun's garment, exposing her bare breasts.

Samak's blood boiled at the sight. He leapt on Niku and stabbed him with his dagger over and over in the back and chest. Niku just had time to exclaim: "Samak!" before he fell dead. Blood poured out of his wounds and soaked the ground under the tent.

Samak picked up a robe and handed it to Ruzafzun to cover herself. She jumped into Samak's arms and hugged him tight.

Samak said: "Ruzafzun, I'm sorry I interfered. I know you would have beaten him in a fair fight. But seeing you like that was more than I could take."

Ruzafzun covered his face with kisses. "O Samak!" she said. "Every time I see you in action, I learn something new. Please let me go and free Kuhyar tonight, the way you freed me."

Samak smiled and said: "Good idea. I'll count on you." Then he added: "Now that I've come this far, why don't I go see if I can abduct Shabdeez and bring him as a gift to his uncle Gurkuhi?"

It was an inspiration he would later regret.

Samak left the tent the way he had entered it. Ruzafzun got dressed. As she was trying to figure out how to make the best of her shredded outfit, the two guards came back in. Ruzafzun gave them no chance. She leapt at them and stabbed them both dead with her dagger, just as Samak had done. Then she cut off their heads.

Ruzafzun emerged from Niku's tent wearing a guard's armor and helmet. In each hand she held a severed head.

Ruzafzun walked through the camp. The first soldiers she passed were the sentries Samak had shadowed. When they saw her coming from Niku's tent holding two severed heads, they stopped and stared. One of them summoned the courage to demand: "What are you doing with those heads?"

Ruzafzun answered coolly, making her voice deeper: "These are the heads of two traitors who tried to kill Niku. He told me to bring their heads to Qatush with an important message."

The soldiers instantly stepped aside. Ruzafzun said: "Don't just stand there. Come with me! There's no time to waste." The soldiers hurried to lead the way, taking Ruzafzun directly to Qatush's tent, which she had visited once before.

When they reached the general's tent, Ruzafzun told the soldiers guarding the entrance that she was carrying an important message from Niku for Qatush. The guards relayed the message and Ruzafzun was promptly shown inside.

Ruzafzun entered the pavilion where Qatush sat in a fine robe on silk cushions, drinking wine. She placed the bloody severed heads at the general's feet. As Qatush stared in astonishment, Ruzafzun bowed and said in a deep voice: "O great commander, these are the heads of two of General Niku's guards. They were plotting to seize the prisoner Kuhyar and bring him back to Gurkuhi for a reward. My uncle Niku found out and killed them both. He told me to bring you their heads along with a message: Kuhyar is not safe where he is. Niku suggests you move the prisoner into his custody, to make sure he is well guarded and won't be abducted by the enemy's tricks."

Remembering how Sorkhvard had been abducted out of his own tent several nights before, Qatush agreed and said: "Since Niku is the one who defeated and captured Kuhyar on the field. I can think of no one better to guard him." He told one of his guards to take Ruzafzun to the tent where Kuhyar was held and escort the prisoner to Niku. Ruzafzun bowed, paid her respects and went out. She had noticed that the general was still wearing Samak's headband.

The guard led Ruzafzun to the tent in which Kuhyar was imprisoned. He was tied to a post, his hands and feet bound with rope. Ruzafzun untied him from the post, retied his hands behind his back, then cut the rope from his ankles. She said: "You're going to walk. Don't try to escape, or you'll be sorry."

Kuhyar said scornfully: "Are you an assassin sent to kill me?"

In answer, Ruzafzun winked at him. Kuhyar recognized her face under the helmet and did not object further.

With the guard's help, Ruzafzun put a rope around Kuhyar's neck and led him out of the tent. She said to the guard: "Stay here and guard the entrance. If you see anyone acting suspicious, question them."

Ruzafzun took Kuhyar some distance among the enemy's tents, then stopped and untied his hands. She pointed toward the foothills. "This is as far as we can go together. Keep going in that direction until you reach a corral. You'll find horses saddled and ready to go. Pick one. Ride up the hill. When you reach the top, you'll see a road to your right. It will take you to Khorshid Shah's army camp. Tell his soldiers Samak sent you and that he and his friends will join you soon. Kuhyar thanked Ruzafzun and left in the direction she had shown him. Once he was out of sight, Ruzafzun headed back toward Gurkuhi's canyon.

• • •

After leaving Ruzafzun in Niku's tent, Samak crept through the darkness of the army camp. As he approached its center, the silence became more profound. Samak passed only a few patrols. Their main concern was to keep out wild animals. The soldiers did not imagine that an outsider would dare to penetrate this far into their stronghold.

Eventually Samak came within sight of a group of tents that stood atop a hill overlooking several canyons. He could guess that the largest of those tents belonged to Shabdeez. It took him some time to climb the hill. When he reached the top, he saw three guards sitting against a boulder, all asleep.

Samak crept around Shabdeez's tent, passing a horse that was tied up, saddled, and ready to go. He continued the rest of the way around the tent, ending up at its opening. Inside, four candles were burning. By their light he could see Shabdeez asleep in his bed on a platform inside the tent.

Samak entered quietly, drew his dagger, and approached Shabdeez's bed. He lifted the dagger, placed his right knee on the young man's chest, and pushed down until Shabdeez opened his eyes. When he saw the stranger holding a dagger, he asked in terror: "Who are you?"

Samak answered: "I am Samak the ayyar! And if you move or raise your voice, I'll kill you."

Shabdeez's voice trembled as he asked: "Are you the one who broke into Twelve Canyons Fortress, freed the prisoners, and made an enemy of Armen Shah?"

Samak answered: "That was me. And tonight I killed your general Niku. I can kill you too, or you can come with me quietly as my prisoner. The choice is yours."

Shabdeez became motionless and quiet. Samak gagged him, bound his hands behind his back, and pulled Shabdeez outside the tent to where the horse was tied. He seated Shabdeez on the horse, mounted behind him, and rode toward Gurkuhi's canyon.

It was after midnight when Samak reached his friends, who were anxiously awaiting his arrival. He was glad to see Ruzafzun there. Tying Shabdeez to a post, he joined his friends and they sat together drinking. Ruzafzun told the story of how she had freed Kuhyar from Qatush's custody and sent him to Khorshid Shah's army camp. Everyone was happy to be reunited.

Soon they all went to sleep. Samak noticed that Shabdeez, even tied up as he was, could not keep his eyes off Ruzafzun. He was riveted by her beauty and followed every movement she made.

The next morning, Samak, Ruzafzun, and Atashak took Shabdeez to Gurkuhi's pavilion. Samak told Atashak to hide Shabdeez behind a rock out of Gurkuhi's view, to surprise him.

Gurkuhi sat with his advisors, discussing the battle plan for the next day's combat. They fell silent as they saw Samak and Ruzafzun approach smiling, hand in hand.

Gurkuhi asked Samak in surprise: "How did Ruzafzun get here? I thought she was captured by Niku with my brother."

Samak bowed and said: "O great commander, thanks to your good fortune, I was able to take Ruzafzun out of that place and put an end to Niku's life. Even better, she was able to free your brother Kuhyar from detention and send him to Khorshid Shah for safety. I hope this fortunate result will lead you to forgive Ruzafzun for her headstrong action and me for disobeying you."

Gurkuhi was so happy that he stood up from his seat, walked to Samak, and embraced him. He exclaimed: "How can I be angry when you have just told me my brother is safe?"

Samak said: "My lord, I have more good news. While in the enemy's camp, I took the liberty of capturing their commander Shabdeez."

Gurkuhi could not believe it. He asked: "Where is he now?"

Samak said: "One of my associates is guarding him outside your pavilion. Shall I have him brought in?"

Gurkuhi thought for a minute, then he drew Samak aside and said: "I don't want to see that no-good bastard's face. And I don't want to hear him beg for mercy in front of my people and remind me I'm his uncle after what he's done. He's nothing but a traitor. If I give him the chance, he'll spew poison and lies in front of everyone. I want you to kill him and get rid of the body, so I'll never have to see him again."

Samak's heart sank hearing that, but he bowed to Gurkuhi and said: "Yes, my lord."

Samak and Ruzafzun left Gurkuhi's pavilion and walked to the place where Atashak was holding Shabdeez. As soon as Atashak saw their grim faces, he knew the news was bad.

Samak said to Ruzafzun: "Go back to Gurkuhi's and wait for me there."

Ruzafzun protested: "Samak, you can't kill him, whatever Gurkuhi said. He's done nothing wrong."

Samak privately agreed with her. But he said: "It's Gurkuhi's decision."

Atashak now spoke up: "I should be the one to do it. Samak, I've done nothing but sit idle while you and Ruzafzun risked your lives for us. I may not be brave or skillful like you, but at least I can show you I'm steadfast and loyal."

Samak looked at Ruzafzun, saw the pain on her face, and knew that he could not bring himself to kill Shabdeez in cold blood. But neither could he contradict Gurkuhi's order. He said to Atashak: "I accept your offer. Take him down to the stream and kill him there." In his heart, he was secretly hoping that if anyone could find a way to fail at such a straightforward mission, Atashak would.

Atashak led Shabdeez away. Samak and Ruzafzun watched with heavy hearts until the two were out of sight. Then they returned to Gurkuhi's pavilion. Samak met Gurkuhi's eyes with a look that their host took as confirmation that his instructions had been carried out.

Gurkuhi said: "Well! I've been keeping some vintage wine for a special occasion. A thorn in my side that has been causing me pain since my brother Turaj died has been removed, thanks to the bravery of our guests. Today we celebrate." He ordered his wine server to bring the special jug, and he gestured to Samak and Ruzafzun to sit beside him in places of honor.

Meanwhile, Atashak led Shabdeez to the stream. He laid the young man on the ground with his head at the edge of the water, in order not to stain the ground with blood. "I'm sorry to do this," Atashak said, and he drew his dagger.

Tears flowed from Shabdeez's eyes and down his cheeks. He cried out in anguish: "What kind of an uncle would show no mercy and order his own nephew's death? To have my throat cut by a butcher like an animal!" Shabdeez went on bemoaning his fate, crying, and begging Atashak for mercy.

Atashak said: "Look, it's not up to me to spare your life. I've been ordered to kill you and I will."

"At least let me have one last wish before I die. Everyone deserves that, especially a man who's innocent and has done nothing wrong. That's not too much to ask."

Atashak considered, then agreed: "That much I can do."

Shabdeez thanked him. He said: "My wish is a secret. I cannot share it with just anyone. It is for Samak's ears alone. If you have the mercy to bring him here to hear my wish, I promise I will go to my death quietly with no complaint."

Atashak told himself that to allow this young man to say his last words before dying was the sort of virtuous deed that Samak might approve of. Samak might even reproach him if he refused it. So he tied Shabdeez to a tree trunk and went to fetch Samak.

When Atashak arrived at Gurkuhi's pavilion, he found Samak and Ruzafzun drinking wine and celebrating with Gurkuhi and his friends. He bent down and whispered into Samak's ear: "Shabdeez asked if you would hear his final request before he dies."

Samak asked Gurkuhi to excuse him. He stood and followed Atashak down to the stream.

When they reached the stream, Samak turned to Atashak and asked: "Where is he?"

Atashak stared at the tree. The ropes lay on the ground. Shabdeez was nowhere to be seen.

45

AN ARMY AMBUSHED

When the commanders of the canyons gathered at Qatush's pavilion early that morning to discuss the day's battle plan, Shabdeez and Niku were not among them. An emissary from Shabdeez's camp arrived, flustered. He bowed to Qatush, paid his respects, and confessed that Shabdeez had vanished in the night.

"Where is General Niku?" Qatush asked. The emissary didn't know. Qatush sent a messenger to summon Niku immediately.

The messenger soon returned with the information that Niku's camp was in chaos. Someone had entered the commander's tent last night, killed him, and beheaded his two guards. Ruzafzun, the female ayyar whom Niku had captured in battle, was missing.

Qatush was so upset that he rose to his feet. He demanded: "What about his other prisoner, Kuhyar? I sent him to Niku last night for safe keeping."

The messenger knew nothing about Kuhyar.

"Samak!" exclaimed Qatush. "He must be behind these disappearances. No one else would dare to even think about such deeds." Qatush sent the commanders of the canyons back to their camps and told them there would be no combat that day. Then he called his scribe and dictated a letter to Armen Shah. In the letter, he described the arrival of Shabdeez's army, the successful outcome of their third day of combat against Gurkuhi, and how these achievements had been undone by Samak the ayyar in a single night. Qatush ended the letter with a request for advice and assistance. When the letter was finished, he stamped it with his seal and entrusted it to his most trusted messenger, a man named Kaycon. Kaycon took the letter, bowed, and headed for Armen Shah's army camp on Zafron Plains.

That day, both armies rested. As Gurkuhi and his friends celebrated under the ironwood tree, Samak took Ruzafzun aside and said: "Shabdeez has disappeared. He must have tricked Atashak and gotten away, I don't know how." He added: "I haven't told Gurkuhi. I hate to spoil his good mood."

"You're right," Ruzafzun said. "Let's enjoy the celebration. She took Samak by the hand and led him back to the group. They sat together with Gurkuhi and friends, eating, drinking, and enjoying what felt to all of them like a holiday.

Soon they were joined by musicians and dancers of Gurkuhi's tribe, and the party became festive. As day turned into night, Samak noticed Ruzafzun looking at him more often, with a certain look. Ruzafzun came and sat next to him, leaned against him, and whispered mischievously in his ear: "Do you remember what's under Gurkuhi's seat?"

Samak remembered. When it got dark, and the party started to break up, Samak rose to his feet and said: "My head's spinning." Staggering as if he were drunk, he said good night to everyone and went back to his own sleeping place. But he did not sleep. He listened until he heard only silence from Gurkuhi's pavilion, a sign that everyone had left or gone to sleep.

Samak got up and crept quietly back to Gurkuhi's pavilion. He looked under the cushion where Gurkuhi usually sat. Hidden beneath the stone seat was a key. Samak took the key, went back to his own camp, and shook Ruzafzun awake. "Want to go for a walk?" he said. He showed her the key. Ruzafzun sat up, delighted. She and Samak slipped out of camp together and headed for the forest.

It was a beautiful night. Samak and Ruzafzun walked along the canyon. The only sounds were the trickling brook and waterfalls and the trees gently rustling in the breeze. The water shimmered in the moonlight. Samak stopped, took Ruzafzun in his arms, and said: "Suddenly I hate to ruin such a lovely night by unlocking that door, and maybe find something unpleasant. We could just rest here by the creek until morning, enjoy the moonlight, and save the mystery for another day."

Ruzafzun said: "I was thinking the same thing. It would be my pleasure to satisfy your desire!" They found a nice spot to lie down by the river, and held each other all night long, until the sky began to lighten and the sun rose behind the canyon.

• • •

Qatush's messenger Kaycon rode nonstop to Zafron Plains, where Armen Shah's army was camped. The vizier Shahran read the message to the king and others in his pavilion. Armen Shah could not believe that once again a handful of outlaws guided by Samak had done so much damage to his interests. He asked those present if they had any suggestions for how to deal with these troublesome ayyars.

When no one spoke, Kaycon stepped forward. He bowed to the king, paid his respects, then said: "Your Majesty, I have worked in General Qatush's service for many years. I believe I could infiltrate the army camp of Chin and spy at Khorshid Shah's pavilion. Perhaps I could learn something there that would be of use to Your Majesty."

Armen Shah said: "This is the kind of initiative we need. Go and bring back some good news!" Kaycon bowed and left the pavilion.

Kaycon took a circuitous route to reach Khorshid Shah's camp, stopping along the way to change his clothes and appearance so that he could pass for a soldier of Chin. He was a master of disguise. As he rode into camp, he greeted the sentries with confidence as if he belonged there. Kaycon played his part so well that he passed through the camp and arrived at Khorshid Shah's pavilion without any problem.

The first thing Kaycon noticed was the great respect the prince showed to Kuhyar, Gurkuhi's brother, who had arrived the day before. He was seated in the place of honor next to Khorshid Shah's throne. The prince and his other generals were asking Kuhyar's advice about the situation in Twelve Canyons and listening attentively to all he had to say.

Kaycon soon learned that Kuhyar would be at the head of an army of thirty thousand warriors that Khorshid Shah was sending to support Gurkuhi, along with two of his top generals, Hormozgil and Samour. Sorkhvard, who had arrived a few days earlier, was going as well. The caravan included royal gifts for Gurkuhi—fifty Arabian horses, fifty beautiful slaves, fifty purses of fifty gold coins, and one hundred sets of armor.

Kaycon left camp, rode back to Armen Shah, and reported what he had learned.

Armen Shah became concerned and called together his generals and his vizier Shahran to discuss how to defend against this new threat. Kaycon bowed to the king and said: "Your Majesty, if I may offer a suggestion, there is a certain canyon through which Khorshid Shah's army must pass. Above this canyon are hills with ridges and rock formations where soldiers could hide out of sight. If Your Majesty were to act quickly and send an army of, say, ten thousand soldiers, I believe they could be in position to demolish Khorshid Shah's army when it passes through the canyon by raining fire and arrows from above."

Armen Shah approved of Kaycon's plan and instructed his generals to carry it out. Within a short time, ten thousand warriors were on their way toward Twelve Canyons, with Kaycon as guide. By nightfall, thousands of soldiers were stationed in the hills above the canyon waiting for Khorshid Shah's army to arrive.

As Kaycon had predicted, shortly after nightfall, Khorshid Shah's army of thirty thousand soldiers commanded by Kuhyar reached the canyon. The night was clear, and the moon was shining bright. Kuhyar, unaware of the enemy's presence, ordered his army to rest in the canyon to be fresh and ready for combat the next day.

Kuhyar's soldiers were still unloading and pitching camp when they found themselves bombarded by rocks and flaming arrows from all sides. The unexpected attack plunged the army into panic. In the darkness, amid fire and smoke, the enemy seemed to be everywhere at once. With blood-curdling war cries, thousands of soldiers streamed down from the hills. A savage combat began that lasted all through the night.

By the time the sun appeared behind the eastern ridge, the canyon floor was black with ashes and red with blood. Dead bodies lay everywhere. Two-thirds of Khorshid Shah's army had been slaughtered, and most of the survivors had fled. Among those captured were generals Hormozgil and Samour, and Sorkhvard. The royal gifts that Khorshid Shah had intended for Gurkuhi were recovered by the enemy as spoils of war.

Only Kuhyar, who had grown up in the canyons and knew every pathway by heart, escaped the carnage. When he knew that the battle was lost, and saw the other generals taken prisoner, he fled. For the rest of that night he rode through the mountains, taking hidden trails and passages to bypass Qatush's army camp. By daybreak he was headed for his brother Gurkuhi's canyon.

Armen Shah's army arrived at Qatush's camp in triumph. When Kaycon informed Qatush what had happened in the canyon that night, the general became happier than he had ever been in his life. He ordered the prisoners taken to his own pavilion for safekeeping, to be sent to Armen Shah in the morning along with the captured gifts in gratitude for his royal assistance.

He asked Kaycon: "When you visited Armen Shah's army camp, what was your impression of the conditions there?"

Kaycon replied: "General, I noticed that the area around the camp had been grazed dry, and the soldiers and horses I saw looked hungry."

Qatush gave a gold coin from one of the sacks to Kaycon as a reward. Then he invited all the commanders and generals of the eleven canyons to gather in his pavilion to celebrate their victory.

46

WINE FOR A FEAST

GURKUHI was happy to hear of his brother Kuhyar's arrival and went out to greet him. When he saw Kuhyar dismount from his horse covered with blood, he knew the news was not good.

Kuhyar sat in Gurkuhi's pavilion under the ironwood tree and related all that had happened since his capture by Niku—how he had been freed by Ruzafzun, welcomed by Khorshid Shah and given command of an army thirty thousand strong, only to suffer a devastating ambush and massacre in the canyon.

Samak had left Ruzafzun sleeping in their special place by the side of the stream, thinking he would come back to camp, get some food, and rejoin her there for a picnic. Then he passed Gurkuhi's pavilion and saw Kuhyar surrounded by warriors with grim faces. Joining the gathering, he was soon caught up on the terrible events of the previous night. Especially troubling to Samak was the news that Sorkhvard had been recaptured by the enemy along with generals Hormozgil and Samour.

The more Samak thought about Sorkhvard's situation, the more worried he became. Ruzafzun had described to him how Sorkhvard had been tied up in Qatush's tent before she rescued her. After the general's humiliation by Ruzafzun on two successive nights, capped by Niku's death at Samak's hands, Qatush now had more motive than ever for reprisal against the ayyars. Hormozgil and Samour were valuable prisoners, but Samak told himself that Qatush would show Sorkhvard no mercy and might kill her.

These thoughts tormented Samak to the point that he could hardly focus on anything else. At the first opportunity, he took Kuhyar aside and said: "Would you take me to the trail you used last night to escape from the canyon?"

Kuhyar said: "That canyon is filled with blood and corpses. Why would you want to go there?"

Samak said: "I want to find a way into Qatush's army camp without getting caught. Perhaps I could somehow manage to take back our hostages."

He cautioned Kuhyar: "If we ask Gurkuhi for permission, he'll say no. We have to do this on our own."

Kuhyar saw a chance to redeem himself for the previous night's losses. He told Gurkuhi he was tired and going to rest. Kuhyar and Samak then left the camp, riding together along the path Kuhyar had taken to escape.

They rode behind the ridges and in the shadows of rocks until they passed above Qatush's army camp. All the while, Samak was scanning the hills and valleys looking for any clue that might help him achieve his goal. In fact, he had left camp without a plan.

Then Samak spotted a caravan in the distance, camped in a meadow off the main road. He suggested to Kuhyar that they ride down and see who these people were. The two rode down the hill and into the meadow.

As they rode closer, they saw a merchant convoy of about twenty men and a hundred mules that had unloaded their merchandise to rest beside a small lake. Samak called out a greeting. He announced: "General Qatush sent us to take inventory of the merchandise. Who is in charge here?"

Kuhyar stared at Samak in astonishment. The leader of the merchants stepped out and said: "I am. My name is Jafar. Would you care to join us for food and wine?"

Samak thanked him. He and Kuhyar dismounted and sat with the group. As they ate, Samak remarked: "General Qatush will be glad you're finally here. I hope you have brought the right merchandise."

Jafar said: "I hope so too! We have brought five hundred jars of honey, two hundred jars of butter, five tons of vegetables, beans, and rice, and two hundred skins of red wine."

Samak said: "What about barley and hay for the horses?"

Jafar looked puzzled and said: "We have no animal foodstuffs. That is being handled by a different merchant."

Samak said quickly: "Yes, of course." They went on eating and conversing until Samak said: "Thank you for your hospitality, but we don't want to keep the general waiting any longer than necessary. Our instructions are to accompany you to camp and watch out for bandits and enemy soldiers." Jafar agreed and ordered his men to load the mules while he and their two guests finished the meal.

Soon the merchandise was loaded and the caravan was en route to the army camp. Kuhyar and Samak rode behind, acting as if they were helping to guard the shipment.

Kuhyar rode alongside Samak and said: "How did you know this shipment was going to Qatush's army?"

Samak replied: "I didn't know for sure. I guessed."

Kuhyar asked: "What happens once we get inside the camp?"

In fact, Samak still had no plan, but he replied: "Stay close to me and I'll tell you what to do."

The caravan soon reached the army camp. Among the first to greet the merchants were the army's cook and Qatush's personal wine steward, both wanting to know what had been brought. Samak said to Jafar: "Why don't you and your men take the food to the mess, while we take the wine to the general's pavilion." Jafar agreed and separated the mules carrying the foodstuffs, while Samak, Kuhyar, and a few helpers guided the mules carrying the wineskins to Qatush's pavilion.

The pavilion was open. Inside, the tent was lit by candles and torches, with thirty men enjoying a celebratory feast. Slaves circulated serving food and wine, dancers and minstrels played. Samak's gorge rose as he saw Sorkhvard, Hormozgil, and Samour lying trussed like lambs with their hands and feet tied together. Rather than feed the prisoners, Qatush and his guests were tossing leftover food, trash, and wine dregs at them and laughing at their humiliation.

The wine server informed Qatush that a new shipment of vintage wine had just arrived. When the messenger returned saying that the general wished the wine jugs refilled for the feast, Samak hoisted one of the bulky wineskins onto his shoulder and carried it into the pavilion. The wine server instructed Samak to fill the empty jugs that stood around the tent.

Amid the merriment, no one noticed Samak slip sleeping powder into each jug as he filled it with wine. By the time he had finished the circuit, the wineskin was empty. He emerged from the pavilion and helped Kuhyar escort the mules to the wine storage tent, where they unloaded the rest of the wineskins.

"What now?" asked Kuhyar.

Samak replied: "Now we wait."

Samak and Kuhyar returned the mules to Jafar in the mess area. They then returned to Qatush's pavilion and sat outside in the open air watching the celebration inside. They could hear the raucous laughter of warriors throwing food and wine at the helpless and hungry captives to torment them.

Soon a few warriors staggered out of the pavilion, feeling the effects of the sleeping powder and wine and judging they had drunk enough. Others stayed inside and fell asleep where they were. When Samak saw the servants put out the torches and candles and close the entrance to the pavilion, he knew the party was over.

Samak waited until all visible lights had been extinguished throughout the camp and the canyon was dark and silent. He sent Kuhyar to the nearby corral to fetch five horses. Then he entered the general's pavilion.

Qatush was sound asleep and snoring in his seat. All around him warriors passed out drunk.

Samak went to where Sorkhvard and the two generals lay tied up, asleep amid trash and spilled wine. Samak put his hand gently on Sorkhvard's back. She instantly snapped awake and said: "Take your dirty hands off me, unless you want Samak the ayyar to cut them off!"

Samak whispered: "My beloved Sorkhvard, it's me, Samak. You don't know how much I've missed you." He untied her, then the two of them untied Hormozgil and Samour. They left the pavilion just as Kuhyar returned with five horses. They all mounted and followed Kuhyar out of the canyon, up the hill to its peak, and onto a narrow trail that led to Gurkuhi's canyon, which they reached shortly before sunrise.

47

A LOCKED GATE

MEANWHILE, in Gurkuhi's canyon, Ruzafzun had awakened beside the stream to find Samak gone. The first thing she saw was the key Samak had left on the flat stone in place of his pillow. Ruzafzun waited a while, then returned to camp, thinking he must have gone back there. She asked Atashak, the butcher brothers, and Neyal if they had seen Samak. They all said they had not.

Ruzafzun's friends told her the distressing news that by then had spread throughout the canyon—a support army sent by Khorshid Shah had been massacred and Sorkhvard, Hormozgil, and Samour recaptured. Only Kuhyar had escaped to tell the tale. Ruzafzun became concerned and thought she should inform Samak.

Ruzafzun had no idea that Samak had left with Kuhyar without telling anyone and was on his way to the enemy's camp at that moment. Instead, she guessed that he might have gone to the end of the canyon on his own to pursue the mystery of the locked door.

Telling the others she was going to look for Samak, Ruzafzun returned to the canyon. She walked through the grove to the waterfall and crossed the river to the locked door.

She called out: "Samak?" There was no answer.

Ruzafzun knew that since Samak had left her the key, he could not have opened the door. But now that she was here with the key in her hand, curiosity overcame her. She inserted the key in the keyhole and turned it.

A rumble like thunder came from behind her. Ruzafzun froze. Slowly she turned. In the meadow stood a hairy, naked giant, with skin as black as tar and vicious long teeth bared in an ugly face. He seemed more animal than human. Ruzafzun's blood ran cold.

The giant's deep voice roared: "Who are you to dare to break into my master's trust?" He strode toward Ruzafzun in several long steps, picked her up with one hand, and dropped her on the ground. Her head struck a rock and her world went black.

• • •

It was early the next morning when Samak, Kuhyar, Sorkhvard, Hormozgil, and Samour arrived at Gurkuhi's camp. Gurkuhi was in his seat under the ironwood tree, about to start the daily gathering, when the five riders arrived. Kuhyar dismounted and presented Hormozgil and Samour to his brother, explaining that they were the two generals who had been sent by Khorshid Shah and captured along with Sorkhvard in the ambush. He then told the story of how he and Samak had infiltrated a merchant caravan and freed the prisoners from the enemy's camp the night before.

Gurkuhi listened to his brother's report and admired Samak for his bold and clever action. He invited the new arrivals to join the gathering and ordered food and wine served for all.

Qatush awakened that morning with a terrible headache to see the guests from the banquet still asleep in his pavilion. He tried to remember what had happened the night before. He called in his guards and demanded: "Where are the prisoners?" No one knew.

Qatush ordered his guards and his trusted servant Kaycon to search the camp for the missing captives. They were not to be found. Qatush's anxiety and frustration mounted. He remembered drinking and singing and throwing wine at the captives, but beyond that his memory was a blank.

Finally he summoned Kaycon and said: "You managed to enter the camp of Khorshid Shah disguised as a soldier of Chin. If you could do that, I'm sure you can get into Gurkuhi's canyon and find out if the prisoners are there and how they escaped. And anything you can learn about Gurkuhi's army—how many soldiers does he have, and how much feed for their horses?"

Kaycon bowed to Qatush and left his pavilion. It would not be so easy to enter Gurkuhi's canyon without being noticed. In Twelve Canyons, everyone knew one another. A stranger would stand out.

• • •

Around noon, Samak and Sorkhvard left Gurkuhi's gathering with Hormozgil and Samour. When they returned to their own camp, Samak noticed that Ruzafzun was missing. He asked Atashak where she was.

Atashak replied: "She said she was going to look for you."

Samak asked: "When?"

Atashak said: "About this time yesterday."

"Do you mean she was gone all night and hasn't come back?"

Atashak looked concerned. Samak guessed where she might have gone, and he felt a pang of worry. Rather than tell the others, he waited until Sorkhvard, Hormozgil, and Samour had gone to sleep. Then he told Atashak he was going to find Ruzafzun.

Samak walked along the canyon and through the grove to the waterfall. He saw a column of thick black smoke rising from the meadow. Crossing the river, he crept cautiously through the grass until he came within view of the fire pit. Next to it squatted a horrid giant chewing on a raw and bloody hunk of meat. Beside him on the ground lay a carcass so badly butchered that Samak could not tell what kind of animal it had been. Samak's heart lurched.

As Samak got closer, to his relief, he saw Ruzafzun lying trussed hand and foot on the far side of the pit opposite the giant. He thought to himself: "This giant could blow me away with one breath. How can I possibly take Ruzafzun out of his enormous hands?"

Samak decided to wait and see what would happen next. He crouched in the grass and watched the giant devour an entire raw lamb and empty a wineskin in a few gulps. Then the giant stood up, towering over him. Samak would not have believed a creature that stood on two feet could be that size. With one hand the giant picked up Ruzafzun, tossed her over his shoulder as if she weighed nothing, strode toward the mountain, and with a few steps disappeared into the mouth of a cave.

Samak had never encountered a situation like this before. He was worried about what might happen to Ruzafzun in the giant's cave. He crept toward the entrance and waited outside, listening.

Soon he felt the ground shake and heard the giant snoring. Samak summoned his courage and stole into the cave.

The giant was asleep on a rock, Ruzafzun lying between his huge hairy legs. Samak quickly untied her. Ruzafzun threw her arms around Samak's neck in relief. As they ran toward the entrance, Ruzafzun suddenly stopped halfway. "Samak," she whispered, "the giant took the key!"

Samak looked back at the sleeping giant. He crept back to where the giant lay and searched for the key, but didn't see it anywhere. Then he saw that one of the giant's hands was closed. He reached out and tickled the huge palm. The hand opened for a moment. Samak saw a glint of metal. He snatched the key before the giant's fingers closed again. To his relief, the giant went on snoring.

When they were safely out of the cave, had crossed the river, and were on their way back up the canyon, Samak handed the key back to Ruzafzun and said: "I'm counting on you to keep this safe."

Ruzafzun hugged Samak, then told him how she had gone looking for him and had fallen into the giant's hands. She said: "I had just turned the key in the door to see what was inside when that monster appeared behind me."

"You're lucky he didn't kill you," Samak said.

Ruzafzun said: "He was going to eat me until he saw I wasn't from this canyon. He got so angry then, you should have heard him roar! He said his master had told him he could eat anyone from this canyon who came into the forbidden place, but any outsiders, he had to take prisoner. I think he was sorry to miss his meal."

Samak said: "I'm sure that's the reason Gurkuhi's people stay away from this end of the canyon. Let's get out of here before anyone finds out we were here."

Ruzafzun said: "O Samak, I'm so curious to know what's behind that iron door!"

Samak said: "If we're meant to find out, we will. For now, let's just thank God we're both safe."

As Samak and Ruzafzun passed through the grove on their way back to Gurkuhi's camp, they heard the sound of snoring. They quickly hid behind a rock.

After a moment Ruzafzun said: "That's no monster, it's just a man!"

Samak crept out and followed the sound to a willow tree. Above him, on a big branch, a man lay sleeping.

Samak shook the branch so hard that the man woke up. He tried to hang on, but lost his balance and fell to the ground. He was none other than Kaycon. After receiving Qatush's order, he had ridden all morning, taking hidden paths behind the mountain ridge to avoid being spotted from the main road. At a certain point, to avoid detection, he had left his horse and continued on foot. Exhausted, he had stopped to sleep for a few hours in the heat of the day and wait until nightfall before trying to sneak into Gurkuhi's camp.

Samak put his knee on Kaycon's chest, drew his dagger, and placed it against his neck. He said: "Who are you and what are you doing here? Tell the truth or I'll kill you."

The stranger stammered: "My name is Kaycon. I lost my way in the canyon. I was just resting here."

Samak said: "This is no place to rest. I know you're not from this valley, which means you're a spy from the enemy. I'll give you one chance to tell me who sent you and your true mission. If you lie or hold anything back, I'll cut your throat. I am Samak the ayyar, I've had a hard day and night, and I'm in no mood to be merciful."

Kaycon turned pale on hearing Samak's name. He said: "I'm no warrior. I know I don't stand a chance against you. I am at your mercy. Will you promise that if I tell you the truth, you'll let me go?"

Samak replied: "Gurkuhi is the master of this canyon. It will be his decision. I can only promise that if you tell me the whole truth, I'll do what I can to persuade him to spare your life."

Kaycon said: "Then I will tell you everything. Three prisoners of war disappeared from Qatush's pavilion last night. Qatush sent me to find out if they came here and anything else I can learn about Gurkuhi's army. How many soldiers, and if he has enough provisions for their horses." This was the truth, as far as it went.

Kaycon did not mention the role he had played in planning the massacre of Khorshid Shah's army.

Samak tied Kaycon's hands behind his back. He and Ruzafzun brought their prisoner to Gurkuhi's pavilion.

After Samak paid his respects, Gurkuhi asked: "Who is this man in shackles?" Samak responded that he was a spy sent by Qatush. Gurkuhi looked at Kaycon and asked him what he had been sent to find out. Kaycon told Gurkuhi the same thing he had told Samak.

Gurkuhi said: "Here is your answer. The prisoners who escaped are under my protection. My brother Kuhyar is here sitting at my right hand, as you can see for yourself. The question is do we send you back with this information, kill you, or put you in prison?"

Samak bowed and said: "O great commander, please excuse me for intruding. This man is neither royalty nor a warrior. He has only followed his master's orders, and he has told us the truth about his mission. If my opinion as the one who captured him has any weight, I suggest we send him back to his commander with a message."

Gurkuhi thought for a minute, then he said: "You are right. He is no danger to us, not he nor a thousand like him." In that, Gurkuhi was perhaps mistaken. Had he known what Kaycon had already accomplished for Qatush, he might have made a different decision.

Samak untied Kaycon and told him: "Now you have seen our canyon and our army. You can go back to your general Qatush and tell him that we have twelve thousand warriors and plenty of feed for our horses, and we thank him for his concern. You can also tell him that I have had the pleasure of visiting his camp three times—once to release Ruzafzun and Kuhyar from his custody, a second time when I left with Shabdeez as my guest, and most recently last night when I escorted Hormozgil, Samour and Sorkhvard from his banquet. In fact, I've enjoyed the general's hospitality so much that I might come back to his pavilion tonight to cut off his head and bring it as a gift to Lord Gurkuhi."

Kaycon bowed to Samak and said: "I will relay your message to General Qatush." Gurkuhi ordered his guards to escort Kaycon out of the canyon. Kaycon bowed to Gurkuhi, Samak, and the others and left with the guard, grateful that he was still alive.

48

MESSAGE FROM A PRINCESS

KAYCON rode through the canyons to Qatush's army camp. He went directly to Qatush, told him all that had happened, and delivered Samak's message as he had heard it. Hearing Samak's words, Qatush began to panic.

Kaycon added: "My own opinion, based on what I saw, is that Gurkuhi can support twelve thousand warriors and horses for no more than three months."

Qatush told Kaycon to get ready to take a message from him to Armen Shah. Kaycon bowed and told the general that he was at his service.

Qatush called his scribe and dictated the following letter:

"In the name of the Creator of the World, this letter is to Armen Shah, supreme ruler of the kingdom of Machin, from his dedicated subject Qatush, who is fighting a war against Gurkuhi, one of His Majesty's enemies. We wish His Majesty to know that after Faghfur Shah sent an army of thirty thousand warriors to defeat us, by His Majesty's good fortune we were able to win a great victory and massacre and scatter the enemy's forces. We captured two generals, Hormozgil and Samour, and an ayyar called Sorkhvard, but the infamous criminal Samak the ayyar penetrated our camp and freed the prisoners. I apologize for my failure to guard against this infiltration. His Majesty knows I am a mountain man and warrior. My place is on the battlefield, and such stealthy actions under cover of darkness are a kind of tactic in which I have no expertise."

Qatush paused, then added:

"On a different subject, I have heard that the area where His Majesty's army is currently encamped has become unsuitable. There is a large grassland above our canyon called Guran Meadow which offers ample surface and underground waters. Should His Majesty wish to migrate his army to this meadow, it would have the further advantage of enabling us to blockade Gurkuhi inside his canyon. We believe their provisions will run out within three months, so this is a good opportunity to starve them into submission.

"The carrier of this message is my trusted servant Kaycon, who is aware of the situation and can provide further details should His Majesty require."

The letter was stamped with Qatush's seal and handed to Kaycon to carry to Armen Shah. Kaycon mounted his horse and headed for Machin's army camp on Zafron Plains. Arriving, he went directly to Armen Shah's pavilion and delivered the letter. The vizier Shahran unsealed it and read it to the king.

Armen Shah asked his advisors what they thought of Qatush's suggestion. As they were discussing the matter, a guard entered and said that an envoy had arrived with a letter for the king. "An envoy from whom?" Shahran asked. The guard replied that the sender's identity would become clear when the letter was opened. Shahran ordered the envoy shown in. Upon being handed the letter, he opened it and read:

"This letter is from the Princess Mahaneh to my all-powerful father, Armen Shah. Ruling as king must be a punishment for you, since you lack the judgment or strength to take care of your own wife and children, let alone a nation. While you lead an army in a pointless war because my brother wanted to take a woman into his bed, have you ever stopped to wonder whether your queen and daughter are alive or dead? Do you not know that your faithful servant Surkhkafar, whom you so wisely entrusted with our safety, abducted us from your harem and brought us in shackles to the valley of Khorjan? He murdered my mother, my handmaiden, and your wine server Delaram, and now comes to me every day wanting to rape me. What a great boast for my brother to make, when he's bragging about his bravery on the battlefield! 'I had a sister and a mother. My sister was raped and my mother murdered by the man I'd tasked to protect them, and I didn't lift a finger to stop it.' Stay happy, you great heroes and kings! I hope you're proud of your precious honor. It has taken me a long time to find a messenger I could trust to bring you this letter. Perhaps now you will remember that you once had a daughter, and spare a thought to deliver her from her torment at the hands of a vile and deceitful monster."

Shahran's voice trembled as he read the letter. Armen Shah and Gezelmalek were white and shaking. Tears rolled down their faces. Silence spread across the pavilion. No one dared to be the first to speak.

Armen Shah looked at the vizier and said with a choking voice: "When I heard that Surkhkafar had betrayed us and joined Khorshid Shah, that was bad enough. I would never have dreamed that our enemies would go this far or that Faghfur Shah would condone such evil. See what they have done to my family!"

Prince Gezelmalek shouted: "I'll ride to the valley of Khorjan right now and cut this Surkhkafar into pieces! Then I'll do the same to Khorshid Shah and his entire family!"

Armen Shah's eyes ranged over the generals assembled in his pavilion and settled on a warrior with strong features and a barrel chest. His name was Abresiah, and he was the commander of the valley Mahaneh had named in her letter, Khorjan, a wild territory on the outskirts of Armen Shah's domain. The king addressed him, saying: "Abresiah, what is your suggestion?"

Abresiah was a respected warrior. His brother Dabur had an even more fearsome reputation. He had not joined Armen Shah's war but had chosen to remain in his territory of Gold Mountain, where he was known as Dabur the Demon Slayer. Abresiah bowed to Armen Shah and said: "If Your Majesty commands it, I will send a convoy of my warriors to the sheriff of Khorjan with orders to find and arrest Surkhkafar and bring him here in shackles. With your permission, I will instruct the sheriff to take the princess to a safe place where she will be well cared for and await Your Majesty's instructions."

The king said: "Do it!"

Within the hour, one hundred of Abresiah's soldiers were on their way to Khorjan with a letter to the sheriff containing these orders.

Once this had been done, Armen Shah told Shahran that he had decided to accept Qatush's suggestion. The vizier suggested that they write a letter to Faghfur Shah informing him of their move so that he would not think they were fleeing out of cowardice. The letter was written, stamped, and sealed and entrusted to Abresiah. Taking fifty guards with him, Abresiah rode across the battlefield plain until they reached the vanguard of Chin's camp. He informed the vanguard commander that he was carrying a message from Armen Shah to Faghfur Shah. Shortly thereafter he was led to the royal pavilion.

Abresiah was amazed by the splendor of Faghfur Shah's tent. He marveled that such a place had been constructed in the middle of a war zone. The pavilion was magnificently decorated as if it were a royal palace. Faghfur Shah and Khorshid Shah sat side by side on two identical thrones covered with gold and jewels on a large raised platform. At their right hand sat the vizier Haman and the prince's brother Farokhruz. To the left of the thrones was an empty seat, which had been reserved for the messenger. Around the tent sat generals on embroidered silk cushions. All stood up to pay respect to the envoy as he entered.

Abresiah bowed to the king and the princes. Faghfur Shah welcomed him and invited him to sit down. When Abresiah took his seat, all of the generals sat back down as well. Food and wine was brought and served on the king's command.

Abresiah then stood up, took out the letter he had brought, kissed it, and placed it on the step of Faghfur Shah's throne. The king gestured to Haman to read it. The vizier picked up the letter, removed the seal, and read:

"In the name of the Creator of the World, this letter is from Armen Shah, the king of Machin, to Faghfur Shah, ruler of Chin. Our kingdoms are at war but until now we have always thought of you as a wise ruler who conducts himself as a king should. Now we know otherwise. A true sovereign would not have sent thieves and bandits to abduct my queen and daughter from the royal palace and bring them to a war zone. God willed it that they escaped your camp and found their way back to the safety of our city, but that was not enough for you. We have learned that the traitor and murderer Surkhkafar, who betrayed us when he swore allegiance to you, abducted them from the palace a second time—we must assume with your acquiescence if not on your direct orders—and murdered my queen and her maidens in cold blood in Khorjan Desert. My daughter is now his prisoner and at his mercy. A king who would allow his servant to carry out such villainous deeds is not worthy of a crown."

As Haman read this, Khorshid Shah and his brother Farokhruz exchanged looks of disbelief.

The vizier continued: "On another subject, we wish to inform you that our soldiers are suffering due to poor conditions in the area where our army is presently camped. We are therefore planning to relocate to Guran Meadow. We tell you this so that you will know where to find us should you wish to face us in battle like honest warriors."

After Haman had finished reading the letter there was silence. Faghfur Shah asked: "What is all this about? Is Surkhkafar not in our camp?"

Haman bowed to the king and said: "Your Majesty, I was informed that after the departure of the queen and princess of Machin, Surkhkafar became troubled and restless. He had sworn allegiance to us in return for Samak's promise to put Princess Mahaneh's hand in his hand, and her disappearance upset him. Rather than wait, he left the camp at night without telling anyone where he was going."

Khorshid Shah said: "From Armen Shah's letter, it seems that Surkhkafar must have gone to Machin, abducted the queen and princess, and taken them to Khorjan Desert. And then . . ." The prince did not finish his sentence. Faghfur Shah lowered his head, imagining how much pain he would feel if such a thing had happened to his own queen and Mahpari instead of to Armen Shah's family.

Khorshid Shah looked straight at Abresiah and said: "Please tell His Majesty that we share his grief and sorrow at the tragedy that has befallen his family, and outrage toward the criminal who committed this act. We had no knowledge of it before now. You are here to witness that we have conducted ourselves honestly and have done nothing to cause pain to your king. I will take it as my personal obligation to return Princess Mahaneh safely to her father and send him Surkhkafar in shackles. I swear this on my father's crown and on the honor of my queen Mahpari."

Khorshid Shah paused, then continued: "As for your army's move to Guran Meadow, we understand your reasons and do not accuse you of fleeing. We will meet you there and look forward to concluding this war face to face."

Abresiah stood and thanked Khorshid Shah and Faghfur Shah for their concern and hospitality. He bowed to both and left the pavilion.

Abresiah returned to Machin's army camp and relayed Khorshid Shah's message to Armen Shah. The king, Gezelmalek, and the generals were amazed that the prince had given his promise to return Princess Mahaneh and capture Surkhkafar. Even Gezelmalek grudgingly admitted that it was noble of him to take on that responsibility.

The following day, Armen Shah ordered the army to relocate to Guran Meadow. One hundred thousand warriors began their migration.

Qatush was happy to hear that his suggestion had been accepted. Leaving twenty thousand warriors to blockade Gurkuhi's canyon, he stationed guards on every road or trail into the canyons with instructions to arrest anyone who was not part of their group. Then he led the rest of his army to join Armen Shah's warriors at Guran Meadow.

SECTION 7

Guran Meadow

49

AN AYYAR'S REWARD

When the giant awoke and saw that his prisoner had vanished, he could not figure out where she had gone. He came out of the cave and searched the meadow but found no sign of her.

Birds and animals took flight as the giant strode up the canyon, shaking the ground with every step. Everyone who heard him coming ran for cover, for they knew and feared him as a man-eating beast. The giant stopped fifty yards from Gurkuhi's pavilion and roared: "Master! Master!"

Samak and Ruzafzun were sitting with Gurkuhi and his warriors, enjoying food and wine, when the giant's voice resounded through the canyon. Samak saw fear in Ruzafzun's eyes and understood that she was afraid the giant might recognize her. Before Samak could do anything, Gurkuhi stood up and said: "Excuse me, I have an important matter to attend to." And he left.

Samak looked around the gathering. Acting innocent, he asked: "What was that wild howl, and why did Lord Gurkuhi leave in such a hurry?"

One of the warriors said: "That's Gurkuhi's giant."

Kuhyar said: "You are a stranger in this place. Some questions it is better not to ask, especially in front of my brother."

Samak thanked Kuhyar for the word of caution. He suggested to Ruzafzun and his friends that they return to their own camp. They stood and said goodbye. When they left Gurkuhi's pavilion, Samak told the others: "You go on. I can't help it, I have a curious nature."

Samak crept closer to Gurkuhi and the giant, whom he could hear conversing from a distance. When he was close enough to hear their words, he hid behind a rock and listened.

He heard the giant say to Gurkuhi in his deep rumbling voice: "Master, when I awoke, she was gone and so was the key."

Gurkuhi said accusingly: "Tell me the truth! Did you eat her?"

The giant said: "No, master! I was hungry, but I obeyed your orders. You told me that if I ever caught anyone who was not from our canyon, I must bring them to you."

Samak heard anxiety in Gurkuhi's voice as he demanded: "What did this person look like? Are you sure it was a woman?"

"I thought it was," admitted the giant. "But now I'm not sure. I only know it was a stranger."

Gurkuhi said: "I want you to go back to your place right now. Stay close to the door, keep watch day and night. And no more wine for you until you have caught this intruder! When you do, bring him or her to me right away."

The giant replied: "Yes, master! But I'm hungry."

Gurkuhi said: "Go to the corral behind the kitchen. You can take ten sheep, but no more. That should last you a few days at least. I want you to concentrate on keeping watch. Do you understand?"

The giant bowed and said: "Yes, master!" Then he set off down the canyon, with earth-shaking steps that echoed off the rock walls.

Samak went back to his friends. Ruzafzun took him aside and asked: "Should we return the key?"

Samak said: "Not until we find out what Gurkuhi is hiding behind that locked door. As a rule, I try to stay out of others' business, but this is a mystery I have to solve."

After leaving the giant, Gurkuhi went straight back to his seat under the ironwood tree and checked his hiding place beneath the cushion. The key was missing.

Gurkuhi could not sleep all that night, worrying about the identity of the intruder who had stolen his key and gone to unlock the forbidden door. The thought that it could have been Samak never occurred to him. A different suspicion formed in his mind and began to torment him.

The next morning, Gurkuhi's men arrived at the pavilion to find their leader quiet and unhappy. When everyone had taken their seats, Gurkuhi looked at Samak and asked: "Tell me the truth. Is Shabdeez dead?"

Samak became uncomfortable. He said: "Atashak took him down to the river, but he had some problems."

Gurkuhi demanded: "What problems? Did he kill him or not?"

Before Samak could answer, Atashak bowed to Gurkuhi and said: "My lord! I took him to the stream and was about to cut his throat, but he told me he had last words that he could share only with Samak. He cried so much I took pity on him. I tied him to a tree and came to get Samak, but when we got there, he was gone. We looked everywhere but could not find him."

Gurkuhi turned pale. Trembling with anger, he got up from his seat and stood over Samak and shouted: "After all I have gone through to help you, this is how you repay me? I asked you to do one simple thing. Shabdeez is my greatest enemy in this world. As long as he lives he will not rest until he has destroyed me and my family. I should kill both of you right now!"

Samak bowed and said: "My lord, the responsibility is mine. I gave the task to Atashak when I should have handled it myself. Please forgive our carelessness."

"Why didn't you tell me sooner?" demanded Gurkuhi.

"I am embarrassed to say that I had hoped to find and recapture Shabdeez and not upset you needlessly. I swear by Khorshid

Shah's head and the food I have eaten at your table that I will find him and bring him to you, even if he is hiding on the peak of Mount Qaf."

Gurkuhi shouted again: "Easy for you to say!" He was now convinced that Shabdeez was the one who had stolen his key and had been caught by the giant trying to open the forbidden door, only to slip out of his grasp yet again. Gurkuhi did not say this to the others, but returned to his seat white with anger.

Samak noticed that Gurkuhi remained upset and distracted throughout the morning meeting. He felt ashamed and decided it was his duty to waste no time in recapturing Shabdeez. At the first opportunity, he took Kuhyar aside and said: "Kuhyar, do you have an idea where your nephew might have run to? Is there a chance that he has returned to Qatush's camp?"

Kuhyar replied: "O my friend, I advise you to forget about Shabdeez. If he has gone where I think he has, he is out of our reach."

Samak said: "You saw the pain in your brother's face this morning. You heard the promise I made to him. I will find Shabdeez or lose my life over it. Just tell me where you think he is and I will do the rest."

Kuhyar tried again to dissuade him, but Samak kept insisting. Finally Kuhyar gave in and said: "My brother Turaj had a summer house in Red Canyon. Shabdeez took it over after his death. I believe this is where he has fled. The canyon is behind the fortress you infiltrated not so long ago." Kuhyar described where the house was located, then added: "To reach Red Canyon you must pass through Qatush's army camp. The situation has changed since we visited it a few days ago. He has been joined by Armen Shah's entire army, a sea of warriors as far as we can see. They have placed patrols throughout the canyons, on every trail and every pass and lookout. There is no way you can avoid being seen and stopped. This is why I advise you to forget the idea and leave my cowardly nephew where he is."

Samak thought for a moment, then he added: "Please don't tell Gurkuhi or anyone else that I've left. Qatush and Armen Shah have sent spies to infiltrate our camp in the past. The fewer people know where I'm going, the better."

Samak then went back to his friends, told Ruzafzun, Atashak, and Sorkhvard that he was going after Shabdeez, and asked them to keep his departure from the camp a secret. They both tried to convince him to take them along, but Samak insisted this was a mission he must do alone. He asked Ruzafzun to help him darken his face and hands with henna so that he looked like an African. They surprised Atashak as a test. He was so startled that Samak laughed and felt confident in the disguise. He took his tools and a jar of sleeping potion, said goodbye to his friends, mounted his horse, and rode out of Gurkuhi's canyon.

No sooner had Samak left the canyon than he was stopped by a patrol from Qatush's army who had seen him from a distance. The scouts demanded: "Who are you and what is your purpose here?"

Samak responded in an African accent: "My name is Ayaz." He knew that Armen Shah had an African slave by this name who had spied for him in the past. He said: "Armen Shah sent me to gather information about the enemy's army. I managed to enter Gurkuhi's canyon in secret and I am returning from there."

The scouts took Samak to their commander. Samak repeated his story. The commander frowned. The story was plausible, but he had no way to verify it. He asked Samak: "What is the size of Gurkuhi's army?"

Samak responded: "About twelve thousand men, with food reserves sufficient for three months."

This answer matched the commander's information, but he had not been told to expect Ayaz, so he still remained cautious. He told the scouts to escort the African through Qatush's army camp and not to let him out of their sight until he had left the area.

Samak thanked the commander and rode through Qatush's camp guarded by the three scouts. Once they were out of the camp, the scouts left him and he continued toward Red Canyon following Kuhyar's directions.

At the entrance to Red Canyon, a group of sentries stopped him and asked his identity and reason for being there. Samak could guess that these were Shabdeez's soldiers. He replied that his name was Ayaz and that he was bringing a vital message for Shabdeez.

The chief guard said: "What proof can you offer that you are who you say you are?"

Samak said: "His Majesty Armen Shah sent me to spy in Gurkuhi's canyon. I was there when Lord Shabdeez escaped by God's will after being kidnapped by Gurkuhi's men."

The circumstances of Shabdeez's abduction and subsequent escape were known to only a few people, the chief guard among them. Hearing Samak's explanation, he felt more confident that he really was a spy. He asked: "What is the message? And what makes you believe Lord Shabdeez is here?"

Samak answered: "My message is for Lord Shabdeez and no one else."

The chief guard told four of his men to accompany Samak to Lord Shabdeez.

As they rode into the canyon, Samak was amazed to see a castle built into the solid rock of the cliff. Curved stone steps led to the gated main entrance, with guards posted on either side.

Entering, the guards escorted Samak through a well-designed inner garden filled with roses and jasmine, and into the reception hall of the summer house. There sat Shabdeez on an embroidered cushion like a king on his throne.

Samak bowed to Shabdeez. Speaking with an African accent and introducing himself as Armen Shah's spy Ayaz, he paid his respects, praised their magnificent surroundings, then said: "My lord, I have come from Gurkuhi's canyon with important news."

Shabdeez said: "Tell me your news."

Samak said: "My lord, I was present when Gurkuhi ordered Samak to kill you. That man has an evil nature and no mercy for anyone, not even his own relatives. When he learned you had escaped, he flew into a rage and threatened to kill Samak and his friends if they did not bring you back to him in shackles. Samak and Kuhyar are now on their way here with a dozen warriors. I raced ahead of them to warn you to be on your guard. I advise you to post soldiers at every road and checkpoint to stop those vicious men before they reach you."

Shabdeez thanked God for sending this spy to warn him of the danger coming his way. He invited Samak to spend the night as his guest, and told him that he would receive a reward in the morning.

Samak said: "My lord, I am only a slave and not worthy of your company. I would be happy for one goblet of wine in your presence as a blessing. Then I will take my meal in the kitchen with your servants and rest from my travels."

Shabdeez ordered one of his servants to bring a pitcher of wine to his hall and another to the kitchen to accompany their guest's meal. He then called in his guards and transmitted Samak's message, instructing them to post additional sentries at the canyon entrance and along the road.

When the servant returned with the wine, Samak said to Shabdeez: "My lord, please let me keep my position as a slave and pour the wine myself." Shabdeez agreed. His servant stood aside while Samak took the wine pitcher and filled Shabdeez's goblet and his own. Neither Shabdeez nor his servant noticed him add sleeping potion to Shabdeez's goblet before he offered it to him. Shabdeez and Samak both drank.

After Samak had drunk with Shabdeez, he asked if he could be excused and go to his proper place in the kitchen with the servants. Shabdeez, who was already feeling sleepy, gave him permission to leave.

Samak, joined the other servants in the kitchen, and ate and drank with them, making them laugh and keeping them entertained with tales of his adventures while he covertly poured sleeping potion into their wine. He encouraged the servants to talk as well, steering the conversation in such a way that by the end of the evening, he knew where in the summer house Shabdeez kept his treasure.

Once all three servants were asleep, Samak looked into the kitchen pantry and found two empty trunks. He took the smaller trunk to Shabdeez's treasure room and filled it with gold coins and jewels, filling his pockets as well. He then took the larger trunk to the reception hall where Shabdeez lay sound asleep. He opened the trunk, put Shabdeez in it, and shut the lid.

It was a clear moonlit night. The sky was filled with stars. Samak dragged both trunks out of the building one by one. He told the guards: "Lord Shabdeez gave me these as a reward. I will need a mule to carry them."

The guards brought a mule from the stables along with Samak's horse, and helped Samak load the trunks onto the mule. Samak handed the guards a few gold coins to thank them for their help and rode away.

On his way out of Red Canyon, each time Samak met a guard or sentry, he handed out a few more gold pieces, explaining that he had been generously rewarded by Lord Shabdeez and was now on his way back to Qatush's army camp. By the time Shabdeez's servants awoke to discover their master missing, Samak was long gone.

50

A LIFE FOR A LIFE

After leaving Red Canyon, Samak stopped at a stream and washed the dye from his face and hands to regain his natural color. He opened the larger trunk to check on his prisoner. Shabdeez was still snoring. Samak filled a container with water from the stream and placed it in Shabdeez's hands. Then he closed the trunk and locked it. His next challenge would be to find a way to pass back through Qatush's army camp without being questioned. He could not afford to take the risk of the sentries opening the trunks.

As he was considering various possibilities, he saw a caravan coming down the road, a hundred camels and mules loaded with merchandise. Samak rode to the head of the caravan, greeted the leader and paid his respects, then asked: "Do you have any wine you could sell me?"

The caravan leader replied: "In normal times I would, but we are taking this cargo to General Qatush's army camp and we are forbidden to sell to anyone else. Not everyone in these canyons is loyal to the king."

Samak took two gold coins from his pocket and showed them to the merchant. "I'm sure Armen Shah wouldn't mind a loyal subject drinking to his health and victory. Selling me two wineskins won't make a difference to the king. You'll still have plenty of wine for his army," he said. The merchant's eyes gleamed at the sight of the gold. He took the coins.

Samak said: "Would you mind if I travel with you? Riding alone with these trunks and two wineskins, I'm afraid I'd be a target for robbers." He pulled out two more gold coins and added: "I don't ask you to protect me for free."

Seeing how readily this rich stranger parted with his gold, the caravan leader said: "You are welcome to ride with us."

Samak thanked him and joined the caravan for the remainder of the journey. They reached the outskirts of Qatush's army camp late that afternoon. The caravan leader ordered the merchants to unload their mules and camels and spend the night there under the army's protection before distributing their merchandise in the morning.

The merchants unloaded their animals and tied them down. Each man found himself a place to sleep. Samak followed their example, sitting on the ground leaning against his own trunks. While no one was watching, he opened the larger trunk and checked on his prisoner. Shabdeez moaned and stirred. Samak put some sleeping potion on his fingers and rubbed them inside Shabdeez's mouth, adding some water from the flask. Shabdeez swallowed it and was soon once again fast asleep.

As night fell, Samak noticed a patrol of soldiers going among the caravan questioning each merchant. When the soldiers approached Samak, he stood and greeted them and asked if they could direct him to the patrol's night commander. The soldiers pointed to a blue tent on top of the hill facing them. They told Samak that the commander's name was Dudkhan.

Samak went to the caravan leader and asked if he could sell him two more wineskins. He explained that he wanted to offer them to Dudkhan, the night commander, as a goodwill gesture.

The merchant, seeing only gain in this proposition, agreed. Samak produced five more gold coins, saying: "Do you have porters who could help me carry them to Dudkhan's tent?"

The caravan leader called over two helpers, who loaded two mules with Samak's four wineskins while Samak loaded his own mule with the two trunks he had brought. They then led the mules up the hill.

Entering Dudkhan's tent, Samak found the night commander giving instructions to two of his men. When he saw Samak, he stopped talking and asked what he wanted. Samak bowed and paid his respects and said: "O commander, I came to bring you a small gift in appreciation for the protection you have offered us this night."

Dudkhan sent the soldiers out of his tent and then asked: "What have you brought?"

Samak said: "Vintage wine to ease your daily burdens. God bless His Majesty Armen Shah." He signaled to his porters waiting outside the tent. They brought in the four wineskins and left.

Samak bowed again, saying: "I am a merchant from Machin, His Majesty's loyal subject. My brother is also a merchant. He went to Gurkuhi's canyon and unfortunately was trapped there when war broke out. He cannot get out because the road is closed to regular traffic. Our mother is old. My brother's absence grieves her terribly and has made her ill. Every day she weeps for him and prays for his return. I promised her that I would try to bring my brother back with me, if God wills it."

While saying these words, Samak pulled out a small sack of gold from his pocket and placed it in front of Dudkhan. He said: "I know it is forbidden to enter Gurkuhi's canyon. I am hoping that for such an innocent purpose, to ease an old woman's grief, you will find it in your heart to make an exception. If you could ask your men to escort me to the edge of Gurkuhi's canyon, I promise I will give you no reason to regret it."

Dudkhan, who had already peeked inside the sack and seen the gold, saw little disadvantage to this proposition. He said: "O merchant, I will do better than that. I will personally take you through the campground so you will not be bothered."

Samak followed Dudkhan through Qatush's army camp until they reached the edge of Gurkuhi's canyon. Dudkhan showed Samak the path down into the canyon and said: "This is as far as I can take you." He took a ring from his finger and gave it to Samak, saying "If you run into any sentries from our army, show them this ring and tell them Dudkhan said you could pass." Samak thanked him and continued on his way.

Once he was safely out of Qatush's domain and in Gurkuhi's canyon, Samak felt able to relax. He started singing in a cheerful voice. The first sentries who saw him rode toward him, ready to challenge him, until they recognized him as Samak the ayyar. They sent word to Kuhyar, who was the watch commander that night.

As Samak rode back toward his own camp, he met Kuhyar on the way. "O brother, I'm glad you changed your mind and came back," said Kuhyar. "I told you you'd never get through Qatush's camp."

"But I did get through the camp," said Samak. "I passed a hundred thousand enemy soldiers both coming and going. And I've brought Shabdeez from his summer house. He's in this trunk."

Kuhyar thought Samak was joking. He said: "Seriously, what's in the trunks?"

Samak said: "Let's go see Gurkuhi and I'll show you."

Kuhyar led the way. Gurkuhi was awake and drinking wine in his pavilion. Kuhyar entered first and paid his respects. Gurkuhi said: "Brother, I thought you were on watch tonight. What are you doing here?"

Kuhyar said: "O brother, Samak has returned and is talking nonsense."

Gurkuhi said: "Bring him in."

Samak entered the pavilion, dragging the smaller trunk. Gurkuhi asked: "What's this my brother says about you talking nonsense?"

Samak smiled and said: "Let's see!" He pushed the trunk in front of Gurkuhi and lifted the lid.

Gurkuhi stared at the glittering gold and jewels. He asked Samak: "Where did you get this?"

Samak said: "My lord, the answer is in the other trunk. It's a bit heavy." Gurkuhi gestured to his servants. Two men went out and returned carrying the second, larger trunk.

Samak unlocked the trunk and opened the lid. Inside, Shabdeez stirred. The fresh air was starting to wake him up. The servants lifted him out and laid him at Gurkuhi's feet. Samak explained: "I found your nephew in his summer house and have brought him back to you as I said I would. The treasure in the other chest is his reward to me for making such a long journey through the enemy's army."

Gurkuhi gaped at his sleeping nephew. Then he looked up at Samak in confusion. "His summer house?" he repeated. "Then he was not hiding in this canyon?"

Samak confirmed that Shabdeez had taken refuge at his summer house in Red Canyon. Gurkuhi fell silent. He was realizing that it could not have been his nephew who had stolen the key and been caught by the giant trying to open the forbidden door. He could find no answer to the mystery. He looked at Samak and said: "Samak, I wish you a lifetime of happiness."

Shabdeez woke up, coughed, then vomited. The first person he saw was Samak. He looked around, saw where he was, and saw his uncles' grim faces. He cried out: "Samak! What have you done? What did I ever do to you to make you want to destroy me? Is this the way of the ayyars—you heroes, protectors of the people, whom everyone praises for their fairness? To kidnap an innocent man out of his home and take him to his death? Where is your mercy?"

His uncles Gurkuhi and Kuhyar avoided each other's gaze. Samak felt a pang in his heart. His pride in his exploit vanished. He thought: "Why did I ever promise to recapture him when I knew Gurkuhi wanted him dead? I should have just accepted the consequences of letting him escape. I don't think Gurkuhi would really have killed me. Even if he had, it would be better than the guilt of innocent blood on my hands."

Shabdeez begged: "Samak, before they kill me, please hear my last words, so that my secret doesn't die with me."

A ray of hope entered Samak's mind. It occurred to him that Shabdeez's secret could be something that would soften his uncle's anger. Otherwise why would he have mentioned it in front of Gurkuhi?

Samak bowed to Gurkuhi and said: "My lord, you are the pride of the whole world and the master of ayyars. I beg you to grant this young man's last request and let him release the pain he is carrying."

Gurkuhi replied: "Samak, if you are on my side, kill this man now before he reveals things no one should know!"

Hearing this from Gurkuhi only increased Samak's curiosity to learn what Shabdeez had to say. He bowed again and said: "My lord, if you already know the secret, perhaps you should be the one to reveal it, so that he can die in peace."

Gurkuhi shuddered. He said: "Samak, you are a stranger here and have no idea what has happened in the past. The secret you speak of is one I have vowed to protect with my life. You are my guest and have done so much for me, I cannot kill you or refuse your request. You leave me no choice but to reveal the secret and then kill myself."

Samak felt trapped. He wished he had never abducted Shabdeez from the enemy's camp in the first place. He fell at Gurkuhi's feet and said: "My lord, I owe you my life and my friends' lives. If you died on my account I could not forgive myself. Please don't kill your nephew. Make him swear an oath never to reveal his secret to anyone, and let him go back safely to his canyon."

There was silence. Gurkuhi's face was pale. Finally he said: "Samak, since you are the one who captured Shabdeez, it is fair that you should be the one to decide his fate. I put his life in your hands. What you do is up to you."

Samak bowed to Gurkuhi again and thanked him for his wisdom and generosity. He then turned to Shabdeez and said: "O Shabdeez, I have captured you twice. Your uncle Gurkuhi has spared your life, and now I spare it too. In return, I want you to take an oath never to reveal to anyone what has happened here tonight and to carry your secret to the grave."

Shabdeez was so relieved that tears streamed down his face. He took an oath on the spot to say nothing more about his uncle unless it was in his praise and tribute. Samak took Shabdeez in his arms and hugged him. Then he led him out of Gurkuhi's pavilion. The two men mounted their horses and rode in silence through the moonlit canyon. Neither said a word until they reached the edge of Qatush's army camp.

Samak said: "Go. You are free."

Shabdeez could not speak, but only nodded his thanks. He spurred his horse and rode toward Qatush's camp. Samak watched until the young man had disappeared from sight.

The sky was already light when Shabdeez reached the army campground and was stopped by Qatush's scouts. When Shabdeez identified himself, they took him straight to the general's pavilion.

Entering the tent, Shabdeez saw the lords of the other canyons sitting together having breakfast. They all stood up to pay their respects and welcome Shabdeez back as their commander. Shabdeez took Qatush's empty seat at the head of the gathering. The generals told him that Qatush had gone with part of the army to join Armen Shah at Guran Meadow, while the rest of them stayed to blockade Gurkuhi's canyon.

Once everyone was seated, the generals asked Shabdeez how he had managed to escape from Gurkuhi. They did not know that he had escaped twice, and that instead of coming straight back to Qatush's camp the first time, he had gone to his summer house in Red Canyon and been recaptured there.

Shabdeez did not tell them all this, but said simply: "My dear friends, my uncle Gurkuhi kept me prisoner until last night. Samak the ayyar, who is a refugee in his canyon, went to him and requested my freedom. Gurkuhi set me free out of respect for Samak, and Samak himself escorted me to the edge of camp. It was Samak who captured me, and Samak to whom I owe my life. Without him, I would be dead now."

When the morning meal was finished, Shabdeez stood up and informed the group that he would take his own army to join Armen Shah's. He then left the tent.

When Armen Shah's and Qatush's armies came together at Guran Meadow, Armen Shah found the new location to his liking. He thanked Qatush for suggesting it. Two days later, scouts brought the news that the army of Faghfur Shah and Khorshid Shah was marching in their direction. Two days after that, both armies had settled into their new camps facing each other across Guran Meadow, ready for combat.

51

IN THE GIANT'S LAIR

AFTER leaving Shabdeez, Samak returned to his friends' camp. They all welcomed him back. Sorkhvard held him tight, told him how much she had missed him, and wished they could be alone together. Samak kissed her and told her he had missed her too, and that they would make up for lost time once they were safely out of Gurkuhi's canyon.

Samak noticed that Ruzafzun was not in the group. He asked where she was. Sorkhvard said: "After you left, she told me she was going for a walk down the canyon. I offered to go with her, but she said she had a lot to think about and wanted to be alone. That was two nights ago and she hasn't been back since."

Samak became worried and said: "It's bad enough that Ruzafzun has no fear for herself. She could ruin our relations with Lord Gurkuhi if she's not careful. Two nights away is too long. Now I have to go and find out what happened to her."

Sorkhvard asked if she could go with him. Samak said: "No. Look for her around the campground, but don't let Gurkuhi know she's missing. He wouldn't like that. I'll go down to the bottom of the canyon and look for her there." Samak could guess where Ruzafzun had gone. While Sorkhvard made a circuit of the camp, Samak headed for the canyon floor and followed the stream to the grove.

It was getting dark by the time he crossed the river into the forbidden meadow. The scent of cooked meat filled the air. From the ashes of the giant's fire pit rose a thin column of smoke. Beside it lay a whole lamb. Samak saw no sign of Ruzafzun or anyone else.

As he stood there, imagining the worst that could have happened, he heard noises inside the cave. Samak hid behind a bush. In the dim light of dusk he saw the giant emerge from the cave, carrying on his shoulder a mace big enough to kill a lion or elephant with one blow. The giant strode across the meadow to the locked iron door, grabbed the handle, and shook it to make sure it was still locked. Reassured, he squatted by the fire pit. He began devouring the lamb, ripping meat from the bones with his sharp teeth.

Then the giant looked up sharply. A dim light was coming down the canyon toward them. The giant picked up the mace, strode to the iron door, and stood there fiercely guarding it.

As the light came closer, Samak saw that it was Gurkuhi carrying a torch. The giant bowed to Gurkuhi as he approached.

Gurkuhi demanded: "Have you seen anyone coming this way?"

The giant responded: "No, master. I have seen no one." Samak noticed that the giant did not meet Gurkuhi's eyes.

Gurkuhi reached for the door handle and tested it to make sure it was locked, as the giant had done. He said: "I want you to stay alert day and night. Someone has stolen my key and I don't know who."

The giant said: "I promise, master, I will not move from this spot." Again Samak thought there was something evasive in the giant's manner.

As Gurkuhi turned to leave, the giant said: "My lord, now may I please drink some wine? I have followed your orders. I haven't touched a drop for days. I am so thirsty."

Gurkuhi replied: "Absolutely not! I need you to stay alert."

The giant fell to his knees, making the ground shake. He begged: "Please, master. I can't live without wine. I am so thirsty I can think of nothing else. I will be a better watchman if you let me drink one goblet, just tonight."

Finally Gurkuhi relented and said: "All right, only one goblet and only tonight. But after that, I don't want to hear any more talk of wine until the intruder is caught!" The giant thanked Gurkuhi profusely and assured him he could count on him. Gurkuhi then left.

As soon as Gurkuhi was gone, the giant went into the cave, brought out a wineskin, sat by the fire, and began eating the lamb and drinking the wine. Samak watched from hiding while the giant finished the lamb and emptied the wineskin. Soon afterward, he began to snore. Samak said to himself: "If servants kept all the promises they make to their masters, my work would be much more difficult."

Samak emerged from his hiding place, took out his lasso, and tied the giant's hands and feet. Then he entered the cave. He saw bones littered on the floor of the cavern, along with empty wineskins, but no sign of Ruzafzun. Samak felt a chill in his heart, and said to himself: "If she did come here, it wouldn't surprise me if the giant has already eaten her and lied to his master about it."

He left the cave and crossed the meadow to the iron door. He was fiddling with the lock, trying to find a way to open it without the key, when he heard a female voice inside call out: "Who is there? If you are not the giant, and you can hear me, for God's sake open the door!"

Samak said: "I would if I had the key."

The woman's voice asked: "Was it you I heard trying to open the door a few days ago?"

Samak said: "That was my companion. Now she has disappeared." She has the key we took from the hiding place.

The voice asked: "Who are you?"

Samak responded: "I am Samak the ayyar, from Chin. Lord Gurkuhi gave refuge to me and my friends. We discovered this place by accident. Now tell me who you are and what is behind this door."

There was a long pause, then Samak heard the voice reply: "Before I say anything, I need to know how trustworthy you are and if I can depend on you."

Samak said: "The one thing my friends and enemies agree on is that there is no one in this world more dedicated than I am. When I say I will do something, I will do it."

There was another long silence while the person behind the door considered these words. Then she asked: "What do you know about Shabdeez?"

When Samak heard this name, he realized that the animosity between Gurkuhi and his nephew must have something to do with this locked door. Their family secrets were darker and deeper than he had imagined. He replied: "That is something best discussed face to face. I'll come back when I have the key."

Samak returned to the fire pit where the giant lay tied up and asleep. He picked up a stout tree branch from the ground, fashioned it into a club, and began beating the giant to wake him up.

The giant awoke and found himself bound hand and foot. He struggled, but he was tied up tight. Even with his great strength he could not break the lasso. He let out a roar of frustration loud enough to shake the trees. He shouted: "Who are you? What are you doing here? You are not allowed!"

Samak said in a stern voice: "Lord Gurkuhi sent me to punish you for breaking your promise to him and falling asleep on watch. You drank a whole wineskin of wine when he told you that you could have one goblet."

The giant looked nervous and guilty. Samak pressed his advantage and said: "What's worse is that you lied to your master when you said you had seen no one. Lord Gurkuhi knows that you caught the intruder. He sent me to tie you up until you tell the whole truth."

The giant hung his head and said in a miserable voice: "I'm sorry. Please tell the master I'm sorry. I lied because the person I caught was a she, not a he. The master doesn't allow me to eat people, but female human meat is so delicious, and I haven't tasted it in so long, I couldn't help myself."

A shudder ran through Samak. "Did you eat her?" he demanded.

"Not yet," said the giant. "I hid her in a hole at the end of the cave. I was saving her for later."

Samak said: "I will untie you on condition that you bring her to me right away!" The giant promised to do this. Samak untied the lasso. The giant reentered the cave. Samak waited for what seemed like an eternity. At last the giant emerged, carrying Ruzafzun under his arm as if she were as light as a package.

The giant placed Ruzafzun on the ground in front of Samak. He felt a burst of joy and relief on seeing her unharmed, but he hid his feelings so as not to awaken the giant's suspicions. He seized Ruzafzun and tied her hands behind her back and said: "Now I'll take you to Lord Gurkuhi and you'll find out how he deals with intruders and spies." He tied the lasso around her neck like a halter.

Ruzafzun understood and played her role. "Please, I'm innocent!" she cried. "I'm not a spy, I just got lost in the canyon."

Samak said sternly: "Not another word!"

Turning back to the giant, Samak demanded: "She had a key that she stole from Lord Gurkuhi. What did you do with it?" The giant guiltily produced the key and handed it to Samak.

Samak said: "You've escaped punishment this time. Be grateful that your master is so lenient. Now that the intruder has been caught, you may drink wine again. Stay on guard and don't let anyone near that door!" The giant thanked him and promised to be vigilant. He picked up his mace, rested it on his shoulder, went to the iron door and stood guarding it.

Samak led Ruzafzun by the rope around her neck until they were on the other side of the river and out of the giant's sight. Then he untied the lasso. Ruzafzun washed herself in the river in the moonlight. When she was clean, they started walking back through the canyon toward their own camp.

Ruzafzun took Samak's hand and said: "I'm sorry I went back without you. I should have waited. But I was so curious about that woman whose voice we heard behind the door! She sounded like she needed help."

Samak said: "Where were you? I searched the cave but I didn't see you."

Ruzafzun said: "The giant put me in a pit and threw down raw meat and water to keep me alive. Then he covered the opening with a boulder. I was in total darkness, like an animal. I couldn't tell day from night. I don't know how long I was down there before he came and brought me out."

Samak said: "My darling, I hope you've learned your lesson and I won't have to come looking for you a third time. I try my best, but if that giant had eaten you before I got there, there wouldn't have been much I could do." Ruzafzun promised to obey Samak and to be more careful in the future.

Samak then told her the whole adventure of how he had captured Shabdeez and brought him back, and how he had persuaded Gurkuhi to spare the young man's life. Ruzafzun praised Samak for his integrity and expressed relief that Shabdeez had not been killed. She kissed him, then asked with a smile: "When can we come back here together and find out what's behind that iron door?"

Samak said: "Listen, my dear. Whatever this secret is that Gurkuhi has gone to such lengths to hide, I feel sure that he will not forgive us if we expose it. We are at war. Our loyalty is to Khorshid Shah, and to Gurkuhi who has given us refuge. I will put the key back where I found it under Gurkuhi's seat until the time is right to explore this mystery." Ruzafzun was disappointed but understood. By the time they reached camp, they were both so tired that they went straight to bed.

The next morning, as Gurkuhi took his seat under the ironwood tree, he saw a glint of metal under the cushion. He lifted the cushion and was surprised to see the key. He sat there perplexed, the key in his hand, going over everything again in his mind. He wondered if the key had been there all along, if perhaps he himself had been the one who took it from its hiding place and failed to replace it. The more he thought about it, the less he was sure of anything. Finally he told himself: "Shabdeez is far from here and has sworn to keep the secret. The door is still locked, and the key is with me. I have more important things to worry about."

The next morning, a messenger came and told Samak that Gurkuhi wanted to see him. Samak told his associates to come with him. They all went to Gurkuhi's pavilion. Samak braced himself for the worst, but to his relief, Gurkuhi stood and greeted him warmly as they entered. He seated Samak on his right side and said: "In all my years I have met no one in the east or west who is as wise, as just, and as ingenious as you, Samak. If I were a young man, I would ask to join you as one of your apprentices."

After expressing his admiration for Samak, Gurkuhi said: "O great ayyar, we have a problem. I can think of no one better than you to turn to in the hope of finding some solution."

Samak bowed and said: "I am proud to be your servant. I will do anything I can to return a fraction of the kindness you have shown me and my friends."

Gurkuhi thanked him, then he said: "Qatush and Armen Shah's armies have blockaded this canyon to starve us into surrender. We have enough food for twelve thousand soldiers and their women and children, horses and animals, for two months at most. We have gold and jewels to spare, but we cannot eat those. This is why I am asking you if you can think of any ideas to get us out of this trouble."

Samak went into deep thought. He asked: "Is there any hidden passage out of this canyon?"

Gurkuhi said: "At the end of the canyon is a narrow path that only my brothers and I know about. But it is not a road suitable for carrying large loads."

Samak closed his eyes and scratched his ear while he thought. At last he said: "I have an idea that might work. If you give me thirty mules and load them with silver, gold, jewelry, and silks, I will take them to Khorshid Shah's army camp and open a supply line that should solve our problems."

Gurkuhi said: "Whatever you want, we will provide. But how will you get through the enemy's army to reach Khorshid Shah's camp?"

Samak responded: "Gold is a key that can unlock many doors."

While Gurkuhi's men organized what Samak had asked for, Samak instructed Hormozgil, Samour, Atashak, Neyal, and the butcher brothers to dress like merchants in felt hats and fine clothes. He told Sorkhvard and Ruzafzun to wear their most elegant outfits. When everything was ready, they mounted their horses and led the convoy of mules up Gurkuhi's canyon.

52

DEATH OF A PRINCE

WHEN Samak spotted the first sentries from Qatush's army riding toward them, he told the others: "Hold the caravan and wait here while I ride ahead and clear our passage."

Samak rode ahead to meet the soldiers. He told them he was a merchant known to commander Dudkhan, and he showed them the ring Dudkhan had given him. The sentries took him to their commander, who said: "I'll need to verify your story with Commander Dudkhan."

Samak handed him the ring and said: "Tell Commander Dudkhan that the person who holds the ring is the merchant who came to him with several wineskins a few days ago, and that he has returned with his brother as he promised."

The guard delivered the message to Dudkhan and showed him the ring. Recognizing it as his own, Dudkhan ordered the merchant and his caravan escorted to his tent.

Upon arriving at the tent, with Sorkhvard and Ruzafzun's help, Samak arranged a tray of gold, jewelry, musk, amber, and exquisite clothes. He told Atashak to help him carry the tray into the tent. As they entered, they paid their respects to Dudkhan. Samak bowed and said: "My lord, this is my brother. Thanks to your help, I was able to find him and take him out of Gurkuhi's canyon, along with some of his merchandise."

Atashak placed the tray in front of Dudkhan. Samak said: "This is a sample of our wares, our gift to you in gratitude. With your permission, we would like to sell the rest in Machin. This will require several trips back and forth through your army camp. Of course it is only fair that you and your men should receive something as well each time we pass through."

The commander examined the merchandise and was impressed. He gave his ring back to Samak. He said: "Keep this ring so that you can show it to the guards each time you pass." He told his men to arrange for the caravan to stay overnight. Samak thanked him and went back to his convoy to rest. Shortly after dawn, Dudkhan and his men escorted Samak and his caravan through Machin's army camp until they reached the edge of Guran Meadow.

As the convoy crossed Guran Meadow toward the army camp of Chin, Hormozgil asked Samak in amazement: "How did you know that would work?"

Samak replied cheerfully: "My lord general, God has blessed me with sharp eyes and observant ears. Everything I see and hear, I think of how I can turn it to my benefit." Seeing the others hanging on his words, he added: "The wealth of this world is not to be stored, but spent to achieve our goals. Gold is a key that opens every door, and conveniently also locks every mouth. Otherwise, how could one live amid so much war and struggle? Without gold, we could not have taken even one step on enemy ground. It was gold that did the job, not me!"

Scouts from Chin's army rode toward the convoy and asked their identity and purpose. When the news reached Khorshid Shah that the merchant caravan was led by Samak, the prince became so excited that he rode to the edge of camp to personally welcome his friend.

As soon as Samak saw the prince coming, he dismounted and ran to him. Khorshid Shah also dismounted from his horse, hugged Samak, and expressed joy at seeing him alive and well. The prince and his men escorted Samak and friends to the heart of the army camp, where they were warmly greeted by Faghfur Shah, Haman the vizier, and Farokhruz, who had fully recovered from his battle wounds.

Faghfur Shah asked Samak where he had come from. Samak responded: "Your Majesty, we have come from Gurkuhi's canyon."

Faghfur Shah asked in amazement: "How is it possible that you and this convoy of goods passed through the enemy's entire army without being stopped by anyone?"

Samak bowed and replied: "Your Majesty, thanks to the good fortune of my king Khorshid Shah, I was able to arrange a relationship with one of Armen Shah's generals so that we can cross their campground as often as we wish. Now that this route has been established, we can go on using it to supply Gurkuhi's army and the people in his canyon with the food they need to continue fighting on our side."

Everyone in Chin's army camp was happy to see Samak and his associates. The valuables Samak had brought from Gurkuhi's canyon were carried by mule to the royal army warehouse. Samak and his friends spent the night drinking and celebrating in Khorshid Shah's pavilion with the prince and his generals and dignitaries.

During the evening, Samak noticed that Khorshid Shah seemed troubled, as if something were weighing on his mind. At the first opportunity, he asked the prince if there was anything he could help with. Khorshid Shah then told Samak how Surkhkafar had left their camp, abducted Armen Shah's queen and daughter to Khorjan Desert, and murdered the queen and her maidens.

Samak's blood ran cold. He said: "I spared Surkhkafar's life in exchange for his oath of loyalty to Your Highness. I promised him I would put his hand in Princess Mahaneh's hand. I should have killed him when I had the chance. I feel responsible."

Khorshid Shah said: "I am responsible. I have given Armen Shah my word that I will deliver his daughter to him and Surkhkafar in chains."

Samak said: "Your Highness, please give me your permission to travel to Khorjan Desert and bring back Princess Mahaneh and Surkhkafar so that you can fulfill your promise to Armen Shah."

Khorshid Shah thanked Samak and said: "You have been my support since the first day I met you in Chin. Do what you feel is right." Samak bowed and promised not to disappoint him.

Samak asked: "Who were the two maidens that Surkhkafar murdered along with the queen?"

The prince answered: "A handmaiden of the princess Mahaneh. I do not know her name. And Armen Shah's wine server, Delaram."

Samak shuddered. He thanked Khorshid Shah for the information. Then he left the pavilion and sat down on the ground. It was for Delaram's sake that his friend Atashak had joined his service and they had shared their first adventures. Samak knew that Atashak had been counting the days until he and Delaram could be together.

Ruzafzun came out of the tent looking for Samak. He did not tell her what was on his mind, but stood up and accompanied her back inside with a heavy heart. Seeing Atashak happy and dancing in the festive gathering, he could not bring himself to break the news to him that night. He told himself that he would find a better moment.

• • •

Early the next morning, the sound of war drums echoed throughout Guran Meadow as the two armies lined up to face each other for combat. Farokhruz rode to Khorshid Shah and asked his brother for permission to be first to enter the new battlefield.

Khorshid Shah said: "Farokhruz, you are my only brother and the light of my eyes. If anything happened to you, my heart would break. We have no shortage of warriors eager for battle. Please stay out of the combat zone and let them do what they've been trained for."

Farokhruz said: "I have fought Machin's army before. I have no fear of their warriors."

Khorshid Shah said: "My dear brother, I know you are fearless. I am the one who is worried. Last night I had a disturbing dream."

Farokhruz said: "We all have dreams, brother. Tell me, what was yours about?"

Khorshid Shah said: "I dreamed I was riding on horseback and fell into a vortex. I was whirling helpless and falling into its depths when you appeared. You grabbed my horse's reins and pulled us out. Later, as we rode and talked together side by side, an eagle swooped down, seized your hat in its claws, and flew up into the sky."

Farokhruz said: "My dearest brother, from the little I know about dreams, this sounds like it might foretell a separation, but not death. Please let me go into the field as an example to our army."

Tears came to Khorshid Shah's eyes. He hugged Farokhruz and said: "You are my older brother. I don't have the right to tell you what to do or not to do. You must make your own decisions. Just know that I am praying for your safety."

Farokhruz thanked Khorshid Shah and bowed to him. Then he spurred his horse and rode into the center of the field, shouting for an opponent to come out and fight him.

A powerful horseman named Qobad rode out of the Machin ranks and toward Farokhruz. He shouted: "It's about time you met a real warrior to stop your boasting!" He rode at Farokhruz, swinging his mace. Farokhruz blocked with his shield and counter-attacked with his own mace. The two battled on horseback, but neither could gain an advantage over the other. They threw aside their maces, drew their spears, and went on fighting.

Farokhruz saw an opening. He plunged his spear into Qobad's chest with such force that it penetrated his breastplate and the point came out his back. The warrior fell off his horse and died. Farokhruz rode toward Machin's army, brandishing his spear and shouting: "Who will be next?"

The next warrior to ride out was Qobad's nephew. He charged toward Farokhruz. "You just killed a hero who was a better man than you! I will make you pay for that!" he cried.

The warrior leveled his spear and galloped toward Farokhruz. Farokhruz did not wait for his opponent to reach him, but hurled his spear with such force and accuracy that it skewered the warrior through his open mouth before he finished speaking. Qobad's nephew fell from his horse. His blood soaked the dirt.

Farokhruz held the field all morning, defeating one opponent after another, while the sun rose in the sky. By the time the sun reached its apex, fourteen of Machin's warriors lay dead or had been carried wounded back to their ranks. Again Farokhruz rode up and down the line, as fresh as if he had just arrived, calling for a new opponent. No one else dared to step forward and enter the battlefield.

Khorshid Shah, who had been tensely watching every combat, was starting to feel relief that it was over, when Abresiah rode out into the field.

Farokhruz recognized the warrior behind his helmet as the one who had come to Faghfur Shah's pavilion. He said: "Aren't you Abresiah who brought a message to my brother and Faghfur Shah?"

Abresiah said: "I am Abresiah! And I am here to avenge the wrongs you have done to my king and prince by putting an end to your life."

Farokhruz said: "You speak with no more honor than your king and prince have shown. My brother gave his word to rescue your princess and avenge your queen's murder, while you sat silent. If you and Armen Shah and Gezelmalek were men, you would have dealt with Surkhkafar yourselves. Instead you attack Khorshid Shah, who has never harmed you, and who fights your battles for you!" He raised his spear and said: "My brother will avenge the wrongs you should have avenged yourself. I will teach you how a real warrior handles his enemies!" He thrust his spear at Abresiah, who deflected it with his shield.

The two fought on horseback, spear to spear, until finally Farokhruz's spear splintered against Abresiah's shield. Farokhruz threw aside the broken shaft and drew his sword. Abresiah lifted his shield to block Farokhruz's first blow. The sword glanced off his shield and struck his horse's neck, nearly severing its head. Abresiah and his horse tumbled to the ground. Falling, he pulled out his own sword and slashed the forelegs of Farokhruz's horse out from under him. Farokhruz went flying from the saddle and his head hit the ground. As he lay stunned, Abresiah jumped on top of him. The two warriors scuffled in the dust.

At the sight, both armies poured onto the battlefield. Soldiers from Machin reached the struggling champions first. Before anyone could stop them, they pulled Farokhruz off Abresiah, tied his hands, and threw him on back of a horse. A bloody brawl ensued. Khorshid Shah's heart tightened as he saw the group of Machin soldiers gallop back to their own ranks with Farokhruz as their prisoner. He shouted the order to beat the war drums to stop the combat. The melee ended as both armies retreated from the battlefield.

The Machin soldiers rode up the hill to where Armen Shah and his son sat on horseback, and dragged Farokhruz before them with his hands tied behind his back. Gezelmalek shouted with joy when he saw who their prisoner was. He drew his sword, exclaiming: "At last—vengeance!"

The vizier Shahran rode forward to block Gezelmalek's path. "My lord! This is Prince Farokhruz, Khorshid Shah's brother. Such a hostage should be ransomed, not killed."

Gezelmalek shouted back: "Get out of my way, old fool! If we had killed our prisoners instead of letting them go free, this war would have been over long ago."

Shahran said: "O great prince, you are young and have not yet tasted true pain. The world holds dangers and sorrows that you cannot imagine. Do not take Khorshid Shah lightly. It is not only I who say this. All who know him would agree he is no ordinary man. For you to kill his brother would bring disaster on our heads. It could destroy our kingdom."

Far from calming Gezelmalek, the vizier's words made him more furious. He shouted: "You're the one who is destroying our kingdom with your cowardly words and bad advice!" He charged at Shahran, swinging his sword. Shahran dodged and fell from his saddle. Gezelmalek's sword struck his horse. Vizier and horse both tumbled to the ground.

Gezelmalek jumped down from his horse. He strode toward Farokhruz and, before anyone could stop him, struck the prince's neck with his sword, cutting off his head in a single stroke. Farokhruz's body fell forward, hands still tied behind his back. His head rolled to a stop in the dirt at Armen Shah's feet.

There was silence. Then a roar went up from the armies—triumph on the Machin side, anguish on the side of Chin as the soldiers realized what had happened.

Khorshid Shah, watching from his hilltop, stared in shock. He dismounted from his horse, threw his crown on the ground and fell to his knees, crying out: "Farokhruz! Farokhruz!"

Samak, Shaghal, and the other ayyars began throwing dust on their own heads while crying out in grief.

Faghfur Shah and Haman, who had dismounted from their own horses, lifted Khorshid Shah to his feet and walked him back to his pavilion. The prince wept and cried out: "Farokhruz! My brother, my friend! Why didn't I listen to my dream? Look what they have done to you, before you could even taste love's sweetness!"

The death of Farokhruz cast a shadow of despair across the army of Chin. Everyone retreated to their tents and stayed quiet out of respect for Khorshid Shah.

That same day, in the ayyars' tent, Atashak learned of the death of Delaram. With the whole camp plunged into mourning, his private grief was his alone. Delaram had been only a wine server, but he had loved her. His sorrow was no less intense for being so little noticed.

53

THE STONE WARRIORS

THE vizier Shahran was deeply hurt by Gezelmalek's actions, and by the insult he himself had suffered. After Farokhruz's execution, the vizier quietly mounted his horse, retreated to his own tent, and composed a message to Armen Shah. He wrote: "As I have been informed that I am an old fool who gives bad advice, I regret that I will be unable to continue serving Your Highness. I ask permission to go into seclusion and spend my remaining days praying for the long life and health of Your Majesty."

When Armen Shah received Shahran's message, he told his son to apologize to the vizier and convince him to return to the court.

Following the king's order, Gezelmalek went to Shahran's tent. The vizier politely stood up and offered his own seat to the prince. Once seated, Gezelmalek said: "O great vizier, I have come to apologize for my unkind behavior. I am young and sometimes my temper gets the better of me. My harsh words to you were unworthy of a crown prince. What's done is done. Today Farokhruz's life came to an end, and I am the one who took it. Our kingdom needs you. Please come back to court with me."

After saying that, Gezelmalek stood up, held out his arms, and embraced the vizier. Then the two of them returned together to

Armen Shah's pavilion. The king was pleased to see Shahran and welcomed him with a smile. Food and wine were brought, and Armen Shah and his generals celebrated the day's victory.

Abresiah sat in silence while the others congratulated him and drank to his health. After hearing them speak his praises, he bowed to Armen Shah and said: "Your Majesty, today in the field Farokhruz spoke words I cannot forget. He brought up the name of Surkhkafar and said that we as a nation have no honor. His words brought me pain because they were just. We should not leave it to our enemy to avenge the death of our queen. The stain on our honor touches me more than anyone, because that villain took refuge in my territory. I am responsible for Khorjan Desert. I should be the one to go."

The mention of Surkhkafar chilled the mood of the gathering. Armen Shah said to Abresiah: "What about the order you sent the sheriff of Khorjan to arrest Surkhkafar and take the princess from his custody? Did he not act on it?"

Abresiah bowed to the king and said: "Your Majesty, unfortunately the news I have to share is not good. I have been told that Surkhkafar has left Khorjan Desert and taken Princess Mahaneh with him to Black Mountain." Seeing that the king and his generals were unfamiliar with this name, Abresiah went on: "Black Mountain is a remote community whose livelihood comes from ten mills. I am informed that Surkhkafar and his group of about fifty warriors have taken over six of them. Their position is so strong that any farmer who takes his crops to be milled must travel with a large escort of well-armed guards if he does not want to be waylaid and his crops stolen by Surkhkafar."

Armen Shah shouted at Abresiah: "Are you telling me that nothing is being done to save my daughter, who is at this villain's mercy?"

Abresiah bowed low and said: "If Your Majesty commands it, I will take an army of four thousand warriors to Black Mountain and bring back the princess and Surkhkafar."

Armen Shah said: "Why are you still sitting here? Go and do it!"

That very night, scouts came to Khorshid Shah's pavilion with the news that Abresiah and four thousand riders were preparing to leave for Black Mountain. Khorshid Shah, in mourning for his beloved brother, let out a cry of anguish and tore his hair when he heard the name of Abresiah, who had taken Farokhruz to his death.

Samak stood up, bowed to the prince, and said: "Your Highness, I promised you that I would bring back Princess Mahaneh and Surkhkafar. Please give me permission to go now. If God wills it and gives me the opportunity, I will capture Abresiah too, for what he did to Farokhruz. The one who most deserves our vengeance is Gezelmalek, for his cowardly and vicious act. But since he is out of my reach, please let me at least do this much."

Khorshid Shah gave his permission.

Ruzafzun, who was among those present, bowed to Khorshid Shah and said: "Your Highness, since Samak is going to Black Mountain, would my lord permit me to go back to Gurkuhi's canyon to investigate a mystery that we discovered there?"

Before Khorshid Shah could reply, Samak shouted at Ruzafzun: "This is not the time! His Majesty has more important things to worry about than satisfying your curiosity."

Khorshid Shah asked: "What mystery are you speaking of?" Samak glared at Ruzafzun. He bowed to the prince, and told him the story of the locked iron door, the mysterious female voice behind it, and the man-eating giant entrusted by Gurkuhi to guard the place. Khorshid Shah listened carefully, then he said: "I too am curious to learn this secret of the locked door."

Shaghal, who had also been listening, bowed to the prince and said: "Your Highness, since Samak is going on another mission, if you command it I will go with Ruzafzun to explore the mystery of Gurkuhi's canyon."

Samak did not dare undermine his master in front of the king. He said to Shaghal: "O great commander of ayyars, I cannot tell you not to go, because you are my master. But I warn you that Ruzafzun is a willful girl who has no fear for herself or others. She disobeys orders and takes reckless risks. I am afraid that if you follow her lead, she will put you both in danger."

Shaghal smiled and said: "My dear Samak, Ruzafzun is young. You were young too not so long ago. Trust your master. I promise you I will be right behind her."

Khorshid Shah gave permission for them to go. Then his head dropped, overtaken by fatigue and the day's grief. Everyone understood and quickly left the prince's pavilion to let him rest.

That night, as Samak prepared for his journey, Neyal, Atashak, and Sorkhvard approached him and said: "Samak, let us come with you to Black Mountain."

Samak said: "No. This mission I must carry out alone." Atashak objected, and began trying to persuade Samak to accept their help. Samak cut him off and snapped: "Do I have to repeat myself and argue with you over everything? You are my disciples. I am the one who ends up having to rescue you when you get into trouble, and then I repair the damage when you disobey my orders."

Atashak, Sorkhvard, and Neyal became quiet. They left without saying anything more. Samak felt a stab of regret for having spoken more harshly than he intended. He told himself that he was right to be firm with his apprentices. They must learn to respect his authority.

• • •

Early the next morning, Samak left on his journey. This time he took a camel rather than his usual horse, since he would be going through a desert. Under his clothes he wore armor and weapons and carried a bag of gold. He rode for two straight days and nights to reach Khorjan Desert before Abresiah and his army.

As Samak entered Khorjan on his camel, residents gathered around him, wondering who this light-skinned stranger was and what had brought him from so far away. Samak told them he had good news. General Abresiah was on his way with four thousand riders to arrest Surkhkafar, the outlaw who had brought so much pain to their territory.

The people of Khorjan told Samak that Surkhkafar had taken the princess to Black Mountain, where even an army of forty thousand could not capture him. He had seized the mills that ground their grain and he was driving them into starvation. Samak assured the residents that Abresiah was a powerful general and would find a way to eliminate Surkhkafar no matter where he was.

Samak rode his camel through the town's bazaar, found a barber shop, and instructed the barber to weave his hair and darken his face to make him look like the locals. When he came out of the shop and mounted his camel, he looked like a Bedouin. Samak continued through the bazaar, bought a large sack of wheat, placed it behind him on the camel, and headed for Black Mountain.

As the mills of Black Mountain came into view, Samak saw that it was like a ghost town. No residents were to be seen anywhere. He passed the ten mills one by one. When he reached the last mill, Samak dismounted from his camel, lifted the sack of wheat onto his shoulder, and carried it to the mill. The mill house was silent, no one inside. Samak, who knew little about milling, took the opportunity to study its workings. He spent some time examining the mill, trying to understand how the grain was ground and the flour collected.

What Samak did not know was that Surkhkafar had been watching him from a distance since the moment he entered the valley. At first, Surkhkafar took him for a Bedouin who had come to grind his grain. But when he saw Samak passing by the mills one after another, then enter the last mill, he became concerned.

Samak was inside when he heard the approaching hoofbeats of Surkhkafar's horse. He quickly set about grinding the wheat he had brought, blowing flour into the air to land on his face and hair like dust.

Surkhkafar entered the mill house, strode directly to Samak, and demanded: "Do you know who I am? How dare you come into my mill? And why did you pass by the others mills?"

Samak was reassured that Surkhkafar did not recognize him. In a Bedouin's accent and a plaintive voice, he replied: "Please, O great lord, I am a poor man with a wife and children to feed. I came to this mill because the others looked deserted. I only want to grind my one sack of wheat into flour so we can bake bread and my family can eat. If you allow me, I promise to leave this place as soon as I am done and go back to the desert."

Surkhkafar said: "So you came from the desert. What news do you bring?"

Samak replied: "My lord, I heard a rumor that four thousand soldiers are on their way to arrest you, led by Abresiah. But I did not see them with my own eyes."

Hearing this, Surkhkafar turned pale. He immediately left the mill house, mounted his horse, and rode toward the end of the valley. Samak waited until he was nearly out of sight, then he left the mill and followed on his camel. In the distance, he saw Surkhkafar disappear into a narrow mountain pass at the end of the canyon.

Samak followed him. The pass was steep and so narrow that it could take only one rider at a time. Rounding a bend, Samak was startled to see fifty warriors on the cliff above with bows and arrows drawn. Samak pulled back his camel and hid behind a rock, heart pounding. He thought: "Those people were right. Surkhkafar could hold off an army. Where on earth did he get those warriors?"

Samak peered out from behind the rock for a better look. Then he noticed something strange. The warriors had not moved. He waited, then stepped out into the path and waved his arms to attract their attention. Still the warriors did not move.

Samak climbed the hill to the top of the canyon. When he got close enough to touch the first warrior, he understood. They were not men but stone statues clad in armor and helmets, and equipped with real bows and arrows to scare off intruders.

Having seen this, Samak returned to the tenth mill to hide and await Abresiah's arrival.

Two days later, Abresiah and his army arrived in Khorjan. The residents informed him that Surkhkafar had taken refuge in Black Mountain. Abresiah took a hundred riders and rode ahead with them to reconnoiter the territory.

Abresiah and his men rode past the ten mills and entered the narrow mountain pass at the end of the valley. As the first scouts rounded the bend, two arrows shot from above killed both men instantly. The soldiers behind them shouted in alarm and retreated behind the rock.

All that afternoon, Abresiah and his warriors made repeated forays into the mountain pass. Each time a soldier stepped into the open, he was felled by an arrow from above. In fact, all the arrows were shot by Surkhkafar himself, who was moving from one statue to another and hiding behind them as he shot at the men below. By nightfall, forty of Abresiah's soldiers lay dead in the pass. Abresiah decided to retreat and come back with a larger force.

Samak had watched Abresiah's army ride past from his hiding place in the mill house. Now he watched it return at sunset reduced in number. He waited until darkness descended on the canyon. Then he took the mountain pass, bypassed the stone warriors, and emerged into a moonlit valley of stunning natural beauty.

Trees and flowers filled the canyon. Waterfalls poured down rock walls into a stream. Birds and wild animals were everywhere. After Samak's long journey through the desert and two nights in the mill house, the canyon seemed to him like a dream. He marveled at Surkhkafar's cleverness in choosing a location that was at once so peaceful and so well protected.

Silently, under cover of darkness, Samak crept from rock to rock and tree to tree until he reached a green meadow. In the center of the meadow stood a tent of red satin covered with ornaments and fastened to the ground by silk ropes secured with golden nails. As Samak approached, he heard a female voice within, singing a song of mournful beauty.

Peering into the tent's opening, Samak saw a bed mounted inside the pavilion. In the bed was Princess Mahaneh, her wrists tied to the posts. She was about to cry out when Samak bowed and said: "Your Highness, please don't be frightened! It is me, Samak, here to save you from Surkhkafar."

He came closer to give Mahaneh a good look at him. She recognized Samak through his disguise. "Where will you take me?" she asked. "Back to Khorshid Shah?"

Samak explained as he untied her: "Dear princess, I am here to take your hand and put it in your father's hand as Khorshid Shah has promised him."

Mahaneh said scornfully: "To hell with my father and my brother! They are fighting a stupid war and care only about themselves."

Samak rubbed Mahaneh's wrists and feet. He said: "I am sure your father and brother care for you dearly. But they are on a battlefield. That is why I have come to take you to them."

Mahaneh said: "I don't understand. You are our enemy. How can you and Khorshid Shah be so kind to me?"

Samak said: "An enemy is an enemy, but no ayyar would allow a noble lady to be mistreated."

Hearing these words, Mahaneh threw herself into Samak's arms and wept: "If only you had come earlier to save my mother and our maidens!"

Samak held Mahaneh in his arms and said: "I wish I had." He released her and asked: "Do you know where Surkhkafar is now?" Mahaneh shuddered at the mention of the name and shook her head.

Samak asked: "Since you arrived here, have you seen him drink wine?"

Mahaneh shook her head again, and said: "I have never seen him touch a drop. And I have never seen him sleep. Each time he visits me, he stays for only a short time, then he leaves to guard the canyon pass."

Samak asked: "What about food? Where does he eat?" Mahaneh pointed to a tray in the corner of the pavilion and said: "He eats halvah from that plate."

Samak looked around the pavilion, taking note of everything. All around were treasures fit for a queen—gold, jewelry, and the finest embroidered silks. In a kitchen area at the back of the tent stood several empty trunks.

Samak took out a jar of sleeping potion he had brought with him and poured some on the tray of tasty-looking halvah. He returned to Mahaneh and said: "Tonight when Surkhkafar comes to you, encourage him to eat as much as possible. I will hide under the bed and come out after he has fallen asleep."

Mahaneh said: "I told you, he doesn't sleep."

Samak just smiled, and tied Mahaneh back to the bed exactly as he had found her. "Tonight will be different from other nights," he said.

54

A PLATE OF HALVAH

SAMAK waited in the tent with Mahaneh until they heard a horse's footsteps outside. Samak whispered: "Remember what I told you!" And he slipped under the bed to hide.

Surkhkafar did not enter the pavilion right away after dismounting but walked his horse for a while to cool him down. He tied up the horse, fed him some hay, and entered the tent.

Mahaneh lay tied up in bed with her eyes closed. She opened them as if she were just waking up. Surkhkafar sat on the bed next to her and said: "Today I had a busy day. Your father sent an army to arrest me. I killed about forty of them. The rest fled." He brought the tray of halvah to the bed and began eating, as he continued: "If they come back, I will trigger the landslide of rocks and boulders that I have prepared to block the pass. Then you and I will be sealed away from the world. We have everything we need here in this valley to live a good life."

Surkhkafar began caressing Mahaneh and said: "If only I didn't need to tie you up, life would be so much more pleasant. When will you stop sulking and be my friend?"

Surkhkafar's touch was odious to Mahaneh, but she said: "O Surkhkafar, I'm almost ready to surrender to you. I know you would make a wonderful husband. But I can't relax or enjoy anything while my nightmares are tormenting me."

A thrill ran through Surkhkafar when he heard her speak these words in such a sweet voice. He asked: "What nightmares, my darling?"

Mahaneh explained: "Ever since Samak the ayyar abducted my mother and me from our harem in Machin, I've had terrible dreams that he comes back. Just as I start to drift off to sleep, Samak's face appears in front of me and I wake up in a cold sweat. If you could bring me Samak's head, I think the nightmares would end and I could sleep, and we could be happy together."

Surkhkafar said: "O my beloved princess, if Samak ever dares to show his face in this part of the world, I promise you I will cut off his head and bring it to you as you ask. But he will not come."

Mahaneh said: "How can you be sure of that?"

Surkhkafar replied: "Samak is a thief and trickster, not a warrior. He doesn't dare to face his enemies head on because he knows that in a fair contest of strength he would lose. He hatches his schemes in secret and in hiding." He reached for another piece of halvah and ate it. "O princess, it was for your sake that I agreed to serve your father, and Khorshid Shah after him," he said. "They promised to put your hand in my hand, but their promises were worthless. I realized that if I wanted you I would have to take you myself."

"At first I hated you," said Mahaneh. "But then I realized I need a man who's strong enough to stand against my father and Samak."

Hearing this, Surkhkafar became excited. He said: "Princess, let me untie you. Give yourself to me tonight, and I will go after Samak and bring you back his head."

Mahaneh said: "I want to, but I can't be completely yours until I know Samak is dead."

Surkhkafar was about to reply when he began to feel his head spin. He stood up, but his legs crumpled under him. He fell to the floor unconscious.

Samak crawled out from under the bed. He untied the princess and used her ropes to tie up Surkhkafar hand and foot. Mahaneh threw herself into Samak's arms. Samak held her politely at arms' length and said: "O princess, I am just an ordinary man. I don't deserve your affection or gratitude for doing my duty."

Mahaneh said: "You are not just strong and clever, but chivalrous! I wish you nothing but joy for the rest of your life for saving me from that filthy beast. Are you going to tie me up again and take me back to Khorshid Shah as your prisoner?"

Samak smiled and said: "Dear princess, I won't tie you up. Prince Khorshid Shah will give you a royal carriage and a majestic entourage to escort you to your father as he has promised. That promise is what brought me here."

Mahaneh asked: "Will we leave right away?"

Samak said: "Not yet, Princess. First I have some unfinished business." He took a jug of cold water and poured it over Surkhkafar. Then he began kicking him until he vomited and awakened to find himself tied hand and foot. Seeing Samak standing over him, his first thought was that he was asleep and dreaming.

Samak placed his foot on Surkhkafar's neck and said in a terrible voice: "You swore you would be loyal to me. Is this how you repay me for sparing your life? By abusing and murdering innocent women?" He began kicking Surkhkafar and shouted: "What did the queen ever do to you? And the maiden Delaram, who did nothing but pour the king's wine. Don't you have a speck of humanity?" He kicked Surkhkafar between the legs so hard that he passed out. Samak added: "Now you won't need to go after princesses or any other women."

Samak dragged the unconscious Surkhkafar into a corner, made sure he was securely bound hand and foot, and gagged his mouth for good measure. He said to Mahaneh: "Keep an eye on the canyon until I come back with General Abresiah."

Mahaneh, frightened, begged Samak: "Please don't leave me alone with him. What if he wakes up?"

Samak said: "Don't worry, he's tied up well. Just stay close to the entrance to be sure you see anyone coming. If all goes as I hope, the next person to enter this tent will be Abresiah. When he does, be sure to show him your gratitude and serve him lots of halvah. And by the way, my name is not Samak, but Azal." Mahaneh understood.

Samak left the pavilion, mounted Surkhkafar's horse, and rode through Black Mountain until he reached Abresiah's army camp at the edge of Khorjan Desert. He told the guards that he was a servant of Armen Shah with an urgent message for General Abresiah. They led him straight to Abresiah's tent.

Samak entered, paid his respects, then said: "O great general, my name is Azal and I am the custodian of the royal pavilion in Black Mountain Canyon. I have been keeping it for His Majesty in case he ever wishes to come here to hunt. I kept it in perfect shape until two weeks ago, when Surkhkafar arrived with Princess Mahaneh and took it over. At first I thought he had the king's permission, but when I saw his behavior toward the princess, I realized that he had abducted her. I begged him to let me live to serve him and the princess. He tied me to a tree outside the pavilion. Every day he unties me just long enough to clean up and feed his horse."

Samak saw that Abresiah was listening closely. He went on: "Today was different. He drank a full skin of wine. I heard the princess crying out inside the pavilion and I knew this was the day he would try to rape her. Thank God, he was drunk and fell asleep. The princess ran out and untied me and together we used the ropes to tie him up. I rode his horse as fast as I could to ask you for help. I am only a custodian, not a warrior. The princess and I tied him securely, but I am afraid he will wake up and somehow get free."

Abresiah looked hard at Samak and said: "I'd like to believe your story, but there is something I don't understand. How did you get past the soldiers guarding the pass?"

Samak said: "Soldiers? The only soldiers in Black Mountain are made of stone. I heard Surkhkafar boasting to the princess that he had killed forty men and scared off an army single-handed with nothing but a bow and arrow, and the help of fifty stone statues."

Abresiah let out an exclamation. He jumped to his feet and barked to his soldiers: "Let's go!"

As the soldiers sprang into action, Samak said: "My lord, Surkhkafar has treasure with him that belongs to His Majesty Armen Shah. You ought to take it before someone else does. Four mules should be enough to carry it all. If you leave, say, twenty soldiers to stand guard along the canyon, you and I can go down to the pavilion and arrest Surkhkafar, then call down the soldiers to load the treasure onto the mules."

Abresiah said: "Good idea. I'll tell Armen Shah of your loyal service and perhaps you'll be rewarded."

Abresiah called for four mules and forty riders. Samak remarked: "Ah, you are a generous commander!" Abresiah asked him what he meant by this. Samak explained: "Surkhkafar is tied up and helpless. An ambitious general thinking only of his own advancement could have gone down into the canyon alone and captured him single-handed. Such an exploit would impress His Majesty and maybe even be rewarded with Princess Mahaneh's hand in marriage. But you think of your men as well, and share with forty of them the glory that might have been yours alone." Abresiah did not respond to this comment, but by the time they set out for Black Mountain, the company consisted of four mules and twenty riders.

When they reached the fifth mill, Abresiah took Samak's suggestion and left four soldiers there to guard it. They left several soldiers at each mill until they reached the last one. By the time they entered the narrow mountain pass, Samak and Abresiah were alone. The general relaxed when he saw that Samak had told the truth. The warriors ranged atop the canyon were stone statues. He shook his head ruefully as he realized how he had been fooled.

Dawn was breaking as they emerged from the pass into the canyon. Abresiah breathed in the morning fragrance and marveled at what a pleasant place this was. As they approached the red silk pavilion, the general stopped Samak and said: "Perhaps I should go in alone." Samak agreed and waited outside.

When Abresiah entered the tent, his heart began to pound at the sight of the princess. He had seen many beautiful women in his life, but Mahaneh was something else. The second thing he noticed was Surkhkafar, tied up and bloody in the corner. The third was that Samak had told the truth about the treasures. Abresiah bowed, paid his respects to the princess, and told her that he had come to bring her back to Armen Shah.

Surkhkafar was awake. When he saw the general, he writhed and tried to speak, but through the gag could only produce muffled noises.

Mahaneh thanked Abresiah for coming to save her from Surkhkafar. She added: "Thank God for my father's servant Azal who has been my help and support through my ordeal." She offered the tray of halvah to Abresiah. He thanked her and began to eat.

As Abresiah sat eating the halvah, he could not stop looking at Mahaneh. His senses were overwhelmed by the sight of this girl, tall and slim like a walking cypress tree, with a face like the full moon and a smile like the dawn. Her belly was as pure and white as fine-milled flour. He became increasingly mesmerized by the princess's beauty and began to think that perhaps it was not so far-fetched that after returning her safely to the king and delivering Surkhkafar in shackles, he might find an opportunity to ask for Mahaneh's hand in marriage.

Surkhkafar's muffled attempts to speak grew more desperate. Abresiah remarked: "He seems to want to tell us something. What do you think? Should we remove his gag?"

Mahaneh replied: "If we do, he will do nothing but insult us with his foul mouth, and ruin the pleasant mood."

Abresiah smiled at her, and ate another piece of halvah.

Suddenly his head spun. He stood up in alarm, then fell to the floor unconscious. Mahaneh called out to Samak: "You can come in now!"

Samak entered the pavilion and bound Abresiah's hands and feet. Dragging forward three empty trunks from the back of the tent, he put Surkhkafar in one and Abresiah in another. Then he told Mahaneh: "Dear princess, I am sorry, but the third trunk is for you."

Mahaneh gasped and recoiled. "You said you would take me to my father in comfort! How will I breathe?"

Samak said: "I promise it will be only for a short while. At least you will be more comfortable than these two, who will have to endure their quarters for the entire journey."

Mahaneh retorted: "It's easy for them, they're unconscious."

Samak raised his eyebrows and said: "If you like, I could feed you some of this halvah."

Mahaneh said: "No, thank you! I don't think I'll be eating halvah for a long time to come."

Working together, Samak and Mahaneh loaded the trunks containing Surkhkafar and Abresiah onto the mules. They managed this with the aid of a large rock that stood outside the pavilion. First, Samak led each mule alongside the rock, then together they pushed the trunk up onto the rock and from there onto the mule's back to be fastened.

Once the first two trunks had been loaded onto the mules, Samak prepared the third trunk by placing soft cushions inside, then used his dagger to punch holes in the sides. He helped Mahaneh inside, closed the top, then fastened the trunk atop the third mule. He returned inside the pavilion and filled the fourth trunk with treasures until the tent was stripped bare. He loaded the trunk on top of the fourth mule, mounted Surkhkafar's horse, and led the mules out of the valley.

After going through the narrow pass, Samak dismounted and climbed to the top of the hill where the stone soldiers stood. Surkhkafar had prepared a trap with rocks and boulders, and a wooden stick to release them. It must have taken him weeks of labor to assemble. Samak pulled the lever, triggering a cascade of boulders, rocks and dirt. When the dust had settled, the path was impassable.

Samak got back on the horse and led the mules out of the canyon to Black Mountain. When he reached the first mill, he told the group of soldiers guarding it: "General Abresiah sent me to tell you that Princess Mahaneh is safe and Surkhkafar in shackles. You can go down now and take your share of Surkhkafar's treasure." The soldiers took him at his word and rode toward the pass. Samak repeated this story at each mill he passed. One soldier, more alert than the others, asked what was in the four trunks he was carrying. Samak replied that it was his share of the loot Abresiah had given him and that theirs awaited them in the canyon below.

The soldiers' descent into the canyon was delayed by the landslide blocking the pass. By the time they had cleared it, reached the pavilion, and found it empty, the sun was low in the sky. Samak was far away from Black Mountain and riding out of Khorjan Desert as fast as he could. When he felt safe, he stopped, took Princess Mahaneh out of her trunk, and placed her behind him on his horse. Thus they left Khorjan and rode onward toward Khorshid Shah's army camp, leading four mules carrying Surkh-kafar, Abresiah, and a trunk full of royal treasure.

55

HEAD OF A HERO

SAMAK and Mahaneh rode all through that night, and the next day and night as well. It was early morning when they arrived at Khorshid Shah's war camp. They rode straight to the prince's pavilion. Samak dismounted, took Mahaneh's hand, and led her inside.

Seeing Samak and the princess, Khorshid Shah rose from his seat, walked to Samak, and embraced him. He exclaimed: "My brave friend, are you a magician?"

Samak responded: "O great prince, I am an ordinary man. It was God, the greatest of all magicians, who helped me bring the princess to you safely." The prince seemed older and sadder than when Samak had left. Samak understood that he was in mourning for his brother.

Khorshid Shah turned to Princess Mahaneh and welcomed her to his pavilion. Samak noticed pain in Mahaneh's eyes as well and felt sorry for them both. He said to the prince: "Princess Mahaneh and I have come a long way, and the princess is tired. If Your Highness commands, she could be taken to Queen Mahpari's pavilion to rest."

Mahaneh was guided to the queen's pavilion. Mahpari received her with open arms. After the princess had been bathed and dressed in royal clothes, the two young women sat together and Mahaneh told Mahpari everything that had happened to her since she had left her pavilion. Mahpari wept when the princess told her how Surkhkafar had murdered her mother and their maidens. The servants who saw them together marveled at the beauty and nobility of the two young women and the warmth of their friendship, and they remarked that in all the land there must be no one more deserving of happiness.

When Mahaneh had left Khorshid Shah's pavilion, Samak told the servants to bring in the three trunks he had brought from Khorjan Desert. The trunks were carried into the tent and placed in front of Khorshid Shah's throne. Samak bowed and said: "To the glory of the prince, I was able to capture these two and bring them here." The servants opened the three trunks, dragging out first Abresiah, then Surkhkafar, then opening the last trunk to reveal the treasure. A murmur of admiration rose from Faghfur Shah, Haman, and the generals who were watching. They could not believe that Samak had been able to do what he had done single-handed. At the prince's urging, Samak told the gathering all that had happened to him since he had left the camp. Everyone was mesmerized by his cleverness and courage and gathered around to heap him with congratulations. Sorkhvard hugged Samak and told him how happy she was that he had returned safely.

Atashak and Neyal listened in silence at the edge of the crowd. No one paid much attention to them.

Samak said to Khorshid Shah: "O great prince, I do not see Ruzafzun and Shaghal here. Is there any news of them?"

The prince answered: "Samak, they left for Gurkuhi's canyon on the day you left for Black Mountain. We have had no news of them since."

Samak became concerned and said: "If the great prince allows me, I would like to go at once and find out what has happened to them."

Khorshid Shah said: "Samak, you are free to do whatever you feel is right."

Samak thanked the prince. He said goodbye to his associates, left the pavilion, mounted his horse, and rode away without staying even long enough to bathe and change his clothes. Sorkhvard stood at the edge of the canyon watching him until he was out of sight.

• • •

The next morning, Mahaneh told Mahpari how much she wanted to go to her father and brother and mourn her mother's death with them. Mahpari understood, and she sent a message to Khorshid Shah asking his permission to send Mahaneh to her father.

The prince ordered a royal carriage prepared along with a special entourage and had Mahaneh dressed in an elegant silk outfit worthy of a princess. His voice was cold as he dictated a message to Armen Shah. He said: "We have fulfilled our promise to you without bloodshed and have brought back your princess from Black Mountain. We are returning her to you out of respect for your royal family."

When Mahaneh entered Khorshid Shah's pavilion for the last time to say goodbye, there were murmurs and gasps of admiration for her beauty. Mahpari felt a pang as she watched the princess say goodbye to Khorshid Shah. She felt sorry that Mahaneh was leaving the camp so soon, but also there was a part of her that was not sorry. Mahaneh and her entourage departed for the camp of Machin bearing the prince's message.

Armen Shah and Gezelmalek received Mahaneh with open arms. She told them everything that had happened to her from the time that Surkhkafar abducted her and her mother from the royal harem in Machin. She wept as she described the murder of the queen and the terror she had felt when she was a prisoner at Surkhkafar's mercy. Armen Shah and Gezelmalek listened in silence as the princess narrated how Samak had rescued her from Black Mountain, captured Surkhkafar and Abresiah, and brought them to Khorshid Shah.

That night, Mahaneh went to bed in comfort in her own pavilion. As she drifted off to sleep, the face she saw before her eyes was Khorshid Shah's.

The next morning, Armen Shah gathered the generals in his pavilion and said: "I am content to leave Surkhkafar in the hands of Khorshid Shah. He will make him pay for his crimes. But what about our great general Abresiah?"

The vizier Shahran bowed and said: "With Your Majesty's approval, I suggest that we send Khorshid Shah valuable gifts to show our gratitude, and ask for the return of Abresiah."

Armen Shah said: "Do as you feel is right."

Shahran went to the treasury and arranged for thirty mules to be loaded with as much gold, precious jewelry, musk, amber, camphor, satin, and other valuable materials as they could carry. He wrote a letter from the king to Khorshid Shah, stamped it with the royal seal, and sent it to the enemy's camp along with the gifts.

The prince received Armen Shah's envoy and the gifts, and he instructed Haman to read the message out loud. The vizier read:

"This message and these gifts are from Armen Shah, king of Machin, to Khorshid Shah, prince of Halab and Chin, to show our deep appreciation for your efforts in bringing our dear daughter Princess Mahaneh back to us. Meanwhile, we request the safe return of our great general Abresiah. He has committed no crime and deserves no punishment. He is not a common soldier but a noble warrior and leader of men who are dedicated to him and would not forgive his mistreatment. We also take the liberty of reminding His Highness that Abresiah's brother Dabur commands an important army in Gold Mountain, which until now has remained neutral in this war. If harm were to come to Abresiah, Dabur would take this as a personal grievance."

When Haman had finished reading there was silence. Khorshid Shah looked at the envoy and said coldly: "It sounds as if Armen Shah thinks your general Abresiah is more important than my brother Farokhruz. His blood is still fresh since Gezelmalek took his life in a villainous and cowardly act. If your king had sent me Gezelmalek's head along with this letter, that would be justice. How dare he lecture me about Abresiah's nobility, as if my brother's death were not worth mentioning? Was Farokhruz not noble?"

The envoy bowed to Khorshid Shah and said: "Your Highness, of course your brother's greatness is well known and needs no elaboration. I believe His Majesty's intention was simply to make sure you are aware that Abresiah is not unknown but rather an eminent nobleman—and that his brother is Dabur the Demon Slayer, the greatest warrior in the east and west. If he were to enter the war, this could affect the balance from a military standpoint."

Hearing these words, Khorshid Shah trembled with anger. He stood up from his throne and shouted: "You try to bribe me with gifts, then threaten me? If you were not an envoy I would cut your head off here and now. Guards! Bring in the prisoners."

The guards brought in Abresiah and Surkhkafar in shackles. Surkhkafar dropped to his knees at Khorshid Shah's feet, begging for mercy. Abresiah stood straight and resolute.

Haman ordered Abresiah: "Bow to the king!" The guards pushed him down onto his knees.

Abresiah replied: "I am a prisoner of war, not a slave. I bow to my own king, Armen Shah."

Khorshid Shah called out: "Send in the executioner!"

The executioner entered the pavilion. A shiver ran through the court at the sight of this man dressed in red. There was silence as the executioner unrolled a leather sheet on the floor in front of Abresiah.

Khorshid Shah said to Abresiah: "If your king thinks I can be threatened or bought, he is mistaken." To the executioner he said: "Proceed."

The executioner tore a piece of cloth from Abresiah's shirt and tied it over his eyes as a blindfold. He raised his sword. Still Abresiah did not speak a word.

Armen Shah's envoy, in a panic, bowed again to Khorshid Shah and said: "Your Highness, if you take the general's life, you will make an enemy of Dabur the Demon Slayer for all time."

Khorshid Shah's anger redoubled. He said: "If you had begged for mercy, I might have spared his life. Here is a message for Armen Shah to show him how much I care for his warnings." To the executioner he said: "Proceed!"

The executioner's sword swung through the air. Abresiah's head rolled on the floor and came to a stop twenty feet from his body. There was silence in the pavilion.

Khorshid Shah said: "Hang his head around the envoy's neck and send him back to Armen Shah along with his other gifts." Nodding to Surkhkafar, he said: "And send him to the same place."

The executioner blindfolded Surkhkafar, swung his sword and decapitated him in one stroke.

• • •

When the envoy returned to Machin's army camp with Abresiah's severed head hung around his neck, Armen Shah, Gezelmalek, and the generals shouted in grief. The envoy told them in detail what had taken place at Khorshid Shah's pavilion.

Armen Shah asked his generals what they suggested. Everyone agreed that the first thing to do was to let Dabur know that they had had nothing to do with Abresiah's death. At Armen Shah's direction, Shahran called in the court scribe and dictated the following letter:

"This letter is from Armen Shah, the king of Machin, to our great hero Dabur the Demon Slayer. As you may know, it has been almost four years since warriors from Halab and Chin, under the command of Prince Khorshid Shah, marched upon our kingdom. Nearly a hundred thousand soldiers have lost their lives since the war began. With sorrow I inform you that your brother Abresiah was captured by the trickery of an ayyar named Samak, an outlaw in our enemy's service. We sent an envoy to Khorshid Shah with valuable gifts and a request to return your brother to us. Instead, Khorshid Shah ordered Abresiah decapitated and sent us his head, which we now send to you with this letter. We share your grief and know how much you loved and respected your brother. We remain here in battle against the enemy to avenge this and their other atrocities. Should you wish to join us, you will be welcome."

The letter was read to Armen Shah for his approval, then sealed, stamped, and given to an envoy to take to Dabur the Demon Slayer. Two hundred soldiers accompanied him, carrying a chest containing Abresiah's head.

The envoy and escort rode for three days and nights to reach Gold Mountain. They arrived at the edge of a vast green meadow filled with wildlife, in which horsemen with bows and arrows were hunting a herd of zebra. When the riders saw the soldiers approaching, they abandoned the hunt, gathered into a group, and rode up the hill to confront the newcomers.

The leader of the hunters, an enormous thick-bearded man riding a red stallion, shouted: "I am Dabur. Who are you and what is your business here?"

The envoy dismounted, paid his respects, and said: "We bring you a message from Armen Shah, the king of Machin."

The envoy handed Dabur the letter and the chest. When Dabur opened the lid and saw his brother's decapitated head, he let out a roar of anguish that echoed through the meadow. He cried out: "Abresiah, my brother! What have they done to you?" He dropped to his knees and sobbed: "My hero, my soul. You left me without saying goodbye!" The other warriors dismounted and gathered around the huge warrior, who wept like a baby, holding and kissing the severed head.

Abruptly Dabur looked up at the envoy and asked: "Who did this? Armen Shah?"

The envoy said hastily: "No, my lord! The letter I gave you explains everything."

Dabur handed the letter to one of his men, who removed the seal and read it out loud. When he was finished, Dabur invited the envoy to join them at their camp. Mounting their horses, Dabur and his men led the envoy and his entourage to a large open courtyard surrounded by sycamore trees and jasmines. There they sat and ate and drank while Dabur asked the envoy many questions about Khorshid Shah and Samak the ayyar. When Dabur had learned all he needed, he turned to the envoy and said: "Syrup is sweet as long as it is not mixed with water. Khorshid Shah and Samak could do what they did because they did not have me to deal with. That will change."

Dabur said goodbye to his men. Taking with him a group of trusted warriors, he rode with the envoy for three days and nights to reach Machin's army camp. Prince Gezelmalek, Shahran, and the generals rode out to welcome him. When they saw Dabur mounted on his horse, looking like he was ten feet tall, all the generals had the same thought: with such a warrior on their side, no soldier from Khorshid Shah's army would dare to even set foot on the battlefield.

TO BE CONTINUED

"GOOD people, thank you for listening to my story.

"If you would like to hear what happens next, may I ask for a small donation of four hundred dirhams?

"If you don't have four hundred dirhams, just pitch in forty dirhams.

"If you don't have forty dirhams, pitch in *four* dirhams.

"And if you don't have four dirhams, then just say 'Long live the storyteller!' four times, and I will continue."

Here ends book 1 of Samak the Ayyar*—an epic tale of ancient Persia, passed down by generations of professional storytellers.*

GUIDE TO KINGDOMS AND CHARACTERS

THREE KINGDOMS

Halab. Home of Khorshid Shah, who journeys across Persia to marry Princess Mahpari of Chin. His father Marzban Shah is wisely counseled by his vizier Haman.

Chin. Ruled by Faghfur Shah, whose daughter Princess Mahpari is coveted by many princes. Manipulated by his treacherous vizier Mehran, he is unprepared when rival kingdom Machin attacks.

The king's poor leadership is counterbalanced by the cleverness and courage of Chin's ayyars, led by Shaghal and Samak. While the ayyars sometimes act against the king's orders behind his back for the greater good, they are loyal to the kingdom, and rulers and citizens alike turn to the ayyars in time of need.

Machin. Ruled by Armen Shah. Against the advice of his vizier Shahran, he allows his son Gezelmalek—driven by obsessive desire for Princess Mahpari—to lead their kingdom into a war with Chin, at grievous cost.

The ayyars of Machin, unlike those of Chin, ruthlessly serve the king and vizier, undertaking kidnappings and assassinations regardless of right or wrong.

CAST OF CHARACTERS

(In alphabetical order)

Abresiah. Warrior from Khorjan desert, who joins Armen Shah's army. Brother of Dabur the Demon Slayer.

Arghonun. Patriarch of Bograi Valley warrior tribe, the first to give shelter to Samak and his friends and pledge allegiance to Khorshid Shah.

Armen Shah. King of Machin. Ignoring the prudent counsel of his vizier Shahran, he starts a war with Chin, and backs his son Gezelmalek by repeatedly escalating the war out of pride.

Atashak. Servant to Qatran, Machin's champion warrior. He betrays his master and joins Samak as his loyal sidekick, in the hope that Samak will unite him with his beloved Delaram.

Behzad. Son of Kanun, leader of the ayyars of Machin. Brother of Razmyar and Ruzafzun.

Benkhan. Edkhan's lieutenant at Falaki Fortress, helped by Tarmashe.

Butcher Brothers. Owners of a butcher shop in Machin.

Chapmar. Farokhruz's stepbrother on his father's side, a champion warrior in Marzban Shah's army.

Dabur the Demon Slayer. Powerful warrior from Khorjan desert. Enters the war on Machin's side to avenge the death of his brother Abresiah.

Delaram. Faghfur Shah's wine maiden, Atashak's beloved.

Dudkhan. Qatush's commander, fooled twice by Samak, who gets past him disguised as a merchant.

Edkhan. Guardian of Falaki Fortress, in the service of king Armen Shah.

Faghfur Shah. King of Chin. Mahpari's father. Attacked by rival kingdom Machin thanks to the treachery of his vizier Mehran, he puts his future son-in-law Khorshid Shah in charge of the army.

Farokhruz. Khorshid Shah's older half-brother, a devoted, loyal and brave warrior.

Fattah the Giant. A giant placed by Gurkuhi under secret orders to guard a mysterious forbidden gate.

Gezelmalek. Proud, headstrong, bellicose prince of Machin, son of king Armen Shah. His passion to marry Mahpari leads their kingdom into war with Chin, at grievous cost.

Golnahr. Queen of Persia, Khorshid Shah's mother.

Gurkuhi. Leader of the warrior tribe of Twelve Canyons, who takes Samak and friends under his protection.

Haman. Vizier to Marzban Shah, king of Halab.

Hormozgil. Warrior champion and general in Khorshid Shah's army.

Jafar. Wine merchant whose caravan Samak uses to sneak into an enemy camp.

Jeldak. Surkhkafar's commander of the watchman's headquarters in Machin.

Kafur. Ayyar of Machin, Kanun's right hand man.

Kanun. Leader of the ayyars of Machin, ruthlessly loyal to Armen Shah. Father of Ruzafzun.

Kaycon. Spy in the service of Armen Shah.

Khatur. Old ayyar with a special talent for tunneling, hired by Kanun for one last mission.

Khomar. Elderly respected citizen of Machin, who befriends Samak after his arrival in the city. Works on the people's behalf in opposition to the corrupt leaders and ayyars of Machin.

Khordasb. General in Khorshid Shah's army, sent as an envoy to Machin in hopes of negotiating an end to the war.

Khorshid Shah. Prince of Persia. His love for Mahpari takes him across Persia to Chin, where he assumes leadership of his father-in-law's army in a war against neighboring kingdom Machin. He matures on the battlefield, learning lessons in strategy and loyalty from Samak the ayyar.

Kirmun. Leader of army detachment sent by Khorshid Shah to Falaki Fortress.

Kuhyar. Gurkuhi's brother. Warrior of Twelve Canyons.

Mahaneh. Armen Shah's daughter, princess of Machin.

Mahpari. Faghfur Shah's daughter, princess of Chin.

Marzban Shah. Khorshid Shah's father, king of Halab.

Mehran. Treacherous vizier to Faghfur Shah of Chin; he betrays his king and joins his enemy Armen Shah.

Mehruye. Grave robber who saves Samak's life and helps the ayyars.

Mugavgar. Guardian of Shahak Fortress in Armen Shah's service. Son of Mahpari's witch nurse Shervaneh.

Neyal. Fortress treasurer in Edkhan's service, who joins Samak.

Niku. Warrior in Armen Shah's army. Captures Kuhyar and Ruzafzun.

Qabiz. Champion warrior of Chin. His father, the king's vizier Mehran, schemes to help realize his ambition of marrying Princess Mahpari.

Qatour. Warrior in Armen Shah's army, Qatran's younger brother.

Qatran. Armen Shah's greatest warrior, general in Machin's army.

Qatush. Machin warrior general, sent by Armen Shah to guard Twelve Canyons Fortress. He is undone by his lust for women, Ruzafzun in particular.

Qobad. Warrior killed in battle by Farokhruz.

Razmoq. Woodcutter of Falaki Fortress. He and his family risk their lives to help Samak and friends.

Razmyar. Son of Kanun, leader of the ayyars of Machin. Brother of Behzad and Ruzafzun.

Ruhafza. Mahpari's loyal handmaiden. A friend to the ayyars, she loves Samak like a godmother.

Ruzafzun. Daughter of Kanun in Machin. High-spirited, brave and ruthless, she repudiates her father and brothers to join Samak and become an ayyar.

Saber and Samlud. Khomar's sons, citizens of Machin who help Samak.

Salim. General of Machin.

Samak. Young ayyar, disciple of Shaghal, leader of the ayyars of Chin. Becomes Khorshid Shah's friend and right-hand man.

Samana. Wife of Mehruye the grave robber, she helps hide Samak.

Samour. The oldest of the generals of Chin. Sent as an emissary to try to negotiate peace with Gezelmalek.

Saum. General of Persia, often seen in a pair with Siaghil.

Shabdeez. Gurkuhi's nephew and rival clan leader, recruited by Armen Shah to his side.

Shabkhiz. Mehran's sneaky servant who digs and spies.

Shaghal. Samak's mentor, head of the ayyars of Chin.

Shahran. Armen Shah's vizier. A good strategist, he conducts the war as best he can while counseling prudence and trying to restrain the worst impulses of his king and prince.

Shervaneh. Mahpari's witch nurse, who abuses her position to dominate and manipulate king Faghfur Shah for her own reasons.

Shirafcan. Warrior who trained Mehran's son Qabiz. Mehran uses his desire for Mahpari to manipulate him.

Shiruyeh. Son of Shirafcan, leader in Faghfur Shah's army.

Siaghil. General of Persia, often seen in a pair with Saum.

Sorkhvard. Aspiring ayyar of Machin, who joins Samak after meeting him through Atashak, and becomes his most loyal disciple and loving friend.

Surkhkafar. Nobleman warrior of Machin, powerful and independent, he accepts king Armen Shah's assignment to capture Samak in exchange for the promise of marrying his daughter, Princess Mahaneh.

Tarmashe. Abusive jail keeper of Machin, who becomes Samak's nemesis.

Tiruq. Champion warrior of Machin. Defeats Hormozgil on the battlefield.

CPSIA information can be obtained
at www.ICGtesting.com
Printed in the USA
LVHW111924300621
691575LV00001B/77

9 780231 198783